DOUBLE BLIND

DOUBLE BLIND

Of Medicine and Malice

John A. Bartlett

Troubador Publishing Ltd
Unit E2 Airfield Business Park,
Harrison Road, Market Harborough,
Leicestershire LE16 7UL
Tel: 0116 279 2299
Email: books@troubador.co.uk
Web: www.troubador.co.uk/matador

ISBN 978 1 80514 130 3

British Library Cataloguing in Publication Data.
A catalogue record for this book is available from the British Library.

Printed and bound in Great Britain by 4edge Limited
Typeset in 11pt Adobe Garamond Pro by Troubador Publishing Ltd, Leicester, UK

Matador is an imprint of Troubador Publishing Ltd

Editor: Jennifer Mathews
(www.ballpointpencil.com)

This book is dedicated to the research, discovery and development of new medicines that assist patients in living longer, healthier lives.

"When a great profession and the forces of capitalism interact, drama is likely to result. This has certainly been the case where the profession of medicine and the pharmaceutical industry is concerned."
David Blumenthal, M.D., M.P.P.

Acknowledgements

My thanks to Linda Boyce for her guidance and for joining me on the journey to bring *Double Blind* to life. She is the personal trainer who helped get the raw narrative pummelled into shape. Without her input, it would have been flabby. Her broad knowledge of a wide range of topics and the writing process helped correct errors that would have gone undetected.

My gratitude to Catherine Lund for her input on the conducting of clinical trials and Dr Bruce Howard for his consultation relating to breast cancer. Their advice was invaluable. The representation of this information is mine, and any errors regarding these aspects are my responsibility.

Thanks to Dr Joe Lund, Dr Damian Largier and Julie Prochassek for additional guidance and information.

Members of my family, Michael, Lindsay and Geraldine, provided their usual critique of my efforts, and their input was all-important. Thank you for your endless patience over the many months it took to plan and write this book.

My sincere appreciation goes to my editor, Jennifer Mathews. Her enthusiasm for wanting to be involved in making my story a reality was both encouraging and motivating. She helped make the task of developing the novel an easier one than I imagined. *Double Blind* would have remained simply an unresolved idea without her dedicated input.

CHAPTER 1

The Envelope

Paul Beresford stared at the white envelope on the desk in front of him. He almost had a sense of disbelief as he read the address:

Dr Paul Beresford
Business Development Director
Harrowgate Pharmaceuticals
Berkhamsted
England

Beneath the address was the instruction, 'Confidential: Only to be opened by addressee'.

Paul had anxiously been waiting for it for the past few weeks, and now that it had arrived, he was quite taken aback. Every morning he had come into his office expecting to see it. Whenever someone knocked on his door, he looked up expectantly, hoping that the person was bearing the report. At last, the couriered document had reached its destination.

Paul's desk was always neat and tidy, unlike so many others in the company, with only the essentials on the warm mahogany surface, so the presence of the envelope was unmistakable. By contrast, David's desk in the adjoining office was eternally cluttered with papers, files and business journals. If David were to be the unknowing recipient of any confidential report, it would take him days to discover it among the debris of management.

On Paul's desk, everything had its place – telephone, calendar, a small printer, and two containers. One held an array of pens – mostly the promotional pens marked with the names of Harrowgate's products; the other had a selection of coloured markers with which he would highlight aspects of reports, emails or letters.

Next to his computer stood a silver-framed picture of a beautiful woman sitting on a couch with one arm resting on the back and the other raised to the side of her face, with an enigmatic smile as she gazed into the camera.

Paul stared at the picture for a moment and then again at the envelope, conspicuous on the bare wood. Its arrival had caught him off guard. He had been at lunch in the canteen and returned to his office deep in conversation with a colleague with nothing more serious in mind than the progress of the Wimbledon men's singles tournament. He stopped in his tracks at the doorway, staring at his desk, then moved quickly to his leather chair and sat down.

Paul picked up the envelope with both hands and, holding it vertically in front of him, tapped it on the desk. He was lost in his thoughts. Thoughts about his past. Thoughts about his career. Both linked by the contents of the envelope.

He thought about Jill – tall, blonde, elegant and sophisticated. Jill with her passion for life. Her innate and natural sensuality beguiling men who laid on the charm in her presence, as Paul was when they met.

They were happy and Paul was content with their life together. He had dealt with the fact that Jill's parents felt their relationship was below her station – and their expectations. It left a deep scar that she had not fallen for one of several affluent or titled men who had pursued her.

Yes, it was fine that Jill's partner was a doctor. It was fine that he was a good-looking man. It was fine that he had a presence in the company of others. But Jill had been a 'golden' child, beautiful as a baby and as a teenager, talented at everything she touched. She had exceeded in academics, debating, and sport and had won a scholarship to Oxford based on merit and potential. Her parents, particularly her father, had hoped she would marry someone with a title. This would have closed the circle on their ambitions for their adored child.

They could envisage Lord and Lady Jill, or Sir Someone and Lady Jill. Early on in their dating days, Paul was made acutely aware of their aspirations for Jill. Was it to deter him or make their point about who they thought he was? He found their ambitions curious because they had no pedigree of this sort in their heritage. Certainly, they were wealthy and lived in a splendid house in the English countryside with the mandatory townhouse in London. But it was new wealth, not old money.

Jill's father, Edward – never Eddie in his successful years – had acquired an ordinary Bachelor's degree in accounting from an average English university and had experienced a fairly uneventful life until he joined a plastics company as a co-partner. The company had invented a breakthrough plastic barrier used in road safety. These barriers minimised the damage to cars during the impact of high-speed accidents by absorbing and reducing the kinetic energy released.

Just before they won a major tender in the UK, Edward's business partner died, leaving him the key beneficiary of the company and its product. His partner's family hotly contested this, and there were rumours that Edward had done their family out of their proper inheritance. The company staff were split on the issue. Many saw Edward as a nasty piece of work who could not be trusted, but they feared for their job security and withdrew into a sullen silence.

The barriers had proved a great success, and soon, export orders and money rolled in. Edward's life changed. His sense of grandeur increased, and he gave his family only the best of everything; good schools, expensive education, and numerous overseas family trips. It was on one of these trips that Jill and Paul met.

* * *

Paul had visited South Africa with his parents on numerous occasions and had many fond memories of their holidays and the country. Paul could not leave boarding school in his final year to join his parents on one of these trips. It was on this trip that his parents were killed. This loss wreaked havoc on Paul. His devastation was heightened as the father he idolised and whose endorsement he craved was taken from him – just as Paul was flourishing at Charterhouse School. He was determined to complete his sporting and academic success to prove to himself and the memory of his late father that he could succeed.

On passing school, Paul chose to return to South Africa to study medicine at the University of Cape Town. The university was a few hours' drive from the scene of his parents' accident, which was near the town of Knysna along the Garden Route on South Africa's beautiful east coast. They had been returning to Cape Town, and on a steep hill outside the town, a heavily laden truck had brake failure on a bend and crashed into their car, killing his parents instantly.

Paul had qualified as a doctor as his mother had hoped and specialised in orthopaedics at Groote Schuur Hospital – the iconic building where the world's press gathered in 1967 to embrace Dr Christiaan Barnard, who had just completed the world's first heart transplant on Louis Washkansky.

There was no press milling around outside the hospital casualty department on a hot Sunday afternoon in January. Only the usual collection of locals waiting for the family member, friend or drinking buddy beaten up on Saturday night while drunk and disorderly or involved in an accident and brought in to be repaired by the medical staff.

Paul was nearing the end of his Sunday shift. It had been a long day with its usual array of broken bones and fractured noses. He would soon take off his white coat and head for Camps Bay beach to unwind and enjoy a bottle of crisp Sauvignon Blanc. On his way to get the wine, resting alongside the insulin vials, anti-coagulants, and other injections in the casualty fridge, the junior doctor on duty called him. Another patient had just come out of the X-ray department with a suspected fractured wrist. Paul cursed his luck and reluctantly trudged to the waiting room. What he saw changed his attitude – and his life forever.

Sitting there was a blonde girl in her twenties holding her wrist. She was breathtakingly beautiful, despite the pain and discomfort etched on her face. Sitting next to her was a large red-faced man, one minute consoling her and the next complaining loudly about the poor service in the hospital compared to the National Health Service in England.

Paul immediately knew they were tourists. His diagnosis was based on the fact that when the British went abroad into sunnier climes, they usually overdid their time in the day's heat. As a result, their complexions usually assumed one of two alternatives: bright pink blotches offset by an alabaster whiteness where the sun had not penetrated or a smooth golden-brown tan. The man was a supreme example of the former and the girl of the latter. Paul remembered the pleasure his father got from the words of Noel Coward's song, 'Mad dogs and Englishmen go out in the midday sun.' How true.

Paul recalled a veterinary friend's advice who, when dealing with Chihuahua owners, would first calm and remove the owner before dealing with the pet. He would need to do something similar with this man. Paul asked the young lady to come through to his consulting room. The father – that's who Paul assumed he was – got up to follow, but Paul swiftly shut the door in the face of the advancing man. Paul wondered in retrospect whether Edward had retained this incident in the back of his mind, holding it against him all those years.

She introduced herself as Jill and said she had fallen off her horse while riding in the leafy Cape Town suburb of Constantia, known for its notable and wealthy elite. Their sect had previously been complemented by a couple of famous Brit residents, namely Princess Diana's brother, Earl Spencer, and Margaret Thatcher's son, Sir Mark. But the latter had brought a whiff of scandal with him, charged in relation to a failed coup attempt.

When Jill turned to face him in the consulting room, Paul was taken by a number of her features. Although he was just over six-foot tall, he found himself looking directly into a pair of blue-grey eyes, so she was five-foot-ten or eleven. Paul had always fancied tall girls with their leggy elegance. Her blonde hair had been firmly pulled back into a ponytail, but wisps of it now broke loose and fell onto her forehead, creating a curtain of gold. She had high cheekbones and an exquisite mouth – the top lip almost in an arch and much fuller than the lower one. She wore a short-sleeved white blouse that bore traces of dirt and a tear – apparently from the fall – and the whiteness of the blouse offset by her tanned arms. She wore a pair of blue jeans that clung to her figure, and a pair of short riding boots completed the outfit.

She held out her left arm for examination. Paul held it and began to palpate her wrist's carpal and metacarpal bones, feeling for the fracture. He had been completely blown away by this girl, and he wanted his first comment to be either something clever to impress her or some deeply serious medical statement that would leave her in awe of him. However, his usual cool and measured approach deserted him. He stumbled between the stools and then heard his almost disembodied voice loudly asking the stupid question, "Does it hurt?"

"Of course it does," she winced. "I think it's broken!"

Paul bit his lip and mentally kicked himself.

He looked up from his examination to see a faint smile in those blue-grey eyes and the closed mouth turn slightly upward in amusement. Jill was obviously accustomed to men becoming flustered in her presence.

Not all was lost!

"Where are the X-rays?" Paul asked, regaining his composure.

She handed him a brown envelope, and he glimpsed the details written on it. Her full name was Jill Collins, and she was twenty-six years old. He took a disk out of the envelope, inserted it into the computer and called the image up onto the screen. She moved closer to the desk – and to Paul – to see what had happened to her wrist.

He was conscious of the fragrance she wore but could not recognise it. He was poor at identifying perfumes but good at identifying wines and their aromas, discerning fully ripe fruit, strong tannin support, and shy varietal character. But perfumes simply fell into two categories for Paul – those he liked and those he didn't – and he definitely liked what she was wearing.

He realised he needed to focus his mind on the medical aspects of the case rather than the allure of the patient, although during his examination of her swollen and bruised left hand, he couldn't help but notice the absence of any rings.

"Hmm," he said, staring at the screen and partly clearing his throat.

He was aware of the girl turning from viewing the X-rays to await his conclusion on the images in front of him.

"Hmm," again.

He reached into the brown envelope and read the covering note from the radiologist: Fracture of the shaft of the second metacarpal bone. It confirmed his clinical diagnosis. Paul took a pen from the top pocket of his white coat and pointed to a tiny dark line on the stark white image of the bones of Jill's hand.

"I'm afraid you've fractured this bone," he said, tapping the screen. "The good news is there is no displacement between the broken parts, so a simple splint will hold them together while they heal, and it will not require surgery."

"How long will it take to heal?"

"I should be able to remove the splint in just over two weeks."

"That's fine," Jill said, "because we are going back home in just under three weeks."

Paul's spirits sank. He had just met the girl of his dreams, and she was about to be taken away from him.

"I assume you are on holiday here?"

"Yes, my family has been in Cape Town for a while now. We are going to Botswana tomorrow, then on to Victoria Falls, returning to Cape Town for a short while, and then back home to London."

"Well, I better start getting your wrist sorted out then," Paul said, deflated.

He could have called on the junior doctor to apply the splint as it was a simple task, but he wanted to prolong this encounter as much as possible. He took his time going to the cupboard, getting the bandages, wrapping her hand, and placing the splint as if in slow motion.

Noticing his faint British accent, Jill broke the silence and asked, "You're also from England. How is it that you are working here?"

"My parents spent quite a lot of time in South Africa and loved the country."

He decided not to mention their death, not to ruin the mood of their exchanges.

"I spent a number of my school holidays here," Paul continued, "and since the medical training in South Africa is first-rate, I decided to do my studies in Cape Town, which is one of the world's most beautiful cities."

"I agree. I've enjoyed it here – except for this accident."

"Well, this should have you right in no time," he said as he put the final touches to the splint. "I hope to see you in two weeks."

"You will, Dr Beresford," she said with a certainty that sent his pulse racing and showed that she had taken note of the name badge on his white coat. He opened the door of the consulting room to let her out.

Immediately the red-faced man rose from the benches, apoplexy etched on his face as he walked towards them. His mouth opened like a goldfish to express his displeasure at how he, a man of means, had been treated by a lowly hospital doctor.

"Don't worry, Daddy. Everything's all right," Jill said, holding up the wrist with its splint.

The man's mouth closed, then opened again, but no sound emerged. It was clear to Paul that she had her father wrapped around her little finger, as many daughters do.

"If you say so," he spluttered.

"I do," she said firmly. "Dr Beresford has done a wonderful job. I need to come back in a couple of weeks to have this removed."

She turned to face Paul and extended her hand to shake his.

"Thank you, Dr Beresford. I will see you again when I get back from Zimbabwe."

She turned and walked away, leaving Paul staring as she and her father disappeared along the long glistening corridor which led to the exit. She walked with an elegant athleticism akin to a rangy model on the catwalk with her father in tow, puffing, complaining and mopping his brow.

As they approached the exit, a group of men gathered there, eyed her up and began calling out, "Hello sweetheart," "Give us a kiss," "What are you doing tonight?" followed by a series of kissing sounds and lecherous looks. Her father turned and glowered in their direction, but Jill looked back and gave them a smile.

"Quite a looker, wasn't she?" said a voice at Paul's elbow. "I can see why you wanted to apply the splint. Registrars have all the fun."

The junior doctor had a knowing grin on his face.

"Yes indeed, yes indeed," Paul murmured.

As Jill walked down the corridor, Paul reflected on the tall, elegant presence of the girl. Not only was he struck by her looks but also by the way she had taken control of the situation with her father. She knew that he wanted to tear a strip off the doctor for shutting him out of the consulting room. Attractive and able to take charge. He liked that too.

Paul took off his coat, went to the fridge for his bottle of wine, placed it in a cooler bag and headed out along the same corridor, walking to his car in the cool breeze of an early Cape South-Easter. The ageing Volkswagen Beetle he called Jemimah was painted a horrendous yellowish-green, which had earned the vehicle the epithet 'The Pukemobile'. Jemimah had served him well towards the end of his student days and through his internship in orthopaedics, but her duties were coming to an end. In only a few more months, Paul would complete his qualification, and his car would be bequeathed to another of the interns.

It was a short journey along the freeway to Camps Bay. In the distance behind him were the University of Cape Town's buildings and the imposing edifice of the Rhodes Memorial, built at the turn of the twentieth century. It was built in the style of a Greek temple as a tribute to Cecil John Rhodes, whose vision of the African facet of the British Empire linked the territories from Cape Town to Cairo. Below the temple run the forty-nine steps, each commemorating a year of his life. A magnificent view of the city spreads below, much to the delight of tourists. Paul often went there alone, remembering times with his parents when they enjoyed the vista together. Now those moments were tinged with sadness and remembrance of happier times.

His journey to Camps Bay beach took him up over the 'Nek' between Table Mountain and Lion's Head, which, together with Devil's Peak, form part of the iconic image of Cape Town when seen from sea or from Bloubergstrand, north of Cape Town. The narrow winding road lined with pine trees led down to the suburb of Camps Bay and its spectacular beach with the backdrop of the Twelve Apostles Mountain range.

As Paul wound his way down, he saw the glistening white sands of the beach coming closer. He could discern small figures on the beach – children at play, families walking their dogs, and the sun glistening off the deep blue waters of the Atlantic Ocean, with a few hardy souls venturing in for a brisk swim. All these images captured his mind, but none as powerfully as the girl he had just met. He forced himself to concentrate as the road zigzagged down the steep decline to the main beach.

Luckily, he found parking on the seafront, took a blanket from the back seat and walked across the road to the beach. Because of the late summer sunsets in Cape Town, many residents flock to the beach even after a day's work during the week. Paul managed to find a quiet spot, settled down, opened the Sauvignon Blanc and filled his glass. He looked out at the bay caught between a series of boulders projecting into the sea on the left, a few yachts and cabin cruisers on the sparkling blue sea, and a projection of land on the right. Despite his striking surroundings, Paul could only picture the girl with those blue-grey eyes and the aura of sophisticated elegance. He was utterly won over. Was this love at first sight? Did such a thing exist? The scientist within him was sceptical.

* * *

Following her family holiday in Zimbabwe, Jill returned to Cape Town and to Groote Schuur to have her splint removed. Paul took her contact details, and before she flew back to London, he invited her for dinner at a chic restaurant overlooking the Camps Bay beach near where he had sat two weeks before, smitten by his first encounter with her. She agreed to join him, and he would collect her from their hired house in the Constantia Valley that evening.

As his Beetle coughed to a halt outside the elegant Georgian mansion, Jill's father stood eyeing the car and its contents with overt disdain. He called out to Jill that the 'doctor fellow' had arrived and disappeared inside to seek solace from a whisky and soda. Jill appeared dressed in a pale blue trouser suit, her blonde hair tumbling down to her shoulders. She looked stunning and smiled when she saw the dilapidated car. Jemimah meet Jill. Jill meet Jemimah.

Their evening together was characterised by easy conversation, laughter, finding out about their common interests and different tastes in music and movies. Jill was intrigued by her date. She was aware that Paul was openly attracted to her – which always gives the woman the advantage in these situations.

Paul was absorbed by how the glow from the candle on the table caught the golden colour of her hair and how her fingers swept it behind her ear with a delicate feminine gesture. Her smile was a dazzle of white teeth, and her blue-grey eyes sparkled.

Complementing this beauty was an incisive mind reflecting her position as an Oxford University-trained solicitor.

As she made her points in their conversation, she often reached out with her hand and rested it on Paul's arm, who tried desperately not to look down at this touch which signalled an exhilarating sense of intimacy.

In turn, Jill was taken by Paul's boyishly rugged good looks. The doctor who sat opposite her was tall, with a shock of dark hair that fell across his forehead, which he constantly swept back by running a hand through it as if lost in thought. He was tanned with slightly angular features – an aquiline nose and a scar below his right eye. His appearance was almost stern when lost in thought, contradicted by his hands with their long delicate fingers. Jill wondered about the hands of a surgeon and how they might feel caressing her body.

He had a confident manner about him, except for her first encounter with him at the hospital, where he was clearly taken with her. His eye contact with her was steady, unwavering and engaging. While he had a ready smile in his brown eyes, she sensed a steely determination in him, which could indicate a stubborn streak.

But above all, Jill was taken by his passion for medicine, that he was a caring human being with an unwavering desire to contribute to the betterment of people's lives. Despite his easy-going outward nature and humour, she sensed a certain reserve about him. At one moment, she felt she knew him, and in another moment, it was gone. He had an elusive quality to him, which added to the intrigue.

"I don't think your father was very impressed with me when you arrived at the hospital."

"Oh, don't worry about Daddy," she replied. "He is always overprotective of me and always on guard – especially regarding boys," she smiled mischievously.

After their meal, they headed back to Constantia as Jill and the family were flying back to London the next day. On impulse, and wanting to prolong the evening, when Paul reached the top of the winding Kloof Road leading up from Camps Bay, instead of heading over the 'Nek', down towards the city and across the face of the beautifully illuminated and imposing Table Mountain, he impulsively turned left onto the road which led to Signal Hill. At the end of this road was the lookout point, with sweeping and breathtaking views of the city of Cape Town nestling in the bowl formed between Table Mountain and Devil's Peak.

It was a clear, crisp night, the stars sparkling in the sky like diamonds on a deep velvet cushion. Paul parked the car, and they got out. Below them, the lights of the city and the suburb of Sea Point glittered and danced in a slight mist drifting slowly in over the seashore. In the distance, the sound of the horns of a couple of ships anchored off Mouille Point growled in a deep bass as a warning to any ships moving in or out of the harbour.

Nothing was said between them as they drank in the majestic beauty of the view that has enchanted generations of visitors to Signal Hill. Jill shivered in the cool night air. Paul put his arm around her waist and drew her closer to him. He smelt the fragrance that she wore when they first met that day at the hospital and made a mental note to ask her what it was.

She leant into him. He turned her face slightly towards him and kissed her lips gently.

* * *

Paul sat in his office, holding the envelope. His mind often recalled the day he met Jill and he frequently thought of when they first kissed. He took a breath, reached for a silver letter opener in his top right-hand drawer and sliced open the envelope, carefully drawing out its contents and reading the cover page of the report:

Report of a Double Blind Study of HG 176 (terpazamab) for the treatment of Metastatic Breast Cancer in women.

He looked at the photograph on his desk, and his mind returned to Jill.

Jill – lying disfigured and dead – in a cold grave in Kensal Green Cemetery.

CHAPTER 2

Talent and Fame

Paul was the only son of Richard and Elizabeth Beresford. Elizabeth was a nurse, and Richard had been a talented sportsman throughout his schooldays. His academics, though, had suffered as a result. Much to his parents' frustration, Richard had underperformed, given his academic abilities. Many fathers admire the love of and ability at sport in their offspring, especially sons, but it is often detrimental to academic achievement. The competing demands of sport and academics are a source of aggravation for parents who feel their progeny are wasting their lives on sport when they need to be rooted in the reality that few of them will become career sportspeople. Richard, however, still managed to gain entry to the University of Bath, where he scraped through a basic science degree while prioritising his sport.

Richard had excelled at all sports, particularly rugby union, where he made a reputation for himself both at the university and later at Bath Rugby Club as a hard-running wing with a tremendous ability to score tries. By contrast with its university, Bath's rugby club had deep roots in the town. Established in 1865, it had a great tradition of producing international players for England. It was this that lured Richard to this charming town set in the county of Somerset in the south west of England, renowned for its thermal springs and the baths the Romans developed after they invaded Britain.

Richard soon caught the England rugby team selectors' eye with his talent and extrovert personality. He was 'capped' to play against Australia in a test match at Twickenham, the home of English rugby. Although England lost that day, Richard retained his position in the team. He went on to make several appearances before being selected for the British and Irish Lions tour of South Africa in 1974, under its charismatic leader Willie-John McBride.

Rugby in South Africa is almost a religion to its massed fans, as is football to the English. The Springboks, as the rugby team is known, had an enviable reputation, having beaten every touring Lions team they had played on their home ground. The 1974 Lions presented the Springboks and South Africa with an opportunity to laud their status over their competition through their rugby prowess and sense of superiority. The Springboks would show the world the stuff they were made of, especially since the world increasingly looked to isolate South Africa for its practice of racial discrimination, Apartheid.

Willie-John McBride's team broke the Springbok winning streak. In a run of twenty-two unbeaten matches comprising twenty-one wins and one draw, McBride's squad criss-crossed the country, denting sporting reputations and completing a humiliating 3-0 test defeat of South Africa. On this tour, Richard made a name for himself as an outstanding athlete, a brilliant rugby player and an invaluable contributor to the team.

As is so often the case with sporting events, relationships are formed among the competing teams. Richard developed a close friendship with one of the Springbok players whose parents owned a wine farm nestled in the Hemel-en-Aarde Valley, near the town of Hermanus, towards the southern tip of Africa.

It was a friendship that impacted Richard's life and, ultimately, that of his family. He left his job as a representative for a sporting equipment company to establish a wine import business back in the UK. Initially, Richard imported only from his friend's farm, but later from other wine farmers across the southern Cape keen to be associated with a rugby legend. The business grew with the increasing UK market demand for South African wines based on their quality and price. Richard's business grew more successful, necessitating frequent visits to South Africa to secure more stock, with Richard and Elizabeth bringing their son Paul with them on later trips.

As their financial position strengthened, the family travelled around the country, developing a love for its varied geography, from the Winelands of the Cape to the majestic Drakensburg Mountains and into the world-famous game reserve, the Kruger National Park. This was interspersed with Christmas holidays spent at Plettenberg Bay in the spectacular Beacon Isle Hotel perched on the rocks between two glistening beaches. It was a far cry from England's bleak winters and soggy summers. Life for the Beresfords could not have been better.

Richard and Elizabeth were at a stage where they needed to decide on a senior school for Paul. Their improved financial state allowed them to consider a private school, which by traditional British quirkiness, are called public schools. Richard's roommate on the Lions tour to South Africa had attended Charterhouse School. He spoke highly of its facilities, discipline, and sound values that the school inculcated in its pupils. Important to Richard was its strong sporting reputation.

Given his background, Richard was tempted to send Paul to Rugby School, the school in the town where the game of rugby football originated, when William Webb Ellis picked up a football and ran with it. Elizabeth, however, while conceding to send Paul to a boarding school, wanted it to be closer to their home in Ruislip, North West London. She was more protective of Paul, who was smaller than his peers and slightly reserved, which is why Richard felt that time away at a boarding school would serve to bolster his son. Although not admitting it openly, Richard had been disappointed in Paul's development. He had hoped that Paul would develop into a sportier, more outgoing son. Charterhouse would soon make a man of him.

CHAPTER 3

Titles and Wealth

Sean Sebastian St Ledger was the second son of the 5th Viscount Talbot and grew up on his family's vast estate, Bellingham Hall. His great ancestor made a fortune from the railroads in the 1850s and 60s. He was honoured with the title of 1st Viscount Talbot by the then prime minister, the Earl of Derby, for his role in developing the Great Eastern Railway.

The 1st Viscount had a keen eye for technology and a keener nose for money. He built substantial family wealth and sustained the St Ledger lineage to live in financial comfort for generations. The splendid family home was constructed on the outskirts of Burnham Thorpe, the tiny village on the eastern coast famous for being the birthplace of Vice-Admiral Horatio Nelson, England's iconic naval hero.

The St Ledger family was immensely proud of their peerage, having come from humble beginnings. The British peerage is the system of titles and nobility conferred by the monarchy or prime minister and are generally hereditary positions passed down from generation to generation.

The title of Viscount dates back to 1440 and ranks below that of Duke, Marquess, and Earl but above that of a Baron. Among the distinguished holders of this title in the United Kingdom were Viscounts Nelson and Montgomery of Alamein. The St Ledgers were highly honoured to be grouped in the same titled category of this exalted earlier company and were not shy of making this point. While the family surname was St Ledger, they often referred to themselves as the Talbots, using their Viscountcy name to identify their upper echelon status. The family were representative of the core of British society. In addition to their titles and wealth, they had served their country in various roles, from judges and justices of the peace to lawyers and colonial administrators.

The St Ledgers inherited from their patriarchal great grandfather a drive and determination to win and succeed at all costs. From schooling, sport, politics, and business, every element of life was seen as a battleground where the St Ledgers triumphed over others. Defeat was not a consideration. If failure appeared a likely outcome, every avenue or ruse could be employed to achieve success. This was a winning formula for the 2nd Viscount, who continued to amass a fortune through the railroads by acquiring and amalgamating smaller railroad operators by fair means or foul.

Despite the great wealth, success and power that the St Ledgers had acquired, their family had been touched by tragedy. Two sons of the 3rd Viscount had died in the Great War of 1914-18.

Henry, the eldest and heir to the title, had perished at Gallipoli in April 1915, leading his troops by example. His Division, the 29th, clambered up from the landing grounds on the beaches at Cape Helles to assail the cliffs amid a hail of Turkish gunfire. Together with the Australian and New Zealand troops who landed at Anzac Cove, all suffered huge losses, and his Division received twelve Victoria Crosses during the campaign.

Henry was posthumously awarded the highest medal for gallantry in the British Army, reinforcing the Talbot legend of personal heroics, even in the face of death. In his military uniform, complete with the Victoria Cross added to his other medals, Henry's portrait hung at the top of the staircase in Bellingham Hall, glowering down upon the next generations of the family, challenging them to succeed.

The second son, Mortimer, died in the mud and blood of the Somme, leaving the youngest, Granville, to succeed as the 4th Viscount. He had a single son, Arthur, who became the 5th Viscount – and Sean's father.

The 5th Viscount, an equally powerful personality, expanded his business interests in addition to his railways with a newly acquired chemical business. A successful political career took him to the position of Leader of the House of Lords for the Conservative Party. He also had two sons, and Sean grew up in the shadow of his elder brother Hugh, heir to the title and three years older than Sean.

The elder St Ledger was a dynamic, gregarious individual with a winning personality, charming all who met him. Although not good-looking by any standard, he was a young man with an outgoing demeanour, and his personable ways made him popular with all ages and groups. As was the family tradition, the intellectually talented Hugh passed through Charterhouse and became Head of School. Following this, he went up to Cambridge to read economics.

Hugh and a group of undergraduates were returning to college after a twenty-first party on a cold December night, shortly before Christmas. The car carrying the raucous and inebriated students overturned. Hugh was flung out and killed instantly, following in the tragic footsteps of earlier Talbot heirs who had perished in a variety of circumstances over the years, giving rise to a sense that the Talbots were cursed.

The continuity of the Viscountcy depended on a surviving male heir, and Hugh's death plunged the family into grief and Sean into the role of heir to the Talbot title. With this came the burden of ultimately being the family flagbearer, with all the expectations and pressures that accompanied it.

By nature moody, sullen, indifferent and intrinsically socially awkward, Sean was forced to adopt a persona at odds with his disposition. Alternating between someone plagued with doubt about his abilities or a braggart with a boisterous and bullying manner, Sean set on an intended path, bludgeoning his way through life.

He was made deeply aware of the role of his predecessors. It presented him with both a burden and a joy. Money and title were potent assets that gave him some sense of confidence. He intended to put these assets to good use – irrespective of the consequences. These characteristics brought Sean welcome attention in the circles in which he moved. Although many of these groups were similar to his own, many other experiences in his growing up were marked by a sense of awe and envy by those around him. It made him feel good.

Sean's lineage, wealth, and physical attributes buoyed him to achieve the successes demanded by his family history and the family motto loosely translated from Latin – Success at all costs.

Fame arising from a family heritage evolves easily but creates challenges linked by surname or title. Sean was acutely aware of his father's financial, political and social success. Sons of famous fathers often struggle to relieve themselves of this burden and move out of the father's shadow. Being linked by name or renown means dealing with an inheritance not of one's own making. It often creates discomforting self-awareness and a complex challenge when measured against a parent. Children of successful parents often hero-worship them and bask in this reflected glory, but being that child can bring enormous hardship if it is impossible to live up to parental success and expectation. Anything less is seen as a failure.

With a pre-eminent family presence, self-identity is always a challenge, especially with the invasiveness of the ever-present parent – whether that parent excels in finance, politics, the arts, or sport. Sean felt the pressure. So too, in his own way, did Paul.

CHAPTER 4

A Rivalry Born

Charterhouse School stands on sweeping two-hundred-fifty-acre grounds outside the village of Godalming in Surrey, where it relocated from London in 1872. The school was originally founded in 1611. It is one of the most prestigious private schools in England and has been the seat of education for a broad spectrum of politicians, businesspeople, sportspeople and artists. The school's motto is 'God having given, I gave'.

On a crisp sunny day at the beginning of September, the Beresfords drove down to Surrey to enrol Paul at Charterhouse. On the way to the school, they stopped for lunch at a pub, The Star, in the quaint Godalming village. As they sat inside the squat white building with its green signage, his parents enjoyed their meal while Paul pushed his fish cake and chips around his plate with limited appetite. The tension of going away to boarding school was starting to gnaw at him. He excused himself from the table and went off to the toilet for the second time during lunch.

Elizabeth turned to her husband and said, "Richie, can you see how anxious he is about boarding school? I do hope it works for both of you because you know how he idolises you. He only wants to attain your approbation, but you seldom give it."

"I know he wants that, but I struggle to give it when he is not as outgoing and sporty as I was," Richard admitted. "I'll get better at praising him. For now, I remain hopeful that the school will bolster his confidence," he said as Paul returned to the table.

After their meal, they went along Charterhouse Road, soon catching sight of the impressive Victorian Gothic buildings of the school, framed by a clear blue sky. Passing the statue of Thomas Sutton, the founder of the school, they parked among a throng of vehicles. Richard and Elizabeth joined the other parents following the signs to registration, their offspring showing signs of anxiety or excitement.

They were shown to the school hall, where new pupils gathered to be allocated to the various school houses. Much to Paul's delight, his father was soon recognised by some parents, teachers and pupils. The adults were keen to engage with Richard, and Paul was the source of considerable attention among the new pupils as the son of Richard Beresford, the famous England and British Lions rugby wing. Paul was soon surrounded by fellow pupils expressing their excitement at knowing they had the son of a sporting great in their midst and that he would surely contribute to the sporting prowess of the Charterhouse rugby team.

This focus on another pupil was resented by the Honourable Sean St Ledger, also enrolling that day. He was used to being the centre of attention due to his title and considerable family wealth. As many sons of famous fathers have discovered, through the fallout from an age-old struggle, it isn't easy to grow up in the shadow of a powerful, famous, and successful father – a living legend – and match up to expectations. Paul initially rebelled against this pressure. When it came to rugby season at Charterhouse, he arrived for the first practice wearing pink bootlaces as an act of defiance against the expectations of his peers. While Paul's start at Charterhouse proved inauspicious, he was later to develop physically and into a leadership role that invoked Sean's ire and loathing.

Much to his fellow pupils' annoyance, Paul decided to withdraw from playing rugby and avoid the comparison to his father and contented himself with swimming as his primary sport.

Over his time at Charterhouse, Paul developed a sense of his own worth. Although he had a reserved disposition, his academic progress and prowess at swimming, and later athletics, gradually raised his confidence and self-belief. However, Paul was still desperate to win his father's approval. He worshipped Richard and later returned to playing rugby to gain his validation.

His father often came through to watch the rugby matches, but Paul's frustration grew as he heard instructions barked from the touchline by Richard. Frequently, these were critical of Paul's actions and generated a sense of anger and annoyance in him. It was bad enough to be the son of a sporting hero, but the struggle to live up to the reputation and demands placed upon him only exacerbated the situation.

* * *

An antagonism existed between Paul and Sean from their first meeting. During one of the rugby matches, this boiled over.

Sean was large, with a full face, puffy features and hair combed forward without the usual neat schoolboy parting. Over their time at Charterhouse, Sean tried to antagonise Paul through their various interactions. Bullying at public schools was commonplace, and Sean excelled at this with his sycophantic group of followers hanging around him. His hostility at finding Paul popular with staff and pupils had gnawed away at him dating back to their first day at school and the attention that Paul had enjoyed.

Sean was hopeful of being appointed Head of School to follow in the footsteps of his brother, father and grandfather but saw Paul as a competitor and a threat to thwart his ambitions. It would not sit well with his father if he did not follow in the tradition of his illustrious family.

Sean decided to teach Paul a lesson during an inter-house rugby match and injure him sufficiently to remove him from the school. With his cronies Digby Newton and Crispin Wake-Armstrong, he hatched a plot to damage Paul.

"We'll teach the asshole a lesson he deserves," Sean snarled. "You two will find an opportunity to hold Beresford down during the match, and I'll kick the shit out of him. He's getting too big for his boots, so I will let him have mine."

"What happens if we get spotted?" Digby asked faintheartedly, showing none of his public bravado. "We could get into a shitload of trouble. You know how the schoolmasters lap him up."

"Stop being such a coward," Crispin piped up, "and do what you're told."

To their relief, none of the schoolmasters or parents appeared to be present as the match kicked off, leaving Sean feeling smugly confident that he could exact his revenge and get rid of his rival.

Nearly three quarters through the match, their opportunity arose. Paul played in the scrum, that complex tangle of bodies with no apparent discernible pattern or structure. He found himself pinned on the ground by the bloated bulk of Digby Newton. Seizing his moment, Sean, pretending to be part of the play, drove his boot at Paul's head, who saw the kick coming but was powerless to prevent it. Sean's boot smashed into his face just below his right eye. The last thing he remembered was warm blood dripping down his face before an array of bright lights closed out his consciousness.

Timing is everything, for just at that moment, the headmaster, 'Slitty' Redford, came striding past the match. Despite his nickname due to his small eyes, he took in everything that had just happened.

"St Ledger!" he roared from the sideline.

The game ground to an immediate halt and the boys froze at the sound of his voice. Despite his mocking nickname, the boys of Charterhouse were in awe of their headmaster and feared him to a degree. His authoritarian demeanour kept the school running efficiently, as only effective headmasters can.

Herbert Redford was of upright bearing and even stiffer

principles. A physically large man, rugged, with a shock of grey hair, he dominated as he bestrode his domain with the air of viceregal authority. After leaving Oxford with a first in History, he worked for the Colonial Service in India and later in East Africa, where he climbed Kilimanjaro. Redford also saved the lives of a group of touring friends from a charging lion while the local porters had scattered in all directions. Keeping his cool as only a strict disciplinarian can, he waited until the lion was right upon him and discharged both barrels of his gun almost into the lion's mouth.

It was rumoured that Redford worked for MI6, but this had never been proved. He had been awarded an OBE for services to Education, but stories circulated it had been for services to Britain's intelligence network.

The headmaster took immediate charge of the situation.

"Nuttall," he bellowed at one of the scholars on the touchline, "go and fetch Dr Keenan to attend to Beresford. Newton, get yourself off Beresford so he can get some air. And you, St Ledger, go to my office immediately and wait for me there."

Dr Keenan and the school nurse attended to Paul, who was taken to the sick bay on a stretcher. On his way to the headmaster's office, Sean paused next to the stretcher where Paul was slowly regaining consciousness.

"I won't forget this, Beresford," he hissed. "I will track you down wherever you are and break you into little pieces. Never think you can get away with humiliating me."

This was the last thing Paul heard before the mists of pain closed in around him again. He was taken to the local hospital, where he was treated for a depression fracture of the cheekbone and a large gash below his right eye. In a move displaying his confidence as headmaster in the face of influential parents, Redford dismissed Sean from the school, much to the chagrin of his long-standing friendship with Viscount Talbot, ending a tradition of three generations of the St Ledger family at Charterhouse.

* * *

Paul recovered from his injury, and blessed with an extraordinary memory, developed both academically and in sports. At last, he felt his father had started to overcome his disinterest in his progress, and little by little, Richard began to offer up the praise that Paul had craved for so long. But that was to come to an unexpectedly abrupt end.

Paul was called into the headmaster's study on a bleak February morning. As he knocked on the door and responded to the curt "Enter," he saw the back of Mr Redford standing in front of the large window, his hands clasped behind his back, staring out across the expansive lawn.

"Sit down, please," he said.

The crackling fireplace did little to warm the room or the atmosphere as Redford turned to face him.

"Beresford," he said, "I have dreadful news. There is no easy way to say this, but I have to tell you that your parents have been killed in a motor car accident in South Africa."

CHAPTER 5

The Beloved Daughter

No one could say that Edward Collins was a fine physical specimen as he approached middle age. He had been once when he was young and growing up in Sheffield. Back then, his lean appearance, sharp looks and lush head of hair attracted the interests of many of the young girls in his circle. And 'Instant Eddie', as he was known, was quick to take advantage of their intrigue. Evenings in the cinema were close encounters, and some fulsome groping led to certain benefits when Eddie took his date back to her place – or his.

Unique among his group of mates, Eddie had attended university where he studied accounting and was taken on by a reputable firm of accountants, Whittaker, Smythe & Partners, in London. His family and friends saw him as a young man on the make.

While burnishing his accounting skills, Eddie saw how the company's principals acquired considerable wealth and enjoyed the good life. He yearned for some of these benefits and worked tirelessly to build his reputation and ingratiate himself with the top management. He was hungry for promotion and access to the inner circle with all the rewards it appeared to bring.

Eddie naively failed to appreciate the role of class in British society and business. He had done well, worked hard and contributed to the firm, but his Sheffield heritage let him down. His manner of dressing, with a penchant for burgundy corduroy shirts and dropping 'the' from his sentences, together with his accent, made him the butt of quiet jokes among the very people Eddie wished to emulate. They recognised his competence, sharpness of mind and ability to see alternative solutions to problems – not all of them above the law – but they believed he would never fit into the culture, mannerisms and 'clubbiness' of the upper echelons of their company, and neither into that of their wealthy client base.

Eddie saw that the burden of work falling on his desk was gathering pace. He was increasingly called upon to devise innovative ways of improving the financial standing of their clients' businesses or the personal wealth of the business owners. Eddie took this as an endorsement of his status within the company and an assurance of promotion. However, Eddie also noted that after developing these creative accounting solutions, he was not invited to go out to see clients and present the work himself. Despite having a twinge of concern, he felt that he still had to serve more time to inculcate himself with the company's upper echelons.

While work was foremost in his mind, Eddie also thought deeply about marriage, but not for the usual reasons. He believed that to achieve higher status in his company, he needed a wife. The union would help him fit in with the social scene and select circles the principals enjoyed and exhibited. At university, Eddie had met an extremely attractive girl from Leeds who came from a good family and his marriage to Alice was swiftly followed by the birth of his daughter Jill. Eddie felt that he now had all the elements to allow him to progress up the ladder in his company. His work occupied most of his time and attention, but his young family was also a source of pride for Eddie. Jill was a beautiful baby with blonde locks and blue-grey eyes, and the mothers in their circle and friends of the family clucked over her looks.

"She is a potential Miss World," his sister crowed.

This sentiment played out among friends or strangers when Alice took Jill out to go shopping or walk in the park. Along with her good looks was an increasing indication that Jill was clever too.

She was a quick learner, devoured the books Alice read to her, and quickly learnt to identify shapes, colours, and objects. Jill was the apple of Eddie's eye, and he doted on her and worked hard to provide for her future but always seemed to come up short financially.

Despite the financial constraints, Jill flourished. She was everything a parent could wish for as she grew up. Beautiful and bright, and with her wonderful personality, she sailed through junior school, winning prizes for academics, culture and excelling at hockey and tennis. These talents carried over into her senior schooling, where she was seen as a pre-eminent pupil. Formidably intelligent, she excelled academically, in sports and cultural activities.

* * *

The passage of some years with no significant change in his position and status at work, and only a minor promotion, started to gnaw at Eddie. Even more alarming was the rapid rise of a recent employee of the firm. Eddie felt that Alasdair did not have the smarts to make him that much of an asset. He would endlessly appear in Eddie's office to ask for assistance and guidance on his projects, but unlike Eddie, Alasdair was a posh boy with all the proper airs and graces.

Eddie's patience snapped one day, and he went into Fergus Whittaker's office – or suite as it was mostly referred to. Uninvited, he flung himself down on one of the plush floral couches.

"Fergie," he said.

Fergus Whittaker flinched at the mutilation of his name, but good breeding did not allow him to show his annoyance. He tugged at the cuffs of his pale blue shirt, peeking an inch and a half out of his pinstriped Saville Row suit. Gold cufflinks with the insignia of his former regiment caught the sunlight streaming in from behind his desk. Eddie often wondered why Fergus never took his jacket off in the office. Initially, Eddie draped his jacket on the back of his chair but soon learnt that this was so working class, as someone in earshot had sneered. He emulated Fergus from then on, wearing his jacket no matter the circumstance or weather.

"Fergie, you and I need to chat about my progress in the company."

"What about it, Edward?" Fergus asked, hoping his employee would pick up on the formal usage of his name and apply reciprocity. It did not resonate.

"Fergie, I have been here for just on six years. Apart from one miserable promotion, I have not been accepted as a partner, yet Alasdair, who has only been here for less than three years, has made it. It pisses me off!"

Fergus flinched again, this time at the coarse terminology.

"You see, Edward, Alasdair graduated from Cambridge, as did I, and I know that the level of qualification is much higher …," his voice trailed off, but the implication was clear. Cambridge one; Sheffield nil.

Eddie blundered on, impervious to the subtleties.

"Haven't I always delivered good solutions to problems?"

"Yes, you have," admitted Fergus.

"Haven't I always found creative ways to help the firm?"

"Yes," again.

"Well then, I need to get out among the clients to show them and the firm what I'm about."

"Right. We will arrange something for you, Edward," said Fergus soothingly as Eddie exited the suite with a satisfied grin.

Fergus picked up the phone to his senior partner.

"Frank, I think we need to put Edward in his place. He is getting a little too presumptuous and far too cocky."

Eddie's eventual demise at Whittaker, Smythe & Partners resulted from a plot hatched by the senior management. In response to his request to get out and present his solutions, Fergus arranged to take Eddie to one of their top clients. Fergus and a couple of partners accompanied Eddie to the meeting, but they had prepped the client to make the presentation extremely difficult. What transpired were an embarrassing few hours where the client set out to criticise every aspect of the proposal and continually asked Eddie to repeat himself, claiming they could not understand his broad Yorkshire accent and dialect.

The taxi ride back to the office was tense and awkward. Eddie recognised the betrayal with brutal clarity, and despite Fergus trying to reassure him, he decided that his days with the firm were over. He had wanted respect, progress and reward but had merely been exploited, embarrassed and humiliated. Eddie handed in his notice despite offers of an increased salary and walked away from the firm embittered and determined to make his mark and fortune elsewhere.

Within a few weeks, he joined Goldner's, a firm making plastic items, as Financial Director. It was here that Eddie's ambitions were to be realised.

During his time at Goldner's, Eddie saw the rising potential of the plastic road safety barrier invented by the company's founder, which would minimise the damage to cars in high-speed accidents. With a few design changes, Eddie could see how its sales would make a fortune for the company. Mr Goldner was taken in by Eddie's ideas and was soon more interested in further developing the barrier than the administration of the business. Eddie talked his way into a co-partnership taking care of all financials, legal documentation and general running of the company.

The sudden and severe illness and consequent death of Mr Goldner provided an opportunity for Eddie to adjust the ownership documents making him a major beneficiary of the company and its product. The owner's wife and family were incensed by what they saw as the reduction in their shareholding. Much to his delight, orders, tenders – and money – climbed steeply. Eddie's desire for wealth was fulfilled.

* * *

An ambitious student, Jill passed her school A-levels with distinction and enrolled at Oxford University into Magdalen College – pronounced Maudlen – and began her pursuit of qualifying with a law degree.

Eddie and Alice exuded extreme pride in their daughter and her achievements. Early on, Jill was awarded an 'Exhibition' – a small financial award – for first-class performance in examinations, although Eddie saw it as a mere token, given the Collins family's financial position. Still, Jill remained a source of conversation whenever her parents' friends asked about her latest accomplishments. She played a prominent role in the college's activities during her three-year law degree, and graduated with First-Class Honours, ranked first in her year across the university.

The lethal combination of intellect and beauty made Jill a target for the attention of a multitude of male students at Oxford, and her dating calendar was extensive. The many suitors ranged from all social classes, and occasionally some of them accompanied Jill for a weekend at her parents' lavish home in the countryside.

As could be expected, Eddie was particularly interested in those with links to the nobility and wealth. He wasn't terribly interested in whether Jill loved the man or not, just in his reputation and status. One such man appealed to him as a fine catch for his daughter, but behind his back, Jill pulled a face when Eddie spoke in glowing terms about him.

"Why don't you like him?" her father asked. "He has all the makings of a suitable husband – wealth, a title. What more do you want?"

Jill took various suitors home to meet her father, hoping that one would misstep and cure Eddie's leaning towards notable suitors.

"I only brought him here so that you could assist in getting him out of my hair. Mother agrees with me, but it seems as if I still need to convince you."

"I still think you are making a mistake."

"Thanks, Dad," Jill said flippantly, knowing full well Eddie would not change her mind.

After completing her BA degree in Jurisprudence, she was accepted for the Bachelor of Civil Law at her alma mater, a degree only available to outstanding students. Upon graduation, she joined Chadwick, Monteith & Robinson, a prestigious firm of solicitors based in Middle Temple, one of the four Inns of Court. In this professional association in London's quiet and secluded legal heartland, Jill began to build her career as a solicitor.

She was so focused on her career that it took almost begging for her parents to convince her to take a December holiday with them to visit Southern Africa.

CHAPTER 6

Separate Lives

After Jill and her family returned home from their Southern Africa safari, she maintained regular contact with Paul. With his time as a registrar coming to an end and before his final exams, Paul took an opportunity to fly to London for several job interviews and to meet up with Jill once again.

She had set herself up in an apartment near Wandsworth Common, and Paul felt a sense of nervous anticipation as the black taxi pulled up outside her address in the leafy suburb. Remembering to gather the bouquet of red roses from the back seat, he exited and paid the taxi driver.

"A special lady?" asked the cabbie.

"Extraordinary," Paul grinned.

He rang the doorbell. Jill's footsteps approached, and she opened the door, looking stunning in a yellow silk dress that accentuated her slender figure. Jill looked just as beautiful as when he had last seen her back in January. Her tan had faded, but this only seemed to accentuate the blue-grey of her eyes and the gold of her hair.

No word was said between them, only smiles exchanged, but the attraction was unmistakable. Paul took a bold step inside, took Jill in his arms, and they embraced with a hungry kiss.

Awkwardly untangling themselves, they went to a chic gourmet pub in Lansdowne Road near the affluent suburb of Holland

Park. A young, fashionable, upwardly mobile crowd chatting noisily outside suddenly quietened as Jill moved through them to enter the premises. The men looked on admiringly while the girls interrogated her from top to toe. She reached out and held Paul's hand to demonstrate her affection and pride in her partner, and they were shown to a table in an alcove under a Picasso print. Paul was pleased to find a South African Chenin Blanc wine on the list, but it was not one of his father's imports, as the business had gone under shortly after his death.

The evening passed similarly to the one they had together in Camps Bay six months earlier. For both of them, it seemed hardly any interval had passed. The passionate chemistry was still there. Paul told her of his progress towards qualifying as a specialist orthopaedic surgeon and his plans to return to London. He was already making enquiries at various hospitals in the city for employment.

"I'm confident of getting a position in at least one of the hospitals I have applied to near here. Hopefully not in Birmingham. That's quite far from you."

"I'm sure that many hospitals would like to have a charming surgeon among their ranks. It would pull in a lot of female patients," she grinned.

"Yes, that would give you a bit of competition," he said provocatively, with a laugh.

"If you are going to make a move, you had better hurry up. Daddy is trying to marry me off to the rich and famous. He says it is what I deserve, and he's already lined up a string of them. I am not sure how he sees an Anglo-South African medic as part of the portfolio."

Although said as banter, the implication struck discord in Paul's mind. Ever resurgent was the knowledge that his late father, whose endorsement he always wanted, did not see Paul as successful. He pondered his self-doubt as he was also aware of the significant difference in their financial positions, which seemed to irk Jill's family. Paul's parents left him a fair inheritance, but most of that paid for his final term at Charterhouse and his Cape Town University studies. He had funds to find himself a place in London, but not a lot. He needed a job.

Jill noticed that Paul had partly withdrawn from the conversation into his thoughts – a feature she had observed on their first dinner date. She sensed that certain topics triggered this introspection, but she couldn't quite identify them.

"Where are you, Dr Beresford?" she teased.

"How are you progressing with your legal career?" said Paul, changing the subject.

Jill's progress towards becoming a solicitor was nearly complete, and she was deciding what aspect of law she should pursue.

"I'm still considering several options. Some colleagues at the practice are beginning to work in property transactions, wills, criminal cases or advising on divorce. These facets strike me as dull or depressing. I am interested in advising businesses and corporate clients on contracts or company mergers and acquisitions. I sense a challenge in getting all the moving parts of a business arrangement together."

"Business is far from my mind while I establish myself as a surgeon, but I am sure you will excel at that. You will be a star," Paul said, suddenly returning to the conversation.

They enjoyed the evening's food, wine, and intimacy, but their minds were racing ahead. Paul paid the bill, and they walked hand in hand up to Bayswater Road to hail a taxi to Jill's apartment.

Even though they had some at the restaurant, Jill asked with a wink, "Do you want to come up for coffee?"

They tumbled through the door and up the stairs into the bedroom, shedding clothes as they went. Jill had slipped out of her yellow dress and stood in front of Paul in an elegant lacy black bra and panties. With her incredible figure, this image of her beauty was more than he had even imagined. She still had her heels on, and as he held her face to kiss her, he looked deep into her eyes.

Paul had thrown off his jacket, and she started unbuttoning his shirt and tore it off him. He slowly backed her up against the built-in cupboard, pinned her arms above her head, and drove his tongue deep into her mouth. Holding both of her wrists in one hand, he used the other to caress her breast. He ground his hips into hers, and Jill gasped as she felt him erect against her.

He turned her around, her back towards him, undid her bra, and cupped her breasts with both hands. Paul's heavy breathing seemed to fill the room as he kissed the back of her neck and shoulders. With her legs slightly apart, he put his hand between them and felt the outline of her mons and lips. She was wet. It only served to arouse him more.

She turned around and purred, "Hors d' oeuvres are over. I want you on the bed."

In the morning, the early July sunlight streamed through the window into the bedroom. Paul woke first and looked at Jill lying there, partially covered by the sheet. He leaned over and kissed her breast. She stirred, put her arm around his neck and pulled him down for a kiss.

"Can I take a look at your hand?" he asked. "I want to see how my orthopaedic skills worked on your fracture."

"Why not? You've examined every other part of me, Dr Beresford," she giggled.

At once aroused, Paul moved on top of her and heard her give a small cry as he entered her. They made love once again.

* * *

Paul thought back to that evening. It was another milestone in his relationship with Jill. Sitting in his office, those memories seemed a mile away. As he held the report document on HG 176 in his hands – putting off the desperate instinct to tear into the findings – the image and sense of Jill came back to him vividly. He could see her, touch her, smell her and feel how her blonde hair fell onto his face and chest when she lay on top of him. How he missed her. How he loved her. Paul was terrorised by a deep subconscious fear that some of his actions might have led to Jill's death.

Besides her intelligence and beauty, Jill was a free spirit with an affinity for people. Often people were in awe of her based on her appearance, but her outgoing nature and ability to relate to young and old showed how approachable she was. Paul often thought that she would have made an outstanding courtroom lawyer, but she had chosen the backroom role of complex business affairs.

On his return to London, Paul was accepted by the Royal National Orthopaedic Hospital in Stanmore, North London, where he began his surgical career.

He and Jill started dating exclusively even though they did not live close to one another. Both were forging their way into their own demanding careers. Paul had bought himself a small apartment in Putney near the Bridge, which he kept as his base and commuted daily to the hospital. The hours were long, strenuous, but rewarding. Over weekends he joined Jill in the Wandsworth apartment.

Jill, for her part, was also coming to grips with her role as a recently qualified solicitor and the tutelage of one of the senior partners. Dealing with the intricacies of corporate mergers and acquisitions required intensity and application. Jill quickly surprised her peers and superiors with her rapid grasp of details; perhaps they had mistaken her beauty and lack of experience for a less penetrative intellectual ability.

During this early period, Paul and Jill had the opportunity to get to know each other more personally and intimately as they grew into their lives. Over time, Jill discovered that besides his passion and belief in the art of medicine's healing science, Paul was a complex, profound, and well-rounded individual. He seemed a man of action but inclined to spells of introspection and reflection. She wondered whether the death of his parents had left its mark on him. He never spoke about it willingly. She had tried on several occasions to broach the topic but was rebuffed. She stopped asking.

Despite his strong qualities, Jill was amazed and delighted to find an unusual crack in his make-up. One evening, she invited him to see her offices at the Middle Temple of the ancient Inns of Court. Since her office was on the third floor, they entered a small old-fashioned lift with a metal gate that had to be pulled shut. The moment he got in, she could see Paul was agitated, and by the time the lift had inched its way agonisingly up to its destination, he had broken out into a sweat.

"What's wrong?" she asked.

"Claustrophobia," he replied.

She laughed as he refused to take the lift back down later in the evening, choosing the stairs.

"Race you down!" she called out.

* * *

Paul's mind had its particular qualities – objective, inquisitive, sceptical. He had an innate sense of curiosity encompassing areas outside that of medicine, including history and world affairs, which set the stage for a number of vigorous debates between him and Jill on political and social issues. He had confidence in trusting his ability to hold his own in discussions on a range of topics. However, he was mostly happy to concede to Jill's opposition to his sometimes unsound arguments. Paul had both the instinct and objectivity to see the error in supporting a lost cause.

He had an impatient manner suppressed by a sense of politeness instilled in him by his mother, but when tested, he gave away his feelings by tapping his fingers incessantly on his thigh or pacing up and down. He possessed a dry and waspish sense of humour, often delivered in a deadpan manner that cracked Jill up.

Some of these attributes were also revealed to his medical colleagues at the hospital at Stanmore and later at Bolsover Street, where he brought high energy into his workplace. He tried, enormously successfully, to cut through the management bureaucracy burdening the hospital. Ultimately, Paul's perseverance improved treatment regimens, giving greater independence to those running the clinics and surgeries.

His peers came to know and respect him, but there seemed to be some protective layers around him that prevented them from ever getting really close to him. He frequently portrayed an air of detachment that presented itself almost as aloofness, but above all else, Paul was determined to be effective in his contribution to the team.

He had a critical demeanour and, after considering all the facts, a sharp decision-making process. He could weigh up the complexity of an issue or problem with fact-based analysis, which became particularly apparent in complicated surgical procedures. When traditional approaches failed, Paul would often identify a radically new perspective to succeed, which it invariably did.

Friends and colleagues were struck by his vivid recall of the minutest details. They often joked about Paul's photographic memory, which he scoffed at, saying, "I simply have the ability to retain information and access it quickly."

* * *

Paul's life after Charterhouse was well on track, but Sean St Ledger's life had taken a different route. After his expulsion from Charterhouse, he had to endure his father's wrath. The words still rang in his ear.

"Why did you have to be so stupid?" Arthur chastised. "You know our family has a considerable history at Charterhouse, yet you embarrass us with your foolishness. I have lost face with the headmaster and my peers because of your idiocy!"

Sean took a breath to speak, but his father continued to scold, "When I die, you are to be the 6th Viscount Talbot. Doesn't that mean anything to you? If this family's role in society, business and politics is to continue, I want not only a successor but someone who can succeed."

Glaring at Sean, Arthur spat, "Now go. Get out of my sight!"

Fuck you, thought Sean as he left the room, partly because he was an entitled brat, but beneath his rebellion, the weight of expectation bore down on Sean. His mood vacillated between frustration, anger and tearful moments when he felt the brief was beyond him. The Viscountcy became a weighty burden.

His father had, through his connections, found Sean a place at another prestigious school where Sean – for once – applied himself and passed reasonably successfully. He even gained a place at Oxford University, much to his and his father's surprise. Perhaps the reprimand had sunk in after all.

And then, the old Sean reasserted himself. He slipped back into his old ways at university, missing lectures and study groups favouring a good-time student's life. Lots of socialising, getting drunk in numerous pubs, dating some of the most attractive and eligible girls all at the same time, and placing himself as the central figure among a large student group.

There was an inevitable crash and burn when exam time came around, and Sean failed dismally. He left Oxford at the end of his first year, once again in disgrace, putting another blot on the family tradition.

Further humiliated by his son's misconduct, Arthur decided Sean needed discipline and toughening up. The only place to provide that discipline would be the Royal Military Academy, commonly known as Sandhurst. It was here that Sean found his métier. The physical activity appealed to his aggressive streak, and his use of firearms and weapons displayed impressive skill.

Even though Sean seemed designed for the armed forces, his arrogance got the better of him. After completing nearly four years of training, he opted against a military career and joined one of his father's companies, Blackheath Chemicals, as Managing Director. Sean was determined to show his father and the aristocracy what he was made of – that he was not stupid or an idiot. He went about acquiring other companies to build a business empire as a testimony to his abilities. He would prove to his father that he could succeed to the title of 6th Viscount Talbot.

* * *

Sean's first few months at the helm of Blackheath Chemicals were fruitful, proving his worth to his father at every opportunity. Never again would his father belittle him.

Relaxing one evening in his apartment overlooking Hampstead Heath, Sean received a phone call from his father inviting him to Bellingham Hall that coming weekend. Arthur said he wanted to hear how Blackheath Chemicals was doing under his leadership and discuss some personal matters.

That Saturday, Sean went through to the London Heliport and was flown in the family helicopter up to Norfolk, landing on the spacious grounds of the manor. His father was out on a hunt, so he occupied himself furtively looking around as he had not been home for quite some time.

One day, all of this will be mine, he thought, smirking as he strolled through the gallery with its myriad artworks collected by his ancestors.

That evening, he and his father had dinner in the austere formal dining room, where they discussed the progress at Blackheath, after which they retired to the Viscount's study for drinks. Sean noticed that his father had drunk a lot at dinner and was now consuming copious amounts of port; this was highly unusual.

"I have something important to tell you," said Arthur, leaning back in his leather chair, eyeing Sean with an air of disdain.

Sean sighed, waiting for yet another lecture.

"After your brother Hugh was born, your late mother refused to have sex with me. She said that giving birth had been too traumatic. I needed an outlet for my appetite, so I initiated a relationship with one of my employees before your mother and I divorced."

Sean's eyes widened with surprise, and he bit his lip nervously.

"From this union, a son was born – your half-brother."

Sean gasped.

"He was born before you, and let me tell you, my boy," his father hissed, "if you do not succeed in your current venture, I will marry this woman to legitimise this other son of mine."

Arthur gulped down his remaining port and declared, "Since he was born before you, that will make him heir to the Viscountcy."

Sean was stunned and mute following this announcement. He ejected from his chair without a word and headed for the door to the parting words from his father, "This is your last chance."

Sean phoned the helicopter pilot and shouted down the line, "We are going back to London now! Move your bloody arse."

CHAPTER 7

Coincidence

Paul and Jill managed, mainly over weekends, to share some quality time and take a break from their pressurised lives. Besides going for an occasional dinner or seeing a play, they also planned time away from London as often as their schedules would allow.

On one such trip to the Lake District, they knew they had fallen deeply in love and talked about taking their relationship to the next level. They had experienced attraction, passion and attachment, and now they knew they were right for each other, ready to take the next steps.

As they set off on a walk around Lake Windermere, Paul raised the subject that had been buried during their time together and broached the discussion.

"Jill, you know that you will have to take me to meet your parents eventually, don't you?"

"Yes, I've been thinking about that."

"Well, I think it's time to act. I'm concerned that your father still dwells on that incident at the hospital in Cape Town."

"I'm sure he does as he tends to hold grudges. I hope Daddy has moved on since then, but I agree we need to act."

"You said he was lining up a number of eligible young men for you? I'd better get in the queue then," Paul grinned.

"Agreed. Leave it to me; I think I can manage him," Jill smiled, pecking him on the cheek.

"Yes, but can I?"

* * *

Getting back from the Lake District, Jill called her parents and had a measure of relief when her mother answered the phone. Her parents spent most of their time at their country home, rarely coming up to London and, therefore, seldom seeing Jill. Her mother was pleased to hear from her, and after general chit-chat about her work and well-being, Jill touched on the subject.

"Mum, I want to bring a boy over for a dinner with you and Daddy."

"Oh," said Alice, "who did you have in mind? Someone nice, I am sure. What's his name?"

"His name is Paul, and he is the doctor who treated me when I fell off the horse in Cape Town."

"Oh," was the reply, followed by an uncomfortable pause. "Isn't he the one who was rude to your father?"

"He wasn't rude, Mum; he was being professional about doctor-patient privilege. Dad just took it the wrong way. I need your support in this."

"If he is nice, that's not a problem. Are you in love with him?"

"Yes, very much so," Jill said with no hesitation.

"Well, let's set up a date. I will prepare your father. We will come up to the house in London."

"Thank you, Mum."

"I know it's your life, Jill, but it's our lives too. Goodbye, darling."

* * *

Jill and Paul were getting ready at the Wandsworth apartment for the dinner date with Jill's parents.

"I'm sure Daddy will take to you – everyone does."

"I'll be on my best behaviour," Paul grinned, "what with all the competition."

"What do you mean?" Jill asked.

"Didn't you say that your father had lined up half the eligible young men in town for you?"

"Oh, that. Yes, he really fancied some of them but was particularly taken with one. He thought Sean had all the credentials."

"Sean?" Paul stalled in his preparations.

"Yes, Sean St Ledger, heir to the Viscount Talbot title. Daddy thought I would make a good Viscountess – so pompous of him."

Paul was stunned. "Where did you get to know Sean?"

"He was at Oxford for part of the time I was there but not in the same college."

"He was dating you?" asked Paul, incredulous at the coincidence that Sean should enter his life once again after their experience at Charterhouse – and especially that he appeared to have dated Jill.

"He might have thought he was dating me, but he dated many women. He used to hold big parties at Oxford to which many people went along, impressed by his wealth and title. He had tried to make it with plenty of girls – some with success."

Paul couldn't bring himself to ask if Jill was one of them.

"Did you like him?" was the closest he could come to the main question on his mind.

"He was fun in a devilish kind of way. He sort of pestered me, as he did many girls, thinking that we'd roll over."

Normally penetrative in his questioning like he would do to gain medical case history, Paul could only muster an "Oh."

Jill was intrigued to see Paul's reaction to her mentioning Sean's name.

"Do you know him?"

"Sort of; we were at the same school together."

Paul decided against mentioning their altercation and history. That could wait until another time after this initial first pass. But

Sean's parting words echoed in his mind; "I will track you down wherever you are and break you into little pieces." Surely that was dead and buried by now? He hoped it was.

Regaining his composure, Paul questioned, "You said you took him to meet your family. How did that go?"

"As I said, my dad was taken by the trappings, but my mother saw through him. I made it clear to Sean that I was not interested in him or his persistence, but I don't think he got the message. He had a type of crafty intellect, but Oxford found him out. He failed and had to leave, and that was the last I saw of him. Such a small world that the two of you should know each other."

"Yes, isn't it?"

* * *

They travelled up to Kensington to Jill's parents' town apartment close to Hyde Park and near the distinctive building of the Royal Albert Hall. They stood under the portico of the imposing building on De Vere Gardens, one of the most expensive streets in England. Jill rang the bell on the shiny black door framed by two marble columns. Paul stood behind her. Jill turned to give him a quick smile and said, "Here we go!" just before her father filled the doorway.

"Jill, my love, it's wonderful to see you again. It's been so long!"

"Hello Daddy. It's lovely to see you too," she said, hugging him.

Paul wondered if her father's opening comment was aimed at him and related to the fact that Jill had avoided seeing her parents for an extended period while they were initially dating.

"Daddy, this is Dr Paul Beresford," she said, avoiding any reference to their previous encounter.

"Good evening," Edward glowered.

"Good evening, sir," said Paul, reaching out to shake his hand and provoke engagement. Edward reluctantly returned the traditional male greeting.

"Mum, this is Paul," she said, turning to her mother, who had joined her husband in the entrance hall.

"Nice to meet you, Paul."

"And you too, Mrs Collins."

Jill took the opportunity to watch her mother's expression as she saw Paul for the first time and was delighted to see her eyes light up as she took in this tall, handsome doctor.

"Come on in," said Edward, speaking more to Jill than Paul. "Don't just stand there; come on through to the reception room."

The elegantly furnished room was decorated with landscape paintings, and the wooden floor covered with an expensive-looking Persian rug, with a view out over a small, neat garden.

"What can I get you to drink, Jill?" asked her father.

"I'll have a glass of dry white wine; thanks, Daddy."

"And you, Alice?"

"I will have my usual whisky."

"And you, Dr Beresford?"

"Please call me Paul. I will also have a glass of dry white; thank you, Mr Collins."

"Oh, I thought you might be a beer man."

"Wine, thank you. My late father owned a business importing wine from South Africa," said Paul, ignoring the innuendo.

Ignoring Paul, Edward asked, "So tell me, Jill, how is it going with my clever solicitor daughter?"

"It's going very well, thank you, Daddy. Despite my Oxford results, I think they first saw me as an attractive blonde bimbo," she laughed.

"I am sure that you quickly corrected any misapprehensions."

"I am certain I did."

"And you, Paul," Alice chimed in, "where are you working?"

"I am at the Royal National Orthopaedic Hospital."

"If I recall the story, you were the doctor who fixed Jill's wrist when she broke it in Cape Town."

"Yes, that is correct."

49

"Can we eat, Daddy? I am starving," said Jill as the sensitive topic floated up into the conversation.

"Right, come on through to the dining room. You can bring the remains of your drinks with you," said Edward.

As they settled down at the dining table, a butler served bowls of Vichyssoise soup to initiate the meal.

"So Jill, tell me what you are busy with at the famous Inns of Court?"

"Well, Daddy, I have decided to focus on company mergers and acquisitions since I find the legal complexity and scale of the work very intriguing."

Jill went on to explain some of the issues and cases at hand.

"Sounds very complicated," said Alice, "but I am sure you will do a great job. And you, Paul, what sort of work keeps you busy?"

Jill was relieved that her mother had brought Paul into the discussion as her father seemed a bit reluctant to engage with him. The atmosphere was not tense but still seemed to have a bit of an awkward edge.

"I have recently been occupied with a lot of paediatric work, Mrs Collins."

"Please call me Alice."

"Mainly reconstructive correction to limb deformities and broken limbs, Alice."

Small talk continued to pepper the conversation until the arrival of the main course of Beef Wellington. Served with it was a bottle of French Gevrey-Chambertin red wine. Paul recognised this prestigious wine region from some of his father's wine collections when developing his importing business. Paul acquired an appreciation of the grape and a small collection of his own later in life.

Seeing the opportunity to connect with Edward Collins on a mutual interest, Paul complimented him on the choice of wine.

"You did mention that your father had a wine importing business."

"That is correct. It triggered my interest in wines which I have tried to maintain."

"Your surname, Beresford; there was a famous rugby player by that name. Any relation?"

"Yes, that was my late father."

"Oh, I recall seeing him play. Not for my team, Harlequins. We played against his team, Bath. There's a coincidence. Hmm."

Jill looked across the table and gave Paul a fleeting glance. Hopefully, this had eased some of the tension. The rest of the meal passed in a slightly more convivial atmosphere – especially as the wine contributed to a sense of well-being.

In the taxi back to Wandsworth, Jill put her arm through Paul's and said she was sure that he had passed the first test.

"Daddy loves his sports. That was a bit of luck that he knew about your father."

"Prognosis is still guarded," said Paul. "At least it was the first step in a therapeutic process."

CHAPTER 8

The Interview

Paul was entering his second year working at the Royal National Orthopaedic Hospital, where he had derived much satisfaction from his surgical procedures – particularly those on young children who had suffered skeletal injury or birth deformities. He had a talented team around him and was highly regarded by his medical colleagues. They admired this skilled doctor with his partial flat-voweled South African accent, acquired after living in Cape Town for nearly a decade. They were amazed at Paul's memory, who often named the page numbers in surgical manuals that his colleagues should refer to. But Paul seemed distracted.

One of his fellow surgeons, Christopher Wellings, had left the hospital to join a pharmaceutical company, much to Paul's surprise; he thought Christopher enjoyed surgery and wondered why he would have moved into the industry. When Christopher invited Paul out to lunch with him to talk about their times together as surgeons, Paul took the opportunity to ask about his new life.

"I love my time at the company," said Christopher.

"How come? I thought you were extremely happy slicing and dicing your patients?"

"Yes, I was, and I miss some of it, but I feel that working on developing new medicines for conditions that might prevent surgery in the first place is a benefit to medicine as a whole. The pharmaceutical industry is often criticised, but great life-saving results are coming from it despite some failings. These failures often seem to be the point of attention rather than looking to the advanced medications used to keep someone alive and well, when previously they could have died."

Paul was intrigued and mentioned that surgery also kept patients alive.

"Yes, that's true," Christopher continued, "but I feel that I can help more people into better health this way than simply working on a few patients at a time. I have opportunities to travel, meet colleagues from the company and other companies in different countries, and swop ideas about improving treatments. In addition, the financial reward is excellent. The hours are long and demanding, but it's very stimulating work. I got to know the head of a small English pharma company. If you are interested, I can arrange an introduction."

Paul was left to ruminate on this conversation for a few weeks. Some of it resonated with him. He felt that improving more people's lives than he could get through in weeks, months or years at the hospital had merit. An increased remuneration above that of a hospital doctor would be a bonus, not a determinant. But it would help him be more financially secure in the face of Jill's obvious wealth.

He raised the issue with Jill one evening when they had finished their meal and were relaxing, enjoying a glass of wine.

"I have had a radical thought about where my life is going."

"Oh," she said, "are you tiring of me so soon?"

Paul laughed. "That's the last thing on my mind."

"So what, then?"

"I had lunch with Chris Wellings a few weeks ago. He left us to join a pharma company and was extolling the benefits."

"Big Pharma? You want to join Big Pharma?" Jill gasped. "I can't believe what I am hearing. It has such a bad reputation."

"I have done some research of my own, and while there are

issues, the overall contribution to human health has been significant. Medicine has overcome the diseases our ancestors lived fearing."

"Dealing with the corporate world in our legal practice, I work on many of the wrongs and injustices in business. Although, I suppose there are a few good things, just not many."

"I see your point, but I am going to continue to look into it."

"That's your stubborn streak coming through again."

"Perhaps, but it assisted me in continuing to pursue you."

"Glad you did," she said and started beating him with a cushion from the couch. He grabbed her arm, pinned her back onto the couch, and kissed her.

"Right, Miss Legal Eagle. It's time to pluck your feathers."

* * *

Berkhamsted lies twenty-six miles northwest of London in the county of Hertfordshire. Its history stretches way back and is recorded in the Doomsday Book of 1086. It was the site of the Anglo-Saxon leadership's surrender to William the Conqueror after the defeat of King Harold at the Battle of Hastings in 1066. The town nestles in the countryside bordering the Chiltern Hills.

In these serene and pleasant surroundings, a small English pharmaceutical company established itself and set off on a quest to develop new and exciting medicines for the benefit of humankind. The reality of its situation did not necessarily match this grand ideal. Compared to the other major British pharmaceutical companies, Harrowgate was low on resources – human and financial. It had been established by John Patrick 'JP' O'Rourke, who had worked for many multinational pharmaceutical companies and came from a wealthy Irish landowner family. He believed in hiring top-class employees dedicated to his vision of finding new cures for old diseases. He had invested most of his wealth in the business and was confident but not assured of success.

Harrowgate had bought the licences of some older medicines

from major companies to create an operating base to generate revenues to sustain JP's research and development goals. These products would keep the business ticking over while the scientists beavered away to find new cures for specific diseases. It was a high-risk, high-reward strategy that characterises the industry.

JP's aims were boosted by the acquisition of a team of researchers who had worked for the English pharmaceutical company Wellcome, and later Glaxo Wellcome, following the company's sale to Glaxo. Wellcome had been unique as a company in that it was owned by a charitable trust following the founder's death. Besides funding the company's own business activities, the Wellcome Trust made grants to other research groups to advance medical research, as set out in the founder's will. The researchers were motivated by the idealism of the Wellcome approach, which also underpinned JP's philosophy. With his vision to create cures for the ailments of humankind, the expanded team embarked on intensive research. So, the human resource issue had been addressed, but the financial resource was still in question.

Besides JP putting his own money into the company, bank loans additionally funded the research, and the repayment of these was a source of great concern to JP. The company had also listed on the stock exchange, and the share price had risen on rumours that Harrowgate may have a new blockbuster drug in its pipeline. Success was crucial to preventing financial catastrophe. JP was hopeful that the drug's favourable outcome would raise the share price, and he could cash in and return to his farm in Ireland. Until then, the clock was ticking. JP was anxious.

* * *

True to his word, Chris Wellings had introduced Paul to JP, and the two met in London for lunch at an elegant restaurant near Wimpole Street to discuss the possibility of Paul working at Harrowgate. JP was a tall man in his mid-sixties, with cropped steel grey hair with a few vestiges of black and formidable dark eyebrows. His upright posture came from serving with the Irish Guards Regiment.

"Chris speaks highly of you," JP began, "and your CV is outstanding in terms of the work you have done and the character references provided, but ..."

"But?" Paul said with a slightly amused and quizzical look.

"You lack the business knowledge needed for the position I have in mind, which is Business Development Director."

"I thought the position was more medical," Paul said, disappointed. "So that rules me out?"

"Not necessarily."

JP had sent Paul for a battery of tests prior to their meeting. The results were impressive. Paul was shown to be decisive and able to manage the complexity informing those decisions. By temperament, people have a preferred way of tackling problems. The so-called 'do-er' rushes in as an all-action physical solver, whereas the 'be-er' tackles the issues through mental application. Paul was a 'be-er'. JP felt that he had enough all-action team members with his sales and marketing staff. He needed someone to think through and apply cerebral wattage to some of the complex problems of negotiating the successful development of new products. The problem could be described as taking a car from 0 to 100 miles an hour while changing all four wheels at the same time. Paul seemed to have the credentials to match that brief.

In addition, Paul's spatial problem-solving technique was one of linear thinking; set a goal through rigorous analysis, determine the necessary steps to achieve it then set off to accomplish that goal. This was critical given the intricate stages and steps essential to successfully develop a new medicine and get it to market. Any procedural missteps could set back the development of the drug or easily terminate the trials, costing time and money. Furthermore, the HR lady who conducted the assessment identified Paul's exceptional memory. JP thought this would be helpful given the detail-orientated nature of the job.

"If we have the right type of person for the job," JP continued, "we can easily fill in the missing skills."

"How do you plan to do this?"

"Simple. I will send you on a top-class business course."

"Where?"

"To Harvard. That's the best, even if it is American," JP chuckled.

"Right. Harvard. That comes as a surprise."

"Interested?"

"Let me reflect on this," said Paul, confirming his analytical nature detected by the assessment tests. "I will get back to you shortly."

He and Jill needed to talk.

Paul knew the conversation with Jill was going to be difficult. His move to the pharmaceutical industry would be a dramatic shift – a game-changing moment for him – and she had many questions. If it didn't work out, could he go back to surgery? Would he still be relevant, or would things have moved on too far for him to catch up? Was he ready to take such a risk?

Jill was against him leaving clinical medicine to join the pharmaceutical industry, and on top of this, he had to go away to Harvard Business School for close to six months. She wanted to support him but had strong opinions about the negative aspects of the pharmaceutical industry and struggled to come to terms with his career change.

"This is a big move, Paul. Are you sure you know what you are doing?" Jill urged.

"Yes. I firmly believe that I can add more value to healthcare this way than through my existing career."

"Oh, Paul, you're such a boy scout. I hope you're not being too trusting of this JP character."

Jill took a deep breath and gathered her thoughts.

"Paul, I must make it clear that I am not really in favour of this move, especially since you will be gone for five months! The only thing making it tolerable is that I have an enormous amount of work piling up to keep me busy. But I still feel very uncomfortable."

"I know it'll be difficult, darling, but I'd appreciate your support. Now is the best time in our lives for me to get these studies done and make a change."

"You will owe me when you get back."

"I always do."

* * *

Paul received a call the following day to let him know that the position was his if he was still interested. Paul accepted.

He realised he had made a major life decision leaving his surgical career – and nothing would be the same again. He would be on a different quest, and it was unlikely that he could go back to orthopaedics. Surgical techniques would advance to the point that he would be left behind. He was assured of a brilliant career in orthopaedic surgery, but faced with a fork in the road, he had to choose the best way to make a difference – and that was by joining Harrowgate Pharmaceuticals. Despite Jill's apprehensions about his decision, he knew he could make it work. He only had to manage his self-doubt and uneasiness about leaving Jill in England for five months.

CHAPTER 9

Harrowgate

Paul's resignation from the hospital was met with surprise and disappointment. The Head of Surgery felt that he and the hospital were losing an exceptional surgeon and was taken aback that he was doing so to join the pharmaceutical industry. The staff held a farewell lunch for Paul and Jill, having come to know them as a glamorous and talented couple who they would sorely miss.

Jill noted their disbelief that Paul was leaving for industry, and that really concerned her. Reflecting on her discussions with Paul, she decided to do her own research on the pharmaceutical industry. Habitually a note-taker, she would document her thoughts on the move, the industry, and her reflections on this dramatic change. Meanwhile, she would support Paul as best she could.

Paul had retained his apartment in Putney as an asset and moved into the Wandsworth apartment temporarily until he was to fly off to Harvard. On his first day at Harrowgate, Jill made him a hearty breakfast, after which he set off to Euston Station for the hours' train journey.

Slowing down, the train passed Berkhamsted's ruined castle and pulled into the station. Standing just outside the exit was an athletic-looking redhead in his mid-thirties holding a small sign saying 'Harrowgate Pharmaceuticals'.

"Dr Beresford?" he asked as Paul approached him.

"Paul," he replied with a smile and a handshake.

"It's very nice to meet you, Paul. I am Tom Hewitt, the Marketing Director. We've heard a lot from JP about you joining us."

"I hope some of it turns out to be true," Paul replied as Tom led him to a BMW sedan, and they set off up the hill overlooking the town.

They pulled up in a gravel parking lot outside a modest double-storey building with an equally modest sign stating 'Harrowgate Pharmaceuticals' in gold lettering. There is nothing flashy here, thought Paul, as he remembered Jill's comments about the reputation of Big Pharma for spending money extravagantly.

He was taken to a first-floor corner office that had an expansive view of the Chiltern Hills.

"Ah, Paul, pleased to welcome you on board," said JP.

"Thank you, JP. I'm looking forward to it."

They enjoyed some coffee brought in by Mildred, JP's personal assistant, and chatted briefly about the company.

"Right," said JP, "I'll have Tom show you around the building and introduce you to some of the key staff. After that, we will have a brief Exco meeting. You will get to meet the rest then."

The staff seemed upbeat and welcoming in the administrative and research divisions, except when Tom led Paul to a door marked 'Dr Melissa James'. Tom knocked, but there was no answer. He could hear a woman's voice on a phone call and knocked again, but the conversation didn't cease. It was clear that Dr James would not be disturbed to greet anyone.

"It looks as if the Dragon Lady is too busy to meet with us," said Tom.

"Dragon Lady?"

"Yes. Dr James heads up the clinical research associate group, which tracks and implements some of the trials with our new products."

"Why has she earned that title?" asked Paul with a grin.

"Wait until you see her. She is a stunner but hard as nails. Don't get things wrong when dealing with her; otherwise, she will quickly put you in your place. Many guys have the hots for her, but I think they fear that, like the Black Widow spider, she will devour them after mating!" Tom laughed.

"I am looking forward to meeting this lady," said Paul. "Sounds like an interesting challenge for someone who doesn't suffer from arachnophobia."

"Good luck," said Tom, "but she has an intriguing background, though. Italian mother, English father, grew up in Switzerland and was educated there. She came to England to further her studies and married her wealthy English professor, much, much older than her. They separated or divorced; we don't really know, but it's rumoured that he basically wrote her doctoral thesis for her. The only thing that seems to interest her is her work at Harrowgate."

Tom looked at his watch and suddenly realised the time. "We had better get back to the boardroom as JP wants to have a brief meeting to formally welcome you and set out your role in the company."

They went through a maze of corridors and into a brightly lit meeting room. Some people Paul had met with Tom, but others were new to him.

Professor Helmut Reich, who had been poached from a German pharmaceutical company in Darmstadt, was a fairly recent arrival. A burly figure in his early fifties, Professor Reich spoke with a strong accent and had a clipped, precise manner. His role was to oversee the research and development section and design the clinical trial protocols for the new products being developed by Harrowgate.

Paul met David Redford, the Sales Director, who came across as a slightly round, cheerful, easy-to-like individual. Ritesh Shah, the Financial Director, was immaculately dressed, clear-eyed, with an intense look about him.

But there was no Dragon Lady among them.

JP wanted to start the meeting, but noticed the absentee. He looked up at the door a couple of times but to no avail.

"Let's start then," he said. "For those who haven't met him, Dr Paul Beresford is our new Business Development Director. He is an orthopaedic surgeon by training and has been working in London for a couple of years at the Royal National Orthopaedic Hospital. Paul has now made the crazy career decision to throw his hand in with the pharmaceutical industry. Perhaps he will regret it later," JP said to smiles around the table, "but he's here with us for now. In his role as Business Development ..."

At that moment, the door opened, and an extremely attractive woman, possibly in her middle thirties, entered briskly. She had sculpted cheekbones, a sensuous mouth, and short dark hair matching her almost black eyes. She wore an elegantly tailored dark pinstripe two-piece suit.

"Ah, Melissa," said JP, "this is our new recruit, Dr Paul Beresford."

"Yes," she said and sat down without extending a hand of introduction.

Dragon Lady, thought Paul.

Despite the frostiness that settled over the boardroom, JP didn't miss a beat. He had seen plenty of office tensions in his career in the industry.

"As Business Development Director, Paul will work closely with you, Herr Professor, and you, Melissa."

The dark eyes fixed on Paul without any emotion.

"But firstly, we need to give Paul a good overview of how the industry works and how we work to carve our place among the Goliaths which, like David, we intend to take on. Paul has an impressive background but needs to get up to speed as quickly as possible on our operations. I will then send him on a business course to complete his re-education."

The meeting wrapped up with a quick round of questions and answers by team members on their projects, who then started exiting the boardroom. Paul looked around to find Dr Melissa James. He intended to force the first move to introduce himself, but she had left.

JP called his attention and brought him over to Professor Reich.

"Paul, I want you to spend some time this morning with Herr Professor talking about the clinical trial process since this will be a big part of your job description. You can meet with Melissa later," he said, looking intently at Paul to see any reaction to how the boardroom incident had registered with him.

"Not a problem," said Paul, fully understanding the intention behind JP's comment.

* * *

Professor Reich took Paul to his office in the research wing of the building. The office had a sense of crisp efficiency. Folders, all of the same appearance and colour, were neatly stacked on the shelves. A clean white surgical coat, mask and goggles hung from a hook on the door. On one wall were two photographs; one of the central town square in Darmstadt, with its statue of Duke Ludwig, and the other of Otto von Bismarck.

Certificates indicating various doctorates and accolades hung on the opposite wall. It was clear that Professor Reich was extremely well qualified for his critical role in developing new molecules for Harrowgate.

"Sit," said Professor Reich.

Paul's mind quickly returned to the job at hand. The desk was so pristinely clean that he felt one could carry out surgery upon it.

"I want to tell you a bit about the process of clinical trials. I am sure you know some of it from your studies, but I would like to explain some of the intricacies," he said, adopting his professorial pose.

Reich explained that the trial process was more complicated than most people think. He felt that a better understanding of this would help dispel some of the inaccuracies attributed to the industry – but not all. Paul listened intently.

"This is a story of the search for unique medicines, called new chemical entities, to improve or save patients' lives," he continued.

"It is a long, drawn-out procedure and a game of high risks and high rewards. Think of it like your famous horserace here in England, the Grand National. There are many hurdles to be safely cleared before the finishing line can be seen. Sometimes the horse you have bet your money on stumbles and falls at the last hurdle."

Reich used the horseracing metaphor to describe the industry, saying, "It could take nine or ten years to develop a unique medicine, and even if the drug has gone through all the testing hurdles, it can still fail at the last stage of development. The industry is littered with new chemical entities that appear to be winners but never make it to market."

"Does Harrowgate have any of these potentially successful products in the pipeline?" asked Paul.

"Yes, we do have a couple. One, in particular, has our hopes riding on it and is in Phase 3 trials as we speak. JP has bet his family farm on this – literally and figuratively."

"What therapeutic area is it in?"

"In oncology, but we will tell you more about it when you have come back from your business training. We will give you the ... what do they say ... the gritty-nitty about it."

Paul decided it inappropriate to correct his host.

"There are several stages that a candidate drug must pass through," the professor continued with Paul's lesson. "Researchers select a target such as a gene or protein and then select a molecule or compound that may act on the target to alter the disease. Once we have synthesised what we believe is an exciting compound, we apply for a patent."

"That gives twenty years of complete protection, I presume."

"That's not entirely correct."

Reich went on to explain that a patent extended the period of freedom in theory, but two aspects impacted this.

The first impact was that it often took eight to twelve years to get a product from early research to successfully trialled. Then the product dossiers needed to be submitted to medicines regulatory authorities, reflecting all the trial results. Reich mentioned that in certain countries, it could take many years for the authorities to work through all the documentation before approving the drug. Only then could the company aim to get it to market. All these processes would eat away at the twenty-year patent protection, leaving a much shorter time for the company to recoup the high level of the investment. Profits would then help pay for those potential products that had fallen by the wayside, as well as fund new research.

The second impact Reich described was that many companies worked with similar active substances. It could be that shortly after a drug is launched, a competitor could go to market with a different product from the same chemical family – think of it as a relative – with the same, similar or even better clinical effects. Unfortunately, the company would have no patent protection against it. He said that small changes in key assumptions could produce large variations in key outcomes, providing competition in a very tight marketplace.

"People are often surprised to learn that the leading pharma company only has about a five percent global market share, whereas companies such as Boeing and Airbus almost equally share the market," Reich added. "There are many examples of breakthrough products launched, only to find that an almost identical competitor launches shortly afterwards. Alternatively, your competitor beats you to the market with their product."

With patent protection misconceptions explained, Paul changed the subject and asked, "What are the various stages on this long journey as you describe it?"

"Well, once we have identified a compound, it goes into pre-clinical trials for efficacy and safety tests for two to three years, where we look for toxicity in computational models. The second step is to look at the absorption, distribution metabolism and excretion – the pharmacokinetics – and develop a final dosage form, either solid or injectable."

"How sure are you we don't have another thalidomide on

our hands?" Paul asked. "God forbid another drug like it causes severe birth defects – or worse. I haven't left clinical practice to be associated with a disaster."

"Yes, that should be avoided at all costs," the professor agreed, "which is why testing is vital."

Reich elaborated that the critical periods were the early toxicity studies and Phase 1 clinical trials, where tolerability would be tested in twenty to a hundred healthy volunteers. This is where they'd look for side effects. Nearly three-quarters of compounds failed at this stage.

In Phase 2, efficacy trials would be done in small groups of patients who had the disease.

Phase 3 would be large-scale therapeutic trials at several trial centres to prove safety and efficacy and demonstrate the therapeutic advantages they had hoped for.

"Only a quarter of the potential candidates make it through Phase 1 to 3," Reich noted.

"How successful have you been in your career in finding breakthrough products?"

"Mixed," Reich stated. "I have worked for German and Swiss companies and have been involved in some successes, but I've seen many products fail. You could consider me a sceptic."

"Even about the Harrowgate products?"

"Yes. I have been around the block too many times to get overly excited."

To Paul, this seemed rather subduing, given that the distinguished professor had been headhunted to bring success to Harrowgate. But then, he was vastly experienced in the reality and difficulty of new product development in the pharmaceutical industry.

"So, where does the development of a new medicine go wrong?"

"It goes wrong because of the high dropout rate from the number of potential trial drugs we start with to the numbers we finish with. For every five to ten thousand compounds we start with, we only end up with one approved medicine."

There was a quick knock on the door, and Tom Hewitt's face appeared in the doorway.

"Excuse me, Herr Professor, but JP would like to have Paul back in his office."

With the discussion cut short, Paul got up and shook the professor's hand, accepting some notes with a "Danke schön" – the total extent of his knowledge of German – and took his leave.

"Making progress?" asked Tom as they walked to JP's office.

"Yes, but a lot of new stuff to absorb. I find the complexity of the issues intriguing."

* * *

Reunited with JP, he took Paul down the corridor to a sparsely furnished office and said, "This will be your home. You can jolly it up when you are back from the States. I will leave you to get the feel of the place."

Paul entered, reflecting on how different his new life would be from the one he had just left. As a small example, there was no clear territorial domain at the hospital. Three or four doctors shared a common room with empty coffee cups, green surgical gowns scattered around, and textbooks piled up on the desks. The office almost felt lonely by comparison.

Dave, the Sales Director, popped his head in and said, "I will be your neighbour when you are permanently back with us. You're lucky you got the corner office; I had my eye on it."

Paul did not appreciate the trivial foibles and petty symbols of corporate life implied by this statement. He just smiled and continued reading the notes Professor Reich had given him.

Later Tom came to his office to drive Paul back to the station for his return trip to London. On the way, he asked Tom about the apparent cold shoulder that Melissa James had given him, especially since, as JP indicated, he would have to work closely with her.

"That's how she usually is in her dealings with people, but there may be another factor at play. Approaching seventy, JP won't stay at the company forever. He has been an inspirational leader who motivates us, but he wants to leave on a high. Succession to his role as CEO will be open one day, and perhaps she feels she is in the running and sees you as a rival?"

"That's ridiculous. I am so new to the company and have a tremendous amount to learn."

"Well, let's see how this plays out," said Tom, offering a parting handshake as the train rumbled into the small station.

As the train moved smoothly through the Hertfordshire countryside, Paul had time to reflect on the dramatic change in his life and lifestyle that the move to Harrowgate would mean. He would miss the interaction with patients; he would miss the surgery. This was a radical change, and he wondered if he had made the right choice. Paul had done his systematic analysis, which had given him grounds to be sure, but his self-doubt still crept in. And, of course, Jill was not entirely comfortable with it, so he would have to manage her expectations.

On the other hand, Paul was excited about this new career and where it would take him. He pondered his early years and where he had come from. He thought about his interaction with his parents and the deep remorse he felt that his father had mostly dismissed him as unsuccessful. This still left residual insecurity in his mind about his abilities that sometimes crept into his thinking. Despite his dramatic change at school, jolted into action by his parents' death leading him to become the top student and Head of School, then on to medical school, Paul still felt uncertain.

What would his father think of him now if he were alive? He had succeeded at school both academically and on the sports field. He had qualified as a doctor, which would have delighted his nursing sister mother. And he had found a beautiful and talented girl. His father had not lived to see any of it, and Paul realised his past had been the primary driver in his desire to succeed.

His reflections were interrupted by the train pulling into Euston Station. He left the carriage to wrestle through the five o'clock evening rush to get back home, give Jill a kiss and feedback from the first day of his new life.

CHAPTER 10

A Persistent Past

Following his first day at Harrowgate, Paul spent the best part of two weeks on induction, visiting the various departments in the company to get a sense of the organisation's structure and workings. He had met nearly all the staff – but not the so-called Dragon Lady. Melissa James had been away from the company, touring the various clinical trial sites worldwide to engage with the doctors and follow up on the promising results of Harrowgate's potential new product. His meeting with her would have to wait until after he returned from his business course.

Paul flew to Boston in late August to enrol at the prestigious Harvard Business School set alongside the Charles River for an intensive leadership development programme. The parting from Jill had been difficult. The image of her tear-stained face waving him goodbye was still with him as he settled into his business class seat on the upper deck of a British Airways 747 flight. She was not in favour of him leaving clinical medicine, and it had been a source of tension and discontent between them before his departure. Paul wanted to make it up to her on his return and show her the benefits that his being part of a pharmaceutical company could bring to a broader spectrum of patients than he could manage in his previous role as a surgeon.

As the air hostess brought him a hot towel and a welcoming

drink, his mind returned to his childhood family experiences that still haunted him. How lucky Jill was to have parents who were so delighted and supportive of her. He wanted to succeed for his late father, which was impossible, but it would drive him – and haunt him. He wanted to succeed for Jill as well and vowed to come away from Harvard with excellent results.

* * *

It seemed strange to Paul to be back in an academic setting, made starker still by the small but well-equipped students' residence rooms. After enjoying the fairly spacious home back in Wandsworth, this was an adjustment. Sitting in the horseshoe-shaped lecture room, he found that most of the participants were from diverse work backgrounds, quite different from the conformity of medical students that he was used to. This was refreshing and stimulating since they all benefited from a broad-based input in their smaller tutorial groups.

As he had no real business experience other than the workings of a government hospital, Paul found that his contribution to the class and tutorials was minimal. Still, he soon grasped the elements of finance, marketing and technological advances. Paul wanted to absorb the strategic insights, risk assessment, global perspectives and leadership skills taught by some of the finest lecturers in the world. Although the world of medicine was his passion, Paul thought that his overall worldview was limited, and as the course progressed, he felt that he was acquiring a broader understanding of the global picture.

Besides his studies, Paul managed to try rowing with some of his classmates on the Charles River flowing past Harvard – not with a great deal of success. How much more he would now appreciate the skills of the Oxford and Cambridge boat race teams on the Thames next time he watched it.

While enjoying the course, he had limited time to wonder

how things were going back home. Communication with Jill was infrequent due to the course assignments and his self-absorption in developing his new life. He would only later realise how much this would cost him.

* * *

Back in England, Sean was easing himself into the offices at Blackheath Chemicals. Viscount Talbot had allowed Sean to head up the company to test his ability to succeed in this venture. He surrounded Sean with many skilled people in the various management areas and left it up to Sean to sink or swim. He felt that the chances of Sean doing well with the support around him were strong but wanted to see Sean's contribution to the enterprise. At least Blackheath was one of the smaller companies in the Viscount's business portfolio. If Sean failed, it would not be a train smash but rather an inexpensive testing ground for his son.

Sean had brought in his two sycophantic crony friends from schooldays and put them on the payroll as advisors. Digby Newton and Crispin Wake-Armstrong would be there to carry out any special tasks and orders he delegated to them. Crispin was bright and valuable; Digby was useful as a gopher to execute Sean's various requests.

"My father has surrounded me with a lot of little grey men to keep me on the straight and narrow," Sean mocked, "and that's not going to work for me. I give you my authority to override any obstacles they put in our way. I have grand plans to grow this little organisation into a big player with some aggressive moves. That will show my unrelenting autocratic father what I am really made of. Let's do it! Over to you."

Crispin, who had completed an engineering degree and had some experience in the chemical industry, had reviewed the company's portfolio.

"Basically, there are some key areas or sectors that we are

currently involved in. These include the primary market with inorganic chemicals, and we have a good range of agrochemicals."

"That all sounds too dull for me," observed Sean. "What we need is entry into a sexy market with lots and lots of profits. Let's change our production to make some of these – whatever they are."

"I am afraid it doesn't happen like that," Crispin indicated. "Our plant equipment is committed to these areas, so that won't be possible."

"Then what are the markets I am looking for, Mister Know-it-all?"

"I don't know it all," Crispin bristled, "but I do know that the pharmaceutical market is a high-profit industry. But we can't make any final pharmaceutical product with the equipment we have."

"Well, let's go out and buy a company then," Sean said flippantly. "I have access to loads of cash and credit. That's why it's beneficial for you to work for me. I can make things happen."

Crispin laughed. "You don't just pitch up at a pharma company with a suitcase full of cash if that's what you were thinking."

"No smart-arse. I would not show my hand like that, but I could if I wanted to. I'd rather find an organisation that will suss out some acquisition opportunities. My guiding principle in life is that everybody has their price."

With that, Sean started searching for a firm dealing with acquisitions and mergers to assist him in finding potential targets for his grand expansion plans, all rooted in an all-consuming desire to impress his father.

* * *

Jill was extremely busy at the Solicitors' practice, as she predicted she would be, and it certainly helped fill the gap in her life with Paul's absence. He had been gone only a few weeks, but it felt much longer. Even though she missed him, Jill was enjoying the complexity of her current brief to look at a potential merger between two energy companies.

The meetings with the top executives were draining, but they appreciated the complex work she had put in, along with the senior partner and multidisciplinary team members. They smoothed the legal path required to avoid any expensive pitfalls. As part of the corporate and commercial team in the practice, Jill's role was to compile the purchase and sale contracts and support the negotiations around due diligence. The partners were impressed with her insightful contributions and found her inquisitive, empathetic and spirited. They saw her as a rising star.

While finalising the merger between the two energy firms, Giles Robinson, a senior member of the Chamber, came into her office. A chemical company had made an appointment to meet with her regarding potential acquisitions.

"They specifically asked to meet with you, Jill, so it seems that your reputation is building already," Giles praised. "They have set the meeting for Monday at ten o'clock. They could potentially be a massive client for us, so I am sure you will work your magic on them."

"Did they say who they were?"

"Yes, but they wanted to keep it confidential until the meeting."

"That's strange, but I guess I will find out shortly."

That Monday found Jill in the meeting room in The Honourable Society of the Middle Temple, ready for her discussions with the important, but yet unknown, potential client. She was facing the window looking out at the Thames when the door opened.

Giles entered and said, "Jill, I would like you to meet the Honourable Sean St Ledger."

Jill swung round in surprise as the familiar figure followed Giles into the room.

"Hello Jill, I don't think you expected to see me again," Sean smirked.

"Oh, you two know each other," said Giles, delighted that a distinguished member of the nobility and the wealthy potential client was on friendly terms with one of his key employees. That seemed to set things up for a possible business arrangement.

"Oh. Hello, Sean. Yes, it's been a while," she responded, taken aback that he should re-appear in her life and after the coincidence of Paul mentioning that he was at school with Sean. It seemed an odd triangulate.

"Right, I will leave you two to catch up and discuss what the Honourable St Ledger has on his mind," said Giles as he exited the room with an expectant smile.

"Sean, please take a seat."

Jill retained her politeness while she processed the figure opposite her. Sean had become somewhat more inflated than in his student days – both in body and attitude. In the expensive attire intended to hide his belly, Sean eased himself into a chair opposite her.

"How can I assist you?" she broke the awkward silence.

"You must be surprised to see me calling on you again?"

"Yes, exactly."

"Well, I'm running a successful chemical business, but I want to grow not only organically but also by acquisition," Sean boasted. "I searched a number of companies dealing in mergers and acquisitions and looked through their staff. When I got to Chadwick, Monteith & Robinson, I recognised a beautiful blonde I knew from my student days. Bingo!"

Jill was unmoved by his observation and remained silent, processing where this was going.

"So, how can I help you?" she said, opening her legal pad as an inveterate note-taker.

"I am looking to add a pharmaceutical company to my portfolio since my existing business can be modified to produce raw materials for the manufacture of medicines. I was hoping that your firm, which has a reputation for identifying potential targets and always clinching the deal, could assist."

"What size company are you looking at? There are substantial companies in this sector – almost beyond acquisition."

"I am looking for a small to medium-sized business. There are a lot of fairly new startups that would easily make potential targets."

Jill was rapidly absorbing how this narrative could evolve. Paul's company fitted this brief along with a few others that the firm had previously identified. What would it mean if Sean tried to buy Harrowgate? From her previous interactions with Sean, she knew that his family had enormous wealth. He would make a valuable client, and as an employee of her organisation, she was obliged to pursue the firm's best interests.

"Well, I will work with other colleagues in the corporate and commercial divisions to see what we can come up with for you."

"Excellent. I consider that a positive first step. Now I would like to take you out for lunch at my club to cement our business arrangement."

"Thank you, Sean, but I cannot accept your kind offer as I have a full day of meetings and projects for today."

"Well, how about dinner? I feel we have some unfinished business."

Jill ignored this comment and, taking up her legal notepad, said, "Let's rather get some sense of what exactly you are looking to acquire so that I can brief my colleagues accordingly. What you have mentioned is only a starting point. From my experience, there are a number of steps, from acquisition strategy to closing, that need close attention. We will need some target screening based on your ideas. You mentioned small to medium-sized businesses. Just here in the UK, or globally?"

"Let's limit the search to locals," Sean began. "I intend to expand once I have a basic footprint."

Jill probed Sean further for details, took copious notes and completed her assessment of his requirements. While she did so, her mind went back to her student days and her interactions with Sean. Even as she focused on her task, Jill was aware of him staring at her intently in a none-too-subtle way, as if he was mentally undressing her. She stood up to indicate that they had completed their meeting.

Sean slithered out of the chair and round the table to stand next to her.

"So, what about dinner?" he asked, moving into her personal space.

"Thank you, Sean, but I'm afraid not."

"You can't be busy day and night. I am sure you will have a free evening somewhere. I am prepared to wait – especially for you."

"Thank you once again, Sean, but I won't be able to manage that."

"Why not? I thought you and I had something going. You even took me to visit your parents."

"Yes, but I took others from Oxford to meet them as well. They were interested in meeting other students from the University, that's all."

"Your father seemed to like me," Sean persisted.

Jill felt uncomfortable with the situation. She needed to keep the practice's interests in mind, but all she wanted was to disengage from Sean, personally and professionally. Professionally, she could not, so she said she would think about dinner as a last resort to end the standoff.

"Good, I am sure we will enjoy a little tête-à-tête."

She moved towards the door to take Sean back to the reception. He followed her, and she could feel him taking her in. She had decided on a whim that morning to wear a shortish black skirt that perfectly showed off her waist and legs.

"Still a very nice figure," she heard from behind her.

"Thank you," she said through gritted teeth.

She took him through to reception, where a number of the staff were lingering to see this distinguished potential client from the nobility. Giles appeared, as if by magic, to bid Sean farewell.

As Sean exited with a "Thank you, Jill," Giles turned to her with a broad smile.

"So, how did it go?" he asked eagerly.

"It seemed to go well. The team needs to start looking for what he is interested in."

"He seemed interested in you, Jill," observed Giles.

"Let me call a meeting to debrief the others and ensure all the details are noted."

"He looked as if he wanted to debrief you as well," said Giles with an uncharacteristic but knowing look.

"I'll call the others."

Jill went back to her office and closed the door. She felt utterly uncomfortable and trapped between her obligation to her employer and having to protect her private life. She regretted opening up an opportunity for him to take her out, but it seemed at the time the only way to get him away from her. That was a mistake because she knew that he would come calling again.

She had decided against mentioning Paul, even though he knew Sean from school. That would open up the prospect of mentioning Harrowgate, and she felt repulsed by the thought of Sean owning Paul's company. She went back to her notepad and recorded some personal thoughts and observations.

With a heavy heart, she went back to the Wandsworth apartment that evening. She missed Paul's company, but in some ways, she felt relieved that he was not there. He would have wanted to diagnose her discomfort and know why she was upset. Jill wanted to manage this in her own way.

CHAPTER 11

Trapped

Nearly a month into his course, Paul was becoming wholly engrossed in the business world. He found his mind as sharp in absorbing the issues revolving around corporate affairs as it had been during his medical studies.

Time off was somewhat limited and mostly confined to weekends, and even then, there were usually preparations to complete for the upcoming tutorials for himself and his group. When he could, he managed to get away for some sightseeing in New York, where he marvelled at the buzz and activity of Times Square or enjoyed a quieter moment strolling through the Metropolitan Museum of Art located in Central Park. While at Oxford, Jill combined her law degree with taking extra classes to study Impressionist artists. She had introduced Paul to art appreciation, and they visited a number of galleries in London together. After his excursions, the return to Harvard was always a jolt but one which he enjoyed.

One jolt Paul didn't enjoy was one night in his quarters in the small hours of the morning. A female classmate slipped into his bed, claiming that she was feeling anxious and depressed by the course pressure and wondering if the class doctor could do anything to relieve these symptoms. It took persuasion and diplomacy to detach her and send her back to her room while maintaining her dignity. She left the course shortly after, and the incident served to remind him that the course's intensity placed great strain on marriages and relationships. He resolved to contact Jill more often to improve the hiatus in their communication.

* * *

Following her encounter with Sean, Jill buried herself in work, keeping the image of their meeting and its demands – personal and professional – out of mind. She started a small workgroup to look at possible prospective companies to suit Sean's requirements and keep Harrowgate outside the frame of reference. She took it upon herself to identify companies and pass these on to members of the workgroup to crunch the numbers and review the opportunities and threats facing them. In this way, she could control which of these companies were reviewed. It seemed to be working well as there were several potential candidates that needed assessment.

Late one evening, due to their time differences, she received a phone call from Paul.

"Hello, my love."

From the tone of his voice, Jill sensed that he was upbeat about how things were going at Harvard. Wanting to keep the mood the same despite feeling a bit down that evening, she replied, "All well this side. How is the course progressing?"

"I'm pleased to say that I am enjoying every moment – despite the pressure it places on all of us. How is your work? I hope they're not overloading you, given all your capabilities?"

There are moments in life when decisions need to be made regarding what is said and what is withheld. This was one of those moments for both Paul and Jill.

Jill decided not to mention Sean St Ledger's visit as she had picked up from their conversation before meeting her parents that the relationship between the two men seemed to reflect a degree of tension. She was also aware that Sean would do all he could to bed her. She was confident that she could deal with that but didn't want to reveal that Sean was looking to buy a pharmaceutical company. That would only serve as a distraction for Paul, given the demands of his course.

By the same yardstick, Paul did not want to raise the incident where his classmate was looking for intimacy with him as he felt this might upset her; he could hear in her voice that she was not as upbeat as she pretended to be. He made a mental note to contact her more regularly as their lives were now running in separate, parallel streams.

"I am missing you," Jill confessed. "All of you."

"Same here, love. I feel that I have become a monk living on Coke and black coffee to keep me going!"

"I hope that none of your fellow female students want more of you?"

"No," he lied.

"At least you have the first month behind you. Just over four to go. It seems like a lifetime."

"It'll go quicker than you think as we are both swamped. It will help the time go by."

"I hope so."

* * *

About three weeks after her encounter with Sean, Jill was informed by Giles that Sean was requesting a visit to gauge the progress of his acquisition investigation. In the interim, Jill had identified three small companies – two in England and one in Northern Ireland which might be suitable. She had provided these names to the workgroup with the instruction to interrogate the opportunities. Her team's focus areas included the company's business background, market size and share and the importance of the numbers – revenues, margins, capital investments – and, most importantly, their product portfolio and their new chemical entity pipeline.

The team had put together a presentation and was ready

to demonstrate the opportunities. Jill felt that the profile of the companies almost resembled Goldilocks' porridge. One was too cold to generate interest but was a marker for the market. The other was too hot as there was overcapitalisation, but the third seemed just right on the necessary metrics. Perhaps she and the team could provide the answer to Sean's needs – though not all of them. She reluctantly reminded herself of his interest in her.

Sean arrived on the designated day with Crispin Wake-Armstrong. When he entered the meeting room, he was disappointed that Jill was not alone but accompanied by a group of colleagues. He hoped to impress Crispin with his interaction with Jill but would now have to deal with a more disparate audience.

Jill welcomed Sean and Crispin and introduced them to her team. As they took their seats around the table, he whispered to Crispin, "I told you she was a looker. I got a bit of her at Oxford."

Crispin looked on enviously as Jill initiated the presentation launch, and her group started running through the options. Sean had enough knowledge and common sense to ask some appropriate and penetrating questions, reminding Jill that he was no fool and would only be sold on what was a viable option. With his engineering background, Crispin was also able to supplement those issues raised by his boss with his own questions. Jill concluded the presentation with an overview of the legal status of the three companies covering agreements, contracts, copyright and product patent status.

As Jill anticipated, the two lesser option companies were seen as not that viable, but the third, a startup in Northern Ireland, InnovoPharm, had merit. Sean indicated an interest in this company which encouraged Jill as she hoped this would prevent any identification of Harrowgate.

"What's the next move?" Sean asked.

"I can contact them and say there is interest in an acquisition."

"You have my permission to do so."

"I first need the team to do a deeper dive, which will precede a due diligence if we progress to that point."

"Right," said Sean. "Can I have a private word with Miss Collins about that next step?"

The group moved out. Sean leered at Jill and closed the door.

"We seem to be making progress – at least in one area," he said, once again moving around the table to be closer to Jill.

"If this lead turns out to be a positive one, I would like to visit the company, and I want you to accompany me. We can use the Talbot company jet. Have you ever been on one?"

"No, I haven't."

"It will be an experience you will never forget," he boasted.

Jill did not acknowledge the offer.

Undeterred, Sean said, "Last time I was here, you said you would have a meal with me. What will it be – lunch or dinner?"

"I'll have to see what my diary looks like and let you know."

Jill felt that a meal engagement with Sean was inevitable to balance her commitment to the practice with her need to shake him off. He was hunting her down like a trapped deer, and she knew it.

"Let's go and join the others," Jill tried to escape. "They must be wondering what is keeping us and whether something is going wrong with the arrangement."

"No, things are coming along nicely," said Sean with a look of smug satisfaction. "Very nicely indeed."

The group reunited in the reception area to make their farewells. The omnipresent Giles was there to bid Sean and Crispin goodbye and, after they left, turned to Jill.

"So, how is it going?"

"We seem to have identified a prospect of interest to him and will carry out a more in-depth view now that we have identified a specific target."

"Excellent, excellent!" said Giles. "Don't forget to keep him happy; there could be a big opportunity for us here."

Jill knew precisely what would keep Sean happy, and she would do her best to avoid it.

Following the meeting with Sean and her group of colleagues,

Jill applied herself with the commercial division for a deeper dive into the workings of InnovoPharm, which, like Harrowgate, was a startup established ten years before. It had some innovative combinations and sustained-release products in the cardiovascular and gastrointestinal fields. It had been the subject of several acquisition enquiries by major pharmaceutical companies – many of these having offices or factories in Ireland. Jill felt that InnovoPharm might be tempted to succumb to an offer from one of the wealthy noble families of the United Kingdom, where some of the large American companies had failed with tentative bids.

The team's research showed that Ireland had attracted pharmaceutical company investments for several reasons, one of them being amongst the lowest corporate tax rates in the world. There was also an attractive tax credit incentive on qualifying research and development, which was a considerable bonus for the pharmaceutical industry's high-risk, high-reward nature.

Jill started to feel confident that this proposition could satisfy Sean's business needs. The downside was that he wanted to take her to Ireland in his company jet, and she guessed he would try to make her a member of the Mile High Club if any of his past actions were an indication. How she wished Paul was there to help deal with this personal and professional dichotomy. Jill always prided herself on her ability to take control of difficult situations, but this one was unique.

* * *

About two weeks after their last meeting, Sean called Jill at the office.

"How is your research going on the Irish acquisition?"

"It's progressing well. I have sounded them out, and they have expressed interest. I think you will find it an attractive proposition."

"Not as attractive as you."

Deflecting, Jill continued, "I'll be able to share some of the information with you and your team shortly."

"Let's combine that preliminary overview with a dinner. I can come and collect you, and I know an exceptional restaurant. We can do the full team briefing later."

Jill decided that she would have to accede to having a meal with Sean to close off these approaches. She did not want to agree to dinner as this could involve a late night, trying to fight off a lustful, alcohol-infused Sean. In addition, she did not want him to know where she lived.

"I'll have a lunch with you, Sean. Give me about a week to finalise some of the information."

"Well, that's a start."

They set a date for the following week, and Jill put the phone down with a heavy heart. She hoped she could tactfully put an end to Sean's advances by finding him a suitable business opportunity that would hopefully take his mind off her by absorbing all his attention.

On the agreed date, she waited in her office for Sean to arrive. She had informed Giles that Sean would be taking her for lunch, which he received with obvious pleasure. Her thoughts were forming around how this would play out – how to disengage with Sean on a personal level without damaging her company's prospects.

She received a call that Sean was in reception and went through to find him in the company of Giles, chatting amiably.

"Hello Jill, I hope you are ready for a good discussion and meal."

"Thank you, Sean, I am," she said, maintaining an air of decorum in front of her boss.

"Good. The Bentley awaits," said Sean, smiling and winking at Giles.

Leaving the building, they took the short walk down Middle Temple Lane to Victoria Embankment alongside the Thames. On the way, Sean called his chauffeur and shortly, a maroon Bentley pulled up next to them. Sean opened the back door for Jill and followed her in.

"Well, at last, we are together," Sean gloated.

"We are together to discuss a lucrative business opportunity."

Jill wanted to take charge of the narrative to focus on the issues and deflect from the personal.

The Bentley weaved its way through the London midday traffic and into Mayfair. Jill had dressed in a demure grey blouse and a checked black and white skirt with black leggings. She had gathered her hair away from her face in a ponytail to create a business-like appearance rather than let her hair tumble down to her shoulders as she often wore it. Jill was disturbed to find that she sank back further than she had expected on the Bentley's plush, spacious rear seats, leaving more of her thigh exposed than she wanted.

"Ah, here we are," said Sean as they approached the restaurant. He put his hand on her exposed thigh. "I am sure you will enjoy this."

Jill wondered if he was referring to the meal or his attempt to seduce her. The chauffeur opened the door for her, and Sean joined her on the pavement while the Bentley drove off.

As they entered the restaurant, the maître d' almost bent double as he welcomed Sean.

"Welcome back, sir and to your lovely guest. Your usual private dining room, of course?"

Jill felt uneasy; she thought they would be in an open dining area with plenty of guests. A private dining room afforded Sean an environment conducive to familiarity. As they walked through the elegant art deco inspired interior with its 1920s glamour of leather seating, oak-panelled walls and brass fittings, Jill felt that she had to credit Sean with taste and money. Their entrance was greeted with nodding and approving glances from the customers. Some of them who knew him raised themselves from their chairs to greet Sean obsequiously. So, this is how the entitled are treated, she thought.

Jill was relieved that the meal started in a business-like manner after the arrival of her starter of Challans Duck and tuna sashimi for Sean. He then ordered an expensive French white wine that Jill saw as the first step in a standard loosening-up tactic.

"So, what can you tell me about my potential acquisition? Of course, I am referring to the Irish company," said Sean expanding on his double entendre. Jill knew that he was also referring to her.

"It's looking favourable," said Jill, keeping it professional. "They've had a few overtures from some of the bigger American companies but have rejected them up to now. But this means that they do have an interest in being taken over. I think that an offer from a UK company which has your family's reputation would have some appeal."

"That sounds like a positive step. It's good to know that the family connections have leverage – as they have had in the past."

Jill gave Sean more of the company's details, explaining that the patent protection on some of their locally developed products would be favourable since there were still several years before expiry. She was pleased to find that the conversation was mainly centred on the acquisition, even though he continually looked to refill her glass in an apparent attempt to loosen her resistance. She countered this by sipping slowly and matching this equally by drinking water.

They ordered their main meal and continued their discussion about the timing of completing the deep dive and approaching the company with an offer. So far, so good, thought Jill. Sean did turn the conversation to some of their Oxford days, chatting about the people they had known and their current whereabouts, but the discussion remained fairly benign with little reference to the more extravagant episodes. As they finished their meal, Jill felt it was a case of mission accomplished, even though she felt slightly lightheaded from the wine.

They left the restaurant with the staff bowing and scraping as they passed through to find the Bentley waiting for them. Once in the car, Jill's concern grew as Sean closed off the partition between them and the chauffeur after telling him to take the scenic route back to the Inns of Court.

"So, we seem to be making the progress we want on all fronts," said Sean as he leaned towards her, placing his hand on her thigh once again.

"We are making progress in the business of finding you the right acquisition. That's all."

"Come on, Jill, you know that you are attracted to me, but you are just playing hard to get."

Jill had a sense of unreality as the car drove through the streets of Mayfair and Chelsea. She looked out of the window to see people going about their daily lives – pausing at traffic lights, queuing for the red London buses, peering into shop windows – everything was normal, but they could not see through the tinted windows the abnormal scene developing within the luxurious confines of the Bentley. Sean moved even closer to her and put his hand further up on her thigh. She did not flinch immediately and hoped her nonresponse would deflect him with some dignity. Sean took her lack of reaction as acquiescence.

"Sean, this approach is inappropriate if we hope to keep our business arrangements moving forward professionally."

"Why not? It's worked for me in the past," he declared and inched his hand even further up her thigh, attempting to prise her legs apart in preparation for a further assault.

"You know your firm is eager to do business with me. Surely you would not want that opportunity to fall through?"

"Yes," Jill winced, "but they would not want it to occur under these circumstances. That's not their way."

"Business is business! Haven't you learnt that?"

"I need to separate my professional from my personal life, and with that in mind, you must know that I am in a relationship." Sean's fingers paused, just short of their target.

"And who is this lucky man?"

"He is a doctor."

"Only a doctor? I thought you deserved better."

"He is a wonderful man, and I am very much in love with him."

"Oh, so what is his name?"

"His name is Paul."

"Lucky Doctor Paul. Where does he work?"

"He works at one of the local orthopaedic hospitals," Jill lied, having anticipated the question.

She did not want to reveal Paul's connection to Harrowgate. She was also mindful of Paul's reaction when she mentioned that she knew Sean. Obviously, something had happened between them, but Paul had not wanted to open up about it, so she didn't want to mention Paul's surname.

"So I have a rival, a competitor. I always enjoy a challenge!"

"There's no competition, Sean. I am fully committed to him."

"We will see about that," Sean snarled, abruptly withdrawing his hand from between her thighs, much to Jill's relief. Hopefully, she could manage his disengagement from her while still keeping her firm's interests on track.

"We can continue to keep our business interests moving forward as I am interested in the opportunity you have identified," he said matter-of-factly.

Despite his setback in wanting to seduce Jill, Sean had another pressing issue on his mind – perhaps even more urgent than wanting to bed Jill – which was the challenge his father had set him to run Blackheath Chemicals successfully. Failure could lead to his father reinstating his illegitimate son and depriving Sean of the Viscountcy. That could not happen. Jill was pivotal in helping him succeed; sex with her would have to wait. He was sure he could overcome the challenge of a lowly doctor once he was progressing with developing his company.

Sean opened the partition to the rear passenger compartment of the Bentley and told the chauffeur that they could return to the Inns of Court. The chauffeur studied Jill in the rearview mirror, expecting to see a dishevelled female readjusting her clothing if previous trips of this nature were anything to go by. He was surprised to see the beautiful passenger fairly composed and sitting sedately. So you failed for the first time, oh Honourable Sean, was the chauffeur's contemptuous thought as he pulled up once again on the Victoria Embankment.

"Let's continue our progress on all fronts," Sean said as the chauffeur opened the rear door for Jill.

"We will assist you in finding the company you need. Thank you for lunch," she said, then the Bentley drove away.

Jill did not feel like going back to the office. Despite her apparent composed demeanour, she was shaking inside. She had succeeded in warding Sean off from molesting her, although he had come close, and she hoped she had done it without wounding his dignity – if he had any. She had also protected Paul and his identity and indicated to Sean that she was in a relationship that mattered. Jill was relieved at Sean's final comments, showing he was still committed to an acquisition through her firm. All objectives were achieved, but she wondered if that was too optimistic, given Sean's nature.

She resigned herself to going back to work. If she didn't, she feared it would create the impression that she had gone off for an indecent rendezvous with Sean, and Jill didn't want to make herself the subject of the gossip chain. As she walked up Middle Inn Lane to the practice, she knew she'd have to maintain an air of propriety even though she could still feel the sensation of Sean's hand between her legs.

Jill realised that Vanessa, the elegant receptionist with the dirty mind, would wonder if the nobleman had plundered Jill's little treasure. She needed to present the perfect picture of composure as she returned to work, walking through reception to the interested glances of the staff. And she did.

As Sean drove away from dropping Jill off, he called Digby.

"I have a project you need to get onto immediately," he ordered. "Find a doctor with the name of Paul – no surname available – who works at one of the orthopaedic hospitals in London. I want his surname. He is dating Jill, and I don't want any opposition getting in the way of my plans for her. I want to sort him out – see how he operates without kneecaps."

"Right, boss. I'll get onto it immediately!"

Sean put down the phone with a sense of gratification and called to his chauffeur with a smirk, "Home, Jeeves."

CHAPTER 12

Triumph

Following the lunch meeting between Jill and Sean, their paths went in different directions. Jill hoped that she had fended off Sean's initial moves on her and had him more interested in acquiring the Irish pharmaceutical company, InnovoPharm. There was still a lot of work to do exploring the opportunity, but at face value, it seemed the company might consider a takeover or merger. She set about getting her team to assess the company further. In addition, Giles kept following up with her on the project as he was keen to see Sean as a client of the practice with all the prestige that would accompany it.

She was still concerned about Sean's reference to them flying to Ireland in his jet. Would she have to fight off his advances again? Would he try to make her a member of the Mile High Club? She had to put these questions out of her mind as she still had other legal cases to work on and found herself almost overloaded, but she welcomed the workload as it helped fill the void in Paul's absence. She wanted Paul to focus undisturbed on his studies at Harvard as this was critical for him to make the transition from clinical medicine into the pharmaceutical industry, and she wanted to do everything she could to support this. He was over halfway through the course, and soon their normal relationship and life would resume. Communication between them had been drastically reduced, but she put this down to their respective work pressures and her reluctance to engage in lengthy discussions in case a reference to Sean might crop up. She made a note to ask Paul to clear up the mystery about Sean when he returned. There was obviously significant friction between them.

In the meantime, Jill continued with the research on InnovoPharm. Sean had contacted her a few times to follow up on her progress, so it was imperative to get the proposition to him as soon as possible, as there was a good chance of success. Jill had another motive for the urgency. If Sean committed himself to the InnovoPharm project, it was unlikely he would make a move against Harrowgate since the cost implications of the Irish purchase would tie Sean up financially – despite his wealth – even if he stumbled on Paul and Harrowgate.

Desperate to advance this, she started taking work home and found that she was neglecting herself. Meals became more erratic and irregular and sometimes even missed altogether. Jill would usually keep her commitments to gym and Pilates classes, but the exercise fell away under these circumstances. Her sharp mind was able to process the legal complexities of the proposed takeover, and she felt confident it would be finalised and tied up shortly before Paul was due to return. She was encouraged by her ability to cut through the issues surrounding a proposal to purchase and felt that this period of extreme pressure was justified in pursuing her goal.

* * *

While Jill worked on the proposal, Sean progressed with overseeing his chemical company. Running it would be too much of an overstatement since his interest in it was minimal. It was simply a means to an end. Crispin had told him it was possible to convert their equipment to make active ingredients for pharmaceutical products. This would create a vertical value chain for input into the Irish company when it became part of the St Ledger business empire.

Sean kept his father informed since a large tranche of money would have to be raised for the purchase besides issuing stock. His father seemed impressed with these efforts, much to Sean's relief since his father would then continue to back him. Sean's business engagement with his father and Blackheath was purely self-serving, and all he really wanted was to teach the old bastard a thing or two by his success.

Sitting in his office, scheming how he could further his success, the phone rang. Sean was expecting it to be from his father regarding the funding issue for the acquisition but was surprised that it was Digby.

"Morning, Boss. I have some news for you. Guess where I am?"

"Don't waste my time with mysteries. Where are you?"

"I am in London at the Royal National Orthopaedic Hospital."

"Get on with it."

"Are you sitting down?"

"For Christ's sake, Digby, get to the point."

"I have found Doctor Paul."

"What?"

"Yes, and here are two more surprises. Guess what his surname is?"

"Don't play games with me."

"His surname is Beresford!"

"What? Are you sure? You're not the sharpest tool in the shed, after all."

"No doubt about it. And here is the second surprise: Beresford left the hospital to join a pharmaceutical company called Harrowgate. And thirdly, they said he was dating a girl named Jill Collins, a lawyer from Oxford University."

"Well, how about that," Sean said, stunned at Jill's deception. "How about that!"

Sean experienced mixed emotions with the news. His old adversary from schooldays had suddenly reappeared, and Sean had a score to settle with him. On top of that, Jill was leading him in a different direction with her proposition about the Irish company. Undoubtedly she was trying to protect Paul, and he wondered why. What did Jill know about the altercation at school and its consequences that so embittered him and reduced his standing in front of his father? Sean believed that Paul had put him in a position to lose what was rightfully his, and now Jill was dating the bastard! The thought of Paul sleeping with the woman he lusted after riled him. He needed to put a plan in place to deal with the situation.

Sean remembered the Talbot family motto and history of winning at all costs, and that's precisely what he would do. He felt elated and exhausted at the same time. Fortunate circumstances had put him in a position to settle old scores and exert pressure on Jill to be intimate with him by threatening to withdraw his engagement with her firm. And at the same time, he would develop a successful business to prove to his father that the lineage of the Talbots could continue through him. He got up from his desk, crossed to the drinks cabinet, and took out a bottle of Veuve Clicquot. "Here's to triumph," he said, toasting himself.

Sean raced to find out about Harrowgate Pharmaceuticals. From their website and in press clippings, he saw a small to medium company on the rise. He found an image of Paul as Business Development Director among the staff photographs.

"So that's who you are now. Let's see what you look like when my guys have finished with you."

Crispin had found some articles in financial publications about the rise of the small British pharmaceutical company and its discovery of an innovative and promising medicine for the treatment of cancer. If the drug passed all trials and registration, the share price, already moving upwards, could skyrocket. This new medicine could be a blockbuster making a fortune for the company. No other information was provided about the product except that it was undergoing trials in some listed sites worldwide.

Sean's mind was scheming how to best use this information. Sitting in his office with Crispin one evening, he had a thought.

"What if we buy Harrowgate instead? I could kill two birds with one stone."

"That also crossed my mind," said Crispin, "so I made some enquiries through friends in the financial sector. They said that other companies had tried to bid for it, but the exponential rise in Harrowgate's share price based on the new product's potential made it non-viable."

"Remind me where the trials are taking place."

Crispin pulled out an article from the Financial Times.

"It says the trials are taking place here in the UK, Nairobi, Hong Kong, Geneva, St Petersburg, Hartford Connecticut and Cairo."

"Interesting," Sean pondered. "I might have a thought or two about that. The Talbot business empire has its presence and contacts across the globe. Everyone has their price or things to hide, and I like to work on people's weaknesses, don't I, Crispin?"

"Yes," came the guarded response.

"The share price going up makes it impossible to buy the company, but I think I might have another plan," Sean grinned as he developed his line of thinking.

The Talbot business empire had interests in a large number of countries and access to powerful people. Could he leverage this to his advantage? He contacted one of the financial people at the Head Office of Talbot International, whom he knew from their Oxford days. He asked about the level of investments, the relationships with the cities and countries mentioned in the Financial Times article and where the Harrowgate trials were taking place.

"We have excellent contacts in Russia, Kenya and China, and many of them are at a government level. Since all three countries have a reputation for dubious dealings, they could certainly extract favours for our companies – if you know what I mean."

"I know exactly what you mean," said Sean. "This is very helpful. Since Hong Kong is now part of China, do we have influence with the Chinese government?"

"Yes, we have substantial investments there, and some very senior officials are close to us."

"Excellent. I'll get back to you."

Sean got Crispin to contact some medical friends in Hong Kong, asking them to find out who was doing the Harrowgate trials and at which hospital. They soon relayed that a Professor Hung Leung-Jin was leading the trial.

Sean Googled him and called out to Crispin, "Look what I have found. As I said, everyone has things to hide. This is very, very helpful."

Sean also enquired from Talbot International about valuable contacts in Kenya. To his surprise, it did not turn up anyone high enough in the echelons of government to be useful, but Russia delivered an unexpected bonus. Talbot International had connections with organisations involved in certain illicit activities in Moscow and St Petersburg, which proved extremely useful when they couldn't get their way with government officials.

"So we can explore the setups in Hong Kong and St Petersburg and see how we can leverage them," Sean smiled. "I may need to travel and cash in some IOUs accruing to the Talbot company empire. Crispin, I will leave you to continue the research here while I head off to do some negotiation."

"Good luck."

"It's not about luck. It's about making things work for you, and I'm good at that."

Sean set off for his apartment to pack and arrange to have the Talbot company jet ready to take him on his business trip.

* * *

Sean arrived in Beijing and was greeted by the Talbot China office CEO, Alexander Leong, who took him to one of the many luxury hotels in the capital. They had arranged a suite for him, and their discussions began shortly after he had settled in.

Sean explained the nature of the trial occurring in Hong Kong and the responsible Principal Investigator's role in the trial.

"Ah, yes, Professor Hung Leung-Jin," Leong acknowledged. "He has made a name for himself. Let me contact one of my high-profile government connections. We may have a way of using his past to your advantage. In fact, I am convinced of it."

The following day Leong arranged a meeting at the hotel between Sean and a leading figure in government, Liu Zhengfu. The suite Sean was staying in had a small boardroom, and in the presence of the government representative and the Talbot China CEO, Sean opened the meeting.

"As you are well aware, our organisation is building a clothing factory outside Shanghai, and you have dealt with us regularly. This contributes to additional employment in the area, and the factory's output will be sold, mainly to the West, providing further foreign currency for your government."

"Yes, this is very useful," agreed Liu, "especially since there was a lot of unemployment in that particular area."

"Excellent because I need some assistance in a project of my own. I can promise an increase in the factory's capacity with the benefit of more jobs and output. You can take the credit, but I need a particular favour from you in exchange for this."

"What is required?" the official asked.

"I believe you have a role on the Central Committee regarding Hong Kong?"

"That is correct."

"There is a clinical trial taking place there by an English pharmaceutical company. Professor Hung Leung-Jin, a former Chinese national, is in charge of the trial."

"Professor Hung! He is well known to the Central Committee."

"Given what I have read, I thought he might have been familiar to you."

Sean explained what he had in mind and how a senior member of the Central Committee could be of assistance in exchange for some additional investment in a part of Shanghai that needed more development.

"Given that, I believe that I can arrange something that could work to our mutual benefit," Liu affirmed.

Sean felt a wave of satisfaction pass over him when he heard what was planned but was tempered by the qualifying response.

"But the professor is what you call a tough cookie," Liu warned, "so we cannot be completely sure that our plans will work – but we don't often fail."

"Neither do I," was Sean's rejoinder. "An additional benefit for you could be a trip through Europe with a few nightspots thrown in on your way to our Head Office in England to discuss our trade deal."

"Sounds interesting," Liu smiled as he, Sean and the Talbot CEO shook hands and went to the restaurant to seal the deal.

* * *

Following his meeting in Beijing, Sean instructed the pilot to fly the jet to Moscow. Once again, he met with the head of the local branch of the Talbot organisation there. The information that Sean had provided to him resulted in a lunch meeting with representatives from the Council of Ministers. Despite Sean's prompting about the trial happening in St Petersburg, the two representatives could not offer much assistance, and their knowledge of the trial appeared minimal. Sean was at a dead end and needed to look elsewhere for assistance.

The local Talbot company representative contacted a member of the local Russian Mafia. It took two days, but a dinner meeting in an exclusive restaurant was arranged. Not one to be thrown by unsettling circumstances, Sean found himself slightly troubled by the heavies who stood in the background keeping watch over the security of the Mafia representative. Dinner was served in the venue, which appeared to have been cleared of all regular customers.

Despite the sinister feel of the meeting, a couple of phone calls made during the meal by the Mafia member threw up some positives regarding the trial in St Petersburg and those involved. In exchange for money laundering through Sean's company in England, some action was promised due to the Mafia's hold on certain individuals. With that arranged and the meal finished, the Mafia representative plus bodyguards exited the restaurant into a convoy of black Mercedes vehicles with tinted windows. They drove off into the congested Moscow traffic.

As Sean got back to his hotel, he put through a call to Crispin and uttered two words before ending the call.

"Pay dirt."

* * *

Jill was working round the clock to get Sean's deal to an advanced stage that would allow her to have this signed and sealed before Paul returned from Harvard. Together with the team at Chadwick, Monteith & Robinson, she put together a dossier on InnovoPharm and was ready to approach them in person with a firm proposal to sound out the prospect of being acquired by Sean's company.

As the intensity of the work increased, Jill found that her communication with Paul had reduced to barely making contact. He seemed to have adopted the same approach as the pressure of the course increased. Rare phone calls, the occasional email and a few text messages were the sum of their interactions. This suited Jill since she did not want to reveal to Paul the nature of the work occupying her time – and certainly not who she was working for.

Her project team and Giles were becoming concerned about the pressure she was under and noticed a change in her demeanour, naturally friendly and charming, replaced by an unusual tetchiness when deadlines were missed, or errors crept into the report.

Besides work pressure and the need to finish it in confidence before Paul's return, another issue played on her mind. One cold evening, coming out of the shower, missing Paul and their lovemaking, she ran her hands over every part of her body, wishing they were Paul's. As she cupped her left breast, she was shocked to find what she thought was a lump. She froze in shock and felt again. Yes, without a doubt, there was a lump there, but it didn't seem large. What to do?

Jill could not afford the time to go to a doctor or be in hospital when she was so close to getting the proposal ready for the Irish company. In fact, she had a date in her diary to go across and meet with them to sound them out. The deadline was tight. She needed to press on and get it done, and then she would attend to the lump in her breast.

She also didn't want to alarm Paul as he approached the final part of his course. She wanted him to get that behind him. Lumps do appear in breasts without a significant threat. They could deal with that once Paul had finished the course, and she had dealt with Sean's investment opportunity while ensuring that the acquisition cost would prevent any move on Harrowgate. She needed to present to InnovoPharm as soon as possible, and on a blustery day, Jill took a taxi out to Heathrow for the flight across to Dublin.

Settling onboard the Aer Lingus A320 Airbus, she reflected that the next flight to Ireland might be in Sean's company jet. She would likely be in a more threatened position trying to fight him off compared to her sedate companion on this flight, her colleague, Richard Nevin. They would do a joint presentation to the board of InnovoPharm. They had expressed deep interest in her communications regarding a potential acquisition by a subsidiary of the Talbot business organisation, which could bring considerable investment into their cash-hungry growing company. She felt confident that she would be able to secure the deal and take Sean out of several areas that intruded on her personal and professional life.

The presentation took place in Belfast and went extremely well. The Board of Directors were taken with the proposal and the figures mentioned, although some internal debates still needed to happen. They were in favour of setting up a meeting with Sean St Ledger to get final details in place before signing heads of agreement to set the process in motion to arrange the marriage between the two organisations.

Jill was elated. Even the thought of flying back to Ireland on Sean's jet did not undermine her feeling of satisfaction. Despite being one of the youngest members of the law firm, Richard had been composed and handled questions on the financials with confidence. Richard also noticed how the primarily male board were taken by Jill's combination of beauty and intellect. They had probed initially to see if they could challenge some of her proposals, but like Richard, she showed mastery of the details, creating a sense of comfort and admiration among the board members.

She contacted Sean following her meeting with InnovoPharm and gave him the favourable feedback. She was surprised that although his response was positive, he did not seem overly enthusiastic about the news. She was concerned that the drawn-out nature of exploring options, generating scenarios, doing the background analysis and preparing proposals had reduced his appetite for the venture. She needed to accelerate the formal proposal to InnovoPharm before Sean's interest waned. From their time at Oxford, she knew that he had a relatively short attention span for extensive detail and tended to jump from one thing to another.

Equally worrying was that after initially finding the swelling in her left breast, subsequent palpations indicated that the lump was increasing in size. She had to attend to it and start sharing this information with Paul, but his course would only finish in another month. Surely it could wait until then, but in her mind, she felt she could be in trouble.

Nonetheless, Jill started working on a heads of agreement document for Sean to review before taking it back to Ireland for consideration by the board of InnovoPharm. Although a non-binding agreement, it was important to get key terms set out for both parties to assess. She was keen to structure it well to avoid the iterative back-and-forth revision, which would take up time.

The issue of intellectual property was critical since InnovoPharm had several patent-protected products both in the pipeline and recently launched. Patents were essential for pharmaceutical products. Once again, this required extensive work, with Jill pushing herself hard to develop an outline she felt would suit both parties. This document would be the basis for the final negotiations between the parties.

Colleagues noticed a decline in her health as she worked on the extensive document. She reluctantly admitted that she needed another meeting with Sean to structure the financial offer in terms of cash and share swaps. She felt run down and unwell, but she needed to press on with the proposal.

CHAPTER 13

Tragedy

Jill continued to work the finishing touches on the heads of agreement document, which she wanted to forward to Sean for his additional input on the structure of the offer. He had, in the interim, provided her with a series of proposals and suggestions, which she incorporated. She recognised these as insightful and helpful and underscored that she was dealing with a decidedly sharp person despite the issues that tended to distract him – his pursuit of her being one of these.

In some ways, she felt sympathy for him that despite his bravado and blustering ways, there was an insecure person under the persona generally presented to all and sundry. However, she would not let this feeling interfere with her plan to get the documentation complete, the deal signed, and Sean's focus taken away from her and Paul and onto his extensive financial commitment to acquire InnovoPharm.

Jill felt that another face-to-face meeting with Sean would be necessary to finalise the proposal. Surprised but relieved, Sean declined and thought that the information swaps could be done via email and version control of the document. While this suited her, Jill wondered about Sean's unusual distancing from her on the project. Her mind returned to earlier concerns when he did not seem as highly interested in InnovoPharm as before. She attributed it to his natural inclination to avoid detail if effort was required. Strangely, she almost wished that Sean would apply to the acquisition the same level of motivation as he did to pursuing her. Then she would feel more assured.

She had a conversation with Sean regarding the trip to Ireland to present the acquisition document. The business aside, his interest in the trip was heightened by his reminder to her that they would take the Talbot jet to impress the company executives at InnovoPharm.

"I am sure you will enjoy every moment of the trip," he emphasised, knowing that the Hawker 800 XP jet had a large couch that could be converted into a bed.

Jill thought she had better be wearing a chastity belt on the trip, but the conclusion of the takeover would be the last hurdle she needed to clear to get her life back to normal and have Paul back with her. The company jet would take off for Ireland in just under two weeks.

* * *

While working at home one evening, Jill again returned to a subject causing her deep concern – the lump in her breast. It was feeling larger than before. She wanted to put off seeking medical attention before getting Sean's acquisition proposal signed, but she could not delay it much longer. She needed to see her gynaecologist to establish the cause of her condition. The next day she phoned Dr Blackwood for an appointment set in a few days giving Jill a sense of comfort that she would be able to get the problem solved and get on with her work and her life with Paul's return.

Jill arrived at Dr Blackwood's rooms in Harley Street on the appointment day. With some concern, she explained to him the results of her assessment. He carried out his own physical examination of her breasts and armpit, and she could see from his troubled expression that he was perturbed.

"I must be frank with you, Jill, this does not look good, but we can only confirm any uncertainties with some follow-up tests."

"What is required?" asked Jill, feeling despondent that she had left the problem for an extended period.

"My examination has confirmed your finding of a lump, with some tissue thickening in the breast. We need to differentiate this from any other conditions. You are also looking in poorer physical condition than when I saw you last year. You seem rundown."

"Yes, I have been working extremely hard at the practice on many projects."

"That's all well and good, but they mustn't work you into the ground," Dr Blackwood warned. "You need to be fit and well to manage any conditions we may uncover."

Jill felt that she couldn't explain the pressures she was under and replied lamely, "I'll try."

"I need you to have a mammogram for imaging the breasts and a fine needle aspiration biopsy to examine the breast tissue cells. I will send you to our radiology section for the mammogram and the biopsy, and then come back to me."

"Yes," said Jill, "we need to get this done as soon as possible."

She went through to radiology, and following the mammogram, the radiologist made Jill lie down on a bed. While steadying the lump in the breast with his hand, he introduced a needle into the node and drew up some fluid and cells. He also drew a blood sample from her for further tests as an extra precaution. Jill returned to Dr Blackwood.

"This will take a day or two as we must be certain of a diagnosis based on all the reports – the imagery, blood analysis and the appearance of the cells from the biopsy." Holding her trembling hand, Dr Blackwood continued, "Jill, please remain calm while we wait for the results. I don't want you jumping to any conclusions until we have all the evidence."

Despite his comforting words, Jill felt growing anxiety about her situation and the severe consequences of the potential clinical findings. Bewildered with sadness, she returned to the Wandsworth apartment.

* * *

After two days of not hearing from Dr Blackwood's rooms, the tension she felt at the consultation was starting to ease. If it were urgent, she thought they would have contacted her by now. By lunchtime on the third day, she felt that perhaps the tests had not proved as dire as she initially thought. She felt optimistic, and on top of that, the finalisation of the heads of agreement document was reaching its endpoint.

Dr Blackwood's receptionist called and asked Jill if she could come through to see the doctor as soon as convenient. Jill's initial response was calm but was quickly replaced by every woman's dread that she had developed breast cancer. She quickly finished the work she was busy with, closed up her office, and headed to Harley Street.

She was relieved not to be kept waiting for long and was shown into the doctor's consulting room. Although he smiled warmly at her, she detected an undertone of tension and bad news.

"I took a little extra time before contacting you as I wanted to have the results of all the tests available before we met again, although not all are in yet."

Jill felt a deadening of her senses as she waited for him to continue.

"You have been coming to me fairly regularly over the years. We have established a good patient-doctor relationship, so I know we can have an honest conversation about the challenges ahead."

Jill nodded. Her mouth was dry.

"While I have the preliminary findings of most of the tests, some are still outstanding, which may alter the situation. It is not all doom and gloom, but the situation is difficult."

"I have breast cancer, haven't I?"

"Yes, I'm afraid so."

Jill took a deep breath, taking in the news.

"How bad is it?"

"It is difficult to tell at this moment. The chance of breast cancer increases primarily in older women. In postmenopausal women, breast cancer is linked to risk factors such as obesity, early menarche or late menopause. However, there is an increase in the condition in premenopausal women, which we call young age breast cancer. This seems to be your situation."

Jill's mind was reeling as she started to run through thoughts about how this conversation would end. Would she be the same woman at the end of the diagnosis and treatment?

"Young age breast cancer is more likely to be aggressive and spread quickly."

He paused to gauge Jill's reaction to the news before continuing. While keeping her composure, he could see the turmoil reflected in her expression.

"I know these are not easy conversations. Do you want me to continue, or should we take a short break?"

"No, I think we need to expose the full extent of the problem and how we can deal with it," Jill said bravely.

"I had a blood sample taken from you to see if there is a genetic link in your family which may add further complexity to our assessment. I wish I could be the bearer of better news, but there are more complications. From the genetic counsellor's report, the blood tests using DNA analysis show a harmful mutation in one of the two breast cancer susceptibility genes, which we call BRCA 1 and 2. There is an increased risk of breast cancer for those who inherit the mutation. Do you know of anyone in your family who has a history of breast cancer?"

"Not that I know of; my mother has certainly not had breast cancer unless she has kept this information from me."

"Is there anyone else in the family who has had breast cancer?"

"I have an aunt on my mother's side, but she is a very private person. I will need to ask my mother about her."

"Although that would be relevant, it will not alter the current situation."

"Are we talking mastectomy?"

"I am not certain at this point. Let's not jump to any conclusions as I wait for more histopathology results. Let's deal with this in smaller portions for the moment and determine the best way forward for you in dealing with the situation."

Jill felt the tears welling up in her. Had she been guilty of neglecting herself in all the work needed to see off Sean St Ledger? How would Paul react to her in the case of a mastectomy? If the chances of breast cancer in women her age were relatively small, why had this happened to her?

"Do you have a support group around you who could help you deal with these developments?"

"My partner is, ironically, a doctor, but he has been away for the past few months as he is attending a course in the United States."

"You need to work with him to help you deal with the next stages of the diagnosis and treatment."

Jill was in turmoil. She wanted to allow Paul to finish his course successfully but needed his love and support to help her deal with her dreadful news.

"Yes, I will," she replied, not knowing exactly how and when she needed to convey the news as Paul approached his final exams.

How would her parents react? In Paul's absence, would her mother be able to support her in this dark moment in her life? Was Dr Blackwood holding back more bad news to help her deal with the situation little by little? The questions kept bombarding her.

"It is easier to say this than to do it, but try to stay positive. Breast cancer is not necessarily a death sentence. There is no need for radical intervention in some cases, as new treatments emerge regularly. I am involved in a trial on a novel product developed here in the UK. There is hope."

"Thank you, Dr Blackwood. I will try my best to be positive," Jill said but thought differently.

"I will have more results for you in a week or so. Try to focus on your work in the interim, but remember, don't let them overwork you."

"I will try, but it might be difficult."

Jill left the rooms in Harley Street and went out into the early dark of the evening. The gloominess and chill of the evening served to reflect her circumstances. Jill hailed a taxi to take her back home as she felt she could not deal with a train packed full of people going about their lives while she was coming to terms with the devastating news she had just received. The cabbie tried to make small talk with her, taken by having a beautiful young client in the back of his taxi, but soon gave up, sensing her sombre mood.

Once back at the apartment, she went to the room and fell on the bed, gripped with despair. Dr Blackwood had urged her to stay positive, but it was easier said than done, as he had noted. How she wanted and needed Paul to be with her, but he was engrossed in preparing for his final exams. She took comfort in that he would soon be back with her.

Jill decided not to call him. She would wait for Dr Blackwood's final assessment to know precisely what she was dealing with. Hopefully, Paul would return to support her with whatever the future held.

CHAPTER 14

No Goodbyes

Jill returned to work the following day determined to maintain an air of someone in control of her emotions and work, although she found both difficult. Both her team working on Sean's project and management were concerned about her health but put this down to the pressure to complete a deal for what would be a trophy client for the practice. A more sombre mood had replaced Jill's earlier tetchiness when aspects of the project slipped, and her colleagues felt this was probably due to fatigue as the documentation to complete the deal was vast.

Jill had avoided contacting Paul and was relieved that he had not communicated with her while preparing for his final exams. She was sure she would reveal the anxiety gripping her about her visit to Dr Blackwood.

A week after that visit, his rooms called asking Jill to come for a further consultation. She made it for mid-afternoon so she wouldn't have to return to work after receiving the latest update on her condition.

Dr Blackwood's greeting was warm and friendly, and he came out from behind his desk to sit opposite Jill in one of the two chairs in front of his desk.

"How are you doing?"

"I'm really tense about today," she admitted, "but I have tried

111

to keep my mind occupied since we last met. Tell me, is it bad news?"

"I am afraid it is not good, but we can manage it through a series of interventions."

"What have you learned from the tests?"

"You have what we call triple-negative breast cancer. It is an aggressive form of cancer and is more likely found in younger women. In technical terms, it tests negative for oestrogen and progesterone receptors as well as excess HER2 protein. The histology, the identification of the cells, has revealed invasive ductal carcinoma, one of the most frequent types of breast tumours. It appears to have metastasised or spread to the local lymph nodes."

As Dr Blackwood spoke, Jill's greatest fears were becoming realised. Her life was unravelling before her.

"What happens now?" she whispered.

"We need to have a surgical and medical approach to see you through this."

"Will this require mastectomy?"

"I am afraid so, and Jill, it needs to be a double mastectomy. It is vital, given that the tumour cells are stage three, which means a faster-growing cancer that's more likely to spread. We need to take action as soon as possible."

Jill gasped. "When are you proposing this be done?"

"I would recommend in the next couple of days."

"As soon as that?" Jill was taken by surprise.

"I believe we should not allow any more time to elapse."

Jill's mind scrambled to assimilate all the elements of the current situation. Paul was stuck in Boston. The work on Sean's proposal was only a day or two away from completion. She was facing major surgery and probable chemotherapy after a mastectomy. She had to tell her parents. How would they deal with this news?

"I need a bit of time to organise my life. I appreciate the need for urgency but give me a day or two."

"I understand, but please do not delay it much longer. I have spoken to an outstanding surgeon colleague, Professor Andrew Barnett, and asked him to be available at short notice to attend to you."

"Thank you. I won't."

In stunned silence, Jill left the doctor's rooms. Although evening was starting to close in, she felt that going back to the apartment would seem an even lonelier place now. She walked up to the nearby Regent's Park. Away from the hustle and bustle of the city, she walked in the tranquillity of the park. Finding a bench near the Queen Mary Rose Gardens, she sat down to gather her thoughts.

Gripped by the advancing winter, the rose gardens seemed to reflect her life. She needed to contact Paul; he needed to know, and she needed him and his comforting presence. The practice would have to be advised of her absence, and someone else would have to take the InnovoPharm document to finality. She felt a sense of relief that she would not have to accompany Sean to Belfast, but the price to be paid for not doing so was immense. She gathered herself emotionally and thought of everything she needed to undertake to adjust to a new life. She left the gardens and walked briskly down to Marylebone Road, where she hailed a taxi outside Madame Tussaud's.

At home, she poured herself a glass of wine and picked up the phone to call Paul. His reply was bright and enthusiastic. She felt her spirits sink at his response and the news she had to convey. She wanted him to finish his exams but provide support, even at a distance. She felt she could deal with the situation with her family.

"Hello, my love, how are you? It's so good to hear your voice again. Sorry, I've been a bit poor at staying in touch, but I'm ready and prepared for the exams, and it won't be long until I'm back home with you."

Jill felt that there could be no pretence about her situation, and she needed to get to the point.

"Paul, I have some bad news. I've been seeing my gynaecologist."

She paused before delivering the blow. "I've been diagnosed with breast cancer."

She struggled to maintain her composure and hold back her tears now the words were out. She was greeted with shocked silence, broken by "When did this happen? How are you?"

"It's apparently been developing over the past few months. I got the final diagnosis this afternoon."

"There is absolutely no doubt about this?"

"No doubt. Dr Blackwood did a number of tests, and it turns out I have ductal carcinoma. They called it stage three, whatever that means."

Paul immediately knew that the situation was dire based on this information and jumped to the potential outcome, asking, "What are they recommending?"

"They say I need a double mastectomy followed by chemo." At that, she broke down. "I won't be the same girl you fell in love with."

"Of course you will. I fell in love with the whole of you."

"Thank you, I love you so much," Jill sobbed.

"When is the operation planned for?"

"They want to do it on Thursday, in two days."

"I'm coming back to be with you."

"No, Paul, you need to finish your course – you are so close to the end. My parents can be with me to see it through."

"No, I'm coming back," he insisted. "The course does not matter to me, given the circumstances."

"Honestly, Paul, I can manage."

"I'm coming back immediately. Stay strong, my love. We will get through this together."

"Thank you, that would be wonderful, but I'm concerned about your course."

"I've got all I need from this course. It's been fantastic, but it fades into insignificance compared to supporting you. I am coming back home immediately."

* * *

The next day Jill went through to the office and asked for a private meeting with Giles to tell him of her situation. He was shocked by her news and incredibly sympathetic. Jill asked that the nature of her condition be kept confidential until she had undergone surgery. She recommended Richard Nevin, who had presented well at the meeting in Belfast, take over from her in the interim until her return.

"Nearly all the work on the heads of agreement document has been completed, and Richard has been an integral part of that. He knows the issues."

"I am sure that the Honourable Sean St Ledger knows how much you've put into the document, and I am sure that he will be pleased with your input. He really appreciated you, and so do we for all you have done since joining the practice."

"Thank you, Giles. I hope to be back here soon, but I may be a different person from who I am now."

"We will welcome you back whoever you are," he said with a smile and gave her a hug which was uncharacteristic of him and the formal nature of the practice.

Jill immediately left for the Wandsworth apartment to prepare to go to the hospital the following day for some more tests and then an overnight stay before the surgery.

Jill felt the time had come to contact her mother to break the news. Alice was devastated, as was Edward. He said he would pay for the best surgeons in London if needed, but Jill reassured him that Dr Blackwood had arranged for a leading surgeon to operate. Jill asked her mother if there was any history of cancer in the family.

"Not on your father's side as far as I am aware, but my sister Carolyn had a mastectomy in her thirties. She has always been discreet about it and has only told me. It ruined her marriage as her husband couldn't deal with her changed physical state."

The information was precisely what Jill did not want to hear and simply added to her anxiety. This is what Dr Blackwood was hinting at when he asked about any family connections to breast cancer. He had seen several young women like Jill who had experienced a familial link to breast cancer, prompting him to order the gene mutation test in advance.

Jill's parents comforted her as best they could, but she longed for Paul to be at her side, and Paul wished the same. He was still reeling from the news, but practicality kicked in, and he knew what he needed to do. He needed to contact JP to tell him he was leaving the course to be at home with Jill in her most trying moment. He needed to advise his course leader that he would not be writing his final exams as other things in life were more important. He needed to book a flight back to London and start packing to leave.

Paul was beating himself up over being away from Jill over the past few months. As a doctor, he would surely have recognised her symptoms much earlier and possibly avoided the trauma she was about to experience. He had put his new career in front of everything else. He had not even been a good communicator during his time away, with the course being all-consuming. He had failed the single most important person in his life for his own interests and ends. The oath he took as a doctor was to take care of people, and he had not done that for Jill. He hated himself and was – as his father had judged him long ago – a failure.

* * *

Jill's parents accompanied her to the University College London Hospital, specialising in breast cancer, to check in for the surgery preparation. Alice had found out from her sister Carolyn that the breast cancer that afflicted her did indeed have a genetic link. This came as a shock to the family and to Edward most of all. His little girl was now in danger. How could Carolyn have kept this to herself and not told the women in the family? Most likely due to the double trauma of her mastectomy and then her husband leaving her for another woman shortly afterwards. Even so, Edward was livid.

Jill spent the rest of the day in her ward being subject to a number of tests. During this, Jill and her parents met Professor Barnett and were comforted by his confident presence. While devastated by the significance of her condition, Jill took heart that Paul would be returning from Boston and would be with her before the procedure. She had given him the hospital name and ward and was desperate to see him before theatre. And Paul was desperate to get there.

He had packed up, taken his leave from members of his syndicate group at the Business School and had a flight booked that evening which would get him to Heathrow early morning the next day. He would at least be able to see Jill before she had her operation, and this would hopefully bring some comfort to each of them.

Paul made his way to Boston's Logan Airport to catch his British Airways flight. Once on board, he felt an urgency and anxiety to get going. It was a relief when the pilot came over the intercom to inform the passengers that the final pieces of luggage were being loaded and that they would be taking off shortly. Finally in the air, Paul availed himself of the drinks trolley but turned down the meal as he had no appetite.

About two hours into the flight, while he was staring aimlessly out of the window at a beautiful starry sky and sickle moon, he felt a slight shudder in the plane's movement. The flight continued, but suddenly there was another shudder. By now, some of the passengers had woken up and stared around the darkened cabin, wondering what was happening.

The cabin lights came on, and over the intercom, the captain's voice announced, "Ladies and gentlemen, I regret to inform you that we have experienced a slight mechanical problem with one of the engines. This presents no immediate danger to the aircraft, but we must return to Boston in the interests of safety. I ask that you ensure your seat belts are fastened should we experience more of the turbulence we had a few moments ago."

A groan went up from passengers. Paul was distraught. It was unlikely that he would now get to the hospital before Jill's operation, compounding his distress. A prisoner of circumstance, Paul could do nothing but fret as the plane turned away from its flight path to London – and Jill – and headed back to Boston. Paul wept in frustration.

Back in Boston, a replacement flight had already been arranged. There would be a short turnaround time, but now the flight would only reach London at ten o'clock the following morning, long after Jill had gone into theatre. Given that it was the middle of the night in the UK, the best Paul could do was send Jill a message that she would receive while he was on the flight. He hoped that she would take some comfort, knowing that he would be there when she came out. It was with a heavy heart that Paul boarded the replacement plane as it set off on its journey.

* * *

Once the plane landed at Heathrow, Paul made his way to the Heathrow Express for a rapid trip to the city centre and then a taxi to the hospital. He dropped his cases off at the reception area and rushed to the ward number that Jill had given him. It was now moving towards midday, but the sister in charge told him that Jill had not yet returned from the operating theatre situated on the floor above.

As he got to the operating theatre entrance, he greeted Jill's parents huddled together, holding each other in the waiting area. They mumbled, "Hello," and stared blankly at him.

At that moment, the doors to the operating theatre burst open, and a nursing sister came rushing towards Paul. He called out to her that he was a doctor and wanted to know about Jill Collins, but she ignored him and hurried down the stairs. An announcement came over the public address system for Drs Edwards and Singh to immediately join Professor Barnett in operating theatre two. They shortly rushed into the theatre, ignoring Paul's pleas for information.

Paul turned to Jill's parents and asked them what they knew. Alice said they were told there were complications with the operation, which was taking longer than expected, and all they could do was wait. Paul paced up and down, desperate for news.

Another hour had passed when Professor Barnett came out in surgical garb.

"Mr and Mrs Collins," he said, approaching them.

They nodded.

"The operation was more complicated than anticipated."

Alice let out a sob, and Paul moved closer, disbelieving what he heard.

"We were nearing successful completion when Miss Collins suffered an unexpected cardiac arrest. Our skilled team tried everything we could do for her," the doctor took a deep breath, "but we could not save her. I am deeply sorry for your loss."

Edward collapsed to the floor, howling and crying out Jill's name. Alice tried to help him up, but she was rendered almost immobile by the news and what was happening before her. Standing stunned for a moment, Paul sprang into action and helped Jill's father up off the ground and back onto his seat.

Alice flung her arms around Paul, wailing, "Oh Paul, how could this have happened?"

Paul was dumbfounded and could only shake his head. "I don't know; I just don't know."

* * *

In the days following Jill's death, her parents made the funeral arrangements. Paul found himself partly involved in assisting with this, even though his contact with Jill's parents had only been sporadic when he and Jill were together. Along with this, Paul notified JP at Harrowgate about what had transpired. He also contacted Giles Robinson at Jill's law firm to give them the news. Giles was incredulous that he had lost one of his shining lights and expressed his deep sorrow for Paul and Jill's parents. The practice was stunned by the news.

Alice had many phone calls with Paul during these days, thanking him for his time with Jill, who had told her mother how much she was in love with Paul and that they wanted to marry when their busy lives had eased up. Worryingly, Alice mentioned that Edward had not completely come to terms with Paul's relationship with Jill having higher aspirations for her married life. He also expressed resentment that Paul, as a doctor, should have been aware of Jill's condition and done something to save her. Paul felt the same, and this sense of antagonism from Jill's father only increased his sense of guilt.

Jill's family and friends gathered to say farewell on a cold early morning at the Church of St John the Evangelist in Kensal Green, North London. It was a sombre affair made more poignant by the deceased's age and by the fact that a brilliant young talent had passed away so soon.

Paul did not recognise too many in the gathering. He had some exposure to the staff of Jill's legal practice through past social interactions and knew most of them only superficially. He took comfort that a number of the medical team from his former orthopaedic hospital had come for their farewells.

Edward gave the eulogy to his beloved daughter, breaking down on several occasions, which only heightened the emotional tension in the church. Paul sat through the service, numbed by the occasion. As he looked around, he saw JP, who had come through from Berkhamsted. He noticed Giles Robinson from the law practice, struggling to contain himself in contrast to his usual reserved demeanour. Paul also noted a large figure at the back of the church who looked vaguely familiar but whose face was partly obscured by the order of service booklet. He racked his brains to place him but was distracted by the vicar bringing the service to an end. The final verse of 'Jerusalem' rang out, and the congregation rose to leave and gather across the road at the entrance of Kensal Green cemetery for the burial.

As the coffin was lowered into the ground, Paul felt his joy for a future life with Jill was buried with it.

CHAPTER 15

HG 176

The day after the funeral, Paul awoke early. He tried to get back to sleep, but the enormity of Jill's death weighed heavily on him. He got up, made himself a coffee, and sat down on the bed – their bed as it used to be. He felt rumpled, dishevelled and crushed, and there was a feeling of complete isolation. It came back to him. This was how he felt that cold winter's day at Charterhouse when the headmaster called him in to tell him that his parents had been killed in a motor accident in South Africa.

Why her? Why had such tragedy struck for the second time in his life? Jill meant everything to him. He knew his life would never be the same again. He would have to try to remake it – if that was even possible.

Staring into his cup of coffee, Paul's mind raced as he thought about his possible contribution to Jill's death. He had gone to Harvard for his own gain and development when Jill was against him joining Harrowgate and going away for so many months. What if he had not joined the company? If he had not been away, he would have been with her when she discovered a lump in her breast. As a doctor, he would have been alert to any danger. To make matters worse, Jill had not told him or done enough about it as she did not want to disturb and worry him while he was away on his demanding course. He was filled with remorse.

The remains of his coffee were now cold. Paul put his cup in the sink. He could not sit around all day with these thoughts; they would destroy him. It briefly crossed his mind that that might be the best option. He had to do something to ease the pain, so he decided to go through to Harrowgate.

Paul got up, stripped off and got into the shower. The first wave of ice-cold water took his breath away before heating up. He took this cold shock as part retribution for the wrongs he may have done. Standing under the water, he thought of Jill and how she used to come out of this shower with a skimpy towel wrapped around her beautiful figure and another wrapped around her wet hair. It looked like an elegant turban and stayed in place, defying gravity despite her movements, unlike the towel Paul wrapped around his waist, which Jill sometimes used to pull off him as he walked past her.

He shaved, pulled on some clothes, not caring about any synchronisation between tops and bottoms and headed out to the Wandsworth Common Station behind the apartment. Yes, the apartment. He guessed that the place would have to be sold as it belonged to Jill – the late Jill! That struck a discordant note. It seemed so unreal.

He remembered the breakfast Jill had made him when he first travelled the route to Harrowgate. His heart ached, but soon he alighted at Berkhamsted Station and phoned Tom.

"Tom, it's me, Paul. Can you come and collect me from the station?"

"Paul? My God! What are you doing back here? I am so sorry to hear about your loss."

"Thanks."

"I'll be down in a flash."

Shortly, Tom's blue BMW 3 series pulled up in the lane outside the station. Paul got in. Tom took in the gaunt figure in the seat next to him.

"You look like death warmed up," he said, immediately

regretting his choice of words. "Do you think you should be coming back to the office?"

"I have to do something to stop me thinking about Jill – if that's even possible."

They drove in silence up the hill, parked and entered the Harrowgate offices. Tom left Paul to go through to JP's office. Mildred opened the door, where JP and Melissa James were in deep conversation. They both looked up, startled to see Paul standing there.

"Please excuse us, Melissa," said JP.

As she passed Paul, she gave no nod of acknowledgement, and no words were exchanged.

"Paul," said JP staring at him.

"Hello, JP. Thank you for coming through to the funeral. I truly appreciate it."

"It was the least I could do, but do you think you should be back here so soon? Please take as much time off as you need."

"Thank you, but I need to keep occupied; otherwise, I will go mad. I need something else to keep my mind distracted."

"I have some sense of your feelings. When I lost my wife of thirty-seven years a while back, I felt the same. That was when I threw myself into getting Harrowgate off the ground, and it acted as a crutch to help me through."

"Mildred," said JP calling out to his secretary. "Please bring us some tea. Come and sit down, Paul," he said, pointing to the pair of wing-backed chairs in the corner of his office, affording a wonderful view over the Chiltern Hills in the distance.

"If you need to get your mind off your current situation, if that's possible," JP continued, "I have the topic for you – HG 176. That's what I was talking to Melissa about."

"Is that our new oncology medicine that Professor Reich told me about before I went to Harvard? He said he would fill me in about it on my return."

"Yes, that's the one. It was going incredibly well in Phase 3 clinical trials at several trial sites internationally but has just hit a minor blip at a couple of these sites. Probably, hopefully, nothing to worry about, but we need to check these trial sites just to make sure."

"What is its efficacy against?"

JP hesitated, "I hate to say this to you, but it is effective against breast cancer."

Paul took a moment to absorb what he'd just heard.

"Breast cancer?" Paul winced. "It's effective against breast cancer!"

"Yes, the early results have been promising, but it's not the final outcome. As I mentioned, we have had some minor setbacks recently."

Paul struggled to come to terms with the fact that the pharmaceutical company he had joined had been trialling a product that might have been able to save Jill.

JP read the thoughts that were going through Paul's mind.

"I know what you're thinking, but we did not know about your personal situation until very late. If it's any consolation, treatment would perhaps have been needed much earlier. We can't really tell if this would have helped. Possibly, but as I told you, we have recently hit a couple of bumps in the road. During a trial, an independent audit needs to be carried out. This provides us with the quality and completeness of the data. Many promising products have failed even at late stages or problems are found even after launch as patient usage expands beyond the statistical requirements of a trial."

Paul's mind still wrestled with the disturbing information he'd received.

Recognising Paul's internal conflict, JP made a suggestion.

"If you need to occupy your mind, I suggest that you meet up with Professor Reich and get him to update you on the overall progress of the trial. After all, the product will be the main focus of your business development role in the company."

"Right," was Paul's flat reply.

JP went back to his desk and phoned Mildred to ask the professor to come through to his office, and shortly afterwards, the burly figure of Reich came in after two formal crisp knocks on JP's door.

"Dr Beresford, my condolences to you on your loss."

"Thank you, Professor."

Paul could see that the warmth in Reich's eyes conveyed genuine sympathy for Paul's situation despite his stiff bearing.

"Let's go through to my office and discuss HG 176 and where we are with the product," Reich said kindly, beckoning Paul to follow him.

* * *

In Reich's clinically clean office, the familiar picture of Otto von Bismarck's intimidating stare seemed to follow Paul as he moved around the room. He adjusted his mind to absorb the information on clinical trial procedures.

"Let me tell you how we try to get medicines from the laboratory to the patient," Reich began. "I recall that I gave you an overview on this when we last met?"

"Correct."

"Then let's deal firstly with how a trial is arranged. Many of our critics think we just begin trials on an ad hoc basis and with minimal oversight to rush or manipulate our way to the finishing line. It is slightly more complicated than that," said Reich, displaying some newly acquired British understatement.

"Firstly, there has to be a Chief Investigator responsible for overseeing the procedure. That is my role and why I have been brought to Harrowgate. Around the CI, as I term my position, there is a Principal Investigator at each site who is charged with carrying out the trial. There are also satellite bodies to ensure that everything proceeds in a disciplined manner. These include some committees, each with a specific role. These are Peer Review, Data

Monitoring and Ethics. Are you still with me, Dr Beresford?" Reich asked, hoping that Paul hadn't become distracted by his grief.

"Yes. Yes, Professor. I'm here," Paul affirmed.

Relieved, Reich went on to explain that as Chief Investigator, he took primary responsibility for the conduct of the trial, developing the trial protocol that would guide how the trial was carried out and making sure the laws, regulations, and policies were correctly implemented.

"This must be done within the guidelines of what is termed Good Clinical Practice, known in the business as GCP. If I get this wrong, JP will put me up against a wall and shoot me!"

There was a pause. "A little German joke," Reich grinned. Paul did too.

"Although I have started explaining my role, this must be preceded by that of the sponsor – that is JP. As I might have told you, he has sunk everything into this project – his own money, bank loans and floating the company on the London Stock Exchange to raise the necessary funds. The share price has gone up recently, making the company more valuable, but if this late hiccup with HG 176 proves to be serious, the company is in severe trouble – it could well go under."

"Where is the trial taking place?"

"Trials," Reich corrected Paul. "We are carrying out what is known as a multicentre trial, so there are several sites in a number of countries. In addition to the one we have here in England, there are others in Hong Kong, Geneva, Kenya, Cairo, St Petersburg and one in the United States."

Paul was surprised. "Why such a disparate group of countries?"

"It is vital to get results across a range of different populations and ethnic groups. Something working well in one population group may not have the same clinical effect in another. Some may even show up with a different side effect profile which could be dangerous, so we spread the net wider."

Paul wondered how Harrowgate, a small developing company,

had the capability and human resources to carry out this extensive task.

"Are our people carrying out all this supervision?"

Reich confirmed that there were significant resource requirements to meet this need – doctors, nurses, clinical research associates, and statisticians. Harrowgate outsourced most of this work to QualiMed, a contract research organisation.

"Yet another acronym for you, Dr Beresford – CRO – contract research organisation. You will get used to the jargon. It means that we do not have our own staff on sites. We have to rely on the skills and abilities of these CROs, which puts the trials slightly at arm's length. We hope and pray that they are competent, honest and successful."

"Have you ever experienced issues with any of these CROs?"

"Once, but otherwise, they have been excellent. As they say, what could go wrong? We simply have to depend on them."

Reich could see Paul's attention beginning to wane.

"I think we have covered enough today, Dr Beresford. I have two files on how clinical trials are carried out. Take them with you and go through them. We can discuss the topic more effectively if you have this background reading. I also suggest you spend some time with Dr James as she visits these sites for us to check on the contract research organisation, or QualiMed, as I've said."

Paul thanked Professor Reich, tucked the files under his arm, and went through to Tom's office to start the journey back to the apartment. Home didn't seem an appropriate term for it now.

Back in the apartment, Paul was confronted by the unmade bed, dishes still in the sink, and the rubbish bin, which still needed to be emptied. He felt ashamed of himself as he was usually disciplined, keeping things tidy and clean, probably a function of his surgical habits. Jill always used to praise him for his contribution.

Ah, Jill; how the memories overwhelmed him. Perhaps he should move out since Jill's presence was still so intense in the Wandsworth property. Paul tidied up the apartment, grabbed a jacket and went out in search of something to eat.

* * *

Paul realised that he had drunk more wine than he should have. He had taken Professor Reich's files to read while having dinner, but the effect of the Merlot had only served to make him more morose. He spent most of the time staring at his food and the passing pedestrians and traffic.

He became vaguely aware of two attractive girls a few tables away, often glancing at him. They were enjoying their drinks and trying to catch his eye. Paul felt a disinterested numbness. He finished his food, paid and got up to go. He had to pass the girls on the way to the exit. They clearly thought he was coming over to them, but as he strode past, head down, they looked at each other with a surprised shrug.

At the apartment, Paul made himself a sobering strong black coffee and picked up the two folders to get himself up to speed with the theory and practice of clinical trial methodology. Paul would have to be well informed as the professor said that he should spend some time with Dr Melissa James, aka Black Widow or Dragon Lady.

She had been offhand and indifferent towards him on both occasions that he had been in her company. There was no sympathy or empathy shown for his loss as other colleagues had. Perhaps she didn't have a strand of human compassion in her DNA. Too bad, he thought, he only had to work with her. He didn't have to like her. He opened the first folder and started reading.

Besides the role of the Chief Investigator responsible for the whole trial, in the case of the multicentre trials that Harrowgate was undertaking, there were other Principal Investigators located at each of the trial sites with oversight responsibility and staff.

Even though responsibilities were delegated to others, Professor Reich carried the full weight on his shoulders. Paul felt a measure of sympathy for this gruff, likeable German. Given the complexity involved in discovering that magnificent molecule, Paul could understand his sceptical approach.

Reich had to oversee many other duties, including ensuring compliance with the trial protocol and how the trial's randomisation should be conducted. He would decide if the trial drug would be compared to the current standard medicine used to treat the condition or a placebo, a product appearing to be a medicine but with no active ingredient in it. Interestingly, the placebo seemed to provoke a positive response in some cases. Was this simply the power of the mind?

Reich would also decide how participants were allocated to groups and which product they received. In a randomised trial, patients were assigned randomly into two groups, each receiving different treatments, one being the trial drug.

Finally, Reich would determine whether it would be an 'open' study, in which case both the doctor and the patient knew which medicine the patient was receiving. Alternatively, neither doctor nor patient would know, hence the term 'double blind', removing unconscious biases that could cloud a clinician's mind.

Paul then turned to the section on the Peer Review Committee and its duties. The name seemed to suggest a sort of thought police. An independent body comprising doctors, researchers and statisticians would review the protocol supplied by the sponsoring company and approved by the Chief Investigator to see the importance of the work and its outcome. They would also check the ease of recruiting participants and whether there were any omissions in the protocol. Paul saw this as another layer of protection and intervention to ensure nothing was amiss. What could go wrong, the professor had said.

Paul put the files aside and got ready for sleep, hoping it would come to him tonight. He looked at the recently made double bed where he and Jill had spent many loving hours. He could not bring himself to sleep there tonight and went to the small study with its single bed, climbed in and thankfully slept.

* * *

When Paul woke up, he readied himself to head off to Harrowgate. With some relief and gratitude, he realised it was Saturday. He felt he needed more time to compose himself and read up on how clinical trials worked. He wanted to be prepared for the Dragon Lady as she would doubtless put him through a tough grilling, and God forbid that he got anything wrong.

Physical exercise was always part of Paul's routine, and he used it as a stress reliever when he was working at the hospital. He had also continued to play rugby at medical school at the University of Cape Town to keep himself fit and trim, but those days were distant. He knew he needed to get back into that routine. He put on his running gear, locked the door to the apartment, tied the key to his shoelace and set off for Wandsworth Common.

Feeling refreshed after his run, Paul rustled up some eggs and bacon for his first good meal in some days, then settled down with the file section on ethical approval. This appeared to be another one of the hurdles Reich likened to the Grand National horserace.

A committee comprising members who were not involved in the trial in any way, alongside members of the public, had many responsibilities. The objective of this body included protecting the rights, safety, dignity and well-being of participants in the trial. Important, too, was deciding whether the potential benefits of the trial were greater than the risks.

The qualifications and experience of the team running the trial were critical. Reich had mentioned that most of the trial implementation had been outsourced to another organisation. Would they be as thorough as the company whose very fate hinged upon the success or failure of the product? Reich had mentioned a bad experience, but only one. Could there be others?

Going through all the structures in place to protect patients, ensure the trial was carried out with diligence and hopefully deliver benefits to patients globally, Paul recalled his debates and sometimes heated discussions with Jill – both about his joining the pharmaceutical industry and its reputation.

"It's an industry with many detractors who all make arguments with substantial merit," she said, adopting the case for the critics. "There are issues of excessive charging, spending too much on marketing, and getting too cosy with the medical profession."

Taking the case for the defence, Paul countered by citing the discoveries that had been of great benefit to humankind, including the discovery and manufacture of vaccines, antibiotics, insulin and penicillin and the lives they had saved. The pharmaceutical industry's spend on R&D as a percentage of sales revenues was amongst the highest of all industries.

"Yes, there are supporters and critics," he rebutted, "but you can argue this about any industry. People's lives have been sustained where in the past they could have been damaged or cut short – just take the case of those with high blood pressure or asthma or diabetes."

"Well, once you are fully integrated into the industry, I want you to tell me the truth."

Of course, their whole discussion had ended with Jill's passing. Was she right? Had he sacrificed a potentially distinguished career as a surgeon for one in an industry riven by malign influences? He would make a judgement call when he knew more.

He would be true to Jill if she were right. If his surgical skills had waned, he could always return to being a general practitioner and contribute that way. However, if there was merit to his side of the story, he would pursue the development of HG 176 to treat breast cancer and see its development as a tribute to Jill and other women suffering from the same devastating condition.

Paul had had enough of the readings. He had some questions for the professor when back at the office, but now he just wanted to close off. He turned on the television and with the remote languishing in his right hand, flicked mindlessly through the channels.

* * *

Paul decided to use Sunday to wander around central London. He realised how much he had missed the enjoyment of taking in the sights and the various museums. He needed to clear his mind as he felt that the next few weeks would be intense in getting to grips with the case of HG 176 and other elements of his work.

He enjoyed a walk down Regent Street, past Hamleys toy shop, where his mother used to take him when visiting London. He strolled past Piccadilly Circus and down to Trafalgar Square. In a nostalgic moment, he went into the National Gallery as he and Jill used to and wandered around the rooms admiring the different exhibitions, finishing in front of the equestrian portrait of King Charles I by Van Dyke. The unfortunate king had unfailing belief in his project – the Divine Right of Kings – which was the belief that the right to rule came directly from the will of God.

JP had an unfailing belief in his project – the success of his new wonder drug. Would Harrowgate's attempt to get HG 176 to succeed also be beheaded by circumstances?

CHAPTER 16

Dragon Lady

On Monday morning, Paul arrived at his office to be greeted by Mrs Meadows, his new shared secretary with Dave in the office next door. She was well nourished, exuded homely charm, and her frizzy nest of greying hair was clamped to her head with bright yellow clips. She was known to be in touch with all the office gossip and preferred to be called Gladys, which Paul did.

"I will sort out your office for you. It looks rather barren with only the bare necessities. I could brighten it up for you with some chairs and prints if you'd like. Do you want to choose any of this?"

"Thanks, Gladys. I'll leave it all to you."

"Your first meeting this morning is with Herr Professor at nine. You had better run along."

"Yes, good point," said Paul, as he looked at his watch and headed to the professor's office with a few questions about the two files he had been studying on the clinical trial process, which he handed back to the professor.

"On page forty-seven of the first file, paragraph three," Paul began, "it says in designing the protocol, discretion is given to the Chief Investigator whether the trial should be carried out with either a placebo or a comparator as a control. What has determined that in our case?"

Reich looked up the reference in the file and said that deciding the control should be the medication currently being used for the condition was because it would be unethical to use a placebo on patients with serious diseases.

"And in the second file, page seventy-three, paragraph six, it states that the Data Monitoring Committee has the right to terminate a study. What are their criteria for this?"

"You seem to know these files very well. You must have spent the whole weekend studying them to know them point by point."

"Sort of."

Reich gave an overview of the criteria, including lack of efficacy or safety issues, but said that Dr James would give him a sense of this – he never referred to people by their first names.

"It is time for me to hand you over to her for the next phase of your introduction to the project."

Reich took Paul again to the door marked 'Dr Melissa James'. No sounds emanated from within – no telephone calls to deal with this time. Reich gave his crisp two knocks on the door, which had become recognised as his signature, and a commanding "Come in" resonated from inside, and they entered.

"Dr James, I have brought Dr Beresford for you to give him some more detail on our trial. I'll see you later, Dr Beresford," Reich said, leaving Paul standing alone.

"Thank you," she said. "Sit down."

Paul took in his second sighting of Dragon Lady and her surroundings. Her office had a light, delicate touch despite her hardened disposition. There was a print of Claude Monet's 'Water Lilies' on one wall and above a bookcase, 'The Dance Class' by Degas. On a small round table, there sat a bowl of petunias.

Paul wondered whether her surroundings showed a softer feminine side in her, but he was soon disabused of this notion. Melissa did not offer to move across to the table and chairs for a more informal setting but sat resolutely behind her desk opposite Paul. She had her laptop in front of her with the screen fully opened, serving as a further barrier between them.

In contrast to her dark two-piece suit worn on their first meeting, she wore a crisp white blouse – or what he could see of it over the laptop. No jewellery other than a silver watch and silver drop earrings with a loop holding what appeared to be a pineapple and no nail polish covering immaculately manicured nails. Her eyes, which Paul initially thought were coal-black on their first encounter, were a rich brown, sheltering under a pair of clearly and delicately defined dark eyebrows.

Her eyes scrutinised him as she proceeded with their meeting.

"You come to us with a very different background. I was expecting JP to recruit someone with a lot more experience in the industry. As an orthopaedic surgeon, you will have to set aside all your carpentry skills and rapidly absorb the nuances of clinical trials and their workings."

"That's the way it appears to be," said Paul, adopting a neutral tone to what appeared to be her provocative approach or sarcasm.

"As you might have heard from Prof Reich, the trial of HG 176 has been proceeding well up to now. We have a multicentre trial; that's a trial in several centres across the globe," she added for clarification. Paul did not let on that he was already aware of this information.

"We are in our third year of a Phase 3 study. I hope Prof explained what this was?"

Paul nodded.

"We have centres in Hong Kong, Geneva, Cairo, Nairobi, the US and St Petersburg, besides the major trial here in the UK. The results appear to have been spectacular. We believe we have a blockbuster product on our hands that will do considerable good for women worldwide suffering from breast cancer. This could be our massive contribution to science and the pharmaceutical industry."

Paul sensed a glimmer of humanity in her claim, contrasting with the image of a woman with ice in her veins.

"Where has the problem arisen?"

"There have been some abnormal results in Hong Kong and St Petersburg."

"Was this established through our own analysis of their results or the reports emanating from the contract research organisation?"

He recalled Reich's comment about his one bad experience with a CRO. Maybe lightning can strike twice.

Melissa suddenly looked up from behind her laptop. He read this as a sign that she was crediting him with more understanding of some of the intricacies of the issues and responded, "Our review of an independent audit of these two sites has shown some sudden questionable outcomes."

Melissa explained that it was likely that she would have to go out to the various sites and check if the results were something as simple as finger trouble, a more serious issue or something catastrophic. She would keep Paul informed in terms of his responsibilities in business development.

"Yours is the easy bit," she condescended, "once the experts have delivered the product into your hands. I would suggest that you start reading up on breast cancer to familiarise yourself with the subject, which will help you understand my reports."

Paul bit his tongue. He was about to break out into a rage born of the anguish of the past few days and lose his composure. He had just witnessed Jill die from breast cancer, and to have this elegant iceberg push that comment his way was infuriating.

"Thank you," he said and abruptly got up. "I will start my studies immediately."

He turned and exited her office. Melissa sat staring for an extended period at the office door that had closed with a louder bang than she was used to.

Gladys met Paul at the door to his office, and even though she did not know him well, she could read his expression and mood.

"How did that go? She's a real one, isn't she, love? I shouldn't have said that. I'll fetch you a nice cup of tea."

"Please go down to the library and ask the librarian for all the company literature she has on breast cancer. Thank you."

Paul closed his office door and aimed a kick at the desk leg, withdrawing in time to avoid fracturing his foot.

* * *

Paul's desk was piled high with the company's hard copy reports on breast cancer and his own internet searches, plus those recommended by Harrowgate. He had done some research since Jill experienced her trauma and suffered so greatly. But there were many types of breast cancer, and he needed to familiarise himself with a range of these to best judge what was emanating from the various trial sites.

Paul reflected on Jill's fate. The almost inconceivable had happened to her. Breast cancer is rare in women in their 20s and 30s but has unique features not seen in older patients. Jill had just turned twenty-eight. In this age group, triple negative breast cancer is the most aggressive malignant disease and spreads quickly. This type of cancer comprises only a small percentage of all cases.

The tragedy for Jill was that the survival rate is much lower than for older women suffering from breast cancer.

Further sealing Jill's fate, her aunt had experienced breast cancer before she was fifty but had kept this from the family. There was thus a familial link that had contributed to Jill's death. The disease had taken hold of Jill and had spread, metastasised, to other parts of her body. Thus, the radical surgical approach was adopted when diagnosed. He felt distraught at the thought of that.

In his medical training, Paul had received some knowledge of breast cancer. He had treated some patients, so he had rudimentary knowledge, but his specialisation in surgery had erased most of that. He recalled Melissa's demeaning comment about surgeons being carpenters. He needed to get up to speed rapidly if he was going to make any contribution.

From his readings, he understood that there were mainly two

categories of breast cancer – ductal and lobular. These could either be invasive, where cancer spreads to other parts of the body, or non-invasive. Invasive ductal carcinoma is the most commonly diagnosed type of breast cancer and in Paul's discussion with Reich, all indications showed that HG 176 had a role in treating it.

While the trauma and fate Jill had suffered were unimaginable to Paul, looking through the numerous papers and documents about breast cancer on his desk and computer, he understood that Jill was one of the millions of women across the world who have to deal with the devastation of this condition.

Harrowgate had developed a potentially unique product they felt could bring some hope and significant benefits to these women. Paul would do anything in his power to advance the cause of this difficult, protracted, and expensive journey to see HG 176 get to the market. Could a relatively small company achieve this? Was this only the preserve of the large companies? Paul remembered Professor Reich's story about Astra. Then a relatively small Swedish company, Astra, came up with the blockbuster drug Losec, which revolutionised the treatment of gastric ulcers and became the leading product globally. It was possible that skill, dedication and a measure of serendipity could deliver the same results for HG 176.

Paul's sense of optimism needed to be tempered since HG 176 was inexplicably knocked with what was described as a few bumps in the road. From medical studies of the absorption, distribution metabolism, and excretion of drugs – pharmacokinetics – Paul knew that the oncology sector had the highest failure rate in developing new medicines.

One large pharmaceutical company gave up the search for new molecules despite having a solid presence in the market, having spent billions looking for the Holy Grail of cancer therapy. This had attracted fierce criticism from those watching the industry. How much more money does one have to keep throwing into a sinkhole before reality dawns? Theirs was a sensible decision but had still been attacked. Damned if you do develop a product, then get attacked for your pricing, and damned if you don't have success and withdraw from the research. Perhaps this would be the fate of Harrowgate in their venture.

Pharmaceutical companies refer to their development of new products as their pipeline. Although Harrowgate had other products in early developmental stages, their pipeline was not flush given their size and essential startup position, compared with many of the big companies which had been around for decades or even a hundred years or more. HG 176 was to be the flagship product.

Professor Reich had said that in his experience, a competitor company could easily be first to market, undermining years of effort. Paul's readings showed that oncology was the largest sector of industry R&D spend – even larger than for cardiovascular or respiratory products – so many companies engaged in oncology research. This added another dimension; there would be a battle to find the correct number of patients needed to complete a trial. It was a game of roulette with high risks and high rewards to fund the following product research, which would then fund subsequent research if successful. The quest to find new cures was relentless.

* * *

Paul had progressed in his grasp of breast cancer and some of the competing forces in this market – the competitiveness and resources spent. It was now necessary to understand the specifics of the product Harrowgate had developed. A quick call to Professor Reich directed Paul to two colleagues in Reich's department who had been intimately involved with the evolution of the product. Dr Ngozi Obefemi was a Nigerian-born University of Bordeaux-trained biophysicist. Dr Sarah Hughes was an American researcher who gained a Bachelor of Science degree in computer science and molecular biology from the famed Massachusetts Institute of Technology and a PhD from the Health Sciences faculty of the University of North Carolina in Charlotte. Paul arranged a meeting with them in the Research and Development boardroom.

Dr Obefemi looked a little like Naomi Campbell with her high cheekbones and an elegant disarming manner. Dr Hughes exuded supreme confidence as she viewed Paul through a pair of dark horn-rimmed spectacles with fairly powerful lenses. Paul thought of his lunch engagement with Chris Wellings that had set off the chain of events leading to Paul joining Harrowgate. Chris had mentioned the benefits of engaging with scientists and others from various parts of a pharmaceutical company, and Paul remembered that as he interacted with these two scientists at the heart of the HG 176 project.

Unpretentiously introducing themselves by their first names, Ngozi opened with, "How much do you know about targeted therapy and the effect of monoclonal antibodies and T-cells in the treatment of cancer, Dr Beresford?"

"At this moment, frighteningly little," was Paul's honest answer. "Please call me Paul."

"These are the evolving frontiers of dealing with viruses and cancers today. There are several treatment modalities, including surgery, radiation, hormone and chemotherapy. These bring with them success but often savage side effects and consequences …"

"… so we have stumbled across, or rather brilliantly uncovered, a new approach," said Sarah, completing Ngozi's sentence, indicative of how this dynamic duo operated in tandem.

"This is targeted therapy," said Ngozi, taking up the next stanza. "This approach is the foundation of personalised medicine. Individuals with the same disease respond differently to the same therapy. It allows the selection of treatment based on a person's genetic make-up. We also use the immune system to fight cancer by stimulating the body's natural defences. It's immunotherapy."

"Our new product is ground-breaking," said Sarah, continuing their double act routine, "in that we have discovered a mechanism to link the cancer cell by a bridge, or coupling, to HG 176 and it to a T-cell, which is the body's inherent defence soldier which cleans up, or as we American's like to say, zaps the bad guys. HG 176 severely damages the cancer cell leaving it susceptible to the T-cell. In this way, both the product and the body's immune system tackle the cancer. It's a double whammy to the cancer cell."

At that moment, Melissa James was framed in the boardroom doorway.

"Ngozi …," she started to say, then saw Paul in the meeting. "Okay, I will contact you later," and the door closed.

Ngozi and Sarah exchanged glances and looked across at Paul.

"Have you worked with her yet?" enquired Sarah.

"We've had a brief exchange."

"She is very efficient," commented Ngozi. "I am sure there is a good person inside her."

"But no one has found it yet," said Sarah, and she and Ngozi giggled at each other.

"Thanks for the lesson," said Paul. "I assume the documents you have in front of you are my homework?"

"Correct. Good luck, and don't lose them; they are confidential. This is a unique product – there is nothing else like it."

* * *

As Paul returned to London that evening with all his readings, he felt he was back in his student days. The course at Harvard had enlightened him on issues of management, marketing and strategy. Now he was studying new frontiers of science to treat a condition that resonated with his very being.

He had given thought to moving back to his Putney apartment because of all the memories the Wandsworth apartment held, but when there, he decided he would stay for as long as possible. The cupboards still had Jill's clothes, and the bathroom, some of her cosmetics. Her presence was close to him. He could vividly recall the erotic moments embedded in the apartment from his first visit and all the wonderful memories after that. He felt he needed to have these memories surrounding him to sustain him and motivate him further to support Harrowgate's new product.

CHAPTER 17

Hong Kong

As agreed with JP, Paul took a few days away from the office to review the evolution, development and mode of action of HG 176. He needed to get up to speed with the product urgently. Between numerous cups of black coffee, takeaway meals and a few outings to a local restaurant – without the confidential documents – Paul felt he had a good sense of the unique product and its efficacy. It was time to get back to Harrowgate and get stuck into the activities needed to bring the product through its trials and to market.

When he got back to Berkhamsted, there was a surprise awaiting him. JP had some feedback from the trial auditors used by the contract research organisation carrying out the trials. The trial sites were delivering excellent or outstanding results, except for Hong Kong and St Petersburg, which showed some aberrations that raised concerns for the validity of the whole trial. JP had decided to send Melissa back out there to investigate; she had flown out the previous evening. JP seemed a bit unnerved by the situation as he had invested everything he had, and the company's viability rested on the success of the trials. He would give Paul feedback as soon as he had heard from Melissa.

This did not take long. As Paul got to his office the next morning, he found JP waiting outside for him.

"Let's go into your office and close the door," he said.

Paul obliged. He could see that JP was in a severely disturbed state of mind.

"Melissa has just contacted me from the Hong Kong trial site. Their audit report has shown that a growing number of patients appear to display decreased efficacy to HG 176. As you know from your readings, the drug is in a double blind Phase 3 head-to-head trial with a comparator product, the current standard treatment with known outcomes. Suddenly, it appears our drug results show a reduction in efficacy against the comparator. We can make this assumption in a double blind study because certain of the patients, who we believe to be on our product, were showing significantly better results than those expected of the known comparator," JP said, disheartened.

"My understanding is that the product has had remarkable success and significantly better outcomes than the comparator," Paul said. "I got the impression that the trial was going to be closed out quite soon to enable the product to get approval, be registered and made available to patients everywhere as soon as possible."

"That was the plan which is why this is such a blow to the stomach for me!" Paul could see the tension in JP, who usually had a relaxed manner.

"I've now sent Melissa to St Petersburg, as an issue seems to have arisen there too, associated with side effects from HG 176 causing issues in the trial patients. Everything was going so well, Paul. I felt this could be a miracle product for treating breast cancer, a major win for science and Harrowgate, showing the value of pharmaceutical research and development. I have only confided this with you, the professor and obviously Melissa. Please keep this to yourself. I don't want panic spreading throughout the company."

"Will do."

JP exited Paul's office with his shoulders unusually stooped but straightened up to give Dave a cheery "Good morning" as he passed him in the corridor.

* * *

The situation in the trials moved rapidly. The following day, Paul was at his desk reviewing more documentation when his phone rang. Mildred asked that Paul come to JP's office, where he was in conversation with Professor Reich. As Mildred quickly closed the door behind Paul, he realised that the trial situation had worsened.

"Melissa has just contacted me from St Petersburg. More difficulties!" JP announced. "What I mentioned to you yesterday has just been confirmed. The patients there are experiencing side effects which are now threatening the trial. The person from QualiMed overseeing the trial there has said that, based on the audit, if the side effects continue to mount, they will abort the trial and scrap the product."

Paul turned to Professor Reich. "Do you have any idea why this is suddenly starting to unbundle?"

"Based on the information available to us at this moment, the answer is no. But I did say I have a sceptical nature and have seen this happen before."

"That's all very well," JP retorted, "but this is my company and my dream. This medicine will help patients everywhere, and I am not giving up on this now!"

"What is the next step?" asked Paul.

JP took a breath. "If I suddenly send the Professor out to these trial sites, the company will think there is a serious problem. Paul, I'm sending you on the pretext that I am doing this to further your knowledge and understanding of clinical trials. I want you to work with Melissa to understand what is going on."

"Work with Melissa? I am still on a steep learning curve about the product and the trial."

"I brought you on board because I thought you could add a different perspective to the team. You are an outsider to this business at the moment, and we need fresh eyes to avoid groupthink and applying the same solutions to new problems. We need you now."

"Right, so when do you want me to leave?"

"I have Mildred booking you a ticket right now. I have told

Melissa to return to Hong Kong, and I want you to meet up with her there and start getting to the bottom of this. And Paul, to quote a famous line, failure is not an option."

Paul acknowledged the severity of the situation and passed by Mildred on the way out. She gave him the documents for a Cathay Pacific flight the following night and a reservation at the Harbour Grand Hotel, where Melissa would also be staying. Mildred seemed about to say something but then held back. Paul paused briefly, waiting for her comment, but then took the travel kit and returned to his office.

He felt this would be an interesting experiment, given his previous interactions with the Dragon Lady, but the seriousness of the situation outweighed any personal difficulties. He wondered how she would react that he had been sent to assist with establishing the cause of the issues with the trial site.

* * *

The next day found Paul at Heathrow's Terminal 3, ready for departure. His flight would arrive early in the morning, with Melissa coming from St Petersburg around midday. He was to take a taxi to the hotel and prepare to meet her. Paul needed to make a good impression, so as the plane taxied out onto the runway and hurtled into the early afternoon London sky, he started reading additional documentation on the HG 176 problems highlighted in the audit.

Arriving at Hong Kong International Airport just after six in the morning, Paul made his way through customs and took a taxi to the hotel. After a shower and breakfast, he had a few hours before Melissa's arrival, so he decided to step outside.

He was immediately struck by heat and humidity. The view across the harbour and the spectacular skyline of tall buildings on Kowloon were breathtaking. The people who bustled around the streets energised him as he returned to the hotel room to freshen up.

On the small desk was an envelope marked with his name,

containing a typed message from JP: "Sorry to spring this on you, but I have not told Melissa about your arrival and function as I thought it best you address the issue without giving her a head's up. Good luck! I have every confidence in you. JP."

Paul stared at the message. He remembered that Mildred was about to warn him about something as he collected his tickets from her. Now he began to understand office politics.

Just after noon, Paul confirmed Melissa's arrival with reception and was told she had booked a table for lunch at one o'clock. Paul decided to wait outside the Terrace Restaurant to meet her.

Melissa also appeared to have showered as her short dark hair was still damp, and she tousled it as she approached. She was wearing an elegant white two-piece outfit with shoes to match. Paul had to admit she was undoubtedly attractive, and some of the waiters paused to take in the view of their guest. Suddenly Melissa saw Paul and stopped in her tracks.

"What are you doing here?" she exclaimed.

"JP asked me to come here to provide an extra pair of hands to assist you."

"How can you be of any value? You don't know a thing about this type of work!"

"I have a sense of the issues and have read up about the product and the concerns."

"Read up?" she criticised. "I am sure Mildred has read up on HG 176, but she would not be of any value either."

Ever polite despite an underlying irritation, Paul refused to respond to this barb. "Well, I am here now at JP's request, so we will have to make the best of the situation. Let's have some lunch, and you can start filling me in on your findings here and in St Petersburg."

Melissa stared at Paul with disdain, then looked at a waiter who had a wry smile on his face.

She snapped, "What are you smiling at? Show me to my table."

Paul followed her into the restaurant. The waiter held her chair for her, and Paul sat down opposite. In an absurd game of personal chess, Melissa moved to another seat so she didn't have to face him. Paul immediately moved his chair to sit opposite her once more. She gave him a withering glance but did not move again, and Paul thought, two can play at this.

"I need a menu," Melissa demanded of the waiter.

"Do you want anything to drink?" Paul offered. She ignored the question and placed her order. Paul did the same before initiating a checkmate.

"Melissa, the challenge facing the company outweighs our personal issues. Our brief is to determine the cause of the problems the two trial sites have encountered. That is our task. I don't know what you dislike about me, but I don't really care. We need to develop just enough rapport between us to work effectively."

She sat silently and looked out the window across the harbour view. Nothing was said as both parties digested the situation. The waiter brought their lunch orders, and both fiddled with them. Appetite did not appear to be on the menu.

Paul broke the strained silence. "JP told me the problem at this site is one of efficacy with the longer-term patients, whereas St Petersburg is one of side effects. With this local trial, what are the different possibilities causing this?"

Once again, there was a pause. "Since there is no alternative to this arrangement, I will give you my opinion based on years of experience in this field. Try to keep up," she said with a calm, vengeful assurance.

"I'll try," said Paul, struggling to disguise his sarcasm, his patience fraying.

Melissa revealed that the trial was being administered at the King George, an academic hospital with an excellent reputation and track record for conducting clinical trials. The Principal Investigator was Professor Hung Leung-Jin, a brilliant cardiologist capable of covering several disciplines under his portfolio, including oncology.

Professor Hung had an interesting background. He was from

the People's Republic of China, where he qualified as a specialist at the top of his class. He then travelled abroad to the US and the UK to further his studies. However, he crossed swords with the Chinese hierarchy over human rights, fled the communist side and took refuge in Hong Kong, where they welcomed him with open arms.

"I have every confidence in Hung and his team," Melissa advocated. "The onsite contract research organisation has been effective but not super-efficient. The organisation has found some patients showing a reversal in terms of efficacy. Even worse, the cancer seems to be reappearing in some of those patients who had been in remission with diminishing lesions."

"Could this be a problem with the drug or a procedural error wherein the medication is working, but the reporting is the fault?" asked Paul.

"That is highly unlikely, as you should know. Professor Reich constructed the trial protocol, and the study went through all the correct contractual stages to conduct the trial. We were actually approaching the close-out by reaching a primary endpoint and developing the safety report when we received news of these incidents. The entire multicentre trial has been suspended, and the impact on the company and its market perception is at risk."

"What is the first step now?"

"I am going up to see Professor Hung. You can come along since you are so far behind in your understanding of the issue," Melissa stabbed. "I have also arranged to meet the representative of QualiMed. You can talk to him as he will be at a level you should understand."

There was clearly no letting up in her insulting him, but Paul would ignore this for now in the interests of progress. He prided himself on being patient under difficult circumstances and keeping his usual impatience in check. This had served him well in his surgical career, where patience was critical when making key decisions.

Paul's driving thought was that the problem was an adverse event rather than a fundamental product failure. If it were only an event, he could still hope that the project would be saved in memory of Jill – and also for JP, who he could imagine was going through hell.

"I will meet you in the lobby in thirty minutes. Don't be late and order a taxi for us to go to the hospital." With that, Melissa turned on her heels and left the Terrace Restaurant.

* * *

The taxi ride to the hospital was completed in silence. Melissa and Paul sat as far apart as possible on the back seat, each staring out of their respective windows, alone with their thoughts.

Melissa wondered what had possessed JP to send Paul to assist her. He did not know enough about the trial process to be of any assistance. He could only delay things and would probably blunder. Would this help or hinder her plans? How to manage the situation was going to be tricky. She wanted to be at the heart of solving the problem. JP clearly had some misguided view about Paul, and she would have to play things carefully not to offend JP but to keep up the appearance of collaboration.

Paul wondered to what extent Melissa would involve him in the investigation. JP obviously had faith in him, but the fact that he had not notified Melissa he would be joining her had some sort of message; he just didn't know what that was.

Their thoughts were interrupted by their arrival at the hospital. They took the elevator to the sixth floor and down a long gleaming corridor towards a sign marked 'Cardiology Unit'. Paul felt a sense of nostalgia being back in a hospital setting. The sights, sounds, and smells all had their allure for him, and he had to remind himself that he had made a significant career change and needed to focus entirely on that.

They arrived at an office door marked 'Professor Hung Leung-Jin'. The door was open, and the professor looked up from his desk to see the two visitors. Hung was a smallish figure lost in a white lab coat with a stethoscope draped around his neck. He wore rimless spectacles sheltering a pair of penetrating eyes that darted around, taking everything in.

"Melissa," Hung smiled. "It is always good to see you – even in these difficult times."

"Thank you, Professor. It is the same for me. I need to get more details on the problems developing in the trial," said Melissa, getting straight to the point of the meeting.

"Ah yes, this trial. It is giving me grey hairs," he joked, completely contradicting his dark hair slicked down on his scalp.

He glanced up at Paul, standing slightly behind Melissa. "I will take you through the cases that are showing declining results." He looked up again at Paul and Melissa questioningly.

"Your friend?"

"He is not a friend," Melissa declared, "but an employee from our company who has just joined and needs to start understanding clinical trials. This is Paul Beresford," she said, omitting his title.

"Nice to meet you, Mr Beresford."

"Thank you, Professor Hung."

Melissa turned back to the professor. "Can you go through some of the case studies for me to explain your thinking on these? Paul can meet with Devon Ridley from QualiMed. I asked him to come to the hospital and start going through the basic aspects of the trial to help my colleague get up to speed," she said, looking at Paul.

"Fine, I will ask my secretary to make the boardroom available for them."

"Thank you. Off you go and have a useful chat with Devon."

"Please excuse me, Professor," said Paul as he followed the secretary back down the corridor to the meeting room.

Paul felt there would soon be a collision between him and Melissa, but he would ride this out for now in the interest of unravelling the mystery of the failing trial. In the meantime, he would gather more information.

The meeting room door opened, and Professor Hung's secretary brought in Devon Ridley. Paul's expectations of what a representative of the contract research organisation entrusted with critical aspects of the trial would look like immediately evaporated. Devon was clearly overweight, with the notches in his belt casting off towards the end. He was red-faced and sweating profusely. His shirt's top button was undone with a drab yellow tie hanging limply against what passed for a rumpled white shirt.

"Hello, I am Devon. You are?"

"I am Paul, Paul Beresford."

"How do you do?" Devon proffered a plump and sweaty hand.

"Can you tell me how and why the trial started unravelling?" asked Paul.

"Of course. What is your background so that I know how to pitch it?"

"I am a doctor and specialised in surgery, but I'm fairly new to the industry."

"Okay, well, I am the one who started finding some abnormal results in some of the patients."

"How did you pick this up? Everything seemed to be going well."

Devon expounded that in a clinical trial, the case report form – known as the CRF – is the official data-recording document used in a study and the basis of the data captured in the trial. It allows for efficient and complete data processing, analysis and reporting. Devon mentioned that only the data fields requested in the trial protocol would be captured.

"I noticed in the report forms on the database that some of the triallists, who had been taking treatment the longest, showed decreased efficacy. The lab report entries on the histology of some showed that instead of a reduction in the cancer, the position was reversing and the cancer increasing. I picked up the trend in my review of the overall results."

"How many patients are involved in the trial here in Hong Kong?" Paul probed.

"I think there are seventy-six being treated in this hospital."

"You think?"

"I'm sure – or seventy," Devon faltered.

"How many of them are showing reversal of treatment?"

"There are ten or twelve in various stages."

"What did you do when you saw this trend emerging?"

"I spoke to Professor Hung as soon as the numbers started increasing."

"What was his response?"

"He seemed disbelieving at first, thinking that the data had been captured incorrectly or that I had made an observational error, and then he suspended the trial pending an investigation."

"When was that?"

"That was a week ago."

"What happened then?"

"The Professor said that he would undertake an evaluation himself."

"Why do you think the Professor would undertake the evaluation when you should be doing this as the CRO responsible for the trial?"

"I don't know. Perhaps he didn't trust me."

Based on his assessment of Devon by appearance and some of his responses, Paul also felt that the CRO representative did not exactly exude an image of clinical or factual confidence. Could Devon have got things wrong? As Melissa had alluded to in an earlier exchange, was this a simple case of finger trouble? Was the whole trial in jeopardy as a result of some gross incompetence? But problems of a different nature had arisen at the St Petersburg trial, so perhaps data input wasn't the issue.

Paul and Devon stared at each other across the table in silence. Devon looked a bit shifty and averted his glance.

"Okay, thank you for your input," said Paul. "I assume Melissa has your contact details, but let me have them too. I might need to follow up with you." Devon handed Paul his business card. "Thank you. I'll need to rejoin Melissa and Professor Hung."

With a handshake, Paul and Devon exited the boardroom, Devon heading out of the hospital and Paul returning to Professor Hung's office, where Melissa was deep in conversation with the professor, who beckoned to him, "Come in, Mr Beresford and take a seat."

"Paul, we must leave now," said Melissa standing up and negating the professor's invitation to him. "Professor, I will be in contact with you shortly. Can you ask your secretary to order a taxi to return us to the hotel?"

They left the hospital, and the taxi headed out into the late afternoon bustling traffic.

"I met with Devon Ridley, and he gave me his view of the problems with the trial," Paul said. "The histopathology appears to be deteriorating in up to a dozen patients, with most of them at stage three. Under earlier therapy, they were reverting to stage one or even in remission."

"Yes, Professor Hung mentioned that he would oversee the review of the clinical status of the triallists and the histology."

"I was not impressed with Devon. He appeared shifty and not on top of the facts."

"Perhaps, but I doubt it. We've used QualiMed before, and they have proved reliable."

"Agreed, but there are many areas where errors could have crept in. Professor Reich mentioned that he had a bad experience with a contract research organisation before."

"I have complete faith in Professor Hung. I know he will get to the bottom of the problem with my help."

"I hope your confidence is not misplaced."

"It won't be."

"Yes," said Paul, "but this is a double blind study. Neither the triallists nor the doctors treating them know which product each patient receives. The problem could be with the comparator drug. Unless the protocol code is broken, we don't know who is getting HG 176."

There was a slight pause. "I knew that," Melissa said, clearly not interested in engaging with Paul.

The taxi arrived at the hotel.

"I am going out for dinner with some friends. You can meet up with me in the morning."

Melissa disappeared through the revolving door, leaving Paul to settle the taxi fare.

In his room, Paul's mind sifted through the facts and issues – both those arising from the meeting at the hospital and his readings about the trial and HG 176. There was a massive complexity at play and many ways in which the trial could be seen to be unravelling. He began working through the range of possibilities starting with the chance that the control drug could be the culprit. He sat hunched over the desk, lost in thought, running his hand absentmindedly through his hair.

The clinician in him went systematically through the potential options using mind maps. His medical training and rigorous thinking allowed him to develop models that might explain what was going wrong. He looked to support or refute a model by subjecting it to selective testing – the art and science of medicine trying to determine the probability of one outcome or the other.

The problem couldn't be solved there and then. Paul decided to go out for a meal and sample the delights of Hong Kong to get his mind off the problem temporarily. He left the hotel and went to the famous Star Ferry terminal to cross Victoria Harbour to the mainland. The short journey from Hong Kong Island to Kowloon afforded a magnificent view of both sides of the harbour with their impressive skylines. Once ashore, he hailed a taxi and asked to be taken to a traditional restaurant where he enjoyed the local cuisine.

As he was finishing his meal, he took out his wallet to pay, and in it, he saw the business card of Devon Ridley. On instinct and wanting to drive the project forward, he took out his phone and punched in the number. "Ridley," came the reply.

"Devon, it's Paul Beresford."

"Hello, Paul. What can I do for you?"

"Just on the off chance, I was wondering if you could spare me some time to meet for a drink and discuss some other aspects of the trial?'

"Yes, I can do. Whereabouts are you?" Paul gave the restaurant name. "I will be with you shortly as I am nearby."

"Hope I am not disturbing you and your family?"

"Not a problem. I am in the middle of getting divorced."

With this piece of information, Paul thought it might have contributed to Devon's demeanour at their first meeting since divorce is almost as traumatic as the death of a loved one. Could Devon be the one making errors in the trial, causing the failure of HG 176?

When Devon arrived at the restaurant puffing from what was apparently a rushed journey, he suggested to Paul that they head off to one of the famous Hong Kong watering holes. He said he knew it well, which increased Paul's critical assessment of Devon as someone who was not giving full attention to the trial. Maybe this was the cause of the problem in the trial – personnel, not product failure.

Devon led Paul through the noisy evening crowd at the Ambassador Bar, into the industrial chic interior, past the padded seats and brushed concrete walls to a quieter corner where they ordered their drinks.

"Tell me," said Paul, "where are the possible areas that the trial could be coming off the rails?"

"There are many. These could include incorrect transfer from the data source files such as patient notes and lab reports to the case report form, deviations from the protocol, statistical errors when analysing the data, and confusion between the dispensing of the control drug and HG 176. Or the trial drug is not delivering as Harrowgate was hoping. It happens, you know."

After this evaluation, Devon looked down into his whisky, swirling his drink around in the glass. The ice cubes tinkled, breaking the silence. Unconsciously, Paul tapped his fingers on his thigh. With his meticulous attention to detail, he could not understand how someone responsible for the trial could not remember the exact patient numbers involved when they first met earlier that day.

Paul noted that Devon did not lay any possible blame at his own doorstep. He looked at him with a forensic, clinical analysis as if studying a potential patient for surgery.

"Do you think you could have made an error in evaluating any of the data in the database and the case report form?"

"No. Unlikely. I have done this for years. Could do it with my eyes closed."

Paul wondered if this was not a possible reason why the trial was in trouble. As they chatted, Devon called the barman, who knew him by name and ordered another round for them both. Paul decided to feed Devon more whisky to see if he would disclose the real issue under the joy of the smoky Laphroaig single malt. It worked. Devon obviously had some gripe against Professor Hung.

"Although the Professor is Principal Investigator for this site, he delegates roles and responsibilities to his team members and me. He oversees performance and product accountability. I told him I had found some errors in the analysis, which I would investigate. He said he would reduce my responsibility in this evaluation and take most of this upon himself since he was the Principal Investigator."

"Does that seem correct?" asked Paul.

Devon shrugged and drew deeply at his drink. Paul sensed the evening had reached its end and was concerned for Devon, who was now appearing a little worse for wear. It reminded Paul of his first impression of him, which did not convey confidence.

"Let's go," said Paul. "You have been most helpful."

Paul felt he had made further progress towards his burning desire to get to the bottom of the mystery. Paul hailed a taxi in the humid but fresh air and navigated Devon into the back seat. Devon mumbled his home address, and Paul slipped the cabbie some Hong Kong dollars sending him on his way. He returned to the waterfront to board a Star Ferry back to the hotel.

Paul had a growing unease about how Devon was performing his role in the trial. A man going through a divorce with a probable drinking problem was not the person Harrowgate needed to be involved in their pivotal trial. He felt that he had the beginnings of a solution to the problem.

* * *

The next morning Paul went down to have breakfast. Melissa was already finishing her meal with a cup of coffee.

As Paul sat down, she said, "I am leaving for St Petersburg this morning as there have been more developments that need my attention. You can finish up here and go back and tell JP what the findings are. You can tell him what you think the problem is with your opinion of Devon Ridley. I must be on my way."

She exited the room in a brisk and purposeful manner, and Paul was left to reflect on his next move.

As Melissa went out to the reception area to collect her luggage and find the taxi, she wondered what JP would make of Paul's assessment that Devon was misreading the trial results, which, in her opinion, was clearly not the issue. Her take on the trial was that statistical errors were the most likely cause, which Professor Hung would soon resolve. Of course, Melissa hadn't shared her opinion with Paul, and if he wanted to come in behind the curve and think he could solve the mystery of HG 176, that was his problem. That would show him up in front of JP. Serves him right, she thought.

Paul started his breakfast and lost in thought about the developments, persistently cracked the shell of his boiled egg. The discussion with Devon Ridley and initial assessment of him gave Paul cause for concern regarding how the trial was being managed on the ground but was this enough to explain the unbundling of the project?

Wanting to get the investigation moving as quickly as possible, he decided he would return to the hospital and have a meeting with Professor Hung. Melissa was trying to keep him away from the professor, but Paul knew he needed more information on the trial problems from a more clinical perspective. Following that, he would contact JP and agree to the next move.

Paul retraced his journey to the hospital and the cardiac unit. Professor Hung's secretary said he should take a seat in the reception area as he did not have an appointment. With a little nostalgia, Paul watched registrars and nurses move back and forth through the unit for nearly an hour until the secretary led him into the professor's office.

"Come in, Dr Beresford. I did not realise at our first meeting that you were also a medic."

"I specialised in surgery, but that skill seems a million miles away from the competencies needed to cure this particular patient," Paul smiled.

"Never to worry. Our basic training helps us adapt to a variety of situations. I have seen many of my colleagues diversify into different fields – the last one went into stock broking. What can I do for you?"

Paul surveyed the almost fragile professor seated behind his incongruently large desk piled high with patient folders and medical journals. The professor's smile was benign and friendly, but the eyes were steely behind his rimless glasses.

"I met with Devon Ridley, and although he was helpful, I had a feeling that some of his attention to detail was lacking. Is that a concern as far as you see it?"

"Yes, it is unfortunate that he has a lot of personal problems to deal with now, but he has proved reliable in the past."

"I believe the reports on the histology from certain patients show deterioration in the efficacy of what we believe were HG 176 patients. Was this unexpected in your opinion?"

"Yes, it was, but I am sure you are aware that the failure rate in new chemical entities is high. There may be certain administrative failings in the recording of the data. As Principal Investigator of this site, I have taken control of the investigation and away from Devon."

"In terms of generating the information, I assume it is your doctors, nurses and pharmacists who are the clinical interface and put together the results, which the CRO then analyses. So at this moment, you have control over the entire clinical chain?"

"That is correct. There is a chain of responsibilities from administering the medicine, collecting blood samples, carrying out biopsies and reviewing the histology, all under my supervision. It is for this reason that I will carry out the investigation."

"How long will this take?" Paul asked as his anxiety grew.

"It should be up to two weeks. We cannot leave this for longer as the medicine course needs to be resumed or, I'm afraid, terminated in case of a proven drug failure."

These words struck a chill in Paul, given all that was hanging on the trial.

"Thank you, Professor. I feel confident you will get to the bottom of this, and I hope the outcome is favourable."

The tiny professor rose from behind his desk to bid Paul goodbye, which necessitated reaching, with difficulty, over a pile of folders. With an inscrutable smile and penetrating look, Hung took leave of his guest.

Despite his friendly demeanour, the professor seemed a bit edgy during the conversation. The trial's success would earn him acclaim in terms of publications and prestige for his university and hospital. Paul assumed the pressure of the possible failure of the trial was starting to weigh on Hung too. There was pressure everywhere, but Paul had to have faith in a medical colleague and trusted that Professor Hung's investigations would get to the bottom of the problem.

Paul returned to the hotel and called JP, remembering the time difference between early afternoon in Hong Kong and early morning in Berkhamsted. As usual, JP was already at the office, and Mildred put Paul through.

"Hello Paul, what is your news?"

Paul decided not to reference his concern about Devon but keep it at a high level.

"I have spoken to both the CRO representative and Professor Hung. There is a sense there could be an issue with data transfer from the primary source files to the case report form. Professor Hung will assume responsibility for the investigation himself."

"That's quite unusual, but Hung is a good man – or a sample of one as he is so small. I met him when we brought all the Principal Investigators to a meeting in London, and he is very impressive. I am sure we are in good hands."

"I am too."

"Paul, I want you to go straight to St Petersburg to join Melissa. I'll inform her that you are on the way this time. As a doctor, I need you to give me a feel for the medical people involved in the trial since Melissa, with a PhD in organic chemistry, may miss this. Besides all the technical and scientific issues involved in trial work, there is also the human aspect. Good luck."

Paul found himself staring at the phone, the sound of the dialling tone filling his hotel room. At least Melissa would be forewarned of his arrival this time, but it was unlikely to change her behaviour. What was it about her, her demeanour towards him? He was reminded of Tom's comment about her on his first day at Harrowgate – 'Dragon Lady'. What did she want in life? What was she missing? Did she have an agenda? Perhaps he would figure her out in St Petersburg.

CHAPTER 18

St Petersburg

Paul set in motion the steps to get him to the next stage of his journey. As there was no direct flight between Hong Kong and St Petersburg, he found flights on Lufthansa to get him to Frankfurt and then on to the trial site as quickly as possible.

St Petersburg is a fascinating city, but it was unlikely Paul would have time to explore its various sights. Founded in 1703 by Tsar Peter the Great, situated on the Neva River and facing the Baltic Sea, it is seen as the cultural capital of Russia.

The city has undergone two name changes. In 1914 to Petrograd, later to Leningrad and finally back again, acknowledging its heritage as St Petersburg. The Tsarist cycle was closed when the remains of the murdered Tsar Nicholas II and his family were discovered in a mineshaft in the Koptyaki forest. They were interred with their ancestors in the Peter and Paul Fortress on Zayachy Island.

Touching down at St Petersburg's Pulkovo International Airport, Paul recognised that much of his life now focused on airports, departure lounges, immigration checks, and trusting the taxi rides to yet another hotel. How simple his previous life seemed by comparison. Yet everything important to him now revolved around his new life. This was about solving the cause of the HG 176 trial problems and getting the product to completion and available to patients. Paul wanted to get this done as quickly as possible as a tribute to Jill, and it drove him on with determination and energy. He could not let this fail, although so much of its success or failure lay in other's hands. In this charged emotional environment, memories of Jill haunted him.

His taxi took him to the Taleon Imperial Hotel on Nevsky Prospect, the main street in the city and the centre of shopping and nightlife. Paul got Melissa's room number from reception, went to his room and phoned her.

When she heard his voice, she answered in her customary cool, detached way, "JP told me that you were coming through here. It seems we are to be joined at the hip in this project whether we want it or not."

"As I said, Melissa, it is our job to see if we can solve this problem with the trial as time is running out for all of us."

"I have a follow-up meeting at the hospital this afternoon; I am leaving in half an hour. I will meet you in the lobby," and she put down the phone.

In the taxi headed to the hospital, Paul asked for background on the trial and the personnel involved.

"Professor Anatoly Pavlyuchenko is the Principal Investigator, but I'm sure he delegates most of the trial work to Dr Sergei Alexievich, the Study Coordinator. Besides being Head of Oncology, Professor Pavlyuchenko also appears to be the Superintendent of City Hospital No. 3, the huge public hospital we are headed to. It's hard to tell with language difficulties and suspicion about Westerners poking their nose into their affairs and trying to identify failings. In this regard, I feel Professor Pavlyuchenko is not giving the trial his full attention. Dr Alexievich is an ambitious, driven practitioner, and I think he has intentions to take over from the professor. He comes across as suave."

"Do we have anyone from the contract research organisation here?"

"Yes, his name is Tanel. He's young, bright and not very

experienced. He's from Tallinn in Estonia. The Russians see the Baltic States – Latvia, Lithuania and Estonia – as part of their territorial interests, which they term the 'near abroad', so I don't think he has much clout here."

The taxi wound its way through the dense traffic – although not as bad as in Moscow, according to the broken English of the taxi driver. Pulling up outside the enormous hospital, they were met by Tanel Valle from QualiMed. He had a bright shiny face with flushed cheeks, probably acquired in the cold morning air. Pale blue eyes behind a pair of red-framed glasses and an earnest but slightly distracted manner accentuated his youthful appearance. He greeted them in perfect English and directed them to Professor Pavlyuchenko's office.

As they passed through the corridors, Paul noticed that the hospital seemed an admixture of first and third-world institutions, unlike Hong Kong, where shiny efficiency prevailed. Russia's difficult financial position had an effect everywhere, clearly impacting the hospital and its efficiency, the possible source of the problem.

The professor rose to greet them in reasonable English as he directed them to a circular meeting table in his expansive office. A stunning-looking woman in green surgical gear with a stethoscope draped around her elegant neck was standing beside his desk, going through some patient folders. He asked her to leave.

"To follow up on our meeting this morning Dr James, I have asked Dr Alexievich to extract more information on the increased number of adverse side effects for you and your colleague ... "

"Dr Beresford," said Melissa, to Paul's surprise. Perhaps the ice maiden was melting at last and prepared to acknowledge his presence and medical background.

"We're concerned that the trial, which has delivered some outstanding preliminary results at an initial review, is starting to fail," the professor began. "We cannot be completely sure as this is a double blind study, but we sense that the patients showing increased adverse reactions are from the HG 176 group as they were initially the ones we believe showed incredible promise. I want you to go through to see Dr Alexievich. He can provide the details."

"Do you have any sense of what the problem could be?" pressed Paul, wanting clarity and urgency.

"Go and see Dr Alexievich," was the response, as he gave Paul a bone-crushing handshake, ignoring Tanel Valle during the interaction.

As they left, they passed the elegant woman who had been in the professor's office. Despite being in unflattering surgical scrubs and a head cover over strands of blond hair escaping beneath it, Paul looked into her piercing blue eyes and was reminded of Jill. She returned his look receptively and went back into the professor's office. Paul had to collect himself and focus on the task at hand.

Dr Sergei Alexievich matched Melissa's description to the finest detail. Lush blond hair combed with agonising detail, elegant clothing featuring top-end international brands, rounded off with a pair of Gucci loafers. He appeared to be a client of GUM, the giant store in Moscow facing Red Square and the Kremlin where the leading political figures and apparatchiks shopped. Perhaps he shopped there too, or maybe he was simply wealthy since, from experience, Paul could not believe a hospital doctor could be so well-heeled. The doctor greeted Melissa with a kiss on each cheek and Paul with a handshake, fortunately not as firm as the professor's. Tanel Valle, lurking in the background, was once again ignored.

"You caught me by surprise coming back this afternoon. I thought you only had a meeting with the professor."

Paul looked at Alexievich's desk, and something among the patient folders struck him as unusual. He wasn't sure what it meant but committed it to memory. The Russian regained his seat and quickly rearranged the folders on his desk.

"So much admin to clutter things," he explained as he moved and shuffled folders and documents on his desk. "I am sure it is not so bad in the West. Here, the State wants to know everything."

"What were the most common side effects noticed?" Paul asked.

"The most concerning – and potentially fatal – was the sudden onset of heart abnormalities with arrhythmias and palpitations. In addition, there were neuropathies with patients complaining of pain and tingling in arms and legs."

Paul was perplexed that two markedly different sets of issues characterised the two sites experiencing problems. "We've just come from Hong Kong, and there the efficacy of HG 176 is in question. Why do you think the efficacy is so different here?"

"My colleague is still new to the world of clinical trials and hasn't had experience with these situations before," was Melissa's quick interjection.

"I definitely think HG 176 is in question, as it is not performing at the level that it was," said Alexievich, "but, over a period, adverse events, such as those which I have detailed to you, are coming to the fore. These side effects are possibly fatal, and my concern is that we could lose patients shortly."

"Are you suggesting that the trial be halted?" queried Paul.

"We are close to it."

Paul could see the anxiety on Melissa's face as she contemplated the possible demise of Harrowgate's groundbreaking medicine.

"Doctor, is it possible to have a look at your clinics where the patients on the trial are treated?" asked Paul.

"With pleasure, let me show you around. Melissa, here are some of the folders of treated patients; you can have a look at these while we are away."

He selected some of the patient folders, and she started paging through them with Tanel peering quizzically over her shoulder.

As they exited the office, Alexievich scuttled down a long passageway, saying, "Let me get you a white coat for the tour."

As Paul waited, the woman he saw in the professor's office walked towards him. She had taken off the surgical cap and scrubs, now wearing tight hospital greens. As she approached him, he was taken again by her delicate and sophisticated look that reminded him of Jill. Paul was shocked by the emotion it evoked in him and embarrassed by the fact that he felt aroused by her. As she passed close to him, she looked deeply into his eyes. He caught the embroidery on her top, which read 'Dr Anastasia', but he could not read the surname below that. She almost brushed him as she went past and said in a low whisper, "Moshennichestvo," and went on her way.

Paul was left puzzled and stunned. She had deliberately set out to say something to him, but what did it mean? She obviously could not, or would not, speak English. His thoughts were interrupted by the return of Alexievich holding an off-colour lab coat for Paul, which looked as if it had been worn for years.

"Russian white," Alexievich said with a smile.

The coat he gave to Paul was in sharp contrast to his own crisp, immaculately pressed garment. They set off through the building to the clinics.

Again, Paul compared the images of the clinics he had known at Groote Schuur in Cape Town and the Royal National Orthopaedic Hospital in London to those in this hospital. The differences here were stark. In some cases, the paint was peeling off the walls, and battered filing cabinets bulged with papers. However, there were up-to-date computers on desks, "Stolen from the West," remarked Alexievich with a laugh.

Several ward nurses busied themselves more actively as the two doctors entered. They looked at Paul with coy approving interest. Alexievich said something to them in Russian, which was met by tittering nervous laughter. Paul looked questioningly at his host.

"I told them not to jump into your pants as they are obviously interested in you."

Ignoring this, Paul asked, "Are these the nurses who record the source data and patient information into the case report forms?"

"Yes, and they report to me."

"What about the person from the contract research organisation?"

"Ah, yes, the Estonian, Tanel. He gets guidance from me as he is inexperienced. I am assisting him so that we will have well-trained staff to help us do our trials after we invade Estonia," came Alexievich's deadpan reply.

Paul did not know if this was black humour or tinged with seriousness.

When the doctor started to chuckle, Paul grinned and said, "Let's get back to Dr James."

Although Alexievich had, at times, a glib, superficial side to him, Paul felt that he could trust a fellow medic, and it would be in Alexievich's interest to see the trial succeed. And, like the clinical team in Hong Kong, be associated with the development of a unique treatment. He would be rewarded with publications in peer-reviewed medical journals and likely to present papers at international forums – the things that academics craved.

As they returned to his office, Alexievich asked Paul for the lab coat so that he could return it. "If I don't do this, the KGB will be onto me," he said with a laugh as they set off again down the passageway and Paul entered the office where Melissa was going through a stack of patient folders.

"This doesn't look good. There are a growing number of side effects being recorded."

Paul assessed that Melissa must be paging through a dozen bulky patient folders. He started picking them up and flicking through them.

"I need you to hand these back to me as I have to summarise the latest findings for the professor's report," said Alexievich gathering them up and returning them to his desk. "Let me see you out."

As they exited the hospital, they met up with Tanel. While Melissa looked out for the taxi, he pulled Paul aside and said quietly, "Dr Alexievich is helping me document the trial. It does seem as if there is a major problem with the product. I am, however, not certain that everything is right with the trial."

"What do you mean by that?"

"Although Dr Alexievich has the main control of the trial rather than the professor, I have seen some strange results in the clinical reports that don't make sense. Although he sees me as inexperienced, which I am, I think he underestimates my intellect. I qualified as the top pharmacist in Estonia. I specialised in pharmacology and clinical studies. I know when there's an issue. I wanted to raise this previously, but the doctor keeps putting barriers in my way. I think I will push the point and get to see the professor privately."

"How will Dr Alexievich feel about this?"

"I won't let him know. Which hotel are you staying at?"

"The Taleon Imperial Hotel on Nevsky Prospect."

"I will call you."

At that moment, the taxi pulled up outside the hospital, and Melissa started getting in.

"We will talk about this later," said Paul as he left to join Melissa.

While he had confidence in his medical colleague here in St Petersburg and Professor Hung in Hong Kong, Paul had concerns about the observation he made in Alexievich's office. Was he mistaken; had his memory let him down? And the strange encounter with Dr Anastasia? What had she meant by that word?

There was no conversation in the taxi on the return to the hotel, not due to the icy tension of previous journeys but because both were lost in their thoughts concerning what they had just seen and heard.

Melissa's thoughts were about the puzzling findings of Hong Kong and now St Petersburg, where the trial seemed to be failing for different reasons. She had been involved in numerous trials, but none showed the type of issues besetting HG 176. She was concerned about the survival of the trial, what it could mean for Harrowgate and her ambitions within the company. She hoped to find the problem and the solution and present herself as the saviour. She had to deal with Paul's presence and her concern – however slight – that he would find the answer, cement his position within the company and endear himself to JP. She could subvert this by throwing Paul false leads to follow and report back to JP, thus undermining his position.

Paul was equally lost in thought. His innate nature to have confidence in his medical colleagues was his baseline. They, like him, were fact-based scientists and applied scrutiny and logic to the problem. He trusted their bona fides. They would have a financial and academic reward if the trial succeeded, so the problem was unlikely to lie with them. The inescapable thought was that HG 176 was failing due to inherent inadequacies, errors in the technique of the trial process, system, or staffing, like Devon in Hong Kong or the front-line staff in what was an underfunded Russian hospital.

The contract research organisation's staff member employed by Harrowgate in St Petersburg did not appear to have the experience to detect errors. Or did he? He felt sorry for Tanel and how the hospital staff treated him. Paul remembered Professor Reich's comment that he had experienced failed CRO operations. But counter to that, Tanel appeared bright and perceptive; perhaps his probing could reveal something unexpected.

Two things, however, troubled Paul on this visit; what he had noticed on Alexievich's desk before he shuffled the folders around and the message Dr Anastasia had passed on to him with that one word.

He hardly realised they were parked outside the hotel when Melissa asked him to settle the taxi fare. As they entered the hotel foyer, she said she was tired and would return to her room and order room service as she did not feel like going to dinner. Paul felt a sense of relief as he wanted to be alone with his thoughts processing all the information he had garnered over the last few days.

In desperate need of exercise, Paul decided against going out for a run on the busy streets of St Petersburg, opting instead for a swim in the hotel pool to unwind. The pool was deserted. He entered the water, began to swim with energy and purpose and felt his mind relaxing. After a good workout, he climbed out and was met by a staff member who handed him a towel, complimenting him on his swim. Since the attendant spoke good English, Paul asked him what the Russian word 'moshennichestvo' meant.

"That's easy, Sir; you pronounced it well. It means 'fraud', something you should look out for in St Petersburg."

* * *

The following day, Melissa called Paul just before he went down to breakfast. "I'm going to stay in my room for much of the day, catching up on some admin and compiling a report on my findings in Hong Kong and here. It will take some time to complete, but in the meantime, I want you to contact JP with my headline findings in anticipation of my report."

"What do you want me to convey to him?"

"Let him know that concerning the trial here and its side effects, I think that we may have to reduce the dosage of HG 176. These side effects may only be detected after a lengthy treatment period. The trial here was one of the earlier ones to kick off after the UK, which is why we could only be seeing side effects now. Titration dosage studies were done in the trial's early stages to see the optimal dose. We may need to return to these to adjust the trial rather than terminate it."

"If you think so."

"I do," responded Melissa.

Paul felt some reservations about this based on his observations at the hospital, but it was in the interest of the project to keep JP informed, given the seriousness of the situation and Melissa's experience and knowledge.

After breakfast, he put in a call to JP.

"How's it going?" was the anxious question from the head of Harrowgate.

"There are definite reports of side effects which we have seen in the case report forms, but perhaps a reduction in the strength of the dose may do away with these."

There was a pause at the other end of the line. "What makes you think that?" was JP's puzzled reply. "I believe there were other dosage studies earlier in Phase 2 trial work."

"Not that I can recall, but I will speak to Ngozi about that."

Paul reflected on where this conversation was going. "I have some other avenues I can follow based on my observations."

"I hope so."

"The representative from the CRO also seems to have a view on the problems; I will meet up with him again."

"Please do, as I don't think you are making progress." Disheartened, JP rang off.

Like Melissa, Paul also decided to work in his room, putting together his thoughts on the two trial sites and his assessment of them. As a doctor, he was constantly developing models that might explain what was going awry in the two trials and seeking to support or refute these models by subjecting them to rigorous scrutiny. It required analysis, deduction and a verifiable conclusion. He had to establish how to use the information and how it would alter the probability of scenario A or B. It was early afternoon when deep in thought, his phone rang again. It was Tanel.

"Dr Beresford, I need to give you some feedback on our exchange at the hospital."

"Go ahead."

"Not on the phone; it's not safe. I need to meet with you."

"Where do you suggest?"

"The Hermitage Museum is close to your hotel. Let's meet in an hour in the Romanov section on the second floor of the Winter Palace. I will meet you in front of the painting of Catherine the Great."

"Right, see you there."

Paul put down the phone with some concern. Tanel sounded anxious – even scared. He said it was not safe to talk over the phone. This trial was about saving lives. It was a serious venture, but nothing about the trial should make anyone associated with it feel threatened.

He was about to get changed and ready for his meeting with Tanel when the phone rang again. It was Melissa. She told Paul that she had just been contacted by Professor Hung about some developments in Hong Kong and that she would leave on the first available flight to see him. She suggested that Paul stay on in St Petersburg to see if he could discover anything new but expressed her doubt he would.

Paul was about to raise the issue of the reduced dosage, which she suggested he report to JP, but she'd already hung up. Melissa's behaviour was troubling considering they were supposed to be on the same team. Paul recalled Jill's comment to him that he was too trusting.

Dressing warmly as winter started to bite, he got ready to meet Tanel. Paul was excited to see the famous Hermitage Museum, but this sense was overshadowed by his concern over Tanel's tone and the urgent and tense nature of their exchange. What had he found that necessitated an offsite, almost clandestine meeting? Paul left the hotel and walked briskly along the English Embankment, next to the icy River Neva, past the massive bronze equestrian statue of Peter the Great.

He arrived at the building of the Winter Palace of the Tsars, which housed the Hermitage Museum. He bought a ticket and went up the giant marble Jordan Staircase to floor two. Entering the Museum, Paul went directly to the portrait gallery of the Romanovs and sought out the painting of Catherine the Great. There was an interested gathering of admirers in front of the painting, but no Tanel. Paul looked around anxiously, wandered further down the gallery, and eventually returned to the portrait.

Paul was about to give up and return to the hotel when he felt a tug at his elbow. It was Tanel. He looked as tense as he had sounded on the phone.

"Let's stay with the crowds as I don't want to be seen alone talking with you." They moved along to stand in front of another painting.

"I tried to speak to the professor, but it seemed that Dr Alexievich was tracking my movements around the department. Luckily he was called away, and I took the opportunity to go to the professor's office. He was not there, but Dr Anastasia Medvedeva was."

Given her brief interaction with him, Paul noted her name and was immediately interested. "What did she say?"

"She said something underhand was going on with the trial, and it seemed to be linked to Dr Alexievich," Tanel began.

"Go on."

"It appears that she and the professor are having an affair, and Alexievich seems to have some sort of hold over the professor because of this. He's interfering with his signing off of the clinical findings as Principal Investigator of the trial."

"That's very interesting since when I was in his office with Melissa, I saw something odd on his desk among the patient folders. There appeared to be two folders with the same patient number. When he saw me looking at his desk, he immediately shuffled them around and stacked them."

"That doesn't surprise me, given the unsettling climate surrounding this trial," Tanel continued. "They are trying to marginalise me because of my inexperience, but I am smart enough to know something is wrong. The results were outstanding for an extended period, and we thought that HG 176 was a winner, when suddenly the wheels started coming off. Alexievich also seemed to undergo a change recently."

"What sort of change?"

"I am not sure. He seemed to be quite, how do you say, twitchy."

"He seemed to be quite a smooth operator based on my interaction. I thought I could trust him to do his best for the trial, but I have lingering doubts that you have now reinforced."

Tanel seemed to tense up as he noticed two men sitting on a bench on the other side of the gallery, ostensibly looking at some of the paintings but casting furtive glances in their direction.

"I must go now. I will make some more enquiries and contact you if I have more news for you tomorrow. Let's meet here at the same place and time."

He set off in the direction of the grand staircase, leaving Paul with an air of concern as he disappeared into the crowd. Paul turned to examine the two men sitting on the bench, but it was empty.

* * *

The following day, Paul retraced his steps to the Hermitage Museum to link up with Tanel. Once again, Paul had to wait for a while until they made contact. He hardly recognised Tanel at first as he had a beanie pulled low over his forehead down to his red-framed glasses and a North Face jacket with the collar pulled up.

"If I have difficulty recognising who you are, I think others will too," said Paul trying to make light of the situation.

"You can never be too careful these days," was Tanel's clipped response.

"What did you find out?"

"There is definitely something irregular happening with the trial. I believe that Dr Alexievich is at the centre of it. I met with Dr Medvedeva as the professor won't see me, and as before, she confirmed that Alexievich has a hold over the professor – probably because of his affair with her. But someone or something seems to have a hold over Alexievich. She thinks he may have gambling debts, and the problem is that most of the casinos in St Petersburg, as in most of Russia, are controlled by the Mafia."

"I don't see the link between that and the trial."

"I don't either," said Tanel, "but my instinct tells me something is going on. More seriously, I can't get access to the case report forms, which I should do since I am the clinical research associate for this trial. Our company is contracted by yours to do this work."

"You must insist!"

"I know, but Alexievich says that I am too inexperienced, and as Study Coordinator, he can pull rank."

"What's the answer?"

"I may have a solution, but it involves some irregular action."

"Such as?"

"I have spoken to Dr Medvedeva about getting you into the

hospital late at night when Alexievich is not there. He keeps the patient folders in the black filing cabinet in his office. She can get a key to his office and knows where he keeps the key to the filing cabinet. Are you up for this?"

Paul thought of all the issues hanging on the success or failure of the trial. Here was a potential blockbuster product that had initially held such promise for women worldwide with breast cancer to be effective and save lives. This had to be successful. He wanted the trial to succeed as a tribute to Jill, but he also wanted to prove to himself that his father had misjudged him. And then there was JP, whose hopes and dreams for the success of Harrowgate and proof of the benefits the pharmaceutical industry could offer hinged on the trials succeeding.

"Are you up for it?" asked Tanel again.

"Of course."

"Right, I will arrange with Dr Medvedeva to do this tonight. I will collect you around nine o'clock and take you to the hospital. Dr Medvedeva will meet you and get you in. I must go now," he said, looking around furtively as he left.

Paul stood looking unseeingly at the portraits of the Romanovs while he digested the discussion with Tanel. He had time to spare before the evening, so he wanted to take in some of the splendours of the Hermitage. As he moved down the gallery, he thought he saw one of the two men from the previous day who were such a concern to Tanel. Paul moved to intercept him, not knowing what he would say if he confronted him, but the stranger quickly blended into a large group of loud American tourists and was gone.

Paul got back to the hotel in the early afternoon. He had spent time in the Hermitage marvelling at the incredible artworks and treasures, but it had not been the joyous occasion he thought it would be. The whole tour had been overshadowed by the engagement with Tanel and all the consequences flowing from it. A sinister element had entered what appeared to be a complicated scientific investigation into developing a new pharmaceutical product.

As a subplot, there was his relationship with Melissa, her initial disdain and the offhand way she had dealt with him. She had modified her approach and become slightly more accommodating and less contemptuous. However, she was giving him information, which he had initially taken in good faith, but now seemed punctured with inaccuracies. Was she trying to set him up for failure? Was he being oversensitive?

Paul felt drained by the recent developments. As there was still a long time before Tanel would fetch him, he decided that a short sleep followed by a run in the crisp St Petersburg air would serve to recharge him and prepare him for the challenge ahead.

Just before the agreed time of the meeting, Paul left his room. He found himself impacted by the suspicion that had gripped Tanel regarding being watched by unknown observers. Looking around the lobby, some men and a lone woman suddenly appeared suspicious to him. In Russia, it was not unusual to find women loitering around hotel lobbies touting for business, but she did not seem to fall into that category.

Get a grip, Paul told himself, as his attention was drawn to a dark green Saab that hooted. The window was partially rolled down, and Tanel shouted, "Please get in quickly!"

Paul remembered just in time that Russians drive on the right, unlike the UK, and moved to the front passenger door.

"Ready for this?" asked Tanel with a tight smile, accelerating away almost before Paul had settled into his seat.

"Of course."

It was only a short trip to the hospital. The grounds were well illuminated, and the presence of traffic and ambulances with sirens blaring caused Paul some consternation if this was supposed to be a clandestine visit.

Tanel apparently read his mind as he said, "We're going around to the back of the hospital."

The Saab navigated a roundabout, a side road running between two wings of the hospital and stopped outside a large roller door that was partially open. The alleyway was fairly dark and full of bins marked 'Hospital Waste' in Russian and English.

"Get out; there she is," said Tanel, pointing to a figure in green surgical overalls just visible in the dim light.

"I will meet you back here in precisely an hour. Don't be late. It is exactly nine twenty now."

Paul exited the car and moved swiftly to the person he immediately recognised as Dr Medvedeva. "Follow me," she said, leading Paul into a suitably dark corridor. He could see that she was carrying something over her arm.

"You speak English?" said Paul in surprise, given their first brief interaction.

"A little. Enough," she responded.

Paul felt relief as he had been concerned over how this mission would work if she could not communicate with him.

As they stopped outside what was a change room or toilet, she gave Paul the bundle she had been carrying. He saw a set of surgical overalls, hat and shoe covers.

"Change," she uttered.

Paul understood how the plan was to work, with him changing into surgical gear to appear he was one of the medical staff. The clock was already ticking to get back to Tanel, so he pulled the protective gear over his clothes and fitted the shoe covers and hat. Fortunately, through exercise and diet, Paul had retained his lithe build and didn't look inflated wearing both clothes and scrubs.

He fitted his surgical mask and exited the change room to find Dr Medvedeva waiting for him. "Come," she urged.

He followed her down a series of corridors and into an elevator. He tensed up when he found staff members in it. They greeted Dr Medvedeva and began a conversation with her. They said something in Russian to Paul, and he just nodded, hoping it was the proper response. Fortunately, they swiftly arrived at their intended floor. Dr Medvedeva and Paul set off down a passageway that he recognised from his first visit to the hospital, stopping outside a door with

Dr Alexievich's name on it as far as Paul could decipher from the Cyrillic alphabet.

Telling him to wait, Dr Medvedeva went down the corridor and disappeared into another office, emerging with a large bunch of keys. She tried one key without success and then another, which also failed. She studied the bunch of keys, selected one and tried again. No success, and then another with the same result. She let out what was apparently a string of oaths in Russian which ended in a universal expletive that required no translation at all. She tried again, and the door yielded.

"Enter," was her command. "Top door." She said, pointing to the desk. Paul looked puzzled. "Top door," she repeated.

Struggling to understand what she was trying to convey, he took a stab at it. "Top drawer?" he suggested.

She nodded vigorously, pointed to a black filing cabinet, then closed the door on Paul, leaving him to investigate once he had located the patient folders. What was nearly lost in translation was rescued.

Paul looked around the office, familiar with its layout from his previous visit. It was moderately spacious, with a large desk set sideways against a wall. There were patient folders on it, but none appeared to be the ones Paul was looking for.

A pair of visitor's chairs faced the desk, and behind them was a large built-in cupboard. Paul opened the door and saw some of Alexievich's elegant outfits, the immaculate white coats he had worn on their first meeting, and a pair of skis and ski poles. Alexievich obviously had time for some relaxation.

On the other side of the office was a bank of grey metal filing cabinets and a single black filing cabinet with several drawers – both were locked. Paul went back to the desk and opened the top drawer. To his relief and surprise, he saw a set of keys under a small diary. Alexievich had slipped up in not protecting these. Perhaps he had left his office in a hurry and forgotten about them.

Paul felt he needed every bit of luck going his way, so he took the keys to the black filing cabinet. The first key he tried failed, but the second one sprang the lock open, revealing the neatly stacked folders in the top drawer. Paul paged through one of them, then another, and realised that these did not refer to the trial.

He opened the second drawer and immediately saw a folder with the protocol number of the trial 'HG 176 – St P' written in a block at the top left-hand corner of the file. Paul sighed in relief. Now he needed to locate the folders he had seen on Alexievich's desk during their first encounter. They had both carried the number 'HG 176 – St P – NV – 023'.

Paul praised his memory, which he was increasingly coming to believe was photographic as he could recall images and details of documents or items for months afterwards. He had dismissed the thought, but it was evidenced to him in various encounters – those with colleagues at the Royal National Orthopaedic Hospital and in his discussion with Professor Reich being the most recent.

Paul started flicking through the patient folders arranged in numerical order according to the subject initials and trial number. He found the file marked with NV and 023. All good so far. Now, he needed to find what he was sure was a duplicate file with the same patient number. He looked at the next file, but its number was 024. Damn, it was too hopeful to expect the answer to the problem to simply present itself. Paul had to look through as many cabinet drawers and folders as possible in the brief time he had.

He had worked his way through the top two drawers. The third drawer had a mixture of folders that did not seem to relate to the Harrowgate trial. Paul started going through the final drawer when he heard voices in the corridor – one of which was Dr Medvedeva's. He accelerated his search through the folders in case his visit had to be aborted.

Paul could not find anything related to the trial and was just about to give up when he detected that the drawer was less deep than the others. He scrambled around its base and was able to lift a false bottom. He could see several folders below this, but before he could raise any of them, the voices in the corridor got louder, and he could hear Dr Medvedeva speaking in an agitated way to an equally irate male. The office door handle shook as if it were going to be flung open. Dr Medvedeva's voice got louder and shriller. Paul looked around the office in desperation. The built-in cupboard! Quickly he took refuge in it just as the office door burst open.

He could hear Dr Medvedeva arguing with the unidentified male, both continuing their argument a few feet away from him. Paul hid behind the array of white lab coats, surgical kit and some of Alexievich's stylish range of clothes. Feeling that he may be safe there, he was suddenly gripped by another concern – claustrophobia! In his haste to hide, Paul had forgotten his fear of enclosed spaces. Almost immediately, he started to sweat as his breathing got heavier and heavier, and the argument continued.

Paul desperately needed to get out and into some fresh air, and he struggled to contain and overcome his panic. He grabbed hold of one of the ties hanging on the rail and stuffed it into his mouth in a desperate attempt to stop himself from gasping or crying out. He was about to pass out or push the door open when the argument simmered down, and the voices receded as they left the office. When the door shut with a click, he managed to wait a few seconds before opening the cupboard door, stumbling out and gulping in stale office air, which seemed sweeter than he had ever known. After a minute or two, he stood there slumped, holding on to the desk, sweating as the surgical scrubs over his clothing had acted as an insulator.

He was still breathing deeply and feeling faint when the door opened again, and he saw to his relief that it was Dr Medvedeva – he was in no position to defend himself.

"Come, we go now!" she said.

"I think I have found some folders," he said, pointing to the black filing cabinet.

"Too late, hurry, we go now!"

"But I need to see these folders."

"Sorry, too late, danger."

Dr Medvedeva closed the cabinet drawer, locked it and returned the key to the desk. She pulled Paul out of the office, and while he leaned against the wall, she locked the office door and ran down the corridor to return the bunch of office keys.

"Problem?" she asked, seeing Paul's hunched figure on her return.

"Claustrophobia."

"Okay, we leave now."

Dr Medvedeva grabbed Paul's hand and tugged him towards the elevator as they heard more voices coming down the passageway. Impatiently she pressed the button four or five times and was relieved as the doors opened and she pulled Paul inside the empty elevator. She looked at her companion and could not resist a laugh. How he had transformed from the attractive male visitor yesterday, who had got the nurses in the clinic so excited, to the dishevelled sweating figure standing next to her.

They exited the elevator and reached the change room where Paul had put on the surgical scrubs, and she pushed him towards the door, urging him to hurry. Paul obliged willingly. When he came out, they set off towards the roller door where he had entered the hospital.

Moments later, they stood in the semi-dark and saw a vehicle approaching. Paul could make out the distinctive shape of the Saab. As it pulled up, Dr Medvedeva stood in front of Paul, put her arms around his neck, pulled him towards her and kissed him, her tongue exploring his mouth. Then she pushed him towards the car and was gone.

"What did you find?" Tanel glanced sideways at Paul as he navigated the roundabout and headed towards the hospital exit. Two police cars, with sirens blaring and lights flashing, passed them coming into the hospital grounds.

"I found some of the case report forms for the trial but did not find evidence of errors in trial data. The patient folders were all in the correct sequence, but going through the last drawer of the black filing cabinet, I found there was a false bottom to the drawer. I saw some patient folders in it, but just as I was about to look at them, someone came into the office with Dr Medvedeva, probably a security person, and I had to hide in the office cupboard." Paul omitted his claustrophobia and the close shave of being detected. "Before I had the opportunity to look at any of them, Dr Medvedeva said that we had to leave urgently as there was a security alert, probably because I was in that office so late. She seemed to placate him for a while but said we had to get out."

"She works her charm on most men, particularly the professor," said Tanel.

Paul reflected on his brief exposure to this. "Yes, I'm sure," he said as he relived the sensation of her tongue in his mouth.

The Saab drove quickly through the streets of St Petersburg, and they soon came upon Nevsky Prospect and the bright lights of the central city. Tanel pulled up outside Paul's hotel.

"What do we do next?" he asked Paul.

"We need to access Alexievich's office and filing cabinet again," Paul replied, "but we will have to think of another approach, and we can't do it immediately. We need things to settle down a bit. But we can't wait too long because there is the risk of the trial being terminated here and in Hong Kong. The trial is being paused at both sites while the results are being assessed, but patients need their treatment soon if things are going to proceed."

"I will try to work with Dr Medvedeva. She is the key to solving this mystery."

Paul thanked Tanel and said they would stay in touch.

He got the key to his room and went upstairs, eager for a shower after his time at the hospital. As he switched on the lights, the first thing he noticed was an envelope on the table in his room. This seemed quite familiar now. He quickly opened it; it was a message from Melissa. "Contact me urgently," was the instruction. Although it was late, Paul contacted her.

"Paul, I need you to come to Hong Kong. Professor Hung is now looking at the early termination of the trial. We need to have a full meeting with him to determine the exact clinical details that support this viewpoint."

Since the St Petersburg investigation would have to be left to cool off for a short period, Paul agreed to get a flight in the morning. He was puzzled by her more accommodating tone and approach towards him. He was sure it was not his charm chipping away at her defences since there was little personal rapport between them, but he was too tired to think it through further. He showered and went to bed after first making a booking to get him back to the former colony.

CHAPTER 19

The Plan

Sean St Ledger felt satisfied his plan would soon bring about the outcomes he wanted. His goals to destroy Paul, impress his father, and acquire Harrowgate Pharmaceuticals were now neatly in place. He would be seen as a true descendent of the Talbot family who had achieved success by any means – fair or foul. The phone call he had received from the head of the Talbot operation in Hong Kong giving him an update on the progress was the basis for his optimism, but another element also drove him on.

Although he knew Jill had tried to hide and protect Paul's company from him, Sean had planned to go through the motions of wanting to acquire InnovoPharm, and then threaten to abandon his bid unless he had his way with her. He was sure Jill would have been desperate to do anything to get the deal to succeed. He had fantasised about ensnaring her in the company jet returning from the meeting in Ireland when she would be in his control.

Receiving the news from Giles Robinson about Jill's death had shaken him and denied him one of his determined desires. He felt embittered, and his anger was directed at Paul. If he was this great doctor, why had he not saved her?

Giles had informed Sean about the funeral, and he had attended the church service taking a seat towards the rear, keeping out of sight of Jill's family and watching Paul with animosity and loathing. He wanted revenge.

* * *

In Hong Kong, Professor Hung sat behind his enormous desk, absorbing all that had happened in the past few weeks. He was distressed at his actions since meeting with a professor of cardiology from mainland China. The meeting was supposed to have been about changes in the algorithm to the approach of the therapeutic guidelines for congestive heart failure – but this professor had another agenda.

When this professor made the appointment, Hung had not heard of him, but he seemed authentic. He had Googled him and found the professor's name and a series of publications that motivated his interest in engaging with a colleague from his old home in China. Hung thought he was just out of touch with the new generation of medical specialists coming through the ranks.

But the visiting professor was not quite who he purported to be, which Hung soon realised as the early evening one-on-one meeting in his office unfolded. This professor was a cardiologist, but he evidently had another role besides his medical speciality. The opening gambit from his visitor set the ground rules for their discussion.

"Professor Hung, your human rights activities and opposition to our government when you lived in Guangzhou are well known to you and the Central Committee of my party, correct?"

Hung remained silent.

"As a result, the Central Committee took note of your activities and issued you several warnings. Correct?"

Again, Hung made no comment.

"You decided to continue with these activities, and when we were about to take the necessary action against you, you fled to Hong Kong. Correct?"

There was nothing that Hung could say to this exposé about his life in mainland China. It was all true.

"But unfortunately for you, Professor Hung, some of your family still live in Guangzhou. Not so?"

Hung stiffened at the reference to his sister and elderly mother.

"Leave them alone. They had nothing to do with my activities on human rights abuses in China. In fact, they opposed them," he said, though not truthfully.

"Well, it doesn't matter whether they did or did not; they, unlike you, are still in Guangzhou and are in our care."

"This goes to prove exactly what my arguments were against government activities. I beg of you, release them. They are of no threat to the government."

"I wish it was as simple as that."

"What do you want from me? What must I do to ensure that they are released and safe?"

"Now you are starting to sound sensible – at last."

Hung could not think of any activity he managed or had influence over that could possibly be of interest to a member of the Central Committee of the Communist Party of China. The next question dealt with this, to his complete astonishment.

"I believe you are currently overseeing a trial on an English company's new medicine for breast cancer?"

"The clinical trial on HG 176?" he responded incredulously.

"I don't know about the number, but I know that it is a trial on breast cancer. There is only one?"

"Yes, but what has a clinical trial to do with my activities in human rights and the imprisonment of my mother and sister? This is absurd!"

"It's not for you to know or understand, but simply to do. No harm will come to them if you follow my instructions and carry out my requests. They will be released safely."

The thought of his frail elderly mother and his sister in prison haunted him. Hung's sister also harboured human rights sentiments, and coupled with a quick temper, she could potentially get herself into trouble. His mind raced to figure a way out of this situation, but the smugly smiling delegate from the People's Republic sitting opposite him held all the cards. Not only was Hung beaten, but also broken.

"What exactly do you want me to do with the trial?"

"Finally, you're asking the right questions. Now, listen closely."

* * *

Paul arrived again at Hong Kong International Airport at midday and took a taxi to the same hotel as his previous visit. Reception provided him with Melissa's room number, and he put a call through to her when he got to his room.

"You must join me for another meeting with Professor Hung late this afternoon," Melissa stated. "He contacted me early yesterday, saying that he felt the trial should be temporarily halted or terminated due to the lack of efficacy. He feels it is unethical to keep treating these patients with HG 176 if the comparator drug, although of moderate efficacy, can provide better results. He wants to discuss this and show some of the results as proof. I want you there to be a witness to his decision if that is how it pans out. I need you to be responsible for stopping him if he wants to terminate the trial."

Paul reacted to this last comment with surprise and concern, but before he could respond, Melissa said, "Meet me at five o'clock in the lobby," in her usual curt manner and rang off.

They met at five, got in the taxi and headed off to the King George Hospital once more. Since the meeting was held late, much of the hospital's hustle and bustle had quietened as they made their way back up to Professor Hung's office.

He greeted them cordially, but Hung was tense. Paul put this down to the enormous weight resting on whether to terminate the trial or sustain it. Paul felt similar pressure if the trial collapsed. He wanted it to succeed as a tribute to Jill and provide women worldwide with the benefit of a more effective drug. He would be devastated if he had left surgical practice only to be involved in an experiment that was going monumentally wrong.

"Is Devon Ridley not going to be part of this discussion?" queried Paul.

"No, I don't think he can add much value to this decision. As Principal Investigator, I am in charge."

"Professor Hung, what are the results that make you conclude that the trial should be terminated early?" prompted Melissa.

"As you are well aware, this has been a prospective, randomised, double blind trial on women with metastatic invasive cancer. We have trialled HG 176 against the standard drug treatment for these cancers. Although this trial has been double blind, we were getting results in one group of patients, indicating results far beyond what we expect from the standard treatment of care. We put this down to HG 176 delivering groundbreaking results – far beyond what we could ever have expected. But about four weeks ago, the follow-up clinical and histopathological signs from a significant number of patients suddenly showed a decline in efficacy."

"That coincides with the same time the St Petersburg trial started giving problems with side effects," said Paul. "That's an extraordinary coincidence."

"I don't know much about that," said Hung, "but here, the cancer recurrence rates were from twelve to fifteen percent, and secondary growths started to present. This set off alarm bells in our team, prompting me to suspend the trial pending investigation. But when the incidence of abnormalities increased to nearly twenty percent, I felt obligated to summon Melissa and tell her I intended to abort the trial."

"Can we see evidence of the sort of issues that you are describing?" asked Paul.

"You don't seem to believe me, Dr Beresford," said Hung with a slightly prickly attitude. "I am the Principal Investigator, and as you admitted to me in an earlier conversation, you are new to trial work."

"Don't antagonise the professor," snapped Melissa, glaring at Paul.

"A lot is hanging on the success of this trial," responded Paul. "I am not necessarily disputing your assessment Professor, but every last piece of evidence needs to be double-checked to support the final decision."

A tension settled over the office, and Paul decided he needed to make his point.

"These multicentre Phase 3 trials have been ongoing for the best part of three years. Other sites are not showing problems and were, in fact, reaching an early endpoint of resolving those specific cases being treated. They were ready to close off so that data could be compiled for submission to the medicines regulatory authorities to get the product registered and made available to patients worldwide," said Paul. "If that is the case, why is this site so different from the others? It is imperative that we are absolutely certain the data is correct."

"Dr Beresford stated that he did not have much faith in Devon Ridley," said Melissa, "and that he could be at fault in terms of the interpretation of the raw trial data in the case report forms."

"I agree that Devon has issues – a probable alcoholic with personal problems, but I know this is not a matter of finger trouble."

"Can you let us have sight of the evidence you mentioned?" Paul requested again.

"Yes," said Hung, visibly annoyed, "I have put a representative sample of patient folders and case report forms in the boardroom where you met Devon. Check them out for yourself."

Melissa and Paul left the office to go to the boardroom.

"What are you doing antagonising the professor?" snapped Melissa. "Your function tonight is to convince him not to terminate the trial. Don't overreach your abilities."

"Let's look at the data," said Paul, not hiding his irritation.

They sat down in front of a mound of patient folders. "Here, try to make sense of these, if you can," said Melissa, pushing some of the folders over to Paul.

In addition to the summary in the folders, there was an overwhelming mass of data to assess: copies of histopathology slides, levels of grading, stage of the cancer, lab reports on blood analyses and clinical reports on patient wellbeing. It was a Herculean task to assimilate this in the short time available.

Paul heard Melissa sigh as she went through the folders. She was experienced in this, and it also seemed a challenge for her. How could he better her in trying to prove or disprove Hung's conclusion?

Having gone through about twelve or fourteen folders, something struck him as out of place. He remembered that in three patient folders he looked at, the histopathology reports, blood profiles, and some clinical findings appeared to be different from the raw data listed at the back of the file. The raw data was the source file for the overall case report form. He checked the three folders again. Yes, he was right; in patients SM-Y, CL and JY, there were differing results. This could not be possible. His memory of picturing and retaining images had not failed him.

He asked Melissa, "Did you spot anything unusual?"

"No, it looks as if Hung is correct based on what I see here." She looked utterly despondent.

Paul decided not to share his findings with her. He wanted to be confident in the facts. In addition, based on what he had experienced in St Petersburg and now the bizarre occurrences in Hong Kong, he was certain that irregularities were occurring. But, if so, how to expose them?

They returned to the professor's office.

"So, what did you find?" Hung asked.

"It seems you are correct," said Melissa after a pause.

"I concur, based on what we have seen in the case report forms," said Paul. "These are the paper-based documents, but I assume there is also an electronic version?"

"Yes, there is, but it simply reflects what you can see in the paper-based results. Trial sites need to do both formats where possible since some sites are only paper-based. Kenya, as an example, does not have electronic capabilities, and it is doubtful the Russians have adequate capacity to ensure an electronic record. We need consistency across all our sites, and paper-based formats provide that. But yes, there is an electronic version."

"What is the next step?" asked Melissa, looking ashen.

"I will give an interval of two weeks before I terminate the trial. I will need this time to write my motivation and communicate it to Harrowgate and the other Principal Investigators at other trial sites to get them to do the same."

Paul and Melissa sat silently, digesting what this meant to them. In each case, these were separate and distinct issues.

"Very well," said Melissa. "We need to take this on board and be in touch with our Head Office."

CHAPTER 20

Conflict

Paul and Melissa left the diminutive figure of Professor Hung sitting behind his enormous desk in a stiff, upright manner. He did not extend the courtesy of seeing them out of his office. The taxi took the short ride back to their hotel.

"Paul, what were you thinking?" Melissa scolded. "I told you to tell Professor Hung that we would not accept the trial results since generally, the trial has progressed well at the other sites."

"You saw the results for yourself," said Paul. "How were we to argue against that? We have less than a couple of weeks before he submits his recommendation to terminate the trial."

"What can we do during that time?"

Paul had some thoughts but was not prepared to share them with Melissa until he had some feedback from Tanel. Melissa was unaware of his after-hours activities in St Petersburg, and Paul wanted to keep it that way. In addition, Paul was wary of Melissa's conduct towards him from their first meeting, but now he suspected she was also giving him questionable information to pass on to JP. Paul had under two weeks to get to the bottom of the failure of the trial at both sites. His instinct told him there were other issues at play. However, time was short.

When they arrived back at the hotel, it was nearly eight o'clock, and Paul suggested they have dinner together to share some thoughts about the results.

"Okay, if you insist, but I am feeling quite drained," Melissa mumbled.

"I'll meet you in the dining room in twenty minutes," said Paul, dismissing her objection and going to his room.

Returning to the dining room, Paul sat waiting for Melissa. In his mind, he weighed up to what extent he could share his thoughts about the irregularities he had noticed in the two trial sites. He was a naturally trusting person, but Melissa's behaviour had created uncertainty in his mind regarding her intentions. Based on one of their earlier meetings, she seemed to share Paul's view that being involved with getting a blockbuster medicine to market to help women dealing with the pain and suffering of breast cancer was a massive contribution. He wondered if he had misread her true motives.

Melissa made no apology when she arrived late, but she seemed less tense than earlier.

"Let's order and decide what steps we need to take regarding both sites and how we should break the news to JP," suggested Paul.

They ordered their meals, and Paul decided on a bottle of Cabernet Sauvignon as he felt he needed to unwind and was sure Melissa probably felt the same, although she offered little insight into her feelings.

After their meals were served and each had had a glass or two of wine, Paul shared some of his experiences from St Petersburg.

"Although I accept that the results in both these sites are clearly indicating a problem, I am not fully convinced that the situation is that clear cut."

"You have so little experience in these matters, what makes you think that you are right and the experts are wrong?" Melissa put particular emphasis on 'you'.

"Certain things in the case report forms, both here and in St Petersburg, don't add up."

"How do you know that?" Again, there was special emphasis on 'you', tinged with sarcasm.

"I have the ability to recall detail. Although I may not understand the significance of all the data, I am confident I have seen something peculiar."

Melissa took another gulp of her wine. "You think you saw something aberrant that neither of the Principal Investigators has picked up?"

"Tanel Valle also believes there is something amiss with the trial."

"What does he know with so little experience?"

Paul felt rising irritation that was not quelled by another mouthful of wine.

"He is more astute than some give him credit for, and I saw some unusual things in the folders that Alexievich showed us."

"This is your remarkable memory again, I assume," she scoffed.

"Yes, that's correct. Tanel is going to investigate for me."

"Ah, yes, the inexperienced Tanel. That's what our whole plan is resting on?"

"That and further scrutiny before any final letter reaches JP. I want to contact Devon Ridley and ask him to check some data for me."

"Ridley? This is the person you said was unreliable and the possible source of the problem; the problem you now say is false."

"The facts have evolved since I made that comment."

"Oh, an epiphany moment, I suppose," came the derisive reply.

Both Paul and Melissa picked up their glasses, drank deeply, and stared at each other across the table. The tension was palpable, amplified by their intake of wine.

"I am going to bed now. I have had enough of this nonsense," Melissa said, rising from the table.

Although neither admitted it, the day's events and the wine's effect had escalated the antagonism of their exchange. Paul thought it best to review matters in the morning. He got up and followed Melissa to the bank of lifts. Often after aggravated personal discussions, it is impossible to avoid that person. There was only one lift available, so they both got in. Melissa punched her floor number with unnecessary force and found their rooms were on the same floor. They stood in awkward silence, watching the agonisingly slow progress of the lift to the seventh floor.

Melissa exited, followed by Paul, whose phone rang as they walked down the long corridor towards their rooms. They paused. It was JP.

"Hello JP, how are you?"

"Not happy," was the brusque response.

"Why is that?"

"Melissa called me earlier and said you did not do as she requested and tell Professor Hung not to terminate the trial at this stage." At that moment, Paul felt a wave of understanding.

"We were going to contact you in the morning and explain the results we'd seen and the steps we have in mind to re-examine this."

"I am disappointed in you, Paul. I brought you on board believing you could add a different perspective to the trial and find out things that perhaps other people had missed."

"There are still some issues that I believe can impact the success of the trial."

"Well, you did nothing to stop Hung, and the termination has been set in motion. We can talk again later about this."

JP rang off without saying goodbye. Paul looked at Melissa, who had listened to Paul's side of the conversation with a slight smirk on her face.

"Now I know why you were late for dinner," seethed Paul. "You wanted to get hold of JP first and blame the failure of the trial on me."

"You seemed to think – and JP thought – that you would be the saviour of the trial. I just wanted to show him that his faith was misplaced."

"You know that was not the case, Melissa. I was sent here to assist you. Unlike you, I am not interested in personal glory, and you've been trying to undermine me from the beginning."

"I've only been defending Harrowgate's best interests and pointing out where it went wrong by employing you."

They continued walking towards the end of the long corridor and paused when they reached Melissa's room. She turned to slip the card into the door lock.

Paul, incensed by the exchange, enraged by her cumulative behaviour and fuelled by the wine, moved towards her as she turned to face him with her back against the door.

"You have continually fed me incorrect information to pass on to JP, making me look incompetent."

"It is my job to save Harrowgate. Soon JP will retire, and it seems he might want to appoint you as his successor. Well, I see that as my role when he leaves."

"I have no interest in that. All I wanted to see was the successful development of a drug to save women the torment of breast cancer which I have seen first-hand."

"Fuck you," said Melissa. "That's your story."

"Fuck you, Melissa," said Paul putting his outstretched arms against the door on either side of Melissa. He was up close to her and heard and felt her heavy breathing.

"That's what you have wanted to do from the moment you first saw me," Melissa taunted.

She put her arms behind her back, pushing her breasts towards Paul provocatively. Her mouth was open as if waiting for him to kiss her. Paul's thoughts raced. Melissa was incredibly attractive and sexually alluring, and he missed the physical contact he had with Jill. How he ached for intimacy, an ache realised through his brief exchange with Dr Anastasia Medvedeva.

Through the mists of anger and alcohol, Paul suddenly saw the trap Melissa was setting. She wanted him to try to bed her, and she would report to JP that Paul had raped her. That would finish his career at Harrowgate. A shaft of clarity passed through his mind. He pulled away from her. She was still breathing heavily, offering herself to him.

"That is the last thing on my mind. I want to understand why the trials are failing and see HG 176 get to market. You can have whatever you want regarding Harrowgate. I will move on after we have solved the problem."

They stood back from each other, digesting what had just happened. Paul felt irritation that he had allowed his feelings to cloud his judgement, and Melissa realised that she had perhaps overplayed her hand.

"We will meet for breakfast tomorrow morning and discuss what action we can take. I don't believe that the trials are over yet," said Paul, taking charge of the situation.

"I am going to bed," said Melissa, opening her room door and closing it behind her with a click rather than the loud bang that Paul had expected.

The morning would tell how the incident would impact their future relationship.

CHAPTER 21

A Theory

When Paul returned to his room, he felt his mind clear from the mist that had nearly overcome him. Earlier in the evening, he wanted nothing more than to sleep, but now he felt wide awake. If he could not sleep, neither would Devon. He removed Devon's card from his wallet and punched the number into the phone.

"Ridley," came the drowsy response.

"Devon, it's me, Paul; we need to chat."

"What's happened?"

"Melissa and I met with Professor Hung earlier this evening. He wants to terminate the trial and may take two weeks or less to write up his motivation and send it out to the other Principal Investigators and JP. Because he is so highly regarded among the Investigators, they are likely to take Hung's word and action his motivation."

"I wanted to contact you, Paul. Are you back in Hong Kong?" said Devon, sounding more awake, but Paul could detect a few slurred words indicating that Devon had renewed his relationship with the bottle.

"Yes, I arrived back late yesterday. Why did you want to get hold of me?"

"As you know, Hung has been forcing me out of the trial, which is strange since we have always had a good relationship working on other trials. I was so concerned about his behaviour that I decided to follow him one evening after work."

"What?" Paul was stunned.

"Yes, I know it sounds odd, but he's not himself. On the first evening I followed him, nothing happened, he just went home. But on the second evening, he went to a small restaurant in a poorer part of Kowloon, not the sort of place I thought he would frequent."

"What happened?"

"Shortly after he got to the restaurant, a black Geely sedan arrived. I don't know if you do, but Geely is a mainland China car brand, and it's unusual to see one in Hong Kong. Two men got out and met with Professor Hung in the restaurant. I could watch what was happening as they were sitting partially outside. They didn't seem too concerned about being seen, although they occasionally scanned the street even though it was fairly deserted."

"Did you see anything that might explain his unusual behaviour towards you and the trial assessment?"

"Hard to tell, but I think so. The professor spent quite a bit of time shouting at the men, who appeared unmoved by his situation. Then he seemed distraught, possibly even crying."

"That seems very strange."

"The two men then got up and left, leaving Hung sitting there. I was tempted to go and speak with him but decided against it."

"Probably the right decision based on the events you described."

"He sat there for a while after the men left, then slowly got up, went to his car, and drove off."

"Right, I will follow this up in the morning. Thanks for taking my call, Devon."

"I had no choice, did I? Goodnight."

Paul put the phone down and considered the events of the evening. The bust-up with Melissa was pivotal since she had now clearly stated her agenda. Again he was reminded of Jill's comment that he was too trusting. "Such a boy scout," were her exact words.

The night's events had been a tipping point for Paul, and he would no longer accept the bona fides of those he had trusted before, especially not his medical colleagues. He would also trust his judgement regardless of Melissa's experience.

The introspection about whether he could or would succeed was diminishing. The conversation with Devon had confirmed Paul's suspicions about why the trials were starting to fall apart. Other elements had to be at play, and he had less than two weeks to try to solve the mystery.

From the room's bar fridge, he opened a small bottle of cognac and knocked it back; he needed something to help get him off to sleep as his mind was racing. There was a lot to do and very little time to do it.

* * *

Awake early the next morning, Paul decided he needed some exercise to clear his mind and set himself up physically and mentally for the day. He put on his running kit and ventured outside. Despite the early hour, Hong Kong was already buzzing. He ran along the path overlooking Victoria Harbour, joining other joggers out for an early run. He went back to the hotel and into the gym for a quick workout, then up to his room. He felt more clear-headed and energised.

Standing in the shower, Paul blasted himself with cold water. The last time he had done this was the morning after Jill's funeral. Suitably refreshed, he decided to call Tanel to ask if he had made any progress uncovering the trial malfunction in St Petersburg.

"I have been working with Dr Medvedeva," Tanel confirmed. "She is trying to get me back into Dr Alexievich's office to explore the filing cabinet you indicated had a false bottom. We'll try to get copies of any folders in there, especially the duplicates you remembered seeing on his desk."

"Be careful. I'm sure other forces are at play wanting to see the trial terminated, although I can't see why this should be. It just defies all logic."

"I will."

He hoped that Tanel would indeed take care. Paul wasn't sure what, but he knew something untoward was going on – he just had to prove it.

Paul went to the Terrace Room for breakfast. There was no sign of Melissa. After months of tension and friction came to a head between them, Paul was curious to see how things would evolve after their incident.

He was finishing his breakfast and pondering the next steps when Melissa entered and sat at his table. Uncommonly for her, she wore a pale blue blouse and a pair of blue denim jeans accentuating her figure. Paul wondered if she had worn this to remind him of the opportunity she had placed in front of him the previous evening.

"Morning," he said as she received the menu from the waiter.

"Morning," was the reply without further comment other than placing her order.

Paul wondered if the apparent frosty atmosphere would still prevail between them.

As part of his conversion from his innate polite, patient persona to someone less trusting and more critical of those around him, Paul was determined to take charge and force the issues and not defer to her extensive experience.

"I spoke to Devon Ridley last night."

"Oh," she replied, not looking up from her breakfast.

"He said he believes something unusual is happening with Professor Hung."

"Oh," was the reply again.

"He followed Hung one evening after work, who met up with two suspicious men and appeared to have a tense meeting with them, which ended in Hung looking most distressed."

That got her attention. Melissa put down her knife and fork, looked directly at Paul and asked, "Devon followed him? What on earth for?"

"Devon's convinced that there's something suspect with the trials regarding the reported failures of HG 176."

"We have seen the decline in efficacy Professor Hung showed us. Surely you accept that?"

"I agree that's what it appears to be, yet as I mentioned, I recall seeing some peculiar results in the folders that Professor Hung supplied."

Melissa did not rebuke him as she had done when he made the same claim the night before.

"So, you are prepared to accept Devon's bizarre actions and explanation?" Melissa asked in disbelief.

"I will treat Devon's opinion with circumspection, but there are perhaps two explanations here. Firstly, the drug is failing, although this flies in the face of the other trial sites, or, secondly, something unnatural is happening here and in St Petersburg. If it is the former, there is nothing that we can do, but if it is the latter, we need to be able to solve the mystery and save the product. Failure would be a disaster for all concerned."

"You said you thought there was something wrong with the St Petersburg trial?"

"Yes, between Tanel Valle and Dr Anastasia Medvedeva, they managed to get me into Alexievich's office at night."

"You did what?" Melissa was incredulous.

"I'm convinced there are duplicate folders for some of the patients. I caught a glimpse of them during our first meeting in Alexievich's office, and he quickly shuffled them on his desk when he saw me looking at them."

"Your whole approach to this is absurd!" Melissa barked. "How do you think Harrowgate will be judged if some of these covert activities become known? It'll make us a laughing stock."

"That will be a small price to pay if it turns out that the trial is being manipulated for some reason," Paul pointed out.

Melissa tilted her head and looked askance at Paul with her dark eyes giving him a penetrating glare before leaping into her questioning. "Who or what do you think is behind this farfetched notion of yours? Why would anyone want to sabotage a trial to bring a successful product to market? Do you think that other pharmaceutical competitors would risk their reputations by trying to sink our trials? The pharmaceutical industry has had its detractors with accusations of selecting some trial results over others to improve efficacy outcomes, but what you're suggesting is the complete opposite. You're saying that perhaps our competitors are trying to sabotage or dumb down the results?"

Paul paused at this inquisition. "I cannot answer that exactly, but I'm convinced there is something wrong, and I intend to follow through with my line of investigation. It's the only option left to us."

Just as they were finishing their breakfast, Paul's phone rang. It was Devon.

"Morning Paul. I wanted to let you know that I visited the restaurant last night after we spoke. Without tipping anyone off, I asked the waitress if she had recently seen a man of Professor Hung's description. A pattern seems to be emerging with his activities."

"What did she say?"

"Apparently, every third night, he meets with the same two men, and tonight is when he is due to see them if he keeps to this schedule. Do you want to come along with me and see for yourself?'

"Count me in."

"I will collect you at seven o'clock," Devon confirmed.

"See you then!"

Paul rang off and related the conversation to Melissa. "Do you want to join us this evening?"

"I will," she confirmed, "if only to see that this theory is absurd."

CHAPTER 22

In Pursuit

Devon arrived at the hotel at seven o'clock as planned. Paul was surprised to see that despite his conservative and crumpled appearance, he was driving a red Subaru sports model. Paul opened the back door for Melissa and then got in next to Devon.

"Nice car," he commented.

"Thanks, it's not new, but it works for me. Let's get going as I don't want to be late."

"Melissa wants to come along as she doesn't believe we're on the right track."

"Yes," Melissa confirmed, "I'm not convinced that what you're proposing is valid."

"Well, let's see," said Devon.

They drove through the early evening traffic until they came to a quieter, slightly run-down area of Kowloon. Paul couldn't fathom that such an area could exist given the array of glittering skyscrapers, the signature of the administrative region.

Devon parked his car on a slight hill overlooking the narrow street lined with some small shops and the tiny restaurant they were there to survey. The view from their location was a little unclear, but Devon wanted to keep his quite conspicuous car as out of sight as possible. It had already attracted the attention of several small boys gathering to admire the car.

"You can't see what is happening in the little eatery," said Melissa. "Let's get closer for a better view."

"This is as close as we can get without being noticed," said Devon. "I have been into the restaurant briefly, but I was definitely out of place. We stay here to avoid any suspicion."

"Well, something better happen," Melissa said impatiently, "otherwise, this is a waste of time and shows up the absurdity of your theory."

They did not have long to wait. A person emerged from another side street and entered the restaurant.

"That's Hung arriving for the meeting," said Devon.

"I'm not sure," countered Melissa.

Paul had to agree that the fleeting glimpse of the person was not conclusive. All he could be sure of was that it was someone with a slight build.

Shortly afterwards, a black sedan pulled up close to the restaurant, and two men in suits got out and entered the building.

"Those look like the two men I saw before," said Devon, peering towards the poorly lit restaurant. "Let's walk down and get a bit closer to identify them."

Paul's hopes started to sink as he wasn't sure they'd even identified the professor, but he agreed with Devon.

The three of them exited the car and pushed their way through the admiring throng of children, one of whom tried to get in behind the wheel. Devon silenced their chattering with a few curt sentences in Mandarin, and they dispersed.

Focusing again on the restaurant, they saw who they thought was Professor Hung getting up and leaving.

"We've missed him," said Melissa. "There goes your chance to prove your stupid theory."

"But the two men are still inside," noted Devon.

"I will speak to them," said Melissa, "and ask if they have just met with Professor Hung."

"You can't do that!" said an alarmed Paul. "We must keep

watching these meetings to see if we can catch the three of them together."

"I don't care," said Melissa as she set off down the hill towards the two men.

Paul and Devon were paralysed for a moment, stunned by her actions. As Melissa got closer, she called out, "Excuse me!" The two men also seemed frozen for a moment as this glamorous woman approached them.

"Excuse me, have you been meeting with …"

Melissa had not finished her sentence when the man nearest her grabbed and dragged her towards their black sedan. The second man opened the car door, and Melissa fought against being pushed into the back seat. Realising what was happening, Paul set off down the hill towards them, followed by a puffing Devon.

"Let her go!" Paul shouted the only thing that came into his mind under the extraordinary circumstances unfolding before him.

Seeing Paul advancing towards them, Melissa was quickly shoved into the back seat. The one man fell on top of her while his accomplice jumped into the driver's seat and pulled away just as Paul reached the car. He grabbed the door handle of the moving vehicle and tried to open the door, but it was locked. Through the window, he saw Melissa's stricken face looking up at him from under the bulky figure lying on top of her, and as the car sped away, Paul was flung to the ground.

He quickly got up and started running back up the hill towards the car. Devon realised his lack of athleticism on the way down towards the incident and turned to go back up towards his car. Despite his lead, Paul quickly overtook him, shouting at him to follow the fast-disappearing Geely.

Devon quickly started the engine, moving off at such a pace that Paul's head was hurled back against the headrest. The Subaru rapidly moved through the back alleyways of Hong Kong, just keeping sight of the taillights of their quarry as it weaved in and out of the narrow streets.

Paul was amazed at Devon's speed and proficiency as he pushed his car in pursuit of the Geely. At a sharp corner, the car started sliding. Paul expected they would hit one of the buildings, but Devon applied a proficient opposite lock and the car straightened up and continued on its course down the street.

"You've driven like this before, haven't you?"

"Yes, I was an amateur rally driver before I got fat and inactive. In fact, I have actually driven in the Monte Carlo Rally."

Surprised, Paul reminded himself not to make stereotypical judgments of people based on appearance. The slightly corpulent Devon obviously had another set of skills, Paul realised as the car careered around another bend. He held on to the dashboard, thankful that he remembered to do up his seatbelt.

They barely managed to keep the Geely in their sights as they raced through the streets, briefly losing the target as it suddenly veered off down a side street. Seeing that he had shot past the street, Devon applied the handbrake to swing the car around. In a haze of smoking and squealing tyres, they continued their pursuit in the opposite direction. Meanwhile, Paul sat white-knuckled, hanging on and watching buildings flash by only inches away from their car as pedestrians and other traffic desperately got out of the way of the two speeding vehicles. Paul was waiting for the sound of a crash.

"Ah, he's made a mistake," observed Devon.

Paul glanced across at his driver, whose eyes were lit up, his face alive with the thrill of the pursuit. It contrasted utterly with the Devon of their initial meeting.

"In what way?" asked Paul as his head jerked from side to side under the car's motion.

"I have been to this part of Hong Kong before. I know a shorter route to cut him off."

"Okay," was all Paul could utter.

The Subaru set off down another road losing sight of the black sedan. Paul hoped that Devon was right.

They saw the sedan starting to cross their path as they entered a small intersection. Devon accelerated, hitting the left rear of the car with a loud crash, sending both cars spinning. The Subaru spun around, colliding with a building, coming to a dead halt. The Geely's bonnet crumpled as it went through a shop window, smoke billowing from its engine.

"Let's go," said Paul unbuckling his seatbelt and opening the car door.

When he got no response, he looked at Devon and saw that he was not wearing his seatbelt. When the car came to a shuddering halt, Devon had hit his head on the steering wheel, which was buckled from the impact. A trail of blood trickled down Devon's forehead, and he appeared unconscious.

Paul realised he must tackle the men alone. Pushing the car door open against the wall that had stopped their momentum, he squeezed out and saw the two men also exiting their car. One was obviously in pain as he was crouched next to the car holding his arm. The other was getting out of the back seat on the opposite side.

Paul opened the car's back door and saw Melissa sprawled across the back seat. Fortunately, his concern that she had been injured was allayed as she looked up at him, calling for help. Paul started pulling her out when he felt a blow to his chest winding him. Just as the next impact was coming, he managed to swing round, blocking it with his right arm and lashing out with his left, connecting the man's jaw. He heard an "oof!" as the man stumbled back against the car.

Paul resumed pulling Melissa out as she started moving to extricate herself from the smoking car wreck. Just as Paul got her out and started steadying her, he felt a blow to his head from his rallying attacker. His closing thought was that it was like Sean St Ledger's boot hitting his head all those years ago on the rugby fields of Charterhouse. The same shower of bright lights disappeared into blackness as he slid down against the car.

* * *

"Paul, Paul, wake up!"

He felt a hand slapping his face. His vision was blurred, and he thought he saw a face in front of him. It was a woman. Was it Jill? No, she's dead. He faded away again. The slapping resumed, and an urgent voice called his name repeatedly.

As the mists cleared, Paul saw that the face belonged to Melissa. She was kneeling next to him. Her blouse had been torn, and he could see a black bra strap. Why had he noticed that? The final volley of slaps brought him back to reality.

"Where are the men?"

"They took off down the street. I was more concerned about you and Devon, who's in even worse shape than you. I hope he's not brain-damaged from hitting the steering wheel."

Paul dragged himself to his feet. He was aware of the crowd surrounding them and the two damaged cars. In the distance, he heard a siren.

"The locals have called an ambulance, thank God. We need to get both of you to the hospital urgently."

"I am okay," said Paul, "just a bit groggy. Fortunately, I keep myself reasonably fit, so I should be fine. It's Devon I am worried about."

Just as he finished talking, an ambulance made its way slowly through the crush of curious onlookers. Two orderlies pushed their way to the cars. Paul and Melissa went over to the damaged Subaru, and to their relief, they found Devon starting to stir, mumbling incoherently. Paul's medical training kicked in; he felt Devon's pulse and pulled his eyelids back to check his pupils, and was relieved to find they were not dilated.

"I'm sure he is just moderately concussed, but he needs a scan to check for neck injuries to make certain." He turned to the ambulance orderlies saying, "I'm a doctor. I think it's a concussion. Put a neck brace on him and get him on a stretcher. I am not sure if he has damaged his cervical vertebrae."

The orderlies brought a stretcher, carefully placing the mumbling

Devon on it. Paul and Melissa also got into the ambulance and sat on the bench seats facing the patient, who was fitted with an oxygen mask.

Paul felt his chin; it was now beginning to ache, and his hand came away covered in blood. The blow landed by the mysterious man had left a gash on his chin. He looked down at his shirt splattered with blood. Melissa pulled a pretty handkerchief out of her jeans pocket and dabbed his chin gingerly.

"I'll replace it," said Paul as he saw the blood.

"No problem," she said as she finished dabbing.

The ambulance arrived at a hospital; the stretcher was slid out, followed by Paul and Melissa. They were taken into casualty, where Devon was taken away for a more detailed evaluation. The cut on Paul's chin was attended to with a local anaesthetic and some stitches.

Paul told Melissa to return to the hotel while he would stay to follow up on Devon's condition and meet her back at the hotel as soon as he was satisfied with the results. Despite her protests, Paul insisted, and Melissa called the hotel, asking them to fetch her.

Paul went to radiology to speak to the attending doctors, informing them of his medical status. They had to sedate Devon for the MRI as he was starting to come to and was thrashing about. It took a couple of the nursing staff to hold him down. Standing in the protected room next to the radiology chamber, Paul was relieved to learn that the MRI scan showed no signs of vertebral injury.

Paul was satisfied that Devon was in good hands and phoned the hotel to pick him up. As he got there, Melissa was in the lobby waiting for him.

"How is Devon?" she asked.

"He should be fine, although he will have the mother of all headaches and will be in more pain once he discovers that his beloved Subaru is badly damaged. I want to notify the police to investigate the accident scene now and see if we can determine anything from the other car. After that, I need to get some sleep."

"Is there anything else I can do to help you?" said Melissa

looking closely at the blood-stained figure in front of her. Paul looked down, remembering the bloodstains on his clothing.

"I suppose I should shower and change after calling the police. We should get to bed. There is a lot to do tomorrow."

"Paul, how can I thank you for rescuing me?"

"No problem. I would have done it for anyone."

Paul headed towards the lifts.

* * *

Paul awoke in the morning feeling battered and bruised. His jaw still ached, and he felt like a heavyweight boxer had pole-axed him. In the bathroom, leaning against the basin for support, Paul stared at himself in the mirror. He looked haggard. Splashing cold water on his face, the cut on his chin stung.

He returned to the bedroom and phoned the policeman he had spoken to the night before to ask what they had uncovered at the accident scene.

"Did you find out anything about the black vehicle and its owners?"

"What vehicle are you referring to?"

"The black Geely, the other vehicle involved in the accident."

"No, Sir, there was only one damaged car, a red Subaru that we towed away to our compound."

"You must be mistaken. I was a passenger in the Subaru that crashed into a black Geely sedan."

"No, Sir, there was only one car at the site."

"When did you get to the scene?" asked Paul, thinking they must only have gone to the scene after a long delay.

"We were there less than half an hour after you notified us last night, and I can confirm that only one vehicle was involved in the accident."

Paul was flummoxed. "Okay, thank you. I'll be in touch with you later."

His mind was reeling. There was no doubt what had happened the previous evening – this was not a case of transient amnesia. This was just another chapter in the deepening mystery associated with the trial of HG 176.

CHAPTER 23

An Abrupt Departure

Paul went down to breakfast and found Melissa already there. "How are you feeling this morning?" she asked.

"I'm puzzled, more than anything else."

"Why is that?"

"I phoned the police this morning to see what they could determine from the wreck of the other car, but they claimed there was only one damaged vehicle at the accident scene."

"They must be mistaken; I was in that car."

"I pressed them, but they were adamant that there was no other vehicle."

"That's bizarre!"

"Either Hong Kong's police are inefficient or are covering up for someone or something, or there's a reason we don't understand."

"How's your wound?"

"Stinging a little, but it will be fine. I need to phone the hospital to see how Devon's doing."

Paul ordered his breakfast then called the hospital. They connected him to the ward, and Paul spoke to the sister in charge. After a brief conversation, he hung up.

"How is he?" asked Melissa.

"The sister says he is recovering but still has some signs of a mild concussion. We need to go and have a chat with him."

"Yes, I agree."

"Melissa, I don't want us to give any feedback to JP or Harrowgate yet. All we have at the moment is a series of unconnected dots, and we must get further clarity on what's really happening in the two trial sites. It's no good to share the findings so far, including the events of last night, when we cannot make any sense or conclusion from them."

"I suppose you are right. I was tempted to contact JP this morning, but I'll go along with your proposal for now. We don't have much time to solve this since the trial will be terminated in about ten days if we don't find any credible evidence to the contrary."

"I am well aware of that and plan to move quickly and follow up on some thoughts I have. We need to bring Devon in on any plans we can develop if he is well enough for us to share them. We owe him a lot for stopping the car that never existed and rescuing you."

* * *

A while later, Paul and Melissa were in a taxi on their way to the hospital. It was not the same one where the trial was being carried out but nearby. They found Devon in a private ward surrounded by several nurses and the ward sister.

"I see you are getting the best treatment," noted Paul.

"Yes, many of them know me from other clinical trials we've done at this hospital."

It was apparent that Devon was a favourite among the hospital staff. He turned out to be quite different from the man Paul had met initially, but he was reminded that Devon was a person with a drinking problem and domestic issues. Thankfully neither of these distracted him as he was reliving his motor rallying days through the streets of Kowloon to rescue Melissa from whatever her fate might have been.

After thanking Devon, Melissa said, "I want to tell you two

that I'm still not convinced that the person we saw last night was Professor Hung."

"So, how do you explain what happened last night?" Paul asked.

"I don't know, but your theory is still unproven. We could have accidentally stumbled on another complicated situation; perhaps the men were gangsters planning a crime."

Paul acknowledged that the argument that Professor Hung was somehow endangering their trials was not an open-and-shut case.

Lying back in his hospital bed, his head swathed in bandages, Devon admitted that based on only a couple of observations, he was not absolutely convinced that it was Hung at the meetings either.

Paul recounted to Devon his covert activities in St Petersburg. "It looks like you and I are each following unconventional paths to get to the bottom of the problem."

Melissa was growing increasingly uncomfortable with the activities of her two colleagues. "Despite the strange happenings last night, we cannot simply treat this as a criminal matter. From my experience – and yours, Devon – we both know that trials sometimes fail; this could be the case here," she reminded him. "The thought that the trials are being deliberately subverted goes against what the Hong Kong and St Petersburg site teams would want. They all have a vested interest in the trial's success; from a financial, medical and publicity perspective. I simply cannot go along with what the two of you are thinking."

"We will keep an open mind on this," Paul responded. "I suggest we go to see Professor Hung when we have finished here with Devon."

After making a final check with the ward staff on Devon's progress and possible release, Paul and Melissa took a taxi to the King George Hospital to meet up with the professor.

When they arrived, Paul cautioned Melissa not to mention the previous night's happenings or probe Hung further on that, but rather discuss his take on the trial status and see if anything unusual could be uncovered.

They retraced their steps to Professor Hung's office, along the corridors that were again a hive of activity. They arrived at the outer office where his personal assistant sat. She was surprised to see them.

"We weren't expecting you here today."

"Yes, apologies, we don't have an appointment," replied Melissa. "We just called in hoping we can have a word with Professor Hung. Is he in surgery at the moment?"

The interleading door to the professor's office was open, and Paul and Melissa could see the large familiar desk piled high with folders. But no professor.

"No, I am afraid the professor is not in the hospital."

"Oh, where is he then?" asked Melissa, wondering if his absence was possibly linked to last night's activities.

"I am afraid he left this morning because he had to return to his family home in China."

"What prompted that?" asked Paul, taken aback.

"I believe one of his family members has taken ill."

Paul and Melissa looked at each other in astonishment.

"But what about the trial?" exclaimed Melissa. "The professor said he was suspending it and writing a motivation why it should be terminated globally."

"Yes, he is still doing that. He left me a message saying he was busy working on the report and should complete it in about a week. He will send it to me from China or bring it back himself if all is fine with his family member."

Paul and Melissa were reeling and shocked at this unexpected development. This trial was now spiralling downwards and entirely out of their control. The professor was out of the country, out of reach, but busy working on the time bomb document that would most likely finish off all hopes for HG 176.

"Are we able to contact him?" asked Melissa, seeing years of work disappearing.

"I am afraid not," came the emphatic reply. "The professor said he did not want to be contacted or disturbed in any way. Sorry I cannot be of any further assistance."

She set about attending to folders on her desk. Clearly, the meeting was at an end.

Paul and Melissa drifted out of the office and into the corridor, looking at each other in stunned silence. Now they could not even challenge the professor about the alleged meetings. Everything had ground to a halt. The trial seemed doomed.

"Let's get back to the hotel. We need to regroup and plan our next move."

Melissa agreed with Paul as they hailed a taxi. "We seem to be running out of options."

On the way, Paul's phone rang. It was Tanel Valle. "Paul, Dr Medvedeva is going to try and get me into Dr Alexievich's office tonight. I think you should come back here to St Petersburg so I can share my findings with you."

"Good news, Tanel. I'll fly out later today. We've had a setback here in Hong Kong, but I'll tell you about it when I see you. Thanks for the update."

"Are you going to play your stupid boys' game of cops and robbers in St Petersburg again?" said Melissa. "You will get us into more trouble than we're already in if you get caught. Not only could we lose our blockbuster drug through these problematic trials, but the reputation of Harrowgate will be tarnished. The media dislike the pharmaceutical industry as it is, and you can guess the field day they will have with the headlines. 'Big Pharma up to their old tricks again'. It'll be utterly ruinous."

"Melissa, we are at a stage where we cannot play by the rule book anymore. I'm convinced that there are irregular elements at play. We must use extraordinary tactics to resolve this; otherwise, we can kiss HG 176 goodbye."

Despite the appearance that he had a specific plan to deal with the situation, Paul felt deep despair about the trial's survival. With its termination, any hopes for the product and what it could have offered women, would disappear. His quest for a treatment that would have been a tribute to Jill was being swept away. The entire Harrowgate episode now seemed to be no more than a fiasco and presented a spectre of failure hanging over him. This was a dark moment, and Paul felt his world closing down around him.

"While I head back to St Petersburg, I want you to link up with Devon when he has recovered a bit more. See if between you it's possible to come up with some ideas of how we can tackle this site. Despite his personal issues, I think he is more resourceful than I first thought."

Melissa nodded her agreement.

"By the way," Paul added, "I can recall the registration plate of the black Geely. I'll write it down for you. Perhaps you and Devon can pursue this lead while I'm in St Petersburg."

The taxi pulled up at the hotel. At the reception, Paul asked for paper and a pen, jotted down the car's number, and gave it to Melissa. She observed him with a puzzled look. Was he serious? That he could recall the number with such clarity after the crazy car chase was unbelievable.

CHAPTER 24

A Sinister Turn

Paul secured a booking to fly back to St Petersburg, and while at Hong Kong International Airport, he went into some of the men's shops to buy additional clothing to supplement his existing set. He had not anticipated being away for so long and also needed to replace those items bloodied by the cut on his chin. At least it was showing signs of healing. He checked in and went to the business lounge, and called Tanel to inform him of his intended arrival.

"Tanel, I'd like you to come to my hotel to discuss the plans to get back into Dr Alexievich's office. I'll get there about six this evening, so come around any time after that."

"Yes, that should be fine. I will need to be careful as I think Alexievich is alert to our moves."

"He doesn't know I'm coming to St Petersburg, so he may not expect us to make contact. But are you sure you will be safe coming to the hotel?"

"I'm fine."

Although Tanel said this, he did not sound confident. Paul heard a tension in his voice that he had not noticed before.

"Are you sure?"

"Yes," said Tanel in a terse reply.

"Right, I'll see you later this evening," said Paul as the muffled sound of the loudspeaker in the lounge summoned him to his flight. He felt a sense of disquiet following his brief exchange with the young Estonian.

* * *

Paul landed at Pulkovo Airport and hailed a taxi for the twelve-mile ride to the hotel. On the journey, his mind went through some options for the evening's return to the hospital. He wondered if he should accompany Tanel as there might be greater safety if both of them went in. Paul would suggest that to him. He was concerned about Tanel and felt his presence might give him more assurance.

He thought about his last late-night visit to the hospital and how Dr Anastasia Medvedeva had assisted him. He couldn't forget their previous encounter – when he exited the hospital, and she kissed him so passionately. What was that all about? He had found her extremely attractive, but had she taken that as a come-on? A ridiculous line of thought, he told himself. He needed to focus on the problem ahead.

Shortly after he checked into his room, his phone rang. It was Tanel calling from the reception. Paul went down to meet him but could not see him among the people there. After surveying the lobby, he saw a figure in an oversized coat with a cap pulled low, standing partially hidden by a pillar. The figure raised its hand in response to Paul's stare and moved towards him. Tanel was obviously doing everything possible to obscure his identity.

"Let's go up to my room, and we can discuss tonight's mission."

Safely in the elevator, Tanel peeled back his hat and jacket. "One cannot be too cautious."

"Is it as bad as that?"

"Yes, it could be and I am taking no chances."

Paul was concerned that Tanel was so troubled by their mission; he was almost afraid. It seemed absurd as this was simply about a clinical trial, not some Cold-War-type spying exercise.

"How has Dr Alexievich been behaving while I've been away?"

"He seems very much on edge, and something is troubling him deeply, although he pretends all is fine. He often shuts his office door on phone calls and goes out more frequently for what he says are medically related meetings."

"And the trial, how is that progressing?"

"He says there are now even more cases of side effects which are likely to cause the trial to be terminated. He said this will happen soon, and he will make his recommendations to the professor, who is likely to agree."

Paul explained Hong Kong's trial situation and the extremely short time scale hanging over both trials before being terminated.

"That's why your investigation tonight is so important, Tanel, but I don't want you taking any risks."

"I will try not to."

"Is Dr Medvedeva going to assist you again?" asked Paul.

"Yes, she is helpful and also feels there's something wrong with the results based on her observations. There seems to be a mismatch between the documented case report forms and the patient experience."

"This fits with my instincts about both trials. Do you want me to come along with you tonight?"

"No, I'd rather do this on my own once Dr Medvedeva gets me in. I must leave now. Here are the details of our office in Moscow. My boss is Sergei Balakin; he knows what I am doing but not all of it."

"Can I see you out?"

"No, I would rather go out alone."

"Right then, I will meet you in the usual place tomorrow at the Hermitage in front of the portrait of Catherine the Great at eleven o'clock."

"Yes, see you there." Tanel put on his cap and large coat and left Paul to his thoughts.

It was a restless night as he thought of Tanel and Dr Medvedeva creeping around the offices in a desperate search for evidence that would expose any wrongdoing and save the trial and probably HG 176.

* * *

Paul awoke early after a poor night's sleep. He had time to spare before meeting with Tanel to hear his findings. Paul was sure that this meeting would prove, beyond doubt, that there was intentional obstruction jeopardising the trial. If this could be established, it would block the proposed termination and cast doubt on the Hong Kong anomalies. In turn, this would buy time to challenge Professor Hung and expose any malfeasance.

Paul decided to use the time before meeting Tanel to clock up some lengths in the hotel swimming pool to maintain his fitness. Based on his experience in Hong Kong, that might stand him in good stead for what lay ahead.

Over breakfast, he wondered how Devon and Melissa were getting on with trying to identify solutions to their challenge. After Paul initially dismissed him as potentially being at fault and misreading the trial data, Devon proved to be an asset.

He also thought about Melissa. Her haughty, disdainful attitude towards him had mellowed a little after the car chase and her rescue. However, her prickly side emerged again when discussing how Paul and Devon were planning to investigate both trial sites. Melissa had revealed her ambition to him when she admitted that she wanted to succeed JP, so perhaps she felt a little threatened by their plans.

Paul realised that he had never given her personal circumstances any thought. Was she married? She wore no rings. Did she have children? Was work her all-encompassing passion? He wondered what would make her a happier person, as she seemed so guarded and private. Or did she have something to hide?

Eventually, Paul saw the time creeping inexorably towards meeting up with Tanel. Reception ordered a taxi for him as the weather outside was too cold to consider his usual walk along the Neva River towards the Winter Palace.

Despite his agonising time-wasting, he got to the museum half an hour before the intended time, so he busied himself exploring other galleries with their incredible art collections. He wandered into St George's Hall, one of the largest rooms in the palace. It had been used by the Tsars as the principal Throne Room and was the venue for the sitting of the Duma, the first Russian parliament, in 1906. Paul stared at the throne emblazoned with the double-headed eagle, the symbol on Russia's royal coat of arms. Tsar Nicholas II sat on that throne, and just over a decade later, he and his family were brutally murdered by the Bolsheviks. Paul wondered if that was an omen.

Paul made his way from the Throne Room to the massive and dazzling Jordan Staircase and the room with the portrait of Catherine the Great. He was still a bit early and occupied himself revisiting some of the paintings he had seen on an earlier visit. He checked his watch. Just after the agreed time, but no Tanel.

He wandered around the gallery once more, starting to feel anxious. Another ten minutes passed; still no sign of Tanel. Paul looked around the gallery for the two men he had seen before, but saw only the usual mass of tourists.

It was nearly an hour after the agreed meeting time, and Paul was starting to panic. He was tempted to phone Tanel but held back. What if Tanel was in a difficult situation? Would a call help or hinder? Paul felt that it would be the latter. He left the Hermitage, which now had the ominous feel of the Throne Room with its chill reminder of the seat occupied by the murdered Tsar.

When he returned to his hotel room, he phoned Tanel. There was no reply, only a prompt for a voice message. Paul decided against this. He wondered how his call might be reflected on Tanel's phone. Did it show 'Dr Paul Beresford'? If so, who was taking note of that? Anyone who could influence the trial? He berated himself for not being more forceful and insisting he accompany Tanel to the hospital. Shit, shit, shit! What if Tanel had run into serious trouble? It looked all too likely as he had always been reliable and punctual. Paul had taken a liking to Tanel with his go-getter attitude and initiative.

Just then, his phone rang. Paul dashed to it and, without looking at the incoming number, called out, "Tanel, are you okay?"

"Paul, this is JP. Who's Tanel?"

Paul's spirits sank that it was not the call he had expected. "Sorry, JP, I was expecting a call from someone else," he said, trying to hide his disappointment.

"I gathered that. Paul, I need you back here at Harrowgate. It will only be for a short time, but I need to talk to you in person."

"JP, we are at a critical stage in our investigations here and possibly near a breakthrough."

"I doubt it, as things are making no progress, only going badly. The other trial sites have also suspended their work pending Hong Kong's and St Petersburg's outcomes, and from what I am hearing, we are in deep trouble."

"But JP ..."

"No buts, Paul, I need you back here for a meeting. A day or two, maximum. I want you to keep this confidential from everyone at Harrowgate, including Melissa."

"What! That will be difficult as she thinks I am in St Petersburg."

"I am sure you can manage," said JP, ignoring Paul's protests. "Mildred is already booking you a ticket and will be in contact. Goodbye, Paul."

Paul stared at his phone in disbelief. His life was in tumult. First, the anxiety about Tanel and now JP insisted he vanish from St Petersburg without letting anyone know.

The message from Mildred came through with his flight details, and he dashed to the airport to catch a BA flight back to London.

* * *

On his arrival at Heathrow, he called Tanel again with the same result. Only a voice message. Paul's anxiety rose further as he imagined all possible outcomes. Exiting Arrivals, he jostled through the crowds and saw a sign with his name on it bobbing in amongst other passenger notices.

"Good morning, Dr Beresford," greeted Dawson, the driver from Harrowgate, reaching to collect Paul's small suitcase.

"Don't worry. I can manage, thanks."

They went to the parkade, exited the airport and headed for the M25 to take them through the early morning traffic around London, joining the A41 to Berkhamsted. After his recent time spent between Hong Kong and St Petersburg, arriving in the parking lot of Harrowgate Pharmaceuticals felt almost surreal. It seemed a serene world away from the front line that Paul had been engaged in: battling with Melissa, doubting Devon, being kissed by Anastasia Medvedeva, swept along in a wild car chase and now the disappearance of Tanel Valle.

As he got out of the car, drank in the fresh country air and heard the birdsong, he had a sense of disbelief as to which of the two was the real world.

He went up to JP's familiar corner office and greeted Mildred. "It looks as if you could do with a cup of coffee," she said with a sympathetic smile.

"Make it strong," Paul replied, catching sight of JP standing at his desk.

"Welcome back. Let's head to the comfortable chairs for an uncomfortable conversation," said JP.

"I don't think too much can faze me at this moment," remarked Paul.

"Wait until you hear what I have to say," advised JP.

"Fire away; I am ready for anything."

"Paul, I'm in negotiations to sell Harrowgate."

Paul was stunned. "What has brought this about?"

"The company's share price is dropping rapidly on the rumours that HG 176 is failing in its clinical trials. I'm sure you know that I started this company and invested most of my family fortune to do so. The debt time-bomb is ticking away. If I do not sell now while the share price is above the benchmark I have set for myself, I will not be able to retire, retain my family farm in County Cork or look after my family."

"But JP, it is not conclusive that HG 176 has failed. In Hong Kong and St Petersburg, I have deep suspicions their negative results are not accurately reflecting what's really happening."

"What firm evidence do you have for this?"

"Nothing conclusive at the moment but my investigations and instincts tell me that there is something very wrong about these results we are seeing."

"None? You have no firm evidence! How does that help me in any way? My whole future is at stake. The farm has been in my family for nearly two hundred years, and I'm supposed to take your word, your instincts, that everything will turn out fine. Really, Paul, I expected much better from you, which is why I invested in you in the first place and then sent you out to investigate."

"JP, I know I am right. Give me a bit more time, and I can prove it!"

"Paul, I don't have time to spare. I have a proposal on my desk that will expire in a week, almost the same time left before the trials are scuppered. I must sign the offer before that news hits the financial markets."

Paul realised that there was no changing JP's mind. "Who has made this offer?"

"I can't tell you; it's confidential. You will only find out when I sign the agreement."

The exchange came to a halt. Looking at JP, who he could see was agitated and emotional, Paul could appreciate this point of view, although he disagreed with the decision. He felt it was no use trying to further his case. JP's mind was made up. To change it, Paul needed the hard evidence JP demanded, which could only be found in either Hong Kong or St Petersburg. Paul needed to get back there urgently.

"I do understand your stance JP. I will get back to the trial sites and see if I can prove my theory. If I can bring hard evidence before you sign away the company, I will do so. Please grant me that."

"Do your best, but I am not hopeful," said a dejected JP.

JP went back to his desk and started rummaging through his papers. Paul left the crumpled figure of his boss, heading out to Mildred's office.

"I need to get back to the sites urgently. Can you get me a flight?"

"I knew you would want that. I can get you a flight to Hong Kong tomorrow morning but only the following day to St Petersburg. Which one do you want?"

"I will take the former."

"Can I book you a hotel here in Berkhamsted for tonight?"

Paul thought about it for a moment as, with all the events of the last day, he had not applied his mind to accommodation for the night.

"Thanks, Mildred, but I'll return to the Wandsworth apartment."

"Are you sure?" said Mildred looking questioningly at him.

"Yes, it might do me some good. Can you ask Tom to give me a lift down to the station? I will take a train back to London."

Tom came through to the office to collect him. Nothing was said between them until they exited the building heading for the car park.

"Can I ask you what's happening?" quizzed Tom.

"Bear with me as I cannot say a lot, and at this moment, I'm not even sure myself."

"Is HG 176 failing?" Tom persisted.

"Again, I'm not sure. My instinct tells me there is something peculiar about the poor results, but I don't have hard evidence."

"JP seems uptight and distraught and even a bit emotional, which is unlike him," noted Tom.

"I know he is under a lot of pressure. Again, I can't say more. You are rational, level-headed, and one of the senior managers.

I must ask you to keep behaving in your normal, calm way and deflect any queries with a positive approach in my and Melissa's absence. We only have a week, maybe less, to resolve this."

"How are you getting on with Melissa?"

"We are managing surprisingly well, considering," he said with a smile, knowing where this line of questioning was going. "Here is my train; I must rush."

On the train back to Euston, Paul found himself dozing off despite his efforts not to. He was desperate to phone Tanel again, but the carriage was full. He did not want to have a conversation, if there was one to be had, drawing the attention of other commuters on a busy West Coast Mainline train.

He awoke with a start as the train pulled into Euston, hoping that he had not been slumped in his seat with his mouth hanging open. On reflection, he didn't really care, given what he had been through.

He connected to Wandsworth Common, and it was with mixed feelings that he stood outside the apartment he had shared with Jill. His entry was overshadowed by the memories of their shared time.

He dropped his suitcase in the bedroom, sat on the bed, took out his phone and tried Tanel again. The message said that the voicemail was full and that he should try again later. Paul's head and shoulders dropped, and he let the phone slip out of his hands and onto the carpeted floor. He was now beginning to fear the worst. As a last resort, he phoned Tanel's boss in Moscow. He was greeted in Russian.

"Sergei, this is Dr Paul Beresford from Harrowgate. I've been working with Tanel on the HG 176 trial in St Petersburg. I am concerned that I have not been able to get hold of him for nearly two days."

"Hello, Dr Beresford," said the voice reverting to English. "Tanel speaks highly of you. Yes, we are equally concerned that we can't get hold of him and I have also had his anxious mother and girlfriend phoning about his absence."

"I am back in London for a short while and should be back in St Petersburg in a couple of days. Please phone me if you get any news of him. I know the weather is freezing there, and he may have had an accident in those conditions."

"Da, I will do so as soon as I hear."

Paul headed to one of his local restaurants for lunch. He found his appetite had diminished but forced some food down to maintain his energy levels. He ordered some wine with his meal which, in his exhausted state, made him feel short of complete control of himself. He returned to the apartment, fell onto the bed, and slept for a few hours.

Once awake, he started going through the cupboards to sort out his, and painfully, Jill's clothes as the apartment would have to be sold shortly. He stared at her row of dresses and other items of clothing. Each of the garments held a memory for him. It would be difficult, if not impossible, to discard them, not at this time at least.

He still had his small place in Putney, which he had used intermittently during his earlier time in London. Paul decided that he would have to relocate much of the personal stuff there, and he might as well use this time to start the process. Once the trial was over, whatever the outcome, he had to decide what to do with his life. At least he had a base for this.

He found some empty boxes from his previous trip to the apartment and started filling them with clothes – both his and Jill's. Once he had filled these, he loaded them into a taxi and headed off to the small Putney apartment. It seemed as if time had stood still from his previous life. The Putney apartment represented an earlier phase in his life. He also needed to decide what to do with the place.

He managed a few more journeys between Putney and Wandsworth, carefully offloading personal items. It was early evening when he decided that he had done enough and again went out for a meal before packing his suitcase for the morning trip back to Hong Kong and the complicated picture that awaited him. Sleep came quickly.

* * *

The alarm startled him into action. He showered, dressed and had a last walk around. He opened one of Jill's cupboards and looked through some of the drawers containing stockings and underwear, which he had left untouched.

Paul sighed, lost in his memories of Jill, when his attention was drawn to what appeared to be a file or notebook lying partially covered below her personal garments. Reaching in, he drew out a legal pad. He flicked through the pages covered with Jill's neat script. It seemed to be a diary of sorts with dates heading up a series of observations. He remembered that Jill was a diligent note-taker; committing her thoughts to paper was part of developing arguments and views on various subjects, both work-related and outside of these.

He stared at the meticulous notes so characteristic of Jill. He could hear her voice as he scanned her words, and it was achingly painful. He wondered if he should take the notepad with him. It was very personal, and although he and Jill had no secrets, he felt that reading her thoughts was an invasion of her privacy. Decisiveness kicked in, and he placed the notepad in his briefcase, locked the door to the apartment and went down to the taxi waiting to take him back to Heathrow.

* * *

The familiar routine of the flight, taxi ride, and arrival at the hotel in Hong Kong was repeated once more. In the taxi, Paul wondered about Devon's recovery and how Melissa was. Would she continue to baulk against the methods he and Devon were resorting to?

In the meantime, Melissa had found herself almost at a loose end, waiting for Paul to return and visiting Devon in hospital. Her attitude to Paul had mellowed – but should not be confused with change.

Even though she resented Paul's presence at the trials, she had to admit there was an attractiveness to him. He had been instrumental in rescuing her from being abducted by the mysterious men in the black sedan, and she was grateful to him for that.

She thought back to the night of their heated altercation in the corridor outside her hotel room. She had tempted him to engage with her sexually for her own ends in destroying his career. He had avoided that, but she wondered what that would have been like if he had gone ahead. She shook her head as if to erase this line of thinking. She wanted to succeed JP as head of Harrowgate and had told Paul so to his face, but he had said he was not interested in that position, so he was not a threat to her. Or was he?

Meanwhile, Devon was making strides with his recovery; tests had determined only a mild concussion. He still suffered from headaches, but his greatest outward manifestation of the accident that night was a neat scar on his forehead where the doctors had stitched him up. He was upset about the damage to his Subaru, but he felt it a small price to pay for rescuing Melissa.

Devon was even more convinced that his hunch about Professor Hung was correct, and he needed to get out of the hospital so that he, Paul and Melissa could strategise about their next move. He had also gone nearly three days without a drink and started to get the yearning for one again. He needed to get out of hospital for that reason too.

It was late at night when Paul got back to the hotel. He contacted Melissa even though it was nearly midnight.

"Let's meet for breakfast tomorrow morning and discuss our way forward. Have you and Devon developed any ideas?" he asked.

"Devon seems to want to follow the approach you adopted in St Petersburg."

"In what way?" he prompted.

"As you may or may not know, the King George Hospital is keeping all the trial records electronically as well as hard copies. Devon seems to be close – perhaps too close – to one of the nurses at the hospital. He believes that through his association with her, he could hack into the system and even into Professor Hung's computer to access the case report forms. He was working on these reports before Hung removed him from the work, so he is familiar with the format of the documents and believes he could detect any manipulation of the results."

"Devon seems more creative than I credited him for," noted Paul.

"I don't agree with this approach, as I have already told you," Melissa insisted.

"Melissa, we are in a time trap here, and we now have to use any possible means to beat the clock. Let's discuss it further at breakfast."

* * *

As Paul dressed for breakfast the following morning, his phone rang. He did not recognise the number.

"Dr Beresford?"

"Yes."

"It's Sergei Balakin from QualiMed."

"Yes, Sergei, please tell me you have news of Tanel?"

"They have made a finding on him."

"That's great news," exclaimed Paul.

"Not really; they have only found part of him."

"What do you mean?" Paul could not comprehend what he had just heard.

"Yes, the police found his head and upper torso in a suitcase in the River Neva."

"My God!" Paul sank onto the bed, reeling with shock and holding his hand to his head.

"Yes, we are all shocked here. The police are investigating and hoping to find the remainder of him so they can do a full pathology analysis and open a criminal case."

"He was investigating the HG 176 trial results with me, which seemed strange given what we know about the product."

"I was aware there appeared to be something unusual, but at the moment, we have no evidence linking his death to the trial."

Paul thought it prudent not to share his knowledge of Tanel's proposed after-hours activities.

"I need to go now, Dr Beresford, as the police want to talk to me again, and I need to contact his family. I will keep you updated. Goodbye."

Paul sat on the bed, staring at his phone. What had just happened? What was supposed to be a routine clinical trial was growing more turbulent and sinister. Paul was still dealing with Jill's death, issues with Melissa, the apparent failure of HG 176, the confidentiality of the possible sale of Harrowgate and now – the murder of Tanel Valle.

CHAPTER 25

The End of the Road?

Paul completed dressing in a daze. He went down to the Terrace Restaurant for his breakfast meeting with Melissa. She looked up as she saw him approaching and reacted with shock at his expression.

"Paul, what has happened?"

"Tanel Valle has been killed, or should I say murdered."

"What? I don't believe it! What happened?"

"We don't know the facts, but parts of his body were found in a suitcase in the River Neva."

"That's shocking. Is this in any way linked to the trial?"

"His boss, Sergei Balakin, says we can't make that assumption yet. Despite being Russia's cultural capital, St Petersburg has a reputation for crime, and the Russian Mafia are active there, involved in drug trafficking. Who knows what occurs in Tanel's private life, but I believe it is linked to the trial."

"If so, you may have played a part and are responsible for what happened to him with your stupid games of creeping around the hospital at night."

Melissa's words cut into Paul as he had been troubled by similar thoughts. He had developed a fondness for the young Estonian. There was nothing that Paul could say to Melissa's accusation.

"What happens now that we've lost Tanel?"

"I have other contacts at the hospital who Tanel introduced me to," said Paul. "I'll be in touch with them for their insights. I need to get back to St Petersburg as soon as possible. But first, we must get Devon out of hospital to get moving with some ideas on how we tackle Hong Kong's problem."

"I don't see many options open to us if Professor Hung is sitting somewhere in China writing the death sentence for HG 176," Melissa pointed out

"Let's go," said Paul. "I don't feel like eating."

They took a taxi to the hospital where Devon was recovering, went to his ward and informed him of Tanel's gruesome fate. He was shocked; they had worked for the same company and knew each other.

Devon looked far better with the head bandages removed and the cut on his forehead healing. He was dressed and sitting on the edge of his bed.

"I am pleased that you've come to collect me, although I've been well looked after here," he said, looking up at the attractive Chinese nurse standing demurely in the corner of his private ward.

"I bet you have," said Melissa with a sarcastic undertone.

"By the way," said Devon, "I have some news for you on the mysterious non-existent black car."

"That is?" asked Melissa.

"The registration plates on the car belong to the People's Republic of China for diplomatic cars, specifically the Commissioner's office. You got the registration plate spot on, Paul. How did you do that?"

"A bit of luck, I guess."

"Luck? I don't believe that. We were hurtling around corners at sixty miles an hour, and still, you remembered the plate."

Ignoring the comment, Paul said, "I need you and Melissa to keep working on a plan for here as I must get back to St Petersburg to see what is happening to the trial." He paused. "And to follow up on what happened to Tanel."

"Why do you think that people from the Chinese Commissioner's office would be meeting with Professor Hung? It's absurd," interjected Melissa. "You must have got the number plate wrong, Paul. You could not seriously have recalled it?"

"No, Paul's correct," said Devon. "I checked what type of car registration plates the Chinese diplomats use, and this one fits the bill."

"But why would they act in such an extraordinary way, trying to kidnap me and to engage in a fight with Paul? What were they planning to do with me?"

"We can't answer those questions now," said Paul. "I must be getting back to St Petersburg. Melissa, you will have to suspend judgement on the tactics we are trying. I need you to support Devon since we're basically out of time. What has happened here in Hong Kong and what has transpired in St Petersburg indicate something sinister. All bets are off regarding HG 176 surviving, and it's up to us to solve the mystery. I need to get going. Good luck!"

* * *

Paul flew back to St Petersburg that evening and went to the same hotel out of convenience and habit. He planned to visit the hospital the following day and speak to Professor Pavlyuchenko and Dr Alexievich. Surely they would have a view on the developments. Paul decided to phone Sergei Balakin.

"Sergei, it's Paul Beresford. Do you have any more news?"

"Sorry, Paul, nothing as yet, but the police are suggesting that it has nothing to do with his work at the hospital but something to do with his private life."

"I don't believe that. Things are happening in these trials that are too out of the ordinary."

"Yes, I agree, Paul. I understand from the clinical research associate handling the Hong Kong arm of the trial that there are abnormalities, but I don't know the details. We're looking into that now, but take it from me, there are issues."

Paul was not about to elaborate on the complex happenings

with the trial and said, "I am going to the hospital tomorrow morning and will update you on any developments."

"Good luck, Paul. We must get to the bottom of Tanel's death. His family are distraught."

* * *

When Paul arrived at the hospital the following day, the building was set in the grip of an icy morning and seemed to have a dark, foreboding atmosphere. Did Tanel die inside it? Was he murdered in there? Like so many Soviet-era buildings, especially the numerous apartment blocks for workers that mark Russia's suburbs, the hospital was built in a drab architectural style; design was too strong a word.

Without Tanel to guide Paul through the hospital, he struggled to make himself understood at the reception desk, where he tried to establish whether Professor Pavlyuchenko or Dr Alexievich were on duty. It seemed that there were two Professor Pavlyuchenko's. After a frustrating exchange and delay, Paul managed to establish that the one he needed was available and was given the floor and section where he was. This was different from their original meeting place as he fulfilled his other role as Hospital Superintendent.

Paul took the tatty elevator to the top floor and was shown to the office after repeating the professor's name to the staff he encountered in the corridors. Despite the run-down feel of the building, the Superintendent's office was a grand affair. Professor Pavlyuchenko was in discussion with several people who looked like police from their uniforms. He looked up to see Paul standing in the doorway.

"Come in, Dr …"

"Beresford."

"Ah yes, Dr Beresford." He spoke to his visitors, who then moved towards the doorway, staring at Paul as they passed him.

"Dr Beresford, you must be here about that unfortunate event regarding the Estonian working on your trial?"

"That's correct, Professor. Do you have any additional information for me?"

"I am afraid not. The police were here asking me about Tanel, but they have no news other than the terrible information we have to hand."

"Do you know why he would have been murdered?"

"Again, I am afraid not. As you can see, I wear a couple of hats in my role here in the hospital. I am dealing with administrative matters, the press and the police. I suggest you talk with Dr Alexievich in oncology. He may be able to assist you more than I can. If you don't mind, I am swamped. Get someone to show you where his office is."

"Thank you, I think I can remember having visited him before," replied Paul recalling his two visits to Alexievich's office, particularly the one in the middle of the night.

He went back to the elevator, squeezing in amongst a crowd of hospital staff, patients in gowns and a trolley with a patient on a drip. He found himself standing next to the patient's exposed foot, covered in calluses and topped with dirty toenails. The elevator was hot, sweaty and rowdy as its occupants chattered. Paul indicated with his fingers the seventh floor, and someone pressed the appropriate button. He was pleased to exit.

Tracing his way back to Alexievich's office, Paul passed Professor Pavlyuchenko's second office. He recalled that Tanel thought Alexievich had some sort of hold over the professor, possibly due to his alleged relationship with Dr Anastasia Medvedeva. Seeing the grandeur of the Superintendent's office and the probable prestige and financial reward that accompanied the position, it was easy to understand why the professor might be pressured by one of his staff to keep his title and position. His thoughts drifted to Dr Medvedeva.

Just then, he stopped outside Dr Alexievich's office. He caught sight of the doctor busy on a phone call. With an expression of surprise and concern, even shock, Alexievich looked up at Paul.

However, this was quickly replaced by his suave and supercilious demeanour. Paul was waved into the office, looking around at the filing cabinets and, with some discomfort, at the cupboard that had been his recent place of refuge the night of his covert mission.

Alexievich concluded his call and, while quickly shuffling some folders on his desk, rose to greet Paul, who felt he was an unwanted intrusion.

"Dr Beresford, how good to see your again."

"And you too, Dr Alexievich," Paul responded, keeping up the façade while they summed each other up.

"What can I do for you?"

Paul thought it was a strange question given the brutal murder of Tanel Valle, a frequent visitor to this office, and his involvement with a trial that appeared to be failing. There was no initial expression of regret or sympathy for the loss of Tanel. It was as if nothing had happened to disturb Dr Alexievich from his daily rhythm.

"I am shocked by the murder of Tanel Valle," said Paul as an opening gambit.

"Oh yes, that," said the Russian as if it was an incident such as a missing file or no toilet paper in the department.

"Yes, that," said Paul. "What are your thoughts on his murder?"

"His death," insisted Alexievich, avoiding the term murder. "His death was, in some way, not a surprise."

"Some way, not a surprise – what do you mean by that?"

"Surely, you must have realised that Tanel was gay. Unlike in your West, some Russians don't tolerate homosexual behaviour. They take matters into their own hands and dish out their own form of justice."

Paul and Alexievich stared at each other like two fighters circling their opponent.

As far as Paul could tell, Tanel was not gay. He could be mistaken, but he thought it was improbable.

"What about the trial results?"

"I am sorry to tell you, Dr Beresford, that it looks like the end of the road for HG 176. I am compiling a final report on the adverse events which will kill off the drug."

Paul was taken by the use of the term 'kill off' as if Alexievich wanted and relished this. This flew in the face of Paul's earlier thought that the hospital and the staff working on the trial would be aching for success to bring them academic fame. They would get requests for presentations about the powerful new tool in the clinical armamentarium against breast cancer. Maybe the hospital and staff were looking for these accolades, but Alexievich undeniably was not.

"When will this report be completed?"

"I hope to have it on Professor Pavlyuchenko's desk in just under a week. He will review it, sign it off and submit it. I am terribly sorry about the trial, Dr Beresford."

Alexievich did not look at all sorry. The statement was made as a matter of fact while looking at Paul to gauge his reaction.

"Thank you, Dr Alexievich."

"It's my pleasure, Dr Beresford."

There was nothing more to add. Paul stared at Alexievich for a few seconds, then turned and left the office, hearing the door close behind him. Things were becoming even more desperate. There was no way that Professor Pavlyuchenko would challenge or change the report if Alexievich had a hold over him.

Making his way towards the elevator, he passed Professor Pavlyuchenko's office. There was a figure standing just inside the open door. It was Dr Medvedeva. She gestured to Paul to come in and quickly closed the door behind him.

"Tanel, terrible!" she said.

She was again in her green surgical scrubs and gesturing with her hands, trying to supplement her feelings due to her limited control of English.

"I'm shocked," said Paul. "Alexievich said he was killed because he was gay – homosexual."

"No, no, no! Not gay; has girlfriend. Not gay."

"Then what, if he was not gay?" asked Paul.

"I think problems with trial."

"Are you sure of that?"

"I think problems with trial." She was emphatic.

"Did you help Tanel get back into Alexievich's office?"

"Yes."

"Were you there with him in the office?"

"Nyet!"

"What happened to Tanel?"

"Don't know. I hiding here after he get in."

"Did you hear anything?"

"I hear him shout out, give cry."

"Then, after that, any sound?"

"Men's voices, whispers, then nothing."

"What can we do now?"

"You must go. Here is mobile contact number. Phone tonight; six o'clock," she said, slipping a piece of paper into Paul's hand.

She leaned forward, kissed Paul on both cheeks, and almost pushed him out the door. He gathered himself after another encounter with Dr Medvedeva and headed once more to the elevators.

* * *

At the hotel, Paul transferred Dr Medvedeva's phone number to his mobile and then called Sergei Balakin from QualiMed.

"Sergei, it's Paul Beresford. Is there any additional news about Tanel?"

"No, Paul, I am afraid nothing."

"Sergei, I want to ask a personal question about Tanel; was he gay?"

"No, definitely not! I know his family, his mother, his girlfriend. He was about to get engaged to her. Why do you ask?"

"I understood there is a tough attitude to the gay community in Russia and was just grasping at straws as to why he was murdered."

"No, Paul, definitely not gay."

"Thanks, Sergei. Please let me know if you have any further news about who did this brutal act."

Paul concluded the call, his view reinforced that Alexievich was lying about Tanel being gay. Why would he lie about that, and why did he seem to take such satisfaction from the imminent failure of HG 176? The answer undoubtedly lay with him and the folders over which he had control.

Paul knew something sinister was at play, but he still wasn't sure where to look. He needed to explore all possible ways clinical trials could be manipulated or falsified and understand the definition of clinical trial misconduct. In doing so, he might get a clearer picture of what – or who – was being manipulated.

He did a Google search which threw up a range of articles. According to the US Food and Drug Administration, misconduct or fraud meant falsifying data in proposing, designing, performing, recording, supervising, reviewing, analysing, collecting clinical research or reporting clinical research results, outcomes and endpoints.

He read that fabrication referred to making up data or results or reporting them and that falsification meant manipulating research materials, equipment or processes, or omitting data or results so that the research is not accurately represented.

Paul was so engrossed in reading the articles that when he looked at his watch, he realised it was past six o'clock when Dr Medvedeva said he should call her. He quickly rang her number and was concerned that she was not answering. Despondent, he was just about to hang up when she replied.

"Paul?"

"Yes, and apologies for phoning a bit late."

"No problem, we must talk, but not on phone."

"Can you come to my hotel?"

"No, too dangerous. You come to me. I give you address."

Paul scrambled to find the hotel notepad and cheap branded

pen. He took down her address which was not too complicated given the difficulties with Russian names.

"You must come here."

"I am leaving now."

Paul handed the taxi driver Dr Medvedeva's address, and they were soon in a reasonably upmarket part of St Petersburg. Paul gave the taxi driver a handful of Roubles which, by his response, was more than sufficient. Paul reflected on a side effect of international travel and dealing with foreign currencies. The taxi driver pointed to number five and shouted, "Phyat, phyat," then drove off.

Paul rang the doorbell, and Dr Medvedeva opened the door with a quick, "Come in," before looking up and down the street to see if anyone was watching Paul's entry.

She led him into a sizeable well-furnished sitting room with a crackling fire in a large fireplace. In contrast to her surgical scrubs, she was wearing a dark one-piece trouser suit and around her neck a velvet broadband choker with a small jewel hanging from it which caught the fire's flickering light.

"A drink, vodka?" she offered.

"Why not? Yes, thanks."

She turned away to pour the drinks, and Paul revised his original view of her when seen in her surgical kit. The trouser suit accentuated her figure, and with her blonde hair elegantly piled up on her head, loose strands hanging down the back of her neck, he understood what Professor Pavlyuchenko was enjoying.

She handed him a crystal glass and clinked it with hers, saying "Na Zdorovie!"

"Anastasia, may I call you Anastasia?"

"Da."

"There is about a week before the trial is terminated. Is it possible that Professor Pavlyuchenko can halt that process?" As soon as he asked the question, he regretted it because he knew about the relationship between her and the professor.

"That not possible. Alexievich knows about Anatoly

Pavlyuchenko and me. He threaten to tell wife and hospital and ruin Anatoly position. Alexievich has all real control of trial."

"I see."

"The professor and me, we similar. Our families related to the Romanovs, the Tsar's family. Mother, father named me after Grand Duchess Anastasia Nikolaevna, daughter four of Tsar Nicholas II, killed with Royal family. We lose everything in 1917 October Revolution. All I have is jewellery and furniture," she said, pointing to some heavy but classical pieces. "I know Anatoly since I was young. He much older than me. He help me qualify as doctor, and I grateful to him. He is very good surgeon; I respect him. He my mentor and lover."

A silence settled on the room, broken only by the crackling of the fire.

"And Dr Alexievich, what about him?" Paul probed.

"He nothing. He a peasant, not even good doctor," she spat.

"But I thought he was wealthy with his fancy clothes and the gold Rolex."

"He gambles; he addicted to gambling. He has problem because casinos he go to owned by Russian Mafia."

"Do you think he is altering the results of the trial?"

"Da, I think yes, that because the clinical evidence I see is not fitting."

"We need to get evidence of any changes to the clinical data, which means getting copies of the patient folders and case report forms."

"Is very dangerous."

"I know, but we, I, must finish the work Tanel was doing," Paul emphasised.

"I help you," Anastasia offered immediately.

"But I don't want you to be in danger."

"Thank you, but drug must survive, and Alexievich be beaten."

"I must go now and get back to the hotel," said Paul, rising from his seat.

"You want dinner?"

He paused. "Thank you, but no. I must leave," he said reluctantly.

"I call taxi for you."

She went to the telephone and spoke briefly in Russian. Shortly afterwards, there was a hoot outside the apartment.

"Thank you for all your help."

"You welcome, like they say in the West," she smiled.

As they walked to the door, Paul wondered how she would take leave of him. On one occasion, she had kissed him on the mouth and, on the other, a kiss on both cheeks. It was the latter. He stepped outside, and a cold blast of Arctic air swiftly brought him back to reality.

CHAPTER 26

In the Project Office

In Hong Kong, Melissa needed to contact Devon to develop an action plan. She put through a call to him.

"Devon, have you had any thoughts on what we can do to try to save the trial?"

"Yes, I have arranged with a nursing sister whom I know well to get into the Project Office tonight to try to hack into the programme where the trial results are stored," he responded.

"So you're going to pursue this stupid, risky plan of yours and Paul's?"

"I can't see any alternative with Hung stuck somewhere in China. Do you have a better idea?"

To her frustration, Melissa had to admit that she was stumped. All her clinical trial experience was of no help under the current circumstances.

"No, I don't," she conceded.

"Do you want to come along with me?"

"I guess I have to make sure you don't screw up."

"Thanks for the vote of confidence. I'll collect you around ten o'clock. Don't be late." He rang off.

Melissa detected some role reversal with Devon's closing comment.

Just before the agreed time, Devon pulled up on the hotel

driveway in a white Volkswagen Golf and shouted to Melissa to get in.

"Are you ready for tonight's fun and games?" he asked as she settled into the seat next to him. For a tense undertaking, Devon seemed unusually relaxed and in good humour.

"I am here to police you so that the police don't."

"Relax, all will be fine," he said with a happy smile. Melissa wished she could share his confidence.

They arrived at the hospital, and despite the late hour, it was still a hive of activity, ambulances flashing red lights as they came and went. Devon avoided the main entrance and went to park the Golf in a quiet, darkened parking area close to a deserted entrance. A figure was waiting just inside the doorway.

"Hello, Selina. Melissa, this is Sister Selina Wong. She will help us get into the Project Office," smiled Devon.

Although there was an elevator available, Selina insisted they use the staircase to the fourth floor to minimise detection as the elevators were still busy at night. They set off, Devon tripping on the first step. Melissa looked at him quizzically. By the time they got to the second floor, the overweight and unfit Devon was puffing and panting. They needed to stop for him to catch his breath, after which he stumbled on another step. Melissa felt they would never get there, frustrated that she had to work with idiots.

Reaching the office, Selina unlocked the door and handed the key to Devon, saying she would meet them back at the car.

The door closed on the darkened office. Devon fumbled in his pockets and said, "Damn, I've forgotten my torch."

Melissa cursed, took out her mobile phone and switched on the torch feature. The illumination showed some desks adorned with computers.

"Now, which is the trial computer, the one on a separate system? Ah, this is it," Devon said, starting up the computer. It was evident there were no trial documents on it.

"Must be this one," he said cheerily, moving to the desk next to it. "Yes, success; I told you I knew my way around."

Melissa groaned inwardly as Devon started searching through the document folders.

"Here it is, HG 176," he murmured. "Let me start going through some of the case report forms to see if there are any discrepancies."

Melissa felt a surge of hope which had been absent up to then.

"Paul remembered some patient folders Hung had shown you in hard copy. I jotted down the references, and I have them here," Devon said as he took out a small notebook and flipped through the pages.

Suddenly, they heard voices approaching the office.

"Quick, hide!" whispered Devon into Melissa's ear.

It was then that she smelt liquor on his breath. They were in a risky situation calling for clear thinking, and Devon was inebriated. He quickly closed the folder, and he and Melissa moved to the far corner of the office to crouch behind a desk.

Melissa felt Devon's weight as he leaned into her back. He seemed to be taking some pleasure from this; she almost expected to feel his hands grope her breasts. She shuddered. There was no knowing what gross acts he might get up to in his state. She regretted wearing a pair of jeans and a sweater that accentuated her figure.

A man entered the doorway and said, "They've forgotten to lock this office. Let's go find a supervisor."

"No, we don't have much time together," replied a woman. "Let's not use this office. I've already cleared my desktop for us. Hurry, let's go. They can sort this out in the morning."

The door closed to Devon's and Melissa's relief, although Devon seemed reluctant to move his adopted position.

"Hurry up and check the folder again," Melissa urged.

Devon quickly scrolled through the files, looking for the references Paul had given him. "Yes, I'm positive there are inconsistencies in the case report forms Paul identified. This one for patient SM-Y shows some discrepancies." He went to some of the others that Paul had noted. "Yes, there are definitely some oddities in these reports as well. I am familiar with the files from my time working on the ... Oh, oh!"

"What's wrong?" asked Melissa.

"There is someone else using this file right now!"

A chat window opened with Professor Hung's username, and a message appeared: "Devon?"

"Shit!" exclaimed Devon, abruptly hitting the log-off button. "Let's get out of here. Hung will have security up here in a flash."

He and Melissa promptly left the Project Office, locking the door behind them. They descended using the stairwell. Devon managed to move at a pace previously unknown to him and was relieved not to hear evidence of security personnel behind them.

Leaving the building, they found Selina waiting with the Golf parked nearby and the engine running.

"Thanks, babe. I owe you one."

"I hope so," she said knowingly.

Devon pulled off with a comparable Grand Prix start. Only when they neared the hotel did Melissa catch her breath.

"We have to get access to that computer again if you say there's hard evidence of misconduct."

"We can try, although it will be difficult," warned Devon.

He dropped her off at the hotel and said he needed to get back to Selina. Melissa did not begrudge him this; it seemed he could indeed be the answer to unlocking the trial mystery.

* * *

In St Petersburg, Paul returned to the hotel needing to take stock of the rapidly unwinding situation. He had scarcely a week to resolve the problems with the St Petersburg and Hong Kong sites. He contacted Melissa to find out what they had done while he had been away.

"Have you made any progress?" Paul asked hopefully.

"We had quite an adventure," she said. "I hate to admit it, but it seems that despite all his drawbacks, Devon has made a significant breakthrough."

"In what way?" prompted Paul, pleased that the Dragon Lady seemed to be humanising.

"He got us into the Project Office at the hospital where the computer with the trial details is located, running on a separate system."

"That's brilliant, and what did you find?"

"Unfortunately, we couldn't make much progress, but Devon noted some inconsistencies in certain folders that you miraculously remembered. But, as we were going through the documents, Professor Hung came onto the system via a chat window."

"What! What did you do then?" pressed Paul.

"We had to sign out, but we're planning to try to get back. Devon said some of the patients you identified, from the hard copy case report forms that Hung showed us, appear to have differences from the raw data in the source files."

"There, I told you the approach Devon and I were following would bring rewards."

"So you say," said Melissa slightly sourly. "It still has to be proved in a fact-based manner."

"I'll return to Hong Kong and work with you and Devon. We are definitely onto something. Goodnight."

Paul had time to reflect on the state of the project and his circumstances at that moment. Within a short time, his life had undergone an extraordinary change; his career and personal arc had altered dramatically. He had seen himself developing as a surgeon, hopefully an outstanding one, but all that changed with his joining a pharmaceutical company. Surgery was his past life, as was Jill. There was no going back to reclaim either of those parts of his life.

His self-knowledge had also changed. Always prepared to accept the bona fides of his medical colleagues, Paul realised how imprudent that had been. Perhaps he had been naive. Now he recognised a growing streak of cynicism in him regarding these interactions. A new cast of characters had now inhabited his life: Professor Hung, Dr Alexievich, Professor Pavlyuchenko and Melissa James; people he thought he could trust in the past. All of them seemed to have ulterior motives. Jill had teased him about being a boy scout with his earnest hopes and idealism. He had initially accepted Melissa's judgment and decisions at the outset as he acknowledged her experience, but now he had taken charge.

What about Dr Anastasia Medvedeva? Paul had to admit he was intrigued by her. He had allowed himself to feel attracted to her, and she seemed to feel the same way about him, but was she part of a group of people with hidden agendas? Was he making a significant mistake by trusting her to help him solve the mystery of the failing trials? Would she betray him because he knew about her relationship with the professor?

Paul wondered what might happen if he went back into the hospital. Would he be caught, chopped into pieces, and placed inside a suitcase like Tanel? He felt he had to take that chance because the trial had to succeed, for him, for JP and Harrowgate, and in memory of Jill.

None of these questions had easy answers, but he needed to keep searching for them.

CHAPTER 27

The Diaries

Sean was also consumed by self-reflection, alternately gripped by elation and moments of depression regarding the unfolding situation. There was much at stake resting on his activities and plans – everything, in fact. If he failed in his scheme to achieve business success, his father would legitimise Sean's half-brother from his affair with one of his employees, thereby supplanting Sean with him in the line of succession to the title of 6th Viscount Talbot. He would lose fame, wealth and influence.

Sean was aware of his personal weaknesses and that he defined himself by who he was seen to be rather than who he was in reality. As heir to the Talbot Viscountcy, his title gave him some influence and brought him the attention he craved. The Bellingham Hall estate offered bountiful wealth and prominence as one of the leading stately homes in England. Driven by ego, Sean could not bear the thought of losing prestige or wealth. And yet, he knew that his image of being self-assured, confident, and bombastic was built on sand.

In moments of despair, he mourned the death of Hugh, his older brother, who had been destined for the Talbot title. Hugh had all the attributes his father wanted in a son and heir. If only Hugh had survived, Sean would have been allowed to get on with his life without the pressures he was currently under. He could have enjoyed the louche lifestyle he found so appealing. He knew he did not manage anxiety and pressure well, but these were his constant companions while he was in this situation.

Then there was Jill. Jill, whom he had adored. She would have made the perfect wife to complete his perceived image. Sean had lusted after her and tried everything to win her over. How her father reacted positively to his visit to their home gave him hope. But she remained ever distant, unlike the other girls who were mesmerised by his wealth and title and whom he had easily bedded. Jill had seen Sean's frailties, but he believed she understood him. She was always polite and friendly in her dealings with him but always just out of reach.

And then there was Beresford, the cause of all his problems. Of all people, Beresford had succeeded where Sean had failed with Jill, which only inflamed him further. Although he could not achieve his original aim of possessing her, he had an alternative. Knowing that Jill had tried to steer him away from the possible purchase of Harrowgate, Sean had developed a plan suffused with revenge. He would have used the leverage of not acquiring the Irish company through her legal practice to blackmail her into succumbing to him on the jet. At least he would have achieved that one desire, but now, even that had been taken away from him with Jill's death. Again, Beresford was to blame. He was a doctor; why didn't he save her?

Sean contemplated his master plan to expand his business, impress his father, and secure his inheritance. He had put in place detailed and complicated arrangements involving elements of the Talbot global business, the government of a major country, and organised crime in another. The threads that held this approach together were tenuous and liable to fray and unravel, but Sean had to persevere. He had to place his trust – if that word held any meaning for him – in a disparate group of individuals over whom he had little or no control. Elements of the plan were criminal and would ruin him if they were exposed. But the risk of losing the Talbot jewel of title and wealth carried more gravity for him.

Sean sat in his office nervously rubbing his sweating hands together, waiting for feedback from Crispin on each of his targeted trial sites. He got up and paced around the office, passing the drinks cabinet several times. Sean realised he was becoming more dependent on alcohol to steady his nerves but resisted it on this occasion.

The door opened, and Crispin entered, looking grim.

"What's happened?"

"There are reports from our contact in St Petersburg that someone seems to have been snooping around the offices involved in the trial," Crispin responded.

"Has the snoop found out anything about what's going on?"

"Our contact isn't sure about that but is deeply worried and says we must take action."

"Then we must do whatever it takes to ensure our plan works!"

"Whatever it takes? Are you sure about that?"

"Everything and anything; I won't be stopped."

"Must I tell our so-called 'friends' that your instruction is to do whatever is needed to secure your goal?"

"Yes! What don't you understand about whatever it takes?" barked Sean.

"You appreciate who we are dealing with?" Crispin persisted.

"Of course, get on with it. What about Hong Kong?"

"All seems to be going well there. Our contact has the person in charge of the trial under wraps, and he is doing what is required."

"At least there is some good news. We'll soon have reports available to enable us to complete the plan. Now, get moving!"

"If you insist."

Crispin left the office, and Sean had a moment to reflect on his decision and any consequences, but the Talbot way was to win at all costs – and that's what he would do.

* * *

Paul had received feedback from Anastasia in an early morning call advising him that it would not be possible to get back into the hospital for some days while the issue of Tanel's death was still under investigation.

In addition, Dr Alexievich was twitchy and on edge, so she did not want to risk accessing his office. Alexievich had let slip to one of the other doctors that he had a bad gambling experience and needed his luck to turn around quickly. She suspected he owed money to the wrong type of people.

While Paul trusted Anastasia's judgement, the clock was running down. The delays simply meant less time to solve the mystery of the sites before Professor Hung's and the St Petersburg reports extinguished HG 176 forever.

Paul decided that he needed to get back to Hong Kong urgently. He could help Devon and Melissa make more progress on their breakthrough in gaining access to the electronic records of the trial and picking up possible errors. If they could delay Professor Hung's report, it would buy time for them to save the trial in its entirety if subversion or error could be proved. He set off once again for the airport. This must be what frequent flyer miles are all about, he thought.

* * *

Once back in the hotel in Hong Kong, Paul contacted Devon to arrange a meeting and decide the next move.

"Devon, it's Paul here."

"Welcome back. I am sure that you are aware of our progress?"

"Yes, but we need to move even faster. Can you get us back into the Project Office?" asked Paul.

"I've spoken to Selina, and she feels we can try again tonight as there were no major repercussions from our last attempt."

"No follow-up from Professor Hung?"

"None," Devon confirmed. "It's strange since he knew someone was on the system and thought it was me. It seems he didn't want to stir things up."

"That's odd since he struck me as a meticulous person who would always do things by the book."

"I expected a large-scale investigation, but nothing happened. Hung was undoubtedly acting out of character when this sudden change in the trial occurred. We had always got on well, and he trusted me to do the work. Suddenly that all changed, and I became persona non grata."

"Despite Melissa's reservations, I'm convinced there is underhand work on the go. If that is the case, there's still an opportunity to save HG 176, as I believe the efficacy is well on target elsewhere. I'll hear from you later about accessing the data tonight," concluded Paul.

Although time was slipping away, Paul had some time before they ventured out that evening. He wanted to assess how and why the trials were unravelling. He ordered lunch from room service and, at the small desk in his hotel room, wrote down his thoughts and drew some mind maps. A logical assessment of the two sites showed significant inconsistencies. One site had efficacy problems with the cancer reoccurring, and the other showed inexplicable side effects. If there was a core problem with HG 176, the issues should be common to both sites.

In addition, trial sites across the world had not demonstrated these problems – another inconsistency. Even though only two sites out of the seven showed these discrepancies, safety was the overarching consideration. The whole multicentre trial would have to be canned, placing Harrowgate in a fragile position. JP had told Paul he was considering an offer to sell the business and get out. The pungent odour of impending failure was everywhere.

After the devastation of the thalidomide tragedy, where an anti-nausea and morning sickness medication caused dreadful deformities in newborns, caution had to be the paramount driver. Major drug failings, in some instances, only manifested post-launch. Although large enough to show efficacy and reveal common adverse events, premarketing studies are not always able to uncover rare side effects. These side effects can often only be detected when the number and type of patients using the product after its launch far exceeds the number of subjects in the clinical trials.

In addition, both these sites had Principal Investigators with disquieting uncertainties attached to them. Professor Pavlyuchenko was clearly not in control of his brief, with Dr Alexievich calling the shots. Professor Hung had been behaving out of character and had suddenly disappeared from the hospital and returned to mainland China.

A rational approach in his thinking led Paul to conclude that it could only be the results that were abnormal and that he needed to join the dots regarding these. He completed sketching out his mind map, resolute in his assumption that HG 176 was safe and effective. He had a last bite of his cold toasted cheese sandwich, put on a tracksuit, and went to the hotel gym for some much-needed exercise.

Refreshed after his exercise and shower, Paul decided to go through his briefcase and pick out some key articles on clinical trial design that he carried as hard copies. They were marked in places with a yellow highlighter where he had focused on important points.

Rifling through his briefcase, Paul saw Jill's diaries that he had found in the Wandsworth apartment and that he had, after some reflection, decided to bring with him. Looking again at Jill's neat script and picking up traces of her scent as he held the documents close to his face, he was racked with pain. Should he go through them or put them back? He felt that reading them would only distress him.

He started replacing them in his briefcase but suddenly changed his mind. He had to see them at some stage and since he had some time on his hands, now was as good as any time, as distressing as that might be. It would upset him at any time.

He opened the first set. The notes covered her thoughts about her time at the legal practice and how she enjoyed her work on the energy company and its attempts to acquire a competitor to expand its market share. There were quite a few pages devoted to this, so he flicked ahead.

Further on, there was a bold heading: "PAUL. BIG PHARMA!" That got his attention.

She had jotted down her thoughts, all negative, about him leaving his surgical career. He felt guilt and remorse, learning how distressed she was by his choice to leave what she believed was a brilliant career in surgery. The succeeding notes covered the positives and negatives of the pharmaceutical industry and how the moniker Big Pharma was used in a pejorative sense. Her list of negatives outnumbered the positives. Big Pharma was simply a money-making business with little care for patients.

What about the opioid crisis in the United States? Pharmaceutical companies had built legions of representatives, primarily attractive women, with the distinct task of winning over doctors to prescribe these drugs for any minor ache and pain to achieve their sales targets. This was irrespective of any adverse consequence to their patients, or victims, as Jill described them. Paul admitted that this could be seen as the unacceptable face of the industry. Or was it? Were patients in the US simply more dependent on and demanding of serious pain medication from their doctors? Perhaps the crisis was patient-driven because this phenomenon did not seem so prevalent in other countries. Paul could not answer that question. He moved on from this analysis, typical of Jill's incisive thought processes. He could hear her voice as he glanced through her notes.

He read further to see another bold heading: "DEED DONE!" Under this, she noted Paul's counterarguments about the benefits of the pharmaceutical industry and her admission that not all was bad. He had quoted some telling advantages. She had written that Paul had joined Harrowgate and that she would support him with all her being because she loved him so profoundly. She believed that if he was prepared to work in that industry, there must be merit as she trusted his judgement. Reading that, Paul broke down and sobbed. His decision to join Harrowgate and leave her for such an extended period led to her cancer being undetected for such a pivotal time frame that it had fatal consequences. He put the notes down and went and lay down on the bed, exhausted by his memories and loss.

After a short nap, Paul returned to the desk to continue reading – as painful as it was. The notes continued about her work and how she missed Paul.

The notes cryptically made references to people by an initial or initials: "'G' wants me to complete the energy acquisition in early September. 'CR' needs complete merger SOP for team. 'G' has a valuable client lined up for me."

Later in the notes, it stated that 'G' brought 'S' to the practice. What a surprise, she noted. 'S' wanted an acquisition within industry. This was all obscure to Paul and obviously all about the practice's workings and clients.

He flicked on further to find another reference linked to the previous one: "'G' wants me to do everything to satisfy 'S'." That would not have meant anything, but "Ugh!" was written behind it, indicating Jill was unhappy about it. Still, that did not make any sense to Paul. He continued reading more internal references, noting that 'RN' was now helping with the industry acquisition. He was young but very competent and easing her workload.

Paul stopped dead and fixated on another reference: "Lunch with 'S'. He tried to finger me. Nauseating!" Paul wondered who 'S' was. How come he was in a position where he could molest her? Why did 'G', who he assumed was Giles Robinson, one of the partners, want her to please 'S', and in what way? Paul felt sick at the possibilities.

There were more references to her work, and then came the entry: "Found 'S' a good opportunity in industry in Ireland. This will distract his attention from getting his hands on 'H'."

Paul wondered which industry was being referred to and who was the person represented by the initial 'H'? Was 'H' another person in the firm who 'S' wanted to molest? It was unclear to Paul, but he was concerned that through her notes, he could see that Jill appeared to be coerced into something she was unhappy with. Paul trusted Jill's intellect and judgement to handle any problematic situation, so he couldn't fathom why this situation was so challenging for her.

He wanted to read on, but it was getting late and nearly time to meet with Devon for the evening's activities. It was with reluctance that he returned the diary notes to his briefcase. He was troubled and confused by all the references – the one in particular.

Shortly afterwards, his phone rang; Devon was downstairs and ready to go. Thoughts about Jill's diaries had to be put aside.

CHAPTER 28

Breakthrough

In the lobby, Melissa was talking to Devon. As they went to the car, Melissa whispered to Paul that at least Devon was sober. Paul smiled at her concerns.

On the way to the hospital, Paul updated his companions about his activities in St Petersburg, leaving out details of his encounter with Anastasia Medvedeva, merely saying that he had a connection in oncology who would get him back into the hospital to look at the patient folders.

"You need to take care, Paul," said Devon. "You know what happened to Tanel."

"It's a risk we must take."

"It's a risk you are taking," Melissa chipped in from the back seat. "You know my thoughts on your misguided methods and how this could trigger a catastrophe if you get caught. It can impact negatively on our industry in general and Harrowgate in particular. If you get caught, it's your issue, not mine. I will tell the press I was against it from the beginning; you know that."

"There is no other way," was Paul's curt reply.

Only he knew that JP was on the brink of selling Harrowgate as the share price slipped with the continued concern that their blockbuster new medicine had hit the rocks.

"Time is running out, Melissa," Paul continued, "and you need to apply your mind to how you can leverage all your experience to help us rather than looking to attribute blame."

A tense silence descended as they made their way to the hospital, broken by Devon whispering in Paul's ear, "What she needs is a good screw."

"Go easy on her," was Paul's whispered response.

Once again, Devon stopped in a dark and deserted section of the parking lot. They waited as a figure approached them; it was Selina with a key to the Project Office. They made their way into the building and up the stairs to their destination, where Selina slipped the key to Devon, whispered something and left them.

Devon opened the office, and they moved directly to the relevant computer terminal. Using his torch – which he remembered on this occasion – Devon partially illuminated the office and logged on to the trial programme.

"How did you do that?" asked Paul.

"My username still has access to the trial data. I guess Professor Hung forgot to remove it, which is odd. But that's how he saw it was me the last time."

A file came up named: Investigator-Initiated Phase 3 Trial of HG 176 (terpazamab) for Metastatic Breast Cancer in women. Paul winced, keenly aware this was the condition that had destroyed Jill. If only he had known much earlier about her condition.

Devon once again referred to the notebook in which he had jotted down the patient folders where Paul had noticed irregular data. He started comparing the raw data of the primary outcome measures to that entered on the case report forms. In the cases he scanned, there were differences in the clinical benefit rates. Where the raw data had shown Complete Response (CR), some of the patient case report form examples recorded Partial Response (PR). Others showed the response (PD).

"CR means the disappearance of all target lesions," said Melissa, "but the case report form displays weaker or retrogressive results. Other assessments in the case report forms reflect PD, which means

Progressive Disease. This suggests at least a twenty percent increase in the target lesions or one or more new lesions. In other words, the drug is failing – which it is not, according to the raw data."

Devon agreed. "There is a complete divergence between the raw data in the source files and that recorded in the case report forms. These form the basis of the conclusions and summary of the trial, and if these reflect retrogressive results, it will justify the trial's termination."

Melissa also observed changes in the secondary outcome measurements, confirming their conclusions. Paul recalled two other patient cases, and Devon looked them up to find similar results.

"That's what I thought," said Paul. "The results have been deliberately manipulated to show the drug in a poor light and failing. Why would anyone involved in a trial want to do this? The industry has sometimes been accused of overstating results by selecting better outcomes to make the product look more efficacious. But this is the complete opposite. Professor Hung and his team should want success which would reflect well on them."

All three sat in silence, confused by their discovery.

"How can we capture these results?" queried Paul.

"I'll see if we can print out some of the discrepancies," said Devon. "It will take some time, but I am sure there is a printer linked to this terminal."

Just at that moment, a chat window appeared.

"Devon, is that you again?"

The three of them froze. "Not again," was the collective thought, not now that they had made a breakthrough.

Paul made a quick decision. "Devon, acknowledge Professor Hung and see where this takes us. Remember, he met with those mysterious men from mainland China and appeared extremely upset by them."

"You are mad!" cried Melissa. "You will ruin everything for us."

Devon hesitated as he, too, was unsure. He looked first at Melissa and then at Paul.

"Go on, do it," said Paul.

Devon typed in, "Yes, Professor Hung. I'm here."

There was no response. The three of them held their breath. How was this going to play out? There was still no response on the screen.

Melissa was about to open her mouth and chastise Paul when the screen lit up with the response, "Why are you accessing the trial data?"

"Professor, are you okay? Can we help?" Devon typed.

The screen activity ceased again for an extended period to their growing anxiety. Then suddenly, a word appeared on the screen.

"Peccavi."

"Peccavi. What on earth does that mean?" asked Paul.

"I know," said Devon. He typed back, "I understand."

"Yes," was the response, and the chat box closed.

"I will explain later," said Devon. "We need to see if we can print out some of the evidence reflecting how data has been manipulated to show the product in an adverse light."

Devon scanned a few of the cases they had examined, searched for examples of discrepancies and selected some of these. The printer in the office whirred, spitting out the critical evidence. Devon had only completed printing two of the seven cases when the workstation was automatically logged out. He was unable to select another case.

"I have a feeling that Professor Hung has allowed us to draw down a couple of examples to prove Paul's theory about the trial, then shut us out," Devon surmised. "I think we need to gather what evidence we have and get out of here."

"But we need more evidence," urged Melissa. "Try to get back into the database; two cases will not be enough."

Although acknowledging Melissa's point, Devon realised that the door had slammed shut, and they had to be grateful they had something, even if not enough to prove their case.

"No, we can't get any more. We need to leave," said Devon, as he shut down the computer, collected the documents from the printer and headed for the door, followed by Paul and a reluctant Melissa.

Back in the parking lot, the Golf approached them. Selina retrieved the key from Devon as he, Paul and Melissa got into the car and drove away from the hospital. All three of them were silent for a while, taking in the events they had just experienced.

Paul broke the silence. "Devon, what was that Peccavi stuff all about? It seemed to be a key to your connection with Hung?"

"Yes, it was a coded form of messaging from him to me."

"In what way?" urged Paul.

Devon explained as they drove to the hotel. "As I mentioned, Professor Hung and I had an excellent working and personal relationship. Then, his behaviour changed for whatever reason, and he suddenly shut me out. Hung and I share a love of history and often discuss and debate historical issues. Our most recent debate was about colonialism and Britain's rule in India. For the argument, I took the position of supporting the value of the colonialist's role, and he, naturally, took the opposite view.

"Our last discussion touched on General Sir Charles Napier and his supposedly famous telegram. The General captured the then Indian province of Sindh and is alleged to have communicated this information back to his superiors in a telegram. It had only the single cryptic Latin word, 'Peccavi' – which means 'I have sinned'. You see, it's a play on words – I have Sindh, as in the province.

"But by stating that word to me, Professor Hung is admitting that he has sinned regarding the trial outcome and wants to give us a clue that is unlikely to be understood by others seeing the word. He's obviously in trouble and trying to help us, which he's done by allowing us to get some proof that the trial is being misrepresented. I'm sure he's being watched, so he's had to shut down all access to the database. We will have to move forward as best we can with the information we have."

Paul was shocked but also relieved. Finally, the sinister forces were being revealed.

"A couple of examples will not be enough to convince the other Principal Investigators," Melissa pointed out. "We need more evidence to make our case."

"That means I must get back to St Petersburg urgently," said Paul, "to see if I can gather similar examples to create a critical mass. It's now or never."

CHAPTER 29

Return to Danger

Paul returned to his room after Devon had dropped him and Melissa off at the hotel. The first thing he did was call Anastasia.

She answered, "Medvedeva."

"Anastasia, it's me, Paul. Paul Beresford."

"Hello, Paul."

"Anastasia, we have found some evidence here in Hong Kong that the trial results are being manipulated to look like the drug is failing."

"That is good news."

"Yes, but it is only a couple of cases. The Principal Investigator here has allowed us access to a small example of the data." Paul could not go into the complexity of how they managed to acquire this. "I need to get more examples from your site. Do you think I can come through to you as soon as possible? Do you feel it would be safe to do so?"

"Not safe, but we try."

"I am desperate, but I don't want to place you in trouble or danger."

"Remember I tell you I want Alexievich beaten. We must risk it. Come tomorrow. We try get into Alexievich's office at night. He is left in a hurry. Looked worried."

"Okay, I will get a flight tomorrow morning. Goodnight."

"Goodnight, Paul."

Paul was pleased they were gathering momentum to solve the problem with the trial. He was about to get changed and get some sleep when his eye caught sight of his briefcase and, within it, Jill's diary. He paused, then reached over and took it out. He flicked through the pages to find the last entry he had seen.

The notes went on: "Getting close to finishing proposal for 'S'. He seems less interested in acquisition than earlier. Worrying. Met with Irish company. Board impressed with proposal, client's wealth and title." Paul stopped. That was a jarring entry. Surely not!

He read on. Jill then documented the emergence of her cancer, her concerns about her health, and not wanting to disturb Paul during his course. Paul winced at that; if only he had known. The diary went on to further detail her medical experience as the severity of the condition emerged.

Her final entry read: "Told Paul; he is coming back to be with me." Paul was racked with guilt and broke down once more, his tears falling on the diary and blurring the ink on Jill's words. He closed the notebook and went to bed.

* * *

The following morning Paul headed to the airport for his trip back to St Petersburg. Would this be the last time he had to make the journey? If he could garner enough examples of the duplicity between the patients' raw data entries and their incorrect transfer to the case report forms – for that's what he thought was happening – he could delay the trial termination until the truth was established.

On the flight and in the taxi to the hotel, his mind was also turning over what he had read in Jill's diary. Besides the harrowing description of how her breast cancer was developing and her unfulfilled hope that Paul would be with her as she subjected herself to the devastation of the operation, there was the issue of her cryptic diary notes.

The references to 'S' seemed ominous. Although obscure, there were hints that these referred to a character from his and her past. It seemed too much of a coincidence – or was it? What steps could he take to establish this? Who could he contact? He could contact Giles Robinson, but he had reservations since if he were the 'G' in the notes, Giles would be backing 'S' to succeed – even if it meant putting damaging pressure on Jill. Approaching Giles might be an unsubtle approach.

He had an obscure thought. Could he contact Eddie Collins? Their relationship had been barbed from their first meeting, and Eddie had not supported Jill dating Paul because he wanted ... That thought hung in the air. Eddie knew of and admired Paul's father from his rugby days, so the ice had been broken – but ever so slightly. They had a few interactions during the time Paul was dating Jill but not enough to build rapport. Eddie also seemed to have a grudge against Paul for the loss of his beloved daughter; if he was a doctor, why wasn't he alert to Jill's condition? But Eddie was a resourceful person. His business success and wealth testified to that. But would he want to help Paul? The debate went back and forth in his head.

Once he got to his hotel room, and since he had time, he called Anastasia to let her know of his arrival and make plans for that evening.

"Get taxi to hospital," she said. "I meet you at nine o'clock, entrance C; we meet there before."

"Right. Are you sure you want to go through with this?"

"Da – that's Russian for yes."

"Thank you for helping me."

"Always pleasure."

Paul reflected on the proposed evening's activity. He could handle the danger himself but was anxious for Anastasia's safety. He had let down one person in his life. Was he about to do it with another?

He returned to the thought of contacting Eddie Collins and decided it was worth the effort. What was there to lose? He was already in poor standing with him, but he needed to know if Sean St

Ledger was in any way involved with Jill's activities and if it had any impact on the Harrowgate trial or himself. He found the Collins' country home number on his phone and dialled it.

"Collins."

"Mr Collins, it's Paul Beresford."

There was silence from the other end of the call.

"Mr Collins. Are you there?"

"Yes."

"Mr Collins, I know this is a tough time for you, but I need your help."

"Why?"

"I am in St Petersburg at the moment following up our company's trial on its drug for breast cancer."

"Breast cancer! Your company has a drug for breast cancer?"

"Yes, I was not aware of it when I joined or when I went to Harvard."

There was another extended silence.

Paul continued, "I want this drug to succeed as a tribute to Jill and try to prevent the tragedy you, Alice and I have gone through."

"So?"

"It seems the trial has run into problems at two sites, St Petersburg being one of them, Hong Kong the other."

"So?"

"I found Jill's diaries when I was going through the Wandsworth apartment. It seems that she was pressurised by her boss, extremely pressurised, to help someone Jill referred to as 'S' to purchase a company, probably a pharmaceutical company. 'S' was also acting in an extremely unpleasant and intimidating manner towards her. She appeared to be risking her health to complete the work to get 'S' off her back, which may have contributed to her delaying having her condition checked as urgently as she should have. I believe 'S' in her diaries could refer to Sean St Ledger."

"The Honourable Sean St Ledger?" said Eddie emphasising his full title.

"Yes, the very same."

"I don't believe it. I have met him, and he was exemplary."

"That's how he may have appeared, but it may not be authentic."

"That's hard to believe," he said dismissively.

"As difficult as this may appear," said Paul, "I have a strong sense that it is true."

There was another extended silence while the information was digested.

"Mr Collins, the favour I need from you is to establish whether St Ledger was looking for an acquisition in the pharmaceutical industry."

"Why do you need this?"

"I have not been able to join all the dots in my investigation, but knowing this may help me put the puzzle pieces together to see if he is playing any role in the issues we're facing with the trials."

"I'll think about it."

"Please, Mr Collins. I know you have excellent business and financial connections. Through these, you may be able to establish the facts. It could play a crucial role in developing our new drug to prevent suffering among women with breast cancer. I want it to succeed in memory of Jill."

"I told you, I'll think about it." The phone went dead.

Paul reflected on whether he had done the right thing. Eddie Collins unmistakably harboured a deep antipathy towards Paul, whereas Sean's charisma and title had impressed Eddie when introduced to Jill's family. Did the call simply aggravate the thin relationship with Jill's father? That didn't seem relevant now since Jill was tragically gone.

Paul felt guilt about the call, given how Jill loved her parents and how they had doted on her, but there was nothing to be gained from agonising over it. He decided to get some rest to prepare himself for the evening's events. Would he still be alive at the end of it?

* * *

That evening Paul asked the reception to order a taxi for him. When he told them he wanted it to take him to the hospital where the trial was taking place, they were concerned about his health and wanting to go to a State hospital instead of a private one. He had to argue that he was only meeting a colleague there.

The debate cost time, and when the taxi arrived, it was already close to nine o'clock, adding another layer of stress to the evening. It was after nine when Paul was dropped at entrance C, and there was no sign of Anastasia. He started to panic, thinking he had messed up the whole evening's plan. He entered the building and stood looking around, drawing the attention of some staff who asked him something in Russian. This was the second time he had been late contacting Anastasia, and she must think he was unreliable. At that moment, another figure arrived dressed in surgical kit, rescuing the situation.

"You late – again," Anastasia reprimanded.

"Apologies."

"Here, put these surgical on."

Paul slipped into the changing room and put on the surgical gown, mask and head cover.

"Let's go," Anastasia said. "All quiet in our section. I have key to his office."

They took the elevator and headed to oncology. Anastasia led the way to Alexievich's office and unlocked it. She looked through the desk's drawers but could not find the keys to the black filing cabinet.

"He must have move it because he worried. He normally sloppy in his habits, but I find it." Finally, Anastasia located the keys after an agonising few minutes, handing them to Paul.

"I leave you to find documents. Will be in Anatoly's office with photocopier ready."

She left, closing the door behind her. Paul immediately went to the black filing cabinet, unlocked it, and opened the bottom drawer. He lifted the top documents out and felt around the base.

Yes! There was the false bottom he found before, which he managed to lift out. Underneath it were several neatly stacked folders headed HG 176 with the patient's initials and number.

Paul had listed on his phone the numbers of the folders he remembered from his first visit. As good as his memory was, he wanted to confirm all the intricate details just in case. He scrutinised the hidden folders, each containing the raw patient data in the source files and the case report form. He needed to compare the original folders to those that had been duplicated. Paul drew out the equivalent numbered patient folders from the second drawer of the filing cabinet and compared the information.

It was clear that in the duplicate copy, the raw patient data had been transferred incorrectly to the case report form. The duplicate folders had been created and substituted, giving the impression that some patients were experiencing severe side effects, ultimately leading to the trial being terminated.

Fuelled by adrenalin, Paul didn't quite grasp the gravity of what he had just uncovered. His only objective was to get the proof. For each of the three patient folder numbers he recalled, Paul put together the case report form from the duplicate file and the raw data from the original, and took these to Anastasia to start copying. There were a lot of documents for each patient, and Paul hoped the photocopier would not falter until they were done.

Now that he had found the patient folder numbers he remembered, Paul returned to Alexievich's office and searched for additional evidence. If he located a significant number of patient folders plus the two he had from Hong Kong, he was sure there would be a factual basis for arguing that the trial should not terminate and, in fact, be resumed since patients needed the continuation of their medication. Going through the other folders, and searching for irregularities, would be time-consuming but had to be done.

Paul had found seven additional folders that he could use when he heard voices speaking in Russian. To his horror, he recognised the one was Alexievich. Anastasia had told him that the doctor was away, but that turned out to be incorrect. They were in deep trouble. Alexievich and Anastasia were speaking in raised voices. Paul switched off the light, hoping it had been extinguished in time. He debated whether to hide in the large built-in cupboard again, but his fear of claustrophobia mitigated that thought. He pressed himself into a corner of the office, out of the line of sight should the door open, but not entirely hidden.

The loud voices in the corridor eased, and Paul heard footsteps going past the office. He breathed a sigh of relief, almost disbelieving they had escaped the scrutiny that would have exposed their actions. In his moment of relief, Paul did not realise that Alexievich had seen the light under the door before it was turned off. The Russian doctor wanted to take action, but not by himself, of course.

Paul rushed to Anatoly Pavlyuchenko's office. Anastasia looked shocked and was trembling.

"I put him off but too close. We must get out quickly. Hurry with more folders."

Paul handed her the seven additional patient folders he had identified and then went back to hurriedly find more to complete the work. It was a painstaking job searching through the various folders to find the discrepancies. He had located one more when the office door burst open, and a figure wearing all black with a hooded mask entered the office. Paul was stunned and taken by surprise as he stood with a file in his hands.

The figure reached him in two steps, landing a punch in Paul's stomach. He collapsed forward, only to be straightened up again by a kick to his chest. He fell back against the desk, papers scattering from the dropped file. Paul had done some serious boxing and judo at school and university and, in this moment of peril, tried to recall some of the tactics used to overcome an opponent. He managed to block a follow-up punch and even threw a left hook to the chin of the sinister individual, but it had minimal effect. His opponent seemed to be made of steel.

Anastasia, hearing the commotion from Alexievich's office, came through the doorway to witness the life and death struggle unfolding before her. She threw herself onto the back of the assailant but, initially taken by surprise, he swung himself around and pushed her off him with force. She collapsed against one of the filing cabinets and lay there dazed for a moment.

The attacker had been distracted, and Paul took the opportunity to pick up a paperweight from the desk and smashed it onto the head of the dark figure. There was a cry of pain, and he stumbled back, partially tripping over Anastasia, still lying on the floor and trying to regain her senses. Paul wrapped his arms around the person's neck in a chokehold and executed a judo throw that flung his opponent to the ground – but only momentarily. He leapt forward at Paul and connected with a blow to Paul's cheek, who saw a spurt of blood shoot into the air as he fell back onto the desk. Paul's mind urged him to recover quickly; otherwise, it would all be over for him, and he would soon follow the fate of Tanel Valle, chopped up and stuffed into a suitcase.

As the figure leapt at him to render the coup de grâce, Paul managed to roll off the desk and onto the floor. As he landed, he saw Anastasia get up and leave the office and briefly had mixed feelings about that. Hopefully, she could escape his fate, but Paul needed help – any help. The attacker lunged at him, hissing a string of Russian words, and firmly placed his hands around Paul's neck. Slowly, Paul started to lose consciousness.

So, this was how it was going to end? He thought of the trial, he thought of Jill, and through the mists clouding his mind, he heard her call out, "Paul, Paul, save yourself!" He rallied in response to her vague presence, and with the last of his strength, he lashed out with his right leg to the crotch of his assailant. He heard an "Aargh!", the same male response in any language to a blow in that area.

Paul managed to get up as his opponent slumped down, but his relief was momentary. He was flung back onto the floor as the figure fell upon him again with his hands searching for Paul's neck. Paul felt his strength ebbing and thought this must be the end. He stared up into the ice-blue eyes of his murderer as they shone in a frenzied fashion through the two eyeholes in his black mask.

Paul vaguely thought he saw Anastasia come back into the office. Or did he? He felt a warm sensation wash over him as he realised this was where his life was to end. Paul looked once again into the eyes staring at him. Suddenly they enlarged with shock and pain – and then closed. The man fell to the side, and Paul saw Anastasia standing there with a scalpel clutched in her hand. She stabbed again, this time deep into their assailant's abdomen, and he let out an enraged cry.

Paul got to his feet, thinking the fight was over, but the man got up and turned on Anastasia, knocking her down. Paul was desperate, and the struggle lay in the balance. He suddenly remembered the ski poles in Alexievich's cupboard. He was sure his memory was not faulty even in his current dazed state. He opened the door, found a pole amongst the clothes and lab coats and pulled it out just as the figure turned to attack him. As his opponent lunged forward, Paul pushed the ski pole into his face and saw the tip of the rod plunge through the mask's eyehole and into the eye of his attacker, who let out a piercing scream and fell to the floor, clutching his face. Paul managed to kick him in the chest as he lay on the ground. Even in this state, the man got up, staggered to the door and out of the office, crying in pain.

Paul collapsed in a heap and lay there for a few moments. There was blood on his face and cuts on his arm where his surgical gown and shirt were torn. He ached all over and had difficulty swallowing where the man's hands had throttled him, but he had to check on Anastasia. He pulled himself up and went across the room to where she lay, concerned that she had been severely injured, but she managed to sit up.

"You are quite skilful with a scalpel, Doctor. You saved my life."

"It is all I can think of."

Anastasia told Paul that she had completed copying the ten

documents he had given her, and Paul knew that would have to be enough. He was starting to weaken from the beating he had taken, and they had to leave.

Paul returned the folders to the black filing cabinet; Anastasia gathered the copies, took Paul by the arm and said, "We're ready; let's go."

"I am surprised no security has come," Paul noted, "there was so much noise. That is very strange; almost as if someone ordered them to leave us alone."

"Come," said Anastasia, "we go now!"

As Paul followed Anastasia out and towards the elevator, he felt increasingly weak. He stumbled and held himself up against the wall.

"You okay?" Anastasia turned towards him with an anxious look.

"I feel a bit concussed but keep going."

Exiting the elevator, they passed the change room where Paul had put on the surgical gear, but they did not stop. Paul followed Anastasia to a Mercedes coupe in the parking area. She unlocked it, and he dropped into the passenger seat.

"Nice car," was all he could manage as he slumped back.

"Present from Anatoly for being a good girl, or maybe a bad girl," was all he heard before falling unconscious.

CHAPTER 30

The Evidence Mounts

Paul had only a vague recollection of the car journey and getting to Anastasia's apartment. He remembered stumbling and falling a few times as he went up the stairs and Anastasia struggling to pick him up. In one moment of clear functioning, he remembered asking her if she had the photocopies of the documents, and her "Da" gave him comfort before he slipped away again.

Paul could not differentiate between day and night. He seemed to have moments of wakefulness followed by dark clouds rolling over him. He thought he heard a voice calling his name, but there was no one. Or was there? When he regained consciousness briefly, he found he was in a bed but could not work out where the bed was. It didn't matter because he was alive and had some of the evidence he needed. He faded away again.

Later, starting to recover, he looked around the room, but it was dark, and he could not discern much. He knew that he was not in his hotel room. A door opened, partially illuminating the room. He saw a silhouette standing in the doorway. For an anxious moment, he feared it was the man in black who had attacked him. He was reassured when the figure spoke quietly.

"Paul, you awake?" It was Anastasia.

"Yes, just about," he croaked. His throat was still sore from where the pair of hands had tried to strangle him.

"Anastasia, where am I?"

"You in my apartment."

"Are you okay? Any injuries?"

"I fine, but you are messed up. I stitch cut on your face and arm while you unconscious. I no need anaesthetic; you were, as they say, counted out."

"You mean out for the count."

"Da," Anastasia smiled.

Against the light coming through the partially open door, Paul could see that she was wearing a gown. She undid the belt, and the gown fell into a crumpled mass of silk at her ankles. She was naked. As she pulled back the bedcover, Paul saw that he was naked too. She slid into the bed next to him.

Paul lay on his back but turned his head to face her, saying, "I must thank you. I thought it was the end for me when he was strangling me."

Anastasia was lying on her side, with her hand stroking his chest. He could feel the warmth of her body next to his.

"We both very lucky to be alive," she said.

"Who was that man, and how did Alexievich come to be in the hospital?"

"Maybe set a trap when he tell me he going away. I don't know. I think the man who attack us was Russian Mafia hitman."

"What does the Mafia have to do with a clinical trial?"

"I don't know link, but remember I tell you Alexievich have gambling problem with Mafia casinos. Maybe they have hold over him. I don't understand."

In the comfort of the bed and with the presence of Anastasia next to him, Paul felt himself falling asleep again. He heard her whisper his name a few times but was too tired or weak to reply. He felt a contentment he had not experienced for a long, long time.

Sometime later, he stirred again. Anastasia was asleep next to him with her arm over his chest. He moved slightly to take in the situation, as did she.

"Paul, how are you feeling?"

"Good."

She put her left leg across his and moved her body to partially lie across him. He felt her breast brush his chest.

"Are you very good?" she whispered.

"Yes."

She pushed herself further up onto him and kissed him, and he reciprocated by pulling her gently to lie on top of him. She kissed him again, and he responded to her tongue exploring his mouth.

"You don't have to do this, Paul."

He paused and kissed her back with the intensity of someone denied affection and the sensation of close bodily contact for months. The trauma of Jill's death, the toxic attitude and conflict that Melissa had brought to their relationship, the stress of trying to save the clinical trial – all had overwhelmed his senses. Now he was lost in this moment. All he could embrace was the sensation of Anastasia's body and how her exploring hands aroused him. She straddled and gently lowered herself onto him and brought their two bodies together with slow rhythmic movements. Their cumulative gasps filled the room until, within a short space of each other, they climaxed.

* * *

When Paul awoke again, weak sunlight filled the room. Anastasia was not in bed next to him. He suddenly wondered if it had been a dream, but he felt warmth of spirit that had been lost to him for so long. Lost in his thoughts, Paul was surprised when the door opened, and Anastasia entered carrying a tray. She put it down on the bed and climbed in, careful not to spill anything.

"I bring you Russian breakfast."

"You are the Russian breakfast," he smiled.

She leant over and kissed him, nearly spilling the tray.

"This is kielbasa sandwich with sausage and slices cheese. You will love it."

Paul was hungry, realising that he had not eaten before leaving the hotel. His jaw ached, making eating difficult, but he managed some of the sandwiches, followed by black coffee made in a French press.

After their meal, they lay back in bed. Paul's mind was starting to stir towards the events at the hospital and the evidence they had gathered.

"I want to look at the documents you photocopied last night."

"In good time. I ran bath for you."

She led him to the bathroom, and a quaint, old-fashioned stand-alone bathtub greeted Paul. Anastasia got in first and lay on her back.

"Come in; water is fine."

"So I notice."

Paul got in and lay on top of her. Soon the water was splashing over the edges of the bath as he made love to her again.

* * *

Paul got dressed, with Anastasia giving him one of Anatoly's shirts to replace his, which was torn and bloodstained. She put on her gown, and they went to the small dining room with its disproportionately large table, an heirloom, he remembered. There was the stack of documents they had photocopied the previous night.

"Since we didn't have much time last night to check these folders accurately, we need to go through them to confirm our suspicion that the raw data has been incorrectly transferred to the case report forms to create the impression that there are problems with the drug."

Paul settled down at the table, carefully examining the documents with Anastasia. She was involved with the trial, having treated some of the candidates.

In one of the duplicate cases they had copied, there appeared to be no side effects listed in the raw data, but the case report form reflected a number of these. The fabricated side effects included some fairly severe reactions like supraventricular tachycardia, atrial fibrillation and blood dyscrasias – all to do with heart conditions and blood disorders. In addition, there were also reports of neuropathies, like numbness, tingling, and muscle weakness.

In other folders, no side effects were recorded in the raw data written down by the nurses or treating doctors, but they appeared in the case report forms. These individual reports were the basis of the compilation of the summary report from the St Petersburg site, which would contribute to the termination of the trial.

Paul was perplexed but felt relief and some satisfaction that his memory had been the basis of detecting the discrepancies. Anastasia found the same questionable deviations in her pile of folders.

"Please, I need you to delay Anatoly signing the report that Alexievich is compiling to say that the trial is a failure. I must get back to Hong Kong and have time to review all the documents we have from the two sites showing the results are being manipulated. I must get a summary of the changes to the authorities before Hung's and Alexievich's reports reach them."

They were nearly finished going through the documentation when Paul was startled by his mobile phone ringing.

"Hello."

"Dr Beresford, this is Edward Collins."

"Hello, Mr Collins," Paul replied, feeling slightly uncomfortable talking to Jill's father with Anastasia, flimsily dressed in her gown, sitting opposite him.

"I found some information about Viscount Talbot's son from my financial sources. You are correct; he is looking to get involved in the industry by buying a pharmaceutical company and looks close to acquiring one. I don't know how this impacts you and your work, but it would appear to be a company in Northern Ireland."

"Thank you, Mr Collins. It is most helpful of you to establish this, and it's much appreciated. I am trying to determine why our trial appears to be in trouble, but I think I can solve it. I want the product to be available and, in memory of Jill, to help other women with this condition."

"That might give us some comfort."

"How are you and Alice … Mrs Collins, doing?"

"We are still struggling to come to terms with our situation."

"I understand."

There were no more words Paul could add to this sentiment. He had lost the love of his life, and they had lost their beloved daughter.

"Thank you, Mr Collins. I will return to Hong Kong tomorrow, where I hope to finish uncovering the evidence needed to finally prove that the drug is not failing."

"Hong Kong, you say. I've spent quite a bit of time there; it's a lovely city. I made many friendships there; important people too. Goodbye, Dr Beresford."

Paul stared at the phone for a while, many thoughts running through his mind. Edward Collins had consistently been formal with Paul. This seemed to indicate that there was still an element of distance and possibly resentment towards him from their early engagements to the circumstances of Jill's death. However, Edward had opened up a bit about spending time in Hong Kong. The brief conversation had brought back the memory of Jill – even if it was never far from his mind.

And then there was the information that Sean St Ledger was trying to get into the pharmaceutical industry. What was the purpose behind that? Parts of the mystery were starting to come together, but the big picture remained vague.

Paul looked up to see Anastasia staring quizzically at him.

"That was my partner's father."

"You married?"

"No, she was my girlfriend."

"Where she now?"

"She died."

"I sorry. From what she die?"

"She died of complications following breast cancer."

"I so, so, sorry."

Anastasia got up and moved around the table to console Paul, who was by now visibly upset.

"I want our drug to succeed so that other women don't have to go through the trauma that devastated Jill, me and her family."

"Now I understand passion to get to truth of the trial and risks you take."

"Thank you. I need the help you are giving me, but I'm concerned about the danger I am exposing you to – such as last night."

"I want help you and fuck Alexievich."

Paul grinned at this beautiful Russian girl in her elegant gown, barely covering her figure, spitting out that expletive.

"Besides the trial, something strange is going on with a person who knew Jill and me. It's too complicated to explain fully, so briefly, he is rich and powerful. He is from a noble family and regards me as lower social status. He also knew and wanted to possess Jill. He wants to get into the pharmaceutical industry by buying a company, and I think I know what he is up to. He probably wants to compete with my company, Harrowgate, and beat us at our own game to show how good he is. He and I had an altercation in our schooldays which brought great shame on his family. He hated me for that and declared that he would destroy me however long it took."

"Destroy you? From your schooldays?"

"Yes, these resentments can last a long time in the English class system."

CHAPTER 31

A Brush with Death

Paul and Anastasia completed sifting through the balance of the documents. Paul was satisfied that there was deliberate interference with the transfer of data showing HG 176 in a poor light which, at face value, would lead to the trial's termination and the drug deemed a failure.

"I had a suspicion of what is going on, and I think the parts of the puzzle are starting to fit together. Here in St Petersburg, Dr Alexievich wants to corrupt the trial to make Professor Pavlyuchenko, as Principal Investigator, look incompetent so that he can replace the professor as Head of Oncology and Hospital Superintendent. As you've explained, Anatoly cannot exercise control over the trial because of his affair with you. But the attack on us in the hospital – probably linked to Alexievich – shows a far more ominous element."

"Da, I think so," Anastasia confirmed.

"In Hong Kong, Professor Hung has some strange personal problem compelling him to alter the trial results. And in another piece of the jigsaw, Sean St Ledger is going to buy a pharmaceutical company in Ireland to compete with Harrowgate, possibly also in the field of cancer, to triumph over me. These two separate events appear to have coalesced to make the trial appear unsound."

Anastasia still had an outstanding issue. "I still think what happened with Tanel Valle and why?"

"Yes, you're correct," Paul agreed, "that is unresolved at the moment. Alexievich did not have much time for him – unjustly – but that doesn't explain the tragedy."

Paul felt that he had gathered sufficient evidence to throw doubt on the erratic trial results; he needed to get back to Hong Kong.

"I need to show these results to Melissa James; she is the ultimate expert in these cases."

"Melissa. She your girlfriend now?"

Paul laughed at Anastasia's response and moved around the table to kiss her. "No, not at all. She is very attractive, but she is definitely not my girlfriend. She is nothing like you," he reassured her.

"Good to know," she smiled.

"I must get a flight to Hong Kong urgently, but first I need to get back to the hotel to collect my things. I must call a taxi."

"I take you to hotel and to airport. I am not work today."

"Won't Anatoly wonder what has happened to you?"

"No, in our relationship, he understand if I am not around."

"Okay, let me contact the airline and get moving."

Paul managed to get a late afternoon flight, and Anastasia took him to the hotel to check out and collect his luggage. He packed the copied folders, which held the crucial information and verification of the trial's efficacy, into his suitcase.

Crossing the hotel lobby, Paul thought he recognised two men standing among the mingling hotel residents as those he saw at the Hermitage Museum when meeting with Tanel. Given the attack at the hospital, Paul was shocked and paralysed for a moment, but time was tight, and he may have been mistaken. He got into Anastasia's car but decided not to mention the two men. He did not want to put additional pressure on her.

Pulkovo Airport lies about twelve miles to the south of St Petersburg, and the journey on the Pulkovskoye Highway usually takes less than half an hour in off-peak hour traffic. Anastasia set off, leaving Nevsky Prospect and the city centre behind.

In a less densified area near the airport, Paul noticed Anastasia kept looking in her rear-view mirror.

"Something wrong?"

"Yes, I think we being followed."

"Are you sure?"

"Yes, a black BMW following for some time. It can overtake but does not. It stay two car behind. If car come between them and us, it overtake to stay two behind."

"Are you sure? Perhaps after what we have been through, you are imagining things," he tried to reassure her, but his thoughts went back to the two men in the hotel lobby.

"I am positive," she insisted.

"Speed up or slow down; let's see what happens then."

The road seemed unusually empty for the time of day, but there was a car behind her, a Lada. Anastasia accelerated the Mercedes, leaving a gap between it and the Lada. Immediately the BMW accelerated and started overtaking the Lada. As it drew parallel with the vehicle, the BMW suddenly swerved, pushing the Lada off the road and into a ditch.

Anastasia couldn't see any other vehicles nearby as the BMW filled her rear-view mirror. Paul looked behind to see the bulky BMW 7 series on their tail.

"Can you go faster?"

"Not much faster if I want feel safe."

Given their situation, the irony of her statement was lost on her. She accelerated again and looked into the rear view mirror; the BMW was right behind her.

"What we do now, Paul?" Anastasia urged, but Paul could not offer any suggestion or solution at that moment.

Anastasia quickly reached into her jacket pocket and pulled out her phone. Alternating between keeping the BMW in sight, her eyes on the road and scrolling through her phone, she dialled a number, then turned the phone off and slid it back into her pocket.

The BMW pulled up alongside their car. Paul looked across to see two masked men in the car, and his mind flashed back to the incident at the hospital with the man similarly masked. These men must be from the same crew, he thought, just as the BMW started to push Anastasia's Mercedes off the road.

The two cars ran in parallel for a while until, with a side road up ahead, the BMW lurched across their vehicle, forcing it down the side road. Hundreds of yards into the side road, the BMW shunted the coupé towards a thicket of birch trees. Anastasia braked urgently, and the two cars came to a halt.

Before Paul or Anastasia could move, the two men stood beside their car with guns drawn. One of the men shouted something in Russian.

"They want us get out and keep hands up," said Anastasia, her voice tense but low.

Slowly, they climbed out of the Mercedes and followed the instructions. Paul felt an overwhelming sense of despair as there was nothing he could think to do to remedy the situation. He could retaliate against the masked man in the hospital, but with guns involved, that was not an option here. And to compound matters, he had placed Anastasia in extreme danger for a second time.

One of the men spoke to Anastasia. "He want you get luggage and put it in his car," she said, trying to remain neutral.

Paul was mystified. He knew that crime was a problem in Russia, but to go to this extreme to rob him of his suitcase was bizarre. Anastasia opened the boot of the Mercedes, and Paul removed his suitcase and briefcase. He was about to transfer it to the BMW when the man shouted something at Anastasia.

"He want you open the suitcase."

Paul did so, and the man pushed him aside and rummaged through the contents. He found the copied folders and held them up triumphantly, waving them at his companion. It became clear what this was all about; the recovery of the clinical trial documents to prevent them from being used as evidence of foul play.

Before Paul could digest the significance of this, the men ordered Paul and Anastasia to stand with their hands resting on the car. They were blindfolded, their hands tied behind their backs, and shoved onto the BMW's rear seat. The men closed the doors, got in and drove off.

For the second time, Paul felt he was facing his untimely end. He tried to loosen his hands from the ropes binding them. It would be better to go down fighting rather than being shot in the head execution-style, dissected and scattered.

One of the men shouted something, and Anastasia said to Paul, "He has gun pointed at me. He shoot me if you try to escape."

Hearing that, Paul conceded there was nothing more he could do. He gave up struggling and whispered to Anastasia, "Please forgive me for what I have gotten you into. I am desperately sorry."

"Don't worry. It not all over yet," she murmured.

Paul could not fathom that statement; she must be an eternal optimist. Hopefully, they might spare her.

In his final hours or minutes, he wanted to focus on his time with Jill and relive their memories together – their first meeting in Cape Town, their lives while at the legal practice and the orthopaedic hospital. He tried to blot out the move to Harrowgate and his time at Harvard, which probably contributed to Jill neglecting her cancer. All this had led him to be imprisoned in a car hurtling to his and Anastasia's death. His mind battled to focus on the good times as he felt deep despair about how he had brought himself to this point.

He was suddenly aware that the car was accelerating. Was it trying to get to its destination quicker to finish them off? They would destroy the patient folders, the central body of evidence of the deceit within the trials. Melissa and Devon would be unaware of Paul and Anastasia's fate or their findings. Without Paul's evidence, they only had the two folders in Hong Kong, which, in all likelihood, would not prove their case. The trial would be jettisoned, and all hopes that HG 176 would successfully be launched in memory of Jill would disappear.

Paul's thoughts were interrupted by the BMW speeding up and driving erratically. Although he could not understand what the two men were saying, their anxious tones were unmistakable, becoming more panicked.

The next moment, Paul heard shots being fired. The car suddenly veered to the right, and there was a loud, repetitive thudding noise. Paul guessed a tyre had been shot out as the BMW swerved wildly. Who could be attacking the BMW? Then shots were fired from their car; the kidnappers were firing back.

The car veered erratically until it came to a halt with a shattering crash. The doors flung open, followed by more shots. It seemed their kidnappers were trying to escape. He heard a scream, more shots and then a final fusillade – followed by silence.

Paul was stunned, not comprehending what had happened. He heard the car's rear doors open and again wondered if these would be his final moments.

A voice called out, "Anastasia?"

"Dmitry!" she cried.

There was an exchange in Russian.

"Paul," Anastasia shouted, "we are saved."

"I don't believe it!"

Relief washed over him as he felt someone untying his hands. Ripping off his blindfold, Paul saw a man in military gear undoing Anastasia's bonds. She, too, took off her blindfold and hugged the man, exchanging words in a brief staccato conversation.

Paul got out of the wrecked vehicle and surveyed the scene. They were in a deserted industrial area. The two kidnappers lay motionless on the ground in growing pools of blood. Despite one of the men's masks, Paul could see a gaping head wound. The other lay in a crumpled mass on his back, sightless eyes gazing up at the sky. Two vehicles and armed men in military uniforms stood nearby except for one crouching down, holding his leg.

Anastasia rushed to Paul and hugged him. "Are you okay?" he asked, hugging her back.

"Yes, thank God. Dmitry my uncle and work in Special Services; one thing that still work in Russia," she explained. "Remember I use my phone when we were chased?"

"Yes, I was wondering what you were trying to do."

"Dmitry give me special number to call if I ever in trouble. I do not have to speak, only call for severe emergency. I think this was emergency. He track our position by my phone."

"I can't believe we have survived this," Paul gasped as he turned to address Anastasia's uncle. "Who were the men who captured us?"

He replied to Anastasia, who translated for him.

"He say it look like Mafia hitmen. They take bodies away to identify."

Despite the extreme circumstances they had just experienced, Paul's mind returned to their primary task.

"I need to get back to the airport; I don't want to miss my flight. I also need to get my luggage from the car."

He opened the boot of the wrecked BMW and retrieved his suitcase and briefcase.

"Dmitry say a car will take you to airport," Anastasia confirmed. He help me get my car. His men take BMW and bodies."

"Please thank him. I am very grateful," said a relieved Paul.

Paul placed the luggage in the unmarked car, and before he got in, Anastasia approached him and kissed him. "This is goodbye? I see you again?"

"I don't know. I need to get back to Hong Kong urgently to gather all the information on the trial."

"And back to Melissa?"

"Yes and no. I need her help, but she is not important to me like you are," Paul smiled as he caressed her cheek.

"Goodbye, Paul."

He got into the car and with a siren blaring, headed off to the airport.

CHAPTER 32

Jigsaw Pieces

On the flight to Hong Kong, Paul reflected on the past few days in St Petersburg, which had changed so many things for him. He thought of the struggle in the hospital and the eventual success in identifying and copying clinical documents that would support his contention that a malign force was influencing the trial.

Then there was the frightening car journey and his and Anastasia's capture and dramatic release. Paul had felt utterly helpless in those circumstances, and for a second time, his actions could have led to perilous consequences for someone close to him – Anastasia. She had done so much to help Paul and had come to mean so much to him.

He had to put all that behind him, as there was now a desperate race to confirm the body of evidence that he, Devon and Melissa had compiled between them. Did they have enough evidence to forestall the termination of the trial? Would it be possible to get more information from Professor Hung? Would a forensic examination of their documentation under less frantic circumstances in Hong Kong prove their case? Paul had to admit he required Melissa's and Devon's review of the St Petersburg information to confirm his beliefs.

In the hotel, Paul phoned both Melissa and Devon, asking them to come to his room to study some documents he had acquired under what he called 'challenging circumstances'. They were intrigued and arranged to meet Paul in an hour.

At the agreed time, there was a knock on his door.

"Good God, what has happened to you?" was Melissa's first comment when she saw him.

With his preoccupation over the past few hours, Paul had forgotten about his injuries from the hospital fight – the stitched cut on his face, the bruising, and the wound on his upper arm staining his white shirt. He realised why he had encountered some strange looks at the airport and on the plane.

"So, what did the other guy look like?" said Devon with a grin.

"Completely untouched," was Paul's dry response. "Come on in. I have something to show you."

He led them to the suite's small lounge, where a pile of documents sat on the desk.

"Have a look at these folders," Paul indicated. "From my interpretation, there is a mixture of strange information. These are copies of the duplicated folders from St Petersburg."

Paul explained that the duplicate folders had identical patient reference numbers to other folders from the trial. In other words, there were two folders for some patients. In these, the case report form showed cardiovascular and neurological side effects, but the raw data in each file did not show these findings. The case report form represented the summary of the patient's clinical profile and would have been used to compile a report justifying the termination of the trial.

"The raw data would not have been looked at again assuming it had been reviewed, so that is probably why nobody picked up the discrepancies," Paul said, "but I need you two experts to confirm your thoughts to see if they match my considered opinion," said Paul.

"How did you manage to get hold of these?" questioned Melissa, staring in surprise at the substantial stack of folders.

"With difficulty," said Paul. He decided to withhold the details of his experiences.

Devon looked at him quizzically. "It must have been a tough ask?"

"Let's not go there," he answered.

Melissa and Devon sat down at the table and started reviewing the folders.

* * *

In St Petersburg, Dr Alexievich was gripped by panic as things began unravelling. His interactions with that Medvedeva woman in the hospital showed that someone was trying to ruin his plans. Was she trying to protect her lover, the professor? Was she acting alone to try to foil his efforts to scupper the trial? Or was there something else at play?

He needed to compile his summary document on the trial and the array of supposed adverse side effects associated with HG 176. The summary would be sent to Pavlyuchenko, and he would have to sign it off if he wanted to keep his position as Hospital Superintendent, his role as Head of Oncology, his marriage and his affair with Medvedeva. This signed document would prove that the medicine was a failure and the trial needed to be terminated immediately.

It would then make its way to the Chief Investigator in England, who would, in turn, forward it to the Ethics Committee, who had approved the trial's go-ahead in the first place. Case closed. That would complete his side of the bargain, and they would let him off. If only it were that simple.

The person Alexievich referred to as his 'minder' contacted him to say that something had gone wrong at the hospital that night with their 'representative'. The minder did not explain what happened, but something must have been awry to cause his anger. Alexievich was told that he had better get on with completing his report, or he might also be taking a trip with his suitcase – but inside it. This sent shivers down Alexievich's spine. He also needed to work on his problem; otherwise, they may come calling again.

Putting a 'Do Not Disturb' sign on his office door handle, he prepared to write his report. He drew out the bundle of folders on the trial. He then went to the black filing cabinet, removed the false bottom and extracted the 'other folders', as he referred to them. He noticed they were in disarray, seemingly out of order. This only exacerbated his anxiety – someone had been interfering with the documents. Probably that damn woman, again trying to protect her lover.

He needed to urgently complete his report and include the serious adverse events he falsely attributed to the product. He sat down at his computer and typed:

Clinical Trial Summary Report: Termination of Double Blind Study of HG 176 (terpazamab) for the treatment of Metastatic Breast Cancer in women.

* * *

In England, Sean St Ledger was digesting the latest news from Crispin Wake-Armstrong, and his mind drifted over the events of the past weeks.

When he contacted Giles Robinson to arrange the trip with Jill on the company jet to the Irish pharmaceutical company, he could not believe it when told that she had taken ill. Not long after, followed the devastating call from Robinson with the news that she had died. Sean's plans to seduce her on the flight had been in place, and the flight was to be the realisation of his yearnings since his Oxford days. He imagined how she would writhe and cry out, begging for more as he pleasured her. Surely she would change her mind about Doctor Paul, given the ecstasy she had experienced – both from a physical and lifestyle point of view. He wanted to win her over, but her death denied him that.

From a distance at Jill's funeral, Sean observed the man who had made his life a misery. Paul, who had delighted in the girl he ached for and placed him in jeopardy with his father, Viscount Talbot; Sean could lose his position as heir to the Viscountcy. His inheritance, title and wealth could be lost to an illegitimate older half-brother. The thought made him sick.

The plan Sean had put in place to prove himself to his father and triumph over Paul was a tenuous one relying on several moving parts. Crispin had brought Sean news of a hiccup in St Petersburg that could cause things to fall apart, but the people he dealt with there had a ruthless efficiency. Sean was confident they would overcome any eventuality that threatened their arrangement. Perhaps he needed to visit St Petersburg and Hong Kong and contact his collaborators to see what was happening on the ground and ensure that none of those foreigners screwed up his carefully laid plans.

* * *

In Berkhamsted, JP sat at his desk, staring at the document in front of him. It was a preliminary offer to purchase Harrowgate Pharmaceuticals. Next to it lay the morning's edition of the Financial Times. Financial institutions track developments in new products from listed pharmaceutical companies, and at the bottom of page three was an article headed 'Blockbuster Drug Failing?'.

The author and healthcare editor, Jason Edwards, lamented the possible demise of a potential leading product from Harrowgate, one of the UK's bright new pharmaceutical companies. He reported that multicentre trials had been put on hold.

Harrowgate, he observed, initially seemed to be following in the footsteps of those UK giants such as GlaxoSmithKline and Astra Zeneca, which were the pride of the country's pharmaceutical skills. The discovery of a new chemical entity would change Harrowgate's status overnight as it had done for others.

With GlaxoSmithKline, it was Zantac, which reduces gastric acid and treats peptic ulcers. By 1987, it had become the biggest-selling prescription drug.

For AstraZeneca, or at least the Astra portion of it, it was Losec. Astra made a radical breakthrough in the understanding of peptic ulcer treatment. It was discovered that ulcers are driven not only by excess stomach acid but also by a bacterium, helicobacter pylori. Losec overtook Zantac and, at its peak, became the biggest-selling prescription medicine worldwide.

Both breakthroughs had put the respective companies centre stage in their industry. Such is the race and pressure to keep finding new chemical molecules to minimise or erase diseases afflicting humankind.

Once a company has discovered a so-called 'magic bullet', a sales and marketing infrastructure is needed to deliver this on a commanding scale. Compared to research and development, the pharmaceutical industry's spending on sales and marketing has often attracted criticism. But JP knew, from his extensive time in the industry, that this is pivotal for success in a highly competitive marketplace. He also knew that Harrowgate, as a small company, did not have deep pockets to fund this type of marketing. He needed HG 176 to succeed to start generating revenues to underpin the massive sales expense and expansion.

JP allowed himself a fleeting thought that the article may not be noticed that much at the bottom of page three but soon dismissed the idea as grasping at straws. Analysts, businesspeople, and government would closely study the Financial Times, and even on page three, this article was a full-frontal disclosure of the current weakness of JP's position.

The article would have a further knock-on effect on the company's share price, which was still under pressure and heading south, and with it, JP's hopes of recouping the family fortune he had invested in the company. He would be devastated to lose the family farm; it would have to be sold to meet his debts.

Not only had he invested in the company itself but also in its people. He had placed so much faith in Paul Beresford, whom he saw as someone with unique skills and the person who could probably succeed him when he retired. JP had hired Paul against internal advice based on his lack of experience, but he had sent him to Harvard and invested in his commercial development. It was tragic what happened to his girlfriend. Perhaps this event had a larger than expected impact on Paul, making him less effective, but all that aside, JP found Paul's feedback miles off course.

There is always an element of risk when you hire someone, as you only really know how they'll turn out once they've worked in the job for a while. In interviews, people project such positive images of themselves that you have to trust they can actually do the work.

But Paul had been different. There were no such pretensions about him. He came across as modest, almost self-effacing, but the sharp mind behind that persona intrigued JP. The pre-employment test results had shown Paul to be exceptional in many areas.

By contrast, Melissa had projected herself as clinical, driven, and cold. She could easily be his successor if he were to retire – which was his plan once HG 176 was successfully launched. But her task-driven lack of empathy worried JP and how it would impact the staff he had come to see as his family.

JP knew he was becoming emotional, and his judgement was under pressure. He was aware that he sometimes let his feelings run away with him. In moments of such weakness, he often shared some of these thoughts with Tom Hewitt, the Marketing Director. He had worked with Tom when they were both at Shire Pharmaceuticals in Dublin. JP had recognised Tom as a creative Brand Manager. When JP resigned from Shire, he took Tom to Harrowgate as Marketing Director.

Despite his role and the stereotypical views of flamboyant marketing personalities, Tom was calm and level-headed and often served as a sounding board for JP when his emotions started to overwhelm him. Tom urged caution and avoidance of any rash moves regarding the company's future.

As JP turned back to the document on his desk, the door to his office opened, and Mildred entered carrying a pot of coffee and some cakes.

"I have brought you some of your favourite goodies to cheer you up."

"It might take a lot more than those, I'm afraid."

"Don't worry. I have faith in Paul to solve the problem."

"Ha!" he snorted. "You just like him because he is so good-looking."

"Yes, that too, as well as his abilities. Enjoy your cakes."

* * *

In Surrey, Eddie Collins sat in the study of his country home, reflecting on life and death. He knew that he and Alice would never get over the loss of Jill. She had been the focus of his life, and he always talked to friends and strangers about his beautiful and talented daughter. He had lived out some of his life through her activities and successes, and her death had left a gaping wound in their lives.

Coming from a humble background, Eddie had striven for success against all odds, becoming a person of status among the wealthy and elite. His business was thriving, and he had established branches worldwide following successful exports to several countries. With the loss of Jill, it meant nothing to him. That occasion when he bumped into his former boss 'Fergie' at Ascot and treated him with an air of disdain; even that counted for nothing.

A parent should never have to bury a child, went the saying. It was so true – and devastating.

Eddie thought he would see Jill married into a titled family to complete his design for her, for that is what she deserved. But that, too, had been derailed. She had met and fallen for this doctor who she met in Cape Town.

So many times, Alice had told him how much in love Jill and

Paul were, but it was hard for Eddie to reconcile. He thought Sean St Ledger the perfect match for Jill, but she had rebelled against this. Why, when St Ledger had everything? But now, based on a conversation with the doctor, it would appear that St Ledger was a destructive force in Jill's life. Could this really be believed coming from the doctor, who, after all, had his own agenda? He even had the audacity to ask Eddie for help.

He thought back to that first encounter with the doctor at the hospital after Jill had fallen off her horse. He was so rude and dismissive. Then they met again when Jill brought him to Eddie's London townhouse.

That evening had revealed something surprising; Beresford was the son of Richard Beresford, the international rugby player. Eddie's passion for rugby developed from his playing days at university, where his bulk made him a valuable addition to any team.

He had followed Rugby League in Yorkshire but swapped allegiance to Rugby Union when he went to London and supported the Harlequins rugby team. Through his support and funding, Eddie got to know many of the players who he now counted as friends. He often travelled to follow some teams when they played in overseas tournaments. It was a fun pastime that his newfound wealth enabled him to enjoy.

Through these rugby associations, Eddie made some valuable business and political connections. He wondered if these may have relevance in the current circumstances.

CHAPTER 33

A Race to the Finish

Devon and Melissa settled down to work their way through the pile of documents. It was time-consuming to match the raw data to its transfer into the case report forms, and Paul ordered some snacks and drinks to sustain them during their task.

While they were casting their expert eyes over the evidence, Paul sat in one of the chairs in the small lounge and pulled out Jill's diaries from his briefcase to reread her notes. As Paul paged through them, he could hear Jill's voice again as she transcribed her thoughts into words.

Suddenly, he heard Melissa gasp as she came across blatant errors in the documentation, which pointed to fraud being exercised against the trial.

"I simply don't believe what I'm seeing here," was Melissa's comment as she took a moment to sit back and digest her findings. "In all my time in the pharma industry, I have never seen such a denial of the facts. These women were progressing outstandingly well on the treatment. To deny them the continuation of HG 176 is not only a perversion of justice; it borders on criminal."

"What or who do you think is responsible, Paul?" asked Devon. "You have been at the heart of the St Petersburg investigation."

Paul did not want to divulge all the thoughts and activities he had experienced.

Melissa chipped in, "There seems to be some internal politics between the Study Coordinator, Dr Alexievich, and the Principal Investigator, Professor Pavlyuchenko."

Based on his findings, Paul was convinced there was a deeper issue involved, even though Melissa had identified only some of the elements at play.

"Those are extreme tactics," noted Devon, who swirled the ice in his glass of whisky.

Paul regretted ordering drinks as soon as Devon registered his preference. He hoped that Devon's penchant for a touch of alcohol would not derail the urgent work that lay before them.

"What are the next steps here, Melissa?" asked Paul, anxious to progress.

Melissa explained that she and Devon needed to complete their assessment of the files and document their findings in a report to go to Professor Reich as Chief Investigator. He would then forward it to the Ethics Committees in each country where the trial was taking place; they had placed the trial on a temporary halt and would need to consider the evidence for resumption. The Ethics Committees would also receive the reports from Hung and Pavlyuchenko, which would argue to terminate the trial.

"This is a race to the finish," Melissa exclaimed. "If the Ethics Committees get the other reports first and terminate the trial, it will be difficult to argue our case since caution and safety will prevail over our efforts."

"How long will it take you two to complete this?" Paul's anxiety was evident in his voice.

There were a number of crucial issues coalescing in his mind. The trial had been suspended for nearly two weeks at the multicentre locations, and women had not been receiving their treatment. They could not be left in limbo much longer. They needed to restart HG 176 urgently, or the trial data would be worthless.

In addition, Paul was privy to the fact that JP was sitting with an offer to sell the business as the company's share price was in freefall.

JP probably had a figure in mind based on an acceptable share price where he could get out, minimising his losses. Who knows what would happen with the company and who would take over? Paul had to head this off at the pass, and the only way to do so was with the report from Devon and Melissa.

Paul suggested that Devon and Melissa book one of the business meeting rooms in the hotel to carry out their work. He was feeling overcome with fatigue as the activities of the past days started catching up with him, and he needed to rest. They agreed and gathered up the documentation, leaving him to sleep.

* * *

Safely ensconced in his office, Dr Alexievich typed away furiously at his computer. There was an urgency to complete his report and doom HG 176 to its final death.

He carefully mixed and matched the various raw data files and case report forms to generate his desired outcome. It was complicated and required intense concentration. He was short on sleep and nutrition, having locked himself away for the best part of two days. There were moments when he transferred data incorrectly because of his fatigue. He rubbed his eyes, put his head down on the desk for a moment's sleep, got another cup of coffee and carried on.

There also seemed to be a tense standoff in the department. The professor and his bitch were ignoring him and were seldom around. He knew that Medvedeva was trying to sabotage his work; she wanted to save womankind with this drug, while he wanted to save his life. Alexievich knew one day his habit would get him into trouble, and that day had arrived with stark reality. He had crossed the wrong people, and they were after him. His only opportunity to get them off his back was by undermining the trial and settling his debt. He must not fail, else he might end up like that nosy, interfering Estonian.

Alexievich needed the professor to be available to sign the trial document, thereby retaining his position as Superintendent and saving his marriage. The signature would seal the deal and get Alexievich off the hook with his so-called 'friends'.

But that Medvedeva woman seemed to be acting as the professor's gatekeeper. She was not his secretary, for fuck's sake. With her aristocratic heritage, she always treated him in an offhand manner. He had disliked her from the time he started working in the hospital. What was she up to trying to delay the report? She must know that the professor had to sign it to keep his position and her as his mistress.

Anastasia was keenly aware that Paul needed time to get the copied documents summarised and a report generated to prove the trial results were being tampered with. The report then needed to be despatched to England and the trial organisers. This would take time, and she had to keep Alexievich away from the professor – and his signature. She persuaded Anatoly to pretend to be ill and take time away from the hospital. Alexievich would not be able to contact Anatoly, which would stall the sign-off of the report. But these tactics could not last forever.

* * *

Sean readied himself for a trip to Beijing and St Petersburg. He knew there were some problems with his scheme in the latter, and he wanted to touch base with those contacts.

He was also anxious to see how the Chinese arm of his strategy was working out. He had not had the level of feedback he wanted from either group, although given the underhand nature of the arrangement, that was not altogether surprising. Sean wasn't sure he could trust these bloody foreigners to do his bidding, and he wanted to make sure for himself that all was on track.

He had readied the company jet for his mission. His father was curious as to why the jet was being used so extensively, to which he responded that it was linked to his acquisition strategy, which his father seemed to accept.

Sean wanted to get a copy of the reports from the two sites before they were formally submitted as he needed to show them to a key person in his plan. He packed, advised Crispin to hold the fort, and set off for Heathrow to meet with the crew and fly to Beijing.

Sean's Hawker 800 XP jet touched down at Capital International Airport in Beijing at the end of an exceptionally long but comfortable trip, punctuated by a fuel stop. He had decided to take the Talbot jet for a particular reason. As a scion of the Talbot family, he would attract too much attention flying on a commercial flight. He needed to maintain a low profile on this trip as he wanted his activities to go as unnoticed as possible.

During the journey, Sean gazed at the couch in the cabin, which could be converted into a bed. He imagined what could have taken place there. That yearning had been denied to him, but he had another strategy in its place, even though it was not the primary one he desired.

Meeting Sean at the airport was Alexander Leong from the Talbot organisation. He had been sworn to secrecy on the threat of losing his job. News of these clandestine activities could not get back to Viscount Talbot in the short term until Sean had achieved his objectives.

Leong took Sean to a luxury hotel with his reservation under an alias. It was arranged that the contact from the Chinese Central Committee would come through in the morning with the evidence that Sean needed.

* * *

Professor Hung sat in the small study in his house in Guangzhou, also known by its English name of Canton, a port city only about seventy-five miles northwest of Hong Kong on the Pearl River. He was exhausted for several reasons.

Hung's elderly mother and his sister were with him, under house arrest. They could not fully comprehend why they were being detained or what crime had embittered powers of the Central Committee, and this weighed on the professor. His mother was unwell, and his sister chafed against the restrictions and wanted to break out one night, but he had to rein her in with untruths.

He was also drained from producing a report on HG 176 that misrepresented its actual findings. He would be discredited in the scientific community if it were ever divulged that he had abused his authority. Who would ever understand that he had been forced to abandon his principles? His sparkling international career would be utterly demolished. He was told that the house arrest might be lifted if he did everything he was instructed to do. However, there were no guarantees – this was an authoritarian state, after all.

Hung had completed his report on the drug trial. He needed to send this to his friend Professor Reich, the medicines regulatory authorities and the Ethics Committees. The committees would recommend the termination of the trial. He understood all that, but the Central Committee representative had passed on a strange request regarding their demands of him. Hung was instructed to hold back for a few days on the electronic copy and produce a signed hard copy of the report that would be collected from him.

He could not follow the intricacies of everything that had befallen him and his family, but he knew he had to try to escape and take his mother and sister to safety. He had initiated steps to achieve this, but there were gaps in the plan, and failure would result in retribution against him and his family.

There were precedents for escaping house arrest, but these were few and far between. A prominent example was Chen Guangcheng, the blind civil rights activist who had climbed over the wall of his house and made it to the American Embassy, but he was one of the lucky ones.

For Hung, Hong Kong and safety were nearby but seemed light-years away. He needed outside help. Who could he turn to? Was Devon Ridley that person? They had been good friends until he had to undermine Devon and remove him from the trial investigation.

Would Devon hold that against him, or would he be dependable? Hung had to take a risk and try to reach out to Devon.

* * *

In St Petersburg, Anastasia was starting to run out of ideas and excuses to prevent Dr Alexievich from gaining access to Professor Pavlyuchenko to sign off the final report recommending the termination of the trial of HG 176. This report would be sent to the Chief Investigator in England, the medicines regulatory authorities in the various countries where the trial was being conducted, and other committees overseeing the results.

Then Alexievich pestered her less and less to see the professor. She was surprised and suspicious of his lack of action, or maybe her delay tactics were working. With Anatoly out of reach, Alexievich couldn't send the report.

However, she was unaware that Alexievich had been contacted by his 'friends' telling him to delay the electronic reports but to get a signed hard copy to them. That created a problem for him. Even if he reached Anatoly, the professor would want to sign off both hard and electronic documents to get him off his back and get on with his life. But to get his 'friends' off his own back, Alexievich had to get a signed hard copy. He had been warned about what would happen if he didn't.

Alexievich decided on a plan to forge the professor's signature on the hard copy. He had some examples of that signature and spent time practising it repeatedly. When the time came to put pen to paper, he sweated and hoped his surgical hand would be steady. It was, and he was satisfied with the result. Nearly home and dry. Now he had to wait for instructions for the meeting later that day with those who had cast a shadow over him.

Anastasia was suspicious of what Alexievich was up to. Why had he stopped asking her to see Anatoly? She arranged for him to be called out to an emergency in the ward, allowing her to access his office and the black filing cabinet. It was locked – no surprises there. She went to his desk drawer, where she knew he kept his keys. They were not there. He must have anticipated her move. She pulled and tugged on the filing cabinet drawers, but they were firmly locked.

Anastasia gave up and was about to leave his office when her eye caught sight of something in his wastepaper bin. She reached in and pulled out a couple of crumpled pieces of paper. Opening one, it was covered with copies of Anatoly's signature. Taken aback, she suddenly understood Alexievich's fallback plan. If she continued to keep him from seeing Anatoly to sign off the report – he would simply sign it himself! However, Anatoly would have to sign off both the hard and electronic documents, and Alexievich couldn't forge the signature on the electronic report; that was a protected file, only accessible by Anatoly.

Anastasia felt confident that Paul still had time to produce the report of evidence of trial results tampering. But she needed to remain vigilant. Alexievich was a cunning individual, and now that she knew he was capable of foul play, she had to make sure she wasn't outmanoeuvred.

* * *

Melissa and Devon booked themselves into one of the hotel's meeting rooms and started their detailed analysis of the documents. They noted the irregularities and started to compile a set of notes to serve as the basis of their report on the manipulation of the efficacy and safety results of HG 176. Melissa was concerned when Devon ordered more drinks and snacks for them.

"Thirsty work this," was his retort. "We'll be here late, so we need to attend to our needs."

They both applied themselves to their tasks. Later in the evening, Melissa excused herself, needing to shower, freshen up, and cancel a dinner date with friends.

"Don't worry, I'll carry on in your absence," reassured Devon.

Meanwhile, Paul was relaxing in his room, reading more of Jill's diaries. Initially, it caused him distress, but he now found consolation in her words. It was like having a conversation with her; even though most of her notes were devoted to her work, there were references to her thoughts on the pharmaceutical industry – and to him. Her devotion to their relationship comforted him, but he ached for what he was missing. Tired from his recent activities and emotional from reading Jill's words, he put the diary down and allowed himself to drift off to a much-needed sleep.

His peace was shattered by his phone ringing and even more by Melissa's anxious voice, "Paul, get down here quickly; there is a problem."

He staggered groggily from the bed and tried to pull himself together to deal with whatever prompted Melissa's urgency. He went down to where the meeting rooms were. There were a number of them, but only one had the door ajar. He entered the room and saw Melissa bending over the slumped figure of Devon, who was in a chair with most of his body draped on the table.

"Has he had a heart attack?" was Paul's urgent question.

"No, dammit, he's drunk!" raged Melissa, trying to shake him. "I left him to go shower. He'd ordered a few whiskies during the evening, but he must have been drinking more on the sly – and now this! I need him to be fully functional to help me compile our report, but he's of no use to anyone now, and precious time will be whittled away getting him sober."

Paul was exasperated. At one moment, Devon could be the most incredible resource and the next of no value to their cause whatsoever.

"And it gets worse," said Melissa. "While I was trying to shake some life into him, his mobile rang. The screen showed who was trying to contact him, and it was Professor Hung!"

"What?" Paul was dumbfounded.

"I was unsure about answering Devon's phone, and it rang off

310

after three short bursts as if Hung was not able or wanting it to keep ringing."

"It looks as if Hung was trying to reach out to Devon," said Paul, "but he couldn't have chosen a worse moment."

"All of this is crippling our efforts to get our report to the authorities," Melissa roared, continuing to shake Devon. "Wake up, damn you!"

* * *

Professor Hung could have wept with frustration. He had risked being caught trying to phone Devon Ridley. He could only chance a brief attempt to make contact which had failed. Devon had not responded, and it seemed all was lost. He and his family would be incarcerated forever as his captors had said nothing further about releasing Hung and his family after their visit. He could accept his role in his detention for going against the State, but his mother and sister were innocent victims.

His captors had called on him that morning to collect the signed hard copy of the Clinical Trial Summary Report, which would see the trial's suspension turn to complete termination. With this falsified document leaving him and being taken through the regulatory system, his reputation would be in tatters if it was ever established that he had manipulated the trial results. Hung was told to delay sending the electronic version for unknown reasons, but that was irrelevant now because the hard copy could seal his scientific fate.

He could try to escape and correct the wrongdoing, but escape seemed impossible. He had contacted underground groups in Canton, who said they could try to get him to the city harbour, but that is where their assistance would end. Professor Hung felt miserable. Should he contemplate suicide? Perhaps with him gone, the authorities would release his mother and sister.

* * *

311

Following his arrival in Beijing, Sean arranged to meet with his Chinese Central Committee contact, who met him at the hotel.

Acting as a translator, Alexander Leong explained to Sean that the signed copy of the trial document would be handed over once Sean had given his assurances that the venture by Talbot International to construct a larger factory in Shanghai would proceed. This was tricky for Sean as his influence over the company's International Division was limited. He would draw up a document to cover this but postdate it, allowing him time to realise his plan.

Sean was pleased that the Chinese representative seemed more interested in Sean's secondary proposal for a trip across Europe in the company's jet with pampering and entertainment along the way – not all of it sightseeing. Sean felt that if he could not confirm the extension to the factory, he could blackmail the official over his illicit trip so that none of the factory business would come out.

The government official extracted the copy of the clinical trial report from his briefcase and handed it over to Sean. He looked at the Executive Summary, where Professor Hung had concluded that the trial must be terminated due to the failure of HG 176. Sean felt a wave of satisfaction sweep over him. Half of his plan had been achieved; now on to St Petersburg.

* * *

Alexievich returned to his office after being called away to an emergency, which thankfully wasn't much of an emergency at all. He told the hospital staff that he would be unavailable for the remainder of the day as he wanted no interruptions while he anxiously awaited details of the impending meeting to hand over the signed report. He retrieved the signed copy from the filing cabinet. Staring at it, Alexievich felt an imminent release from the pressures that had afflicted him the past couple of months.

Startled by a text message from a special number, he was told to go downtown to a specific low-key intersection at the designated time that evening with the signed hard copy. He would be collected from there by 'friends' in a black Mercedes and taken to the meeting place. No tricks or funny business, or else. Alexievich was quite aware of what that meant.

He tarried at the hospital until quite late, then made his way to the parking garage. Unexpectedly, he passed Medvedeva in the corridor, just starting her evening shift. Anastasia studied his face closely and could see it was wracked with anxiety. Something was eating away at him.

She raised her eyebrows quizzically as if to address him, and his response was to swallow nervously and be on his way. Anastasia stared after him as he scurried away down the corridor. Alexievich was undeniably up to something.

* * *

Paul and Melissa managed to drag Devon upright. He mumbled something with a big grin on his face. Situations where someone is recovering from too much drink, are frequently entertaining. This situation was not one of those.

They needed to get Devon sober – and quickly – to help compile their report. They managed to stumble to the elevator and punch the button to get them to Paul's room, where Paul started stripping Devon of his clothes to get him into the shower.

"Order plenty of strong black coffee from room service," Paul yelled at Melissa.

She looked up just in time to see the naked form of Devon being pushed into the shower.

"That's gross," she muttered as room service answered.

Between getting him into a cold shower and making him swallow cups of coffee, Paul and Melissa managed to return Devon to a semi-sober state. He was intensely apologetic, but the damage had been done, and precious time had been squandered. When they felt Devon was in reasonable shape again, they resumed working on the pile of documents that Melissa had carried with her from the meeting room. Devon was still not fully functional and impeded the pace of work.

While ploughing through the files, Paul remembered that Professor Hung had tried to call Devon while he was out for the count. When Paul told Devon about the missed call, he was devastated.

"He's in trouble, I'm sure of it, and was looking for help. I've let him and you down by my stupidity," Devon agonised.

"Do you think we can risk trying to call him back?" suggested Paul.

"You're taking a chance and putting him in danger," was Melissa's blunt comment.

"Agreed, but the stakes are high at the moment. Hung must also be aware of his situation when he tried to phone," Paul responded. "Devon, try sending Hung a text message and see what comes of it."

"Right, will do," said Devon, sobering up rapidly.

"Prof. It's D here," was the message.

They waited. No response. Devon tried again with the same short message; again, no response. The mood in the room plummeted.

"Hung would know what is truly happening with the trial, and his earlier Peccavi message indicates that. I am convinced he is trying to escape," was Devon's summary of the situation.

Silence from Paul and Melissa indicated their agreement.

"Okay, we can't do any more with Hung," said Paul, "so let's get on with the files and the report. Melissa, Devon, I'm in your hands."

The two gathered the files and returned to the meeting room while Paul was left in his room to reflect on developments.

* * *

Dr Alexievich climbed into his silver Porsche in the basement parking of the hospital. If all went well tonight, he was hopeful his 'friends' would let him keep it. He set off for his rendezvous, frequently checking his rear-view mirror to ensure that the Medvedeva woman was not following him. That was the last thing he needed.

He did not have to worry. As tempted as Anastasia was to do exactly that, she had patients to see urgently, and her sense of duty to them would not allow her to break that contract, as frustrating as that was.

Alexievich made his way through St Petersburg's streets to the meeting place. He looked across at the passenger seat where the folder containing the hard copy of the report with the forged signature lay. It was his passport to freedom. Finding the intersection, he parked the Porsche and waited.

Before long, a black Mercedes pulled up behind him. A man wearing a mask, his hat pulled down low on his head, got out, his right hand in his pocket, obviously holding a gun. He told Alexievich to get out of his car and walk to the Mercedes. He did so, gathering up his folder.

He was blindfolded and guided into the back seat with the man getting in beside him. Alexievich had to admit that he was now shitting himself. Were they just going to take his folder, exact their revenge and blow his head off? The car pulled away to its unknown destination.

After a short journey, they stopped, and he heard large doors opening. The car moved forward a short distance, and Alexievich assumed they were now in a garage of sorts as he heard the doors closing behind them. The car door opened, and he was led out, still blindfolded, and made to sit on a chair. His blindfold was removed, and he was seated at a table in a darkened room.

A masked man was sitting opposite him, and two figures stood in the shadowy background. Alexievich was asked for the folder, which he put on the table. He saw a sweaty hand mark on the manila cover where he had been clutching it.

The man picked it up and said, "Here it is, lord."

He was immediately reprimanded and told not to use the word 'lord', and this person approached the table, snatching the folder.

Retreating into the shadows, he appeared to give it to the other person in the room, saying in broken English, "Your report, you check it."

This other figure was a bulky individual who started looking through the report. Nothing was said. Only the flicking of the pages broke the silence, but the tension remained.

Alexievich found himself shivering uncontrollably in the icy room, anxiously hoping the report would be accepted. He was keenly aware that his life lay in the balance, and he swallowed nervously. The sound attracted the attention of the men, who let out a round of contemptuous sniggers.

After an agonising period, the man holding the folder, discernible only by his outline, said in an English accent, "This is good; deal done."

Alexievich exhaled and slumped forward onto the table. More sniggers. He was roughly pulled up into a standing position, blindfolded once more and led back to the car. Alexievich had no idea where they were taking him, but soon the car slowed to almost a halt, the door opened, and he was thrown out onto the street. He rolled a few times, landing hard against the kerb and ripped off his blindfold. He was back at the intersection where they had fetched him, with his Porsche parked where he had left it. He had survived the ordeal and almost cried with relief. He expected his 'friends' would keep their side of the bargain and erase his debts.

His joy was only briefly restrained by blood flowing from a gash on his eyebrow, sustained when he was thrown from the car. He needed to get to the hospital to stitch himself up. Alexievich got into the Porsche and set off.

At the hospital, he went to his office and cleaned the congealed blood off his face. He injected local anaesthetic around his eyebrow and waited for it to take effect before stitching the cut. He reached into the bottom drawer of his desk, pulled out a bottle of vodka and poured himself a generous helping to numb his shattered nerves.

The anaesthetic had still not fully taken effect, so he poured another tumbler of vodka. Alexievich could afford to celebrate; he had completed the critical and nerve-wracking part of his bargain and felt content and good about himself. He would wait a day or so before instructing Pavlyuchenko to approve the electronic copy.

The vodka was beginning to have an additive effect on the local anaesthetic. As he stitched his eyebrow, Alexievich felt euphoric and on top of the world. He was getting a little drunk, but he did not care.

Anastasia walked past his office on her way back from the theatre. She heard the singing of the Russian national anthem coming from inside. She opened the door to see Alexievich sitting at his desk with a glass in his hand, belting out the anthem.

"Ah, Doctor Nastya Medvedeva," Alexievich chuckled, using the diminutive of her name as if she were a child.

Anastasia stared at this transformed figure out of character from anything she had seen before. The smooth persona he always projected had slipped. There was a significant cut above his eye, which was starting to swell and blacken. Feet up on the desk, a glass of vodka in his hand, Alexievich waved a toast to her. She was, at that moment, speechless. He was not.

"So all your little plans to interfere with my life have fallen apart," he gloated.

Anastasia could not find a comment to respond to this. He was drunk and in a belligerent mood, and his self-righteous attitude and condescension annoyed her.

"Nastya, soon your lover will sign the death warrant of HG 176, and my report on the trial is going everywhere. It will go to the regulators, who will terminate the trial. Then Anatoly will keep his job – and his playtime with you! There is a name for women like you, Nastya," he slurred gleefully at her.

Anastasia was outraged. She knew exactly what that name was, and she was not a whore or a plaything! He had no understanding of the relationship between her and Anatoly. She was livid that this obscene individual could crow over her, but Alexievich had not finished his rant.

"And the English lord will be happy too. He is 'real' nobility, not like you and your lover. You are only extremely distant relatives of the deceased Romanovs, or so you claim," he smirked.

Anastasia was disgusted with him. There was no value in arguing with him in his state. She left, slamming the office door behind her and stormed off to the sound of him laughing.

She was angry, but something Alexievich had said left her puzzled; she thought to contact Paul about it. But he was drunk and deliberately making inflammatory statements, so perhaps she should just let that go. She wanted to block the entire scene from her mind; it had revealed Alexievich's true nature – and he was a repulsive, vulgar character.

CHAPTER 34

Strange Encounter

Melissa and Devon continued to make headway in evaluating the copied files. Despite her frustrations, Melissa silently acknowledged that Devon, when sober and functional, was good at his work. He was picking up the contradictions in the data, capturing them on his laptop, and structuring a report format that would explain the inconsistencies. She made her notes and observations and fed them into his report.

They were progressing well when Devon suddenly stopped. "I am going to contact Hung. I am positive he wants me to help him."

"And possibly put him in danger if he is caught," was Melissa's irritated response.

Devon ignored her, pulled out his phone and typed, "D here, Prof."

There was no response. Devon stared at his phone, willing a reply, but none came. He put the phone down with a sigh and continued with his work.

About an hour later, Devon's phone suddenly pinged with the message, "In Canton. Need help. Get me out. Use HK."

Devon showed the message to Melissa. "There, I told you he needs help."

"Yes, but what can we do?"

"I don't know, but I'm going to tell Paul."

Asleep on his bed, Paul was again woken up by his phone ringing. "Yes, Devon, what is the problem now? Are you still sober?"

Consumed with guilt, Devon ignored the question. "Paul, Professor Hung has just sent me a message. He is in Canton in mainland China and wants help to get out. He said we should use Hong Kong, whatever that means."

"That's incredible. What can we do to help?"

"That's what I was hoping you could suggest."

"Give me a few minutes to wake up and collect my thoughts. I'll call you back."

Although he sounded confident to Devon, Paul's mind was blank. He paced up and down the room, his mind screening several thoughts and alternatives, going back through conversations. Could any of these have relevance? He suddenly focused on one exchange. It was a long shot, but he had to try it. He picked up his phone and dialled a number.

"Collins," was the sleepy response.

"Mr Collins, I am sorry to disturb you. It is Paul Beresford."

"Beresford, what on earth are you doing phoning me so late; it's just gone midnight here. Have you lost your mind? Goodbye."

"Please, Mr Collins, don't hang up. This could be crucially important."

"It may be to you, but not to me," Eddie said gruffly. "Goodbye again."

"Please bear with me for a moment. It could be a matter of life and death."

There was no reply from the other end of the call – but no click either.

Paul used this momentary gap to make his case. "You mentioned that you had been in Hong Kong and had made a circle of influential friends."

There was no response. "There is a professor from Hong Kong who is doing our trial and appears to be held captive in Canton City. He needs to escape to explain that the trial is not a failure.

Perhaps some of your important contacts in Hong Kong could be of assistance. Canton is quite close to Hong Kong."

Again there was no reply. "Mr Collins, are you still there?"

"Yes."

"I know this is improbable, but you were the only person I could think of in a desperate situation, given your connections here."

Again there was a long pause before Eddie replied.

"You know of my interest in rugby. I regularly visited the city to watch the famous Hong Kong Sevens rugby tournament. I even met your father briefly on one occasion. Many wealthy influential figures – businesspeople, politicians and even some celebrities – would come to the tournament as they liked to get up close and personal with some of the rugby stars."

Eddie revealed that he had befriended many of these people and got involved in some of their activities. Among these, coincidentally, was Operation Yellowbird. The organisation was based in Hong Kong and used to get Chinese dissidents who had participated in the Tiananmen Square protests safely out of China and to Hong Kong.

"The operation came to a halt many years ago," Eddie continued, "but there may be some vestiges left in terms of people and organisation which may, and I repeat, may, be of assistance. I will give it some thought. Goodbye."

This time there was a click, and the phone went dead. Paul hoped that something might evolve from his conversation with Eddie Collins, of all people.

* * *

Sean St Ledger felt immensely pleased with himself as he relaxed in his St Petersburg hotel suite. He had ordered an expensive bottle of champagne and sipped it from his crystal flute.

"Nectar from the Gods," he said. "What is the line from that stupid TV series – I love it when a plan comes together."

How appropriate to his situation. On the table next to his chair lay the two reports – one from Hong Kong and the other freshly obtained that evening from the Russians he had been dealing with. He would have to consider how he would keep his side of the bargain regarding money laundering through his company. They probably wanted to use it to buy up the part of Mayfair they didn't yet own. Like his Beijing deal with the people helping him achieve his goal, he would have to work out carefully how to arrange this.

The Chinese side of the arrangement was more straightforward as they were a bit naive, but with the Russians, he would have to tread carefully – they were dangerous. Sean needed to delay or modify the so-called promises he had made until after he had completed his plan and proved to his father that he was sharp and competent. That should secure his inheritance and place in society.

He had arranged with the head of the Talbot organisation in Russia to organise some female entertainment for his evening's pleasure. There was a knock on the door of his suite. He opened it and admitted two stunning Russian girls. The evening was now complete.

* * *

The following morning, Sean staggered through to the bathroom. Copious champagne and a night of sexual indulgence had rendered him sluggish, but it had all been most satisfying. He quenched his thirst with gulps of water from the tap and splashed some on his face, then called the pilot of his jet to finalise their departure time.

"Sorry, Sir, we have a problem at the moment. There was a severe snowstorm last night, and flights – even the commercial ones – have been delayed until the weather and the runway clears."

"That's not the news I want to hear. I need to get back to London urgently."

"I understand that Sir, but our hands are tied by the authorities."

"Tell them that the son and heir to Viscount Talbot needs to get back to London urgently."

"I have, Sir, but the answer is still negative."

"Well, tell them again if you want to keep your job."

* * *

The room was still dark even though it was early morning. Paul lay sound asleep, making up for all the sleep deprivation and recent exhausting activities. He was woken by his cellphone ringing. He shook off his tiredness, fumbled in the dark for the light, and saw that it was Anastasia calling.

"Hello, Paul."

"Hello, Anastasia. What time is it?"

"It half past seven."

"I was still asleep."

"All alone, no Melissa?" she teased.

"Yes, Anastasia, all alone. I needed some sleep this time," Paul chuckled.

"Paul, I need tell you something of Alexievich. It is very strange. I think he hiding something. I see him in hospital yesterday night, and he look tense, nearly scared. He left to somewhere, but I cannot follow him."

"Do you think it was related to the trial?"

"I am sure. I delay him seeing Anatoly to sign off report for trial. You ask me for this."

"Yes, thank you, because we need to buy time to complete our alternative report, but we had a setback."

"I see him later back in hospital, drunk and looks like from a fight. I no see him like that before. He insult me and saying strange things. He say his report on trial is gone everywhere."

"But Anatoly has still not approved the signing off of the HG 176 trial report. If that is the case, we are safe and have some time to finish our own report."

"No, he hasn't approved. I keep him away from Anatoly."

"I think Alexievich must be imagining things in his drunken state. Anything else you want me to know?"

There was a pause. "No, Paul, not anything."

"Thank you, Anastasia; you might have saved the day by delaying the report."

After the call, Paul readied himself for the day and went to the hotel meeting room. Devon and Melissa were still there working on the folders. Empty coffee pots and cups littered the table. Both looked exhausted, given that they had obviously worked through the night. Even Melissa's refined elegance looked frayed.

Devon looked like Devon – crumpled. But his sharpness had not deserted him, and he managed to get in a dig at Paul. "So, management has been sleeping while the workers have been slaving away."

"Enough of that – you have caused us anxious moments. How are things going, Melissa?"

"We need most of another day to finish our report. There is compelling evidence here to show that there is nothing wrong with the safety and efficacy of HG 176. The trial must be restarted urgently."

"I am going to make a strange request, Melissa," Paul said, "but I want you to trust me on this. Please print out a hard copy of the Executive Summary of your report and give it to me as soon as possible. I need to take it back to London with me urgently."

"What is it for?" asked Melissa, suspicious of Paul's motives. Was he trying to show that he was the saviour of the trial and not her?

"All I need is an overview of the report you are compiling. Not the official report; you can deliver that, Melissa, to the authorities and JP and Harrowgate. I know you want to be the bearer of this news."

Melissa stared at him, knowing he had read her thoughts. She detected some sarcasm from Paul but was too tired to put up much of an argument. As long as she could deliver the full report, the recognition would accrue to her.

"All right, we can arrange that. Come on, Devon, get going."

"Paul, any feedback on Professor Hung's problem?" was Devon's retort.

"Yes, it may be too early to tell, but there is a small chance that something may come of an initiative I have launched to see if we can help the professor. He must be released because, despite our report, I think we need to get Hung in front of the authorities to corroborate what we have found. He will be the most credible witness for us since Professor Pavlyuchenko is compromised to a certain extent. I hope to have feedback on the initiative soon."

"Thanks, Paul," sighed Devon, getting back to preparing the overview for Paul to take to London.

CHAPTER 35

Endgame

Devon and Melissa took a short break to catch up on some much-needed sleep before continuing their work summarising the data and compiling their report. It was starting to evolve into a decisive repudiation of the notion that the trial should be terminated on safety and efficacy grounds. But there was still work to be done, and Paul was becoming anxious about getting the essence of this report back to London, or more accurately, to Berkhamsted.

For the first time in the past few weeks, Paul found himself at a loose end with nothing he could do to help facilitate progress. He decided to go for a run, followed by a swim in the hotel's pool. Feeling refreshed and with time on his hands, Paul wanted to take the ferry across to Kowloon to explore that part of the city. He felt guilty leaving Devon and Melissa, but there was no value he could add to their work. He checked in with Devon before he left for the ferry to see how far he and Melissa were with the report.

"We should have a substantial document ready for you by this evening, according to Melissa."

"That's great news. I'll book a flight back to London. Hopefully, I can get out tomorrow."

Paul booked with British Airways for the seven o'clock evening flight and noticed his phone battery was almost flat. At the risk of missing the ferry, he plugged it into the charger and set off. Paul felt a rare sense of freedom; no work to carry out and no one to bother him with phone calls.

The Star Ferry took Paul across Victoria Bay to Kowloon. Once ashore, he wandered through the Sham Shui Po, one of the oldest districts in the city with its cluttering of shops and eateries. He took a short ride on one of the famous Hong Kong trams with its familiar 'ding, ding' ring as it navigated the streets, warning unsuspecting pedestrians of its approach.

Paul felt like a tourist on holiday after all the recent tensions, but he knew important tasks would need his attention soon, so he should enjoy this brief respite, or day off, as he thought to call it. His final visit was to the Tai Kwun Centre for Heritage and Arts, in keeping with his interest in history and arts.

While he enjoyed his time off, it was nearing lunchtime, and he needed to get back to the hotel to see what headway was being made on the report.

Melissa showed Paul the report when he returned, which looked positively solid. He suggested that the three of them take a quick lunch together as a small celebration of their efforts. Melissa and Devon agreed, and Paul went to his room to change.

He had almost forgotten he'd left his phone behind to charge. To his consternation, there were six missed calls – all from Anastasia. His relaxed mood evaporated, gripped by panic that something had happened to her. He immediately dialled her number, and she promptly answered.

"Anastasia, are you all right? Are you safe?"

"Yes, Paul, is no problem with me," she assured him.

"So then, why all the calls?"

"Something still bother me since last time I see Alexievich. I think not important, but I think maybe yes."

"And what is it?"

"When he talk of trial report, he say English lord will be happy to get it from him."

"What? Did you say the English lord and the trial report?"

"I think is what he said. First, I think he talking about drug lord because sure he is mixed up with them, but I am sure he say English lord."

Paul was stunned as several dots in the mystery were suddenly joined together to form a more coherent picture: Jill's notes in her diary about the mysterious 'S', probably being Sean St Ledger, and her father's confirmation that Sean was looking to gain entry into the pharmaceutical market, possibly through the acquisition of an Irish company. Or could it be Harrowgate? JP had disclosed he had an offer to purchase the company on his desk.

And now it seemed Sean might be in St Petersburg, with links to Alexievich and the HG 176 trial. Alexievich had told Anastasia about a trial report that the English lord would receive, but surely that couldn't be true if Pavlyuchenko had not signed it off. Sean must be trying to find out about the product to decide whether to purchase Harrowgate or not. None of this was good news.

Paul thought even further back to their school days and the coincidence that Jill had known him at Oxford. He thought about Jill's funeral and the person he saw fleetingly at the back of the church. Paul was now certain it was Sean. He had cast a shadow over them without fully appreciating the intrusion in their lives.

"Paul, are you still there?" Anastasia asked. Preoccupied with his recollections, he had forgotten that Anastasia was on the line.

"Sorry, I was lost in thought. What you've told me is absolutely important."

"I should have mentioned first time."

Paul felt so too, and given this new development, there was no time to waste.

"Thanks for telling me about this, Anastasia. It's most helpful. I must get back to London tonight if possible."

"Please keep in contact."

"I will," he assured her.

Paul reflected that valuable time had been lost because Anastasia had not mentioned this obscure but vital clue earlier. He berated himself for spending valuable time acting like a tourist and being without his phone.

He had to get back to London urgently and called the airline to change his booking to fly out that night. Unfortunately, there were no seats available in business or economy class. Frustrated, Paul ended the call but phoned back a moment later to ask if any First Class seats were available. There were, on the late flight.

Paul knew he would have to explain this expense to Ritesh Shah, Harrowgate's Financial Director, but getting to London was critical. He needed to show JP and Professor Reich the Executive Summary of the report. It was no good emailing the summary or phoning JP to tell him what he had uncovered; he had to present the evidence in person. Paul was well aware that JP had lost confidence in him after he conveyed tainted information given to him by Melissa in her quest to discredit him. He naively believed her initially, not realising that she'd been setting him up for failure – corporate politics at its most insidious.

Paul had changed over his time at Harrowgate and his involvement in the trial. He had undergone an inner journey in which he had grown and evolved. Jill said he was a boy scout wanting to save the world by joining the company, and this idealistic view was part of his decision to move to Harrowgate.

But now, Paul had a harder edge and scepticism about people and their actions. Life and death events had scarred him – both physically and emotionally. He thought about Jill's suffering and death, Tanel's brutal murder and his and Anastasia's close escapes. He realised that he could not succeed if he kept to the utopian path on which he began. Perhaps the world of a surgeon was a safer place. He'd have to reflect on this once the hurdle of HG 176 was all over. But first, he had to secure a positive outcome for Harrowgate, and in memory of Jill, he knew he had the wherewithal to do it.

Paul quickly went to see Melissa and Devon, telling them the celebratory lunch was off and the report needed to be finalised urgently. There was limited time before his revised flight time, and he needed the Executive Summary before he left for the airport. Melissa looked confused, trying to understand the sudden change of plan.

"I can't explain it now, but it's a hunch. I will let you know as soon as I'm back in London."

Melissa didn't seem convinced, but she realised Paul's conviction in his assessment was all-consuming, and she now had less influence over him. She and Devon set about finishing their report, and Paul returned to his room, packed his belongings, and readied himself for the flight.

When he thought of London, it seemed to exist in a different world to his present situation; calm, tranquil and pleasant. With this in mind, Paul tried to relax for a couple of hours, mentally focusing on the task ahead.

It was almost time to leave when he got a call from Melissa to let him know the document was ready. He gathered his luggage and went downstairs.

"The report is not complete," Melissa explained, "but the results so far all point to the manipulation of the trial. We have captured this in the Executive Summary, and we are confident that this summary will reflect the essence of the main report. It's the best we could do, given that you wanted a hard copy."

"Thank you – both of you. We'll have a celebration soon enough."

Devon handed over the document, which Paul put in his briefcase alongside Jill's diary and asked reception to call a taxi to take him to the airport. He shook hands with Devon. Melissa seemed to expect a different goodbye from him, but he shook her hand too and departed for the airport.

Paul was ushered into BA's First Class lounge, which he had to admit was impressive with all the trimmings. He chose to eat his meal there so that he would not be disturbed or woken on the flight. Early boarding before all the other passengers and being shown to an enormous, comfortable seat in the nose of the plane completed the First Class experience.

If he had been in a different mood, he might have appreciated all the pampering more than he did. His focus was on getting to London and then to Berkhamsted. Paul was relieved when the plane pushed back from the stand, nosed its way onto the runway, and thundered towards the stars.

* * *

In St Petersburg, Sean fumed that his repeated calls to his pilot had not moved his departure forward. Not that the pilot could have done anything since a snowstorm had halted all flights, and Sean had to spend another day cooped up in his room. He was in a foul mood when his plane was given the all-clear to take off late that night, the snowstorm having eased its wintery grip and the runways cleared to allow smaller planes to depart.

Finally, Sean was on his way to Heathrow and onward to finalise the critical part of his plan. A meeting had been scheduled, and he had the evidence with him to conclude his goal. To pass the time in the air, Sean helped himself to some drinks and then converted the three-seater couch into a bed to allow him to sleep off some of the effects of the alcohol. Soon he would be touching down at Heathrow.

* * *

Despite the luxury and comfort of the flight, Paul had a restless night. For what reason would Sean have been in St Petersburg? Alexievich had made mention of a report given to a lord. If Sean was also heading back to the UK, Paul was anxious about the time he might have lost before realising that Sean could be involved in something devious.

Paul was relieved when the plane crossed the channel, and he could see the White Cliffs of Dover followed by the patchwork of fields and meadows which characterised England. The Boeing 747 touched down smoothly at Heathrow and taxied towards Terminal 5.

Paul was impatient to disembark but prepared himself for the inevitable wait at customs and immigration. As a benefit of flying first class, Paul was shown to a VIP Fast Track zone to facilitate his rapid clearance through customs, a definite advantage given his race against the clock. Although the name suggested very fast clearance, several international flights arrived at the airport in the early morning, so there was a relatively long queue. Still, it was moving quite quickly, much to Paul's relief.

Looking towards the front of the queue, Paul could not believe his eyes. There was a person who he thought might be Sean St Ledger. Paul's hunch was confirmed when he caught a full facial look at him as he turned to speak to one of the Terminal staff as there was some dispute on the go. Although Paul had not seen Sean since school, there was an undeniable familiarity about his face. It was still the schoolboy face but rounder. It dawned on Paul that this was the face of the individual at the back of the church at Jill's funeral.

It seemed that Sean was arguing about being kept waiting. However, this was quickly resolved, and Sean, if that is who it was, cleared the usual checks and moved off. Paul was desperate to follow him but was further back, awaiting his turn for clearance. He decided to jump the queue and moved towards the front despite the apoplectic complaints all around him.

He used a well-worked line at the front of the queue. "I am a doctor, let me through. It is an emergency."

The customs lady confirmed the title in Paul's passport and, taken by his rugged good looks, waved him through. He set off after the fast-disappearing figure of Sean. He realised he had not collected his luggage, but Paul had no time to waste. He would try to retrieve it later, hoping it would be held by the airline. He had his briefcase with the powerful Executive Summary document. That was all he needed.

Paul rushed towards the exit just in time to see the burly figure climb into a maroon Bentley, which pulled away. Fortunately, a taxi was in the parking area with a yellow light on the roof indicating it was available for hire. He shouted through the front window at the driver, "Follow that Bentley," then got into the back seat clutching his precious briefcase containing Jill's diaries and the all-important Executive Summary. He hoped the driver took him seriously and didn't think he was playing out some Hollywood fantasy.

The taxi driver embraced the spirit of the occasion and set off to close the distance between the two cars. He soon caught sight of the Bentley and followed it, remaining a few cars behind as they weaved their way through the early morning London traffic.

"I don't think they'll be aware of us – there are lots of taxis around. Do you know where he is going?

"I suspect he may be heading out Watford way."

"I hope so because that is my football club. Do you like football?"

"I do, but I have other priorities in my life right now."

Paul was puzzled when the Bentley did not take the M25 ring road that would launch him in that direction. Their journey was complicated by a thick early morning mist which had settled over the city. They continued to follow the car and the taxi driver skilfully managed to maintain a discreet distance behind the Bentley without losing it – despite a couple of close shaves at traffic lights and Belisha beacon pedestrian crossings.

As they continued their journey, the driver volunteered, "I think he is heading for central London."

Paul was mystified; this did not coincide with what he thought would happen.

Later the driver said, "He is now heading for the East End."

Paul couldn't understand this. Perhaps he was mistaken, it wasn't Sean, and this was simply a wild goose chase. Fatigue settled over him as the adrenaline-fuelled rush of the initial chase started to wane. How he wished he had a cup of coffee to revive him. They passed the tower blocks of Canary Wharf, their tops obscured in the morning mist.

"I think he might be heading for the London City Airport," volunteered the driver.

"That makes no sense," said Paul. "He has just come off an international flight."

"Besides the usual airlines, private planes also use that airport."

Paul thought of Sean, the show-off who would want to flaunt his position and wealth. Perhaps he had a private plane or helicopter at the airport, his preferred mode of transport, vaunting his self-importance. That would fit perfectly with his character.

"No, definitely not the City Airport," said the taxi driver, surprised that his prediction proved incorrect.

He followed the Bentley past the airport grounds. They continued until they saw a sign for the London Docklands Heliport. The Bentley turned in, and the taxi followed.

"Wait here for me here," Paul told the taxi driver as the bulky figure quit the Bentley and disappeared into a building. Paul set off after him. Inside, he went into what appeared to be a VIP lounge or holding area, and Paul followed.

"Sean," he said.

Sean swung round. "Well, well, well; if it isn't the famous Doctor Paul," he smirked.

For the first time, Paul took in the figure of the Honourable Sean St Ledger. He also noticed two other men in the lounge, and he guessed they were Crispin Wake-Armstrong and Digby Newton – the unholy trinity from Charterhouse were all together again.

"What have you been doing in St Petersburg, Sean?"

"That's none of your business, or, to put it more correctly, that's not your business anymore."

"What are you trying to do in the pharmaceutical industry?"

"I'm not trying; I am acquiring a pharmaceutical company." Sean could not keep himself from gloating.

"So what has a company in Northern Ireland got to do with a drug trial in St Petersburg?"

"Or a trial in Hong Kong, hey, Paul? It has everything, and nothing, to do with it."

With despairing clarity, Paul realised Sean was the puppeteer behind the obstruction of the HG 176 trials in St Petersburg and Hong Kong. Malevolent, vindictive, spiteful – and powerful.

"So what are you trying to achieve?" asked Paul, aware that Crispin and Digby were moving closer to him.

"I have an appointment this morning with JP O'Rourke," Sean grinned. "On his desk, he has an offer to sell Harrowgate to me. Thanks to my intervention, the company's share price has plummeted, and he wants to get out before it collapses. In my document bag, I have reports from the two trial sites you mentioned, showing that HG 176 is a failure. I will show them to JP, and the ink will soon be dry on the contract. When that's done, I will destroy the documents and intercept the electronic versions. Once I have bought the company for a much lower price, I will reinstate the trials, and Harrowgate will be a roaring success. I see it as the next GSK or Pfizer. You, of course, won't be part of my success."

Paul felt contempt and disgust at the person in front of him; nothing about him had changed since their schooldays – bombastic, duplicitous and self-aggrandising. He thought of all the disruption and angst that Sean had created. It was clear that he had somehow been pulling the strings to bring about the failure at the two trial sites.

"Well, Sean, I have a report here that shows that the poor results of the two trials have been rigged. JP knows me, and the evidence I have is overwhelming." Paul raised his briefcase to make his point.

"Yes," said Sean, "but the pity is that you won't get to show him those results." He indicated to Crispin and Digby to move in on Paul.

As they tried to grab hold of him, he managed to hit Digby on the jaw, who fell back, but Sean and Crispin tore into Paul. His fitness allowed Paul to deal with the struggle initially, but the odds were against him. This was a replay of that day at school when the three of them attacked Paul on the rugby field. With a sense of panic, Paul realised he could not fight them off.

Pinned on the ground, Sean kicked Paul in the chest and then in the groin, saying, "I told you I would break you into little pieces, and that day has come."

He lashed out at Paul in a frenzy, delivering one blow after another. His years of seething hatred for Paul found their outlet.

Holding Paul down, Crispin said, "Go easy, Sean; we don't want to kill him, just incapacitate him."

"Why not, for all the damage this bastard has done to me?" said Sean, aiming a last kick into Paul's groin. "That's for using that thing on Jill," was the last thing Paul heard before he felt himself slipping away.

Sean was in a blind fury, kicking at Paul's prone figure. As Crispin pulled him away, Sean was gasping and panting, patently deranged.

"Give me his briefcase. I want to destroy the evidence he has." Digby handed Paul's briefcase to Sean. "I need to board the helicopter for my flight to Harrowgate. I want to impress them when I land at their offices and sign the purchase agreement. Get the Bentley to take me down to the helipad. I need to leave now!"

Digby went outside and called the Bentley driver who collected Sean for the brief drive to where the Talbot Airbus ACH 135 was on the helipad with its rotors slowly turning.

Sean got out of the car and climbed aboard, shouting at the pilot, "Let's get this thing moving!"

"Sir, we have a weather problem. The morning mist is too thick and low to take off now. We need to wait for it to lift."

"Take off now, damn you! I have an urgent meeting in Berkhamsted."

"Sir, it's not safe."

"I don't fucking care. It seems as if all the company's pilots are shit scared to do anything."

"But Sir …"

"Don't bloody 'but Sir' me! Get moving or lose your cushy, overpaid job with Talbot," Sean raved.

The pilot looked at the co-pilot and shrugged. "Should we chance it?"

"I guess we'd better."

The pilot activated the engine, and a steady roar emerged with the familiar 'chop, chop' sound of the rotor blades spinning, louder and louder as the rotors approached sufficient speed to begin a takeoff.

Crispin and Digby could hear the sound in the reception building as they watched Paul slowly recover. Despite his allegiance to Sean, Crispin did not have the same vindictive attitude towards Paul. He told Digby to get some water for Paul, who was slowly getting to his feet.

Suddenly, the taxi driver who had been waiting for Paul entered the building.

"Struth, what's going on here? What's happened to my customer?" His concern arose both from Paul's condition and not being paid for his trip across London.

"Just a small incident," shouted Crispin over the deafening roar of the helicopter taking off.

Paul staggered to his feet and smelt defeat. All his efforts were in vain. The precious hard-won evidence he needed to show JP that the trials were being misrepresented had been lost. Sean was headed for Berkhamsted with proof of trial failure, and based on that, JP would sign away the company. He thought of JP and Mildred, Tom, Professor Reich and the two scientists in R&D and all the hard work to initiate the trial. They would all be at the mercy of Sean St Ledger. Paul could have wept in frustration.

The sound of the helicopter was starting to fade. Paul took another sip of water and saw blood on the rim of the glass as he put it down. At that moment, there was a dull thud that shook the building. All four men stared at each other in disbelief.

"That was an explosion," said Crispin.

"Oh my God, that could be the helicopter!" exclaimed Digby, his face pale with shock. "The boss – he's gone!"

CHAPTER 36

For Jill

Television crews and the media were at the site almost immediately and reported that a private helicopter had crashed into one of the cranes in the London docklands. This was the second incident of this type in London within three months. It was understood that the helicopter had taken off in a heavy mist with poor visibility. Experts said it was suicidal to have considered flying in the prevailing conditions.

Eyewitnesses reported that the wreck of the helicopter plunged into the Thames, sinking rapidly. Three people were believed to have been killed. One of the bodies had been recovered, but police divers were still searching for the two others supposedly on board. Identifying the victims would take some time, but it was confirmed that the helicopter belonged to the well-known Talbot business empire, headed up by the 5th Viscount Talbot.

A battered and bruised Paul wondered if he would ever recover from his pummelling and contacted JP with a brief overview of what had happened. JP was aghast at the machinations against his company and its product.

Paul had the taxi driver take him back to the Wandsworth apartment, rewarding him generously. Fortunately, Paul had a spare key with him and was able to gain access. He cleaned himself up and set off for Berkhamsted to meet with JP and the team.

Tom met him at the station and commented, "Every time I see you, you seem to be in a bad way!"

"Yes, that would seem an accurate description. I think I should stick to surgery; it seems a safer line of work."

They drove up to the Harrowgate building, and Paul went straight to JP's office, where Mildred greeted him with a hug.

"I knew you would come through for us," she beamed.

"It was closer than you might've thought."

She opened the door to JP and Professor Reich. JP gave Paul a firm handshake and a pat on the back. No hugs from a former member of the Irish Guards.

"Well done, Paul. I can't thank you enough. I was about to sign the sale of the company this morning," he said, pointing to a document lying on his desk.

"Congratulations, Dr Beresford," said Professor Reich. "It seems you were paying attention when I taught you about clinical trials. At least I won't need to put you in front of the firing squad." He paused and, with a slight smile, added, "Another German joke."

"I cannot believe that the not-so-Honourable Sean St Ledger had such a devious plan to get me to sign away the company to him."

"It is in some ways astonishing, but what you didn't know when you hired me is that Sean and I had a history. We were at Charterhouse School together. There was a major dispute between us which impacted him and his family. Of course, I had no idea how much he despised me, even after all these years. By coincidence, our paths crossed again, and he took it upon himself to lash out at me, causing Harrowgate and HG 176 to be caught in the crossfire. St Ledger was the keystone in the arch of the product's supposed failings."

"Dr Beresford, you said that you had proof that the trial results were being manipulated?" asked Professor Reich, anxious to see the hard evidence that would save the trial.

"I am afraid I do not have that with me anymore," said Paul, watching as concern crossed the professor's face. "The Executive Summary document that I had, showing the false reports from Hong Kong and St Petersburg, was snatched away from me by St Ledger just before he boarded the helicopter and was lost when it crashed," Paul said ruefully.

Paul suddenly realised that when Sean took his briefcase, he also took Jill's diaries. These were now lost to him forever. He was devastated, and it showed on his face.

"What's the problem? Don't we have the proof?" asked JP, assuming that Paul's reaction was about the Executive Summary and the loss of evidence.

"No problem. I've just realised that some deeply personal documents from Jill were also in the briefcase," Paul mumbled, "but Melissa should be arriving tomorrow with the full report showing the falsifications. I will have achieved my goal of preventing the sale of Harrowgate, and she will have achieved her goal of saving the trial. She has been instrumental in analysing the data, and the trial is sure to be resumed given the information she has with her."

"Humph," JP quickly retorted. "At least we have the evidence. Rapid communication to the relevant authorities must be made so the trial can resume."

"I need to leave now," said Paul. "All the evidence is in place to support our case. I need some time to recover, but there are still a few details I need to follow up on in Hong Kong and St Petersburg. Can Mildred ask Tom to take me back to the station?"

On the way, Tom mentioned rumours circulating in the company that Paul had intervened to save the trial but that the company was about to be sold.

"Some of that is incorrect – especially the last part. Harrowgate is not being sold, and JP will still retain majority ownership of the company. And while I did intervene, I certainly had help."

"That's a relief; the staff is completely behind JP and hopes for his success as well as that of Harrowgate. He is an inspirational leader."

"It will all be revealed soon enough. Thanks for the lift. Here comes my train – the timing is perfect. Cheers."

Paul spent the journey to Euston Station thinking about his first day at Harrowgate, his return home on the very same train, and his eagerness to tell Jill about his experience there. So much had changed, bookended between these two journeys. Despite the likely success of getting HG 176 to market, there was the loss of Jill, which superseded all his subsequent experiences.

Back in the apartment, Paul gazed around at the elements of his recent past. Opening the cupboards, he looked at some of Jill's clothing still left hanging on the racks. He found the yellow dress she had worn on their first date in London and held it to his face. Suddenly his phone burst into life; he answered it.

"Dr Beresford, Collins here."

"Good evening, Mr Collins. Do you have any news for me?"

"Yes, I do, and it's positive. Vestiges of the Hong Kong underground organisation to get dissidents out of mainland China are still in place. I've been in touch with some friends in Hong Kong who have taken up your cause as they know this Hung fellow through his medical work and admire him. It seems he was the cardiologist to a number of them."

Eddie explained that the people from Operation Yellowbird who arranged this sort of activity would organise to get Hung and his family from their home in Canton to the harbour and out in a small boat. They would be met at sea by a fishing boat that would bring them back to Hong Kong.

"If all goes well, Hung will be back in Hong Kong tomorrow night or the next morning."

"Thank you, Mr Collins. You don't know how important this is for the clinical trial. Professor Hung will give evidence of the damaging manipulation of the results creating an unfavourable image of our breast cancer drug. He's highly regarded internationally, and I believe the product will be saved through his presentation."

"Very well then, Dr Beresford. Goodnight."

* * *

Over the following few days, as Paul relaxed and recovered in Wandsworth, events moved rapidly.

Melissa triumphantly returned to Harrowgate with the documentation to prove the results from the Hong Kong and St Petersburg trials were a sham. Professor Reich immediately communicated with the medicines regulatory authorities and Principal Investigators in the other trial site countries and with the various Ethics Committees. These authorities urgently processed the new information as the need to resume the trial was imperative, given the hiatus in providing the triallists with medication.

Professor Hung's escape from China with his mother and sister received international headlines, most reports focussing on the treatment of dissidents sometimes embellished by the Western news media. Professor Hung's live press conference was watched by JP and Harrowgate staff, with the diminutive figure sitting alongside the larger and beaming Devon Ridley, who enjoyed some credit for assisting with Hung's escape. No mention was made of Eddie Collins's role in the rescue to protect the organisation which tried to evacuate dissidents from the mainland.

In the aftermath of the helicopter accident, Crispin Wake-Armstrong provided information to the authorities on Sean's recent activities. He confided that Sean had been involved with certain clandestine groups in Hong Kong and St Petersburg to interfere with the clinical trial of a new breast cancer treatment developed by an English company. The police immediately passed this information to the Medicines Regulatory Authority (MRA) overseeing the UK, who already had Harrowgate's evidence of criminal interference and manipulation of the trial results. The MRA guaranteed that the trials would be resumed based on the evidence provided, and they would contact the other medicines regulatory authorities involved in the trial to discuss the findings of Melissa and Devon's report.

Given the current activities surrounding the product, Paul

could no longer languish in his injuries. He needed to be involved. He decided to phone Anastasia to update her on the developments.

"Hello, Paul. Is so good to hear you!" she exclaimed. "I miss us talking. My English improve while we together. Now I go back to being all Russian."

"I miss our conversations too. My apologies for being scarce. I have been resting after a hectic end to our work."

"What happened? I been anxious to know."

"A lot has happened. Thank God you phoned me with your concern about the English lord. Your intuition was spot on. It seems he was behind the strange results we were getting with your trial and in Hong Kong. He planned to take false reports from the two trial sites to my company and get the owner to sell it to him for very little. He was likely killed when his helicopter crashed on its way to Harrowgate to sign the deal."

"This story is like script for a movie. Are you okay?"

"Yes, Anastasia, I am fine. I am recovering from a chaotic few weeks – as you well know."

"Are you coming back to St Petersburg?"

"I don't know at this stage. I need to spend some time at Harrowgate to catch up with the latest developments. I am not sure until I know about the resumption of the trial. Anatoly should be getting some information soon about restarting the trial."

"I hope so. I think the drug work very well."

"Take care, Anastasia."

"I hope you come to St Petersburg. I miss you, Paul."

"I miss you too."

* * *

Paul spent time with JP and Professor Reich, filling them in on his exploits at the two sites but omitting some of the more extreme activities that led to how he, Melissa and Devon successfully gathered their evidence.

Melissa came to Paul's office to see how he was doing and catch up on what happened after he left Hong Kong. She had changed her attitude towards him, but the legacy of their earlier clashes still left an awkward undercurrent.

"How are you managing with starting things up for the product launch?" Melissa enquired.

"Surprisingly well, thank you. We are working on the assumption that the trial outcome will be positive and planning for going to market rather than holding everything back until we hear."

"JP was delighted when I presented the report showing how the trial was sabotaged. The MRA and the other medicines regulatory authorities accepted the document as justification for the continuation of the trial."

"Yes, well done," Paul congratulated.

"You must tell me the full story of how you and the Medvedeva woman managed to secure proof of wrongdoing."

"I will, in time."

Paul allowed Melissa to revel in her moment of triumph; he was more interested in the bigger picture that Harrowgate had narrowly escaped falling into the hands of St Ledger and that the trials had been given the green light to continue. Despite Melissa's prominence in providing the critical evidence, JP made Paul the contact person to receive the report on the trial's outcome, given what the product's success meant to him.

It took only a few days for the various ethics and regulatory authorities to approve the continuation of the trial.

Professor Reich arranged a meeting in London, and all the Principal Investigators from the different trial site countries were flown in to attend. Reich felt it best to explain, in person, the trial report falsification and all the machinations by Sean St Ledger to avoid any rumours that might affect the trial going forward. The group were astonished at the sabotage but delighted that the trials would continue, given the outstanding early results anticipated or expected of HG 176. At the various trial sites, all patients were seen and put back on the medication they received during the trial's initial phases.

Paul took the opportunity to catch up with Professors Hung and Pavlyuchenko at the London meeting.

Without breaching confidentiality, Paul mentioned to Hung his association with the escape from the mainland. "I am relieved that you were able to escape your captors. We needed your input to persuade the other Principal Investigators that there were underhand activities."

"Yes, it was miraculous. Perhaps my friend Devon was behind all this."

"He played an important role, and I had a contact that may have assisted."

"Thank you, Dr Beresford. I must also thank Devon once more."

At his meeting with Pavlyuchenko, Paul asked about Drs Alexievich and Medvedeva.

"I have suspended Dr Alexievich." Paul noticed a sense of relief in the professor, knowing the hold Alexievich had over him.

"And Dr Medvedeva is back on duty after her lucky escape from the kidnappers. I believe she worked closely with you and seemed to know you remarkably well." This comment was accompanied by a penetrating stare, suspecting Paul's carnal knowledge of his mistress. Paul hoped this would not interfere with the clinical trial or affect Anastasia.

Hearing that Alexievich had been suspended, Paul was interested to know what had happened to him. He called Anastasia for more information. She told him that the police and medicines regulatory authorities had questioned Alexievich.

"He had big gambling debt for his luxury lifestyle," she relayed. "The mafia control casinos, and Alexievich told debts could be cancelled if he manipulate trial results for the English lord."

"That would have been Sean St Ledger, the man I told you about, who wanted to buy the pharmaceutical company. He was working with the mafia to get the false report."

"I remember; the one from schooldays," she said. "The police also want to ask Alexievich what he knows about murder of Tanel Valle, but he disappeared before that."

"Perhaps the mafia found him once they realised the trial had resumed. If his interference with the trial didn't work, I'm sure they would have reinstated his gambling debt," Paul speculated.

"Maybe we find Alexievich in suitcase one day."

"Maybe," Paul chuckled before telling Anastasia he hoped they would see each other again soon.

* * *

The media reported on every development as the investigation into the helicopter crash continued. Police divers eventually located the wreckage after a prolonged search as the movement of the river had carried it away from the site of the crash. In it, they found one body still strapped into his seat, identified as the co-pilot. There was no sign of the third passenger. If the current had moved the helicopter, it could surely have swept away the third person.

According to Mr Wake-Armstrong, who was present when the helicopter took off, the missing passenger was the Honourable Sean St Ledger, heir to the 5th Viscount Talbot. The press ran the story that the title would die without a male heir to continue the lineage. In some ways, the papers likened the Talbots to the Kennedys; both families were fated to experience tragedy. They quoted the deaths of Sean's older brother and the current Viscount's two relatives lost during the First World War.

They painted Sean as a successful businessman running a thriving chemical company and looking to invest in pharmaceuticals through an Irish company. England had lost one of its nobility and a potential captain of industry. If only they knew the truth, Paul thought. Sadly, only Sean knew the whole truth behind his devious plan, and it seemed he would never have to answer for its consequences.

As the weeks passed and there was still no sign of Sean, a short article appeared in The Times newspaper, reporting that the bereaved 5th Viscount had lodged an application to the High Court under the recently passed Presumption of Death Act, which allowed for a declaration that a missing person, thought to have died, be presumed dead. Based on Mr Wake-Armstrong's statement that Sean St Ledger was definitely on the flight, Sean was declared deceased. It was also noted that the 5th Viscount had recently re-married, and hope was expressed that he would find solace in this.

* * *

The trial resumed, and the gathering of the raw data commenced, with the case report forms regularly updated and thoroughly checked against the source files to avoid any further manipulation of the data.

There were several steps to go through before the approval and licencing of HG 176 to be made commercially available. It would take time to reach the critical mass of trial data required to analyse the efficacy of HG 176. Once enough data had been gathered, the trial would then come to a close. The protocol code governing the double blind trial would be broken so that patients and doctors would know which of the two groups were getting the trial drug or the comparator. Then statistical data analysis would be carried out on the results by QualiMed. Only then could it be determined whether HG 176 had fulfiled Harrowgate's expectations of the drug.

If QualiMed's final report showed positive results for the efficacy of the drug, registration dossiers would then be submitted to the Medicines Regulatory Authority for final approval – and even that was not guaranteed. As the weeks passed, the tension slowly grew at Harrowgate about the outcome and interpretation of the trial. It was purely a waiting game.

With enough clinical data gathered, the trial closed early due to the exceptional results in certain patients, and QualiMed began assessing the trial data.

Paul remained optimistic, and as Business Development Director, he started anticipating the licensing approval process of HG 176 and the company's sales and marketing resources. However, he and Harrowgate were still on edge, waiting to receive the report from QualiMed once their analysis had been finalised.

Finally, the results from QualiMed came through. HG 176 had clearly delivered ground-breaking results. Now the task was to compile the registration dossiers, submit them to the MRA, and await their approval of the product. It was never clear how long that might take. At one of their first meetings, Professor Reich told Paul that in certain countries, it could take many years for the authorities to review all the documentation before approving the drug. Paul could only hope it wouldn't take that long; unfortunately, all they could do was wait.

With the passing of time and no news forthcoming, Harrowgate slipped back into its operating mode of trying to develop new products and seeing the existing product portfolio succeed to keep the business afloat.

Spring moved into summer, and the All England Lawn Tennis and Croquet Club hosted one of its sporting highlights, the Wimbledon Championships.

Paul had been watching the tennis in the canteen, and when he returned to his office after lunch, he found a large couriered envelope on his desk. He sat down, picked it up and was gripped by tension. The envelope carried the stamp of the Medicines Regulatory Authority. Reflections about Jill consumed him. He reached for his silver letter opener and sliced open the envelope.

He drew out the document and stared at its heading on the first page:

Report of a Double Blind Study of HG 176 (terpazamab) for the treatment of Metastatic Breast Cancer in women.

Paul turned to the table of contents of the bulky document, found the Executive Summary listed and flicked through to that page. His mind seemed numb at that moment. He could only discern a mass of words, none appearing in the proper order. He was so overcome and anxious that his mind could not grasp the content or meaning of the text.

He glanced away from the document and out of his office window across to the Chiltern Hills and drew a deep breath. Looking at the words again, they slowly came into focus, and he found the line:

"Based on the evidence provided, detailed positive results from the head-to-head Phase 3 trial, the efficacy and safety of HG 176 (terpazamab) in a randomised, double blind study demonstrated superior progression-free survival for the treatment of metastatic breast cancer. The Medicines Regulatory Authority grants a licence for the product to be made commercially available. The submission of additional data will further enhance the claims made for the product."

Paul sat back and re-read the words for a second and third time. HG 176 had been approved for usage in the UK. A smile crept across his face as the gravity of the document settled.

The summary of the report gave Paul comfort. The results of HG 176 were indeed ground-breaking. Based on the confidence displayed by the MRA, the product was likely to be registered soon in several other countries where registration dossiers had been lodged. HG 176 was a success, and Harrowgate's hopes had been vindicated.

Paul quickly called JP's office, asking if Mildred could assemble JP and Professor Reich – he was bringing some information through to them. Paul found JP and Reich anxiously waiting for him in JP's office. They were not prepared to let their hopes run away with them, and JP was particularly tense.

Paul held up the document and declared, "The MRA has approved HG 176 for use in the UK. We have made it to the finish line! Congratulations, JP and Herr Professor."

Their faces beamed with relief. JP was drained; the long-awaited result had taken its toll on him – both financial and reputational. The professor's usually gruff exterior creased then uncreased.

"Thank you, thank you, Paul!" JP cheered. "Well, this is where your job description really kicks in; the launch of new products. All the other stuff you have done up to now has just been peripheral," he said with a grin.

JP was thrilled, and Paul expressed how pleased he was that the trial had succeeded in memory of Jill.

"Mildred, I want you to inform the staff that there will be a special meeting in the auditorium at two o'clock."

Paul left JP and Professor Reich to discuss the internal and external progression of the product and its communication. As well as the scientific community, the financial markets needed to be informed as the company's share price had slipped badly – just as Sean had intended. The company's value was low, and the banks and shareholders were reflecting negatively. The latter had been offloading their shares below the price they paid.

Paul went to his office and closed the door. He swung his chair around to face outwards to the Chiltern Hills. He drank in the tranquillity of the scene, then closed his eyes and said to himself, "Jill, this is for you."

* * *

Over the subsequent few months, preparation was made for the product's launch in the United Kingdom. Paul was occupied with aligning the marketing, sales and production teams to ready the business for making the product available. Paul drew on his experience and learning from Harvard and worked closely with the dedicated staff across the various divisions within the company.

The pressure of the work left him little time for reflection about his life and where it would lead now, but during this time, he made regular visits to Jill's grave in Kensal Green cemetery to tell her about his progress. This left him with mixed emotions. He ached for her presence and took some comfort in being near her. But he often left the cemetery with a sense of emptiness.

One of the decisions that had to be made was selecting a name for the product. HG 176 was only the company's code for the product, determined by its R&D department. Harrowgate was already working on HG 181, a product for Alzheimer's that showed promise in this most difficult of therapeutic areas. A sobering reality, however, was that HG 177 to 180, identified as lead compounds, had all failed along the path of testing, reinforcing the difficulty of achieving success in the pharmaceutical industry.

As Business Development Director, Paul was given control over the launch scheduled in a few months. It had always been his intention that the successful development of HG 176 should be a tribute to Jill, and he wanted to reinforce this through the naming of the product. JP had given him carte blanche in this regard. Paul had earlier selected the name 'Terajil', a combination of her name and the product's chemical structure. Once the name had been approved by the medicines regulatory authorities, passing their guidelines on invented names that avoided any confusion with other named medicines or misleading with regards to its composition or action, the name was revealed to the company and the market.

The release of publicity to the financial and scientific community about the company and its product had buoyed its share price and profile. In a recent press conference about the UK's business strengths, the Prime Minister mentioned Harrowgate as a shining example of British innovation and ingenuity, further increasing the company's value.

JP walked around his organisation like a man reborn, encouraging his staff in their endeavours to manufacture and launch the product. Shoulders firmly back, posture upright, a twinkle in his eyes lurking under dark bushy eyebrows, this was the moment he had dreamed of when he established Harrowgate. Speculation mounted among the staff that he might see the launch as the end of his time at the company. As to who would succeed him, the general feeling was that it would be either Melissa or Paul, but Tom Hewitt was the dark horse in the race.

When the time came to launch Terajil, the company arranged a major function at a London hotel. Professor Reich hosted the event attended by leading oncologists specialising in breast cancer from all over the world, together with representatives from the medical press. Some of the patients who had been treated with the product also gave their personalised testimonials. The function concluded on a decidedly positive note about the product's merits and how it would benefit women with breast cancer.

Similar functions were to be held in the major cities where the trials had been conducted. A 'Roadshow', as it was known in the industry, would be rolled out to promote the product and its indications. All seemed to be going well. JP was ecstatic, and Paul was delighted for him. After committing himself emotionally and financially to developing the product, he deserved the success.

When Paul got home later that evening, he phoned Anastasia to tell her of the outcome of the launch.

"Hello, Paul, how did it go?"

"Brilliantly. The product launch would not have been possible without all the help you gave me to prove the falsification of the trial results. I am grateful to you, Anastasia."

"I am glad I am part of helping you and HG 176."

"It's called Terajil now."

"That is wonderful! It must provide comfort to you."

"How are things in St Petersburg?"

"Quiet now you gone. Things are so boring."

Paul chuckled. "Given what we went through, perhaps it's for the best."

"Dr Alexievich is disappeared. We don't know what happens to him."

"Perhaps his friends have caught up with him."

"Maybe."

"Anastasia, would you like to come to London to spend a few days sightseeing here?"

"I would love to, Paul, but …"

"But?"

"Anatoly ask me to marry him. He want to leave his wife and also position as Superintendent of hospital for me."

Paul was silent. Careful to contain his disappointment, he said, "Oh, then he would be a very lucky man. What did you say to him?"

"I tell him I will think about it."

"Right."

"I will always think of our times together – all of them."

"Perhaps you should blot out some of those memories," Paul laughed.

"Agree, but not all of them."

"I must go now. Take care, Anastasia."

"Goodbye, Paul – I will love you always."

* * *

In the months following the launch of Terajil in the United Kingdom, Paul was involved in the product's global launch in several other countries, which kept him occupied. The product uptake was outstanding, and the results from a larger group of patients internationally supported those found in the smaller number in the multicentre trials.

The company's share price had surged, and JP was often away from the office visiting 'The City', the name by which London's financial district was commonly known. Terminology heard around JP's office was of 'market capitalisation', 'discounted cash flows', and 'financial ratios', especially when Ritesh Shah, the Financial Director, was with JP behind closed doors.

With the great success of Terajil, the company suspected that JP would soon be leaving, and they wondered about his successor.

There were already three in-house candidates who the staff thought were in contention. But in many companies, when the CEO left, an outsider would often be brought in to carry the company, supposedly to another level. Would such a person fit the culture of the company?

Corporate culture is a powerful but often underestimated force. JP had recalled an example of a highly successful German who was brought in to head up a smaller subsidiary of a British pharmaceutical company with a relaxed 'country club' type culture. He failed within a year of his placement at the company's head office and left due to his workaholic ways being at variance with the easygoing company culture. "Poor fit," JP had emphasised, adamant this would not happen to Harrowgate.

* * *

Six months after the launch of Terajil, Paul was in his office when he received a call from Mildred to see JP. They had been talking earlier that morning about the Alzheimer's product, and Paul had promised to get JP some of the statistics showing the pervasive nature of this irreversible, progressive brain disorder.

He had not yet gathered all the information but took what he had to JP's office, knowing that he was not fully prepared for the conversation to meet JP's demanding standards. JP asked Paul to take a seat in the wing-backed chairs in the corner of his office, affording the spectacular view of the English countryside.

"Do you remember when we sat here on your first day at Harrowgate?" JP asked.

"Yes, I do. I was wondering what I was letting myself in for," Paul reminisced.

"Perhaps that is an insightful thought, given what we need to chat about."

"Yes, but I've not yet got all the data you wanted on Alzheimer's."

"That can wait. As you know, I have always had it in my mind to go back to my farm in Ireland. I feel that I have had my time in the industry, and having seen my company grow and the successful launch of Terajil, I feel that now is a good time to move on. My son has been running the farm, but he needs some help now that he has a young family competing for his time. Also, I can't wait to get back among my Charolais cattle. They are so much easier to deal with than people!"

"I am sure they would love to have you back there, but you are needed here to steer the company to other successes."

"Paul, I was hoping you'd be the one to do that for me."

About the Author

Dr John Bartlett was born in Pinner, England and relocated to South Africa with his parents as a young child. He grew up in Durban and later qualified as a veterinary surgeon at the University of Pretoria.

He left practice to join Wellcome's veterinary pharmaceutical company and transitioned to the human pharmaceutical industry, where he held senior scientific, marketing and strategic management positions.

Between occupying these positions, he ran a healthcare consultancy, providing services to a wide range of organisations associated with the healthcare industry.

During these periods, he lectured in marketing and strategy at the local campus of De Montfort University. He was also elected Chairman of the Healthcare branch of the Institute of Marketing Management.

John has a passion for history and fulfilled this interest through completing a part-time BA degree in History and Economic History at the University of KwaZulu-Natal. He has also completed a part-time MBA at the Wits Business School of the University of Witwatersrand.

John's interests include travel, current affairs and following most sports. He is an avid long-term supporter of Tottenham Hotspur football club, despite the challenges associated with this pursuit.

John is married to Geraldine, has a son Michael, a daughter Lindsay and lives in Johannesburg, South Africa.